GOD'S PLENTY:

A STUDY OF HUGH HOOD'S SHORT FICTION

W0259416

GOD'S PLENTY

A STUDY OF HUGH HOOD'S SHORT FICTION

W.J. KEITH

BIBLIOASIS
WINDSOR, ONTARIO

Copyright © W. J. Keith, 2015

All rights reserved. No part of this publication may be reproduced or transmitted in any form or by any means, electronic or mechanical, including photocopying, recording, or any information storage and retrieval system, without permission in writing from the publisher or a licence from The Canadian Copyright Licensing Agency (Access Copyright). For an Access Copyright licence, visit www.accesscopyright.ca or call toll free to 1-800-893-5777.

FIRST EDITION

Library and Archives Canada Cataloguing in Publication

Keith, W. J. (William John), 1934-
God's plenty : a study of Hugh Hood's short
fiction / W.J. Keith.

Issued also in electronic format.
Includes bibliographical references and index.
ISBN 978-1-927428-47-4

1. Hood, Hugh, 1928-2000--Criticism and
interpretation. I. Title.

PS8515.O49Z734 2013 C813'.54 C2010-904596-3

Typeset by Chris Andrechek
Cover designed and copy-edited by Kate Hargreaves

Canada Council for the Arts　Conseil des Arts du Canada

Canadian Heritage　Patrimoine canadien

Biblioasis acknowledges the ongoing financial support of the Government of Canada through the Canada Council for the Arts, Canadian Heritage, the Canada Book Fund; and the Government of Ontario through the Ontario Arts Council.

PRINTED AND BOUND IN CANADA

Here is God's plenty.
(John Dryden on Chaucer in *Fables Ancient and Modern*)

My work demands to be read silently and with close attention by mature men and women ... and a single reading won't do.
(Hugh Hood)

Hood's stories are easy to read but sometimes difficult to understand.
(Kent Thompson)

For Hiroko, my wife
and for Noreen Mallory, Hugh Hood's wife

Contents

Preface

Hugh Hood's fiction was remarkably extensive, both in quantity and kind: four early novels; the 12-volume series *The New Age / Le nouveau siècle* (which I have discussed at some length in *Canadian Odyssey*, 2002); 129 short stories; and two novellas. These last are "Weight Watchers," published as the concluding story in *August Nights* in 1985, and *Five New Facts About Giorgione*, which appeared separately in 1987. My exclusive concerns here, of course, are with the short stories and novellas.

The short stories are spread over ten volumes, from his first book, *Flying a Red Kite* (1962), to his last, the posthumously published *After All!* (2003). In 1987, publication of *The Collected Stories* was initiated. Each volume was to contain an introduction by Hood in which he explained the circumstances of writing and offered a later evaluation of, and commentary on, his earlier work. Unfortunately, the series was never completed. The first two books of stories, *Flying a Red Kite* and *Around the Mountain* (1967), were reprinted, and two volumes of juvenilia also appeared: *A Short Walk in the Rain*, consisting of early work never before published, and *The Isolation Booth*, containing stories that had been printed in magazines but not hitherto gathered into volume-form. *After All!*, the posthumous collection, was also published in the series, though Hood had not written an introduction. The intervening volumes were *The Fruit Man, the Meat Man & the Manager* (1971), *Dark Glasses* (1976), *None Genuine Without This Signature* (1980), *August Nights* (1985), and *You'll Catch Your Death* (1992). Two gatherings of short stories from previous volumes have also appeared: *Selected Stories*

(1978), and *Light Shining Out of Darkness and Other Stories*, selected by John Metcalf for the New Canadian Library (2001).

A few words now about the aims of the present book. It attempts to provide both information and evaluation. I make no effort to describe and analyze every story. In his earlier productions, Hood experimented to find out where his main strengths lay, and this led to his discovering what he could not do or what, after due consideration, he found he did not want to do. Many of these early attempts need not detain us. Surprisingly few of his later stories can be considered failures, but there are a number of others that, though competent and readable, are relatively unambitious and present few challenges. These will be passed over briefly. I concentrate my attention on stories which depend on a particular context—biographical, geographical, intellectual, stylistic, or whatever—and for which readers can profit from some assistance in terms of background. But my main concern will be to offer readings of the more subtle and intricate stories, employing literary-critical approaches that will vary according to the needs of the individual instance.

This is the first book in a position to consider Hood's short fiction in relation to his total *oeuvre*. Patricia Morley's *The Comedians*, a comparative study of Hood and Rudy Wiebe published as early as 1977, was necessarily limited, so far as short fiction is concerned, to his first three volumes of stories. She chose to focus on comedy in the religious (Dantesque) sense as well as on more worldly humour, but Hood's more recent publications have inevitably rendered the book out of date. Its main merit is that, with its focus on comedy, it avoids the excessive solemnity of many of its successors. Keith Garebian's Twayne study (1983) covers material up to and including *None Genuine Without This Signature*. (The same writer's study in the ECW Press *Canadian Writers and Their Works* series, published two years later, proceeds no further and recycles most of the same material; moreover, because of limited space it is less detailed, and I refer to it only in passing here.) Garebian's emphasis falls upon Hood's allegorical proclivities, and although his accounts generally contain useful insights, he tends to play down what I consider to be Hood's all-important variety of response.

Susan Copoloff-Mechanic's *Pilgrim's Progress* (1988) is the most substantial study to date, and covers the stories up to and including *August Nights*, but it appeared before both the last two collections and the two volumes devoted to early work. She concentrates narrowly on the supposed unified structure of each volume, a procedure that too often results in ingenuity rather than persuasiveness. (I discuss this matter in more detail in Chapter two below.) I am bound to state that I find her study frustratingly unhelpful. I would prefer to pass it over in dignified silence, but have been forced to refer to it often, generally in terms of disagreement, in the course of my own discussions. Because my intention here is to provide readings of Hood's finest short stories that bring out their best qualities, it became necessary, in order to do this effectively, to refer to incomplete interpretations or even patent misreadings already in circulation. Copoloff-Mechanic, unfortunately, provides the most conspicuous and accessible examples.

In addition to these book-length studies, there have been several useful reviews of Hood's individual collections, and a number of perceptive readings of specific stories have appeared in books and critical journals. I am indebted to many of these, and they are listed under the stories in question in my "List of Short Fiction" and under their authors in "Other Works Cited" at the end of this book. The alphabetically arranged list gives details of the location of each story, the date of writing, and both the place and date of first publication (if applicable).

My two opening chapters are devoted to a short literary biography and a discussion of literary-critical issues important in a full discussion of Hood's work. General readers looking for guidance in the understanding and appreciation of specific stories may prefer to pass immediately to the later chapters, which are mainly informative and interpretative. After a chapter on his early stories, most of them not published in book form until the late 1980s and early 1990s, subsequent chapters proceed in chronological order of volume-publication.

In order to avoid excessive footnoting or parenthetical insertions, I provide inclusive page references when stories are discussed in detail. All other citations are given as briefly as possible, using abbreviations listed immediately following this preface. So far as texts are concerned, I follow those of the first editions with the exceptions of *Flying a Red Kite* and *Around the Mountain*, where the texts of the *Collected Stories* are used. In these two cases, page references to the first editions follow in square brackets. These *Collected Stories* texts are generally superior since they were subject to additional copy-editing and some (though by no means all) typographical errors and inconsistencies were corrected. The other three volumes in the series, of course, *are* the first editions.

There is no such thing, I would argue, as a typical Hugh Hood short story—hence the emphasis on "plenty" and variety as indicated in my title. He was primarily interested in exploring the numerous kinds of story that appealed to him, in experimenting with form, style, and nuance to find the way of telling a particular story most effectively. His ideal reader is one prepared to be flexible, open to fresh approaches, and above all sensitive to the sounds and rhythms as well as the precise meanings of his carefully chosen words. John Metcalf tells an anecdote about Hood as a fellow member of the Montreal Story Tellers (a group devoted to reading short stories in high schools and universities) that seems appropriate here:

> Hugh would stop in the middle of a paragraph, sometimes in the middle of a sentence, and start to chuckle at some rediscovered felicity. Sometimes he would shake his head as if amazed that he had got off such a perfect shot. He would say,
>
> "You know, that's a *honey* of a sentence. I think I'll read that again."
>
> And did.

Metcalf originally considered this a "tremendous fault" in a reader, but subsequently changed his mind: "When I first heard him do it, I cringed. Later, I found it endearing. Now, my love of him is such that I would feel deprived if he read without indulging this mild eccentricity" (*Kicking* 72).

For my part, the important aspect of this anecdote is not so much the "eccentricity" itself as the fact that it couldn't exist if Hood were not a master of stylistic "felicity." He possessed strong convictions and, unlike Metcalf, was not averse to writing a story that unabashedly had something important to say. However, although many of his stories are strongly affected by his Catholic, allegorizing perspective, I recognize no need to fit all his short fiction into a rigid *schema*. Instead, I prefer to follow the clues provided by the words on the page (without forcing them in preconceived directions), and try to reveal how a sensitive creative artist chooses and arranges them for his own immediate purpose. As a result, parts of this book, especially the later chapters, may seem full of abrupt shifts and transitions. This I consider inevitable. Each story must be read, just as it was written, in a unique way consonant with its own logic or tone. Responsive readers and critics should be prepared to follow the author's lead, trying so far as possible to avoid confining themselves to their own predilections. Such an approach does not, of course, preclude comparative value judgments between story and story, but it should take care to recognize the diversity within Hood's work

One curious feature of Hood's work was noted by Sheldon Currie in his review of *None Genuine Without This Signature* for the *Antigonish Review*. He shrewdly observed that the short stories are so individual that they are "difficult to describe without retelling them" (104). This I have found to be true. I would therefore like to assure readers at this point that I never recount the plot for its own sake; when I appear to be doing so, it is a necessary prelude to making a critical point that depends upon plot details.

Finally, I wish to acknowledge the considerable help I have received from the following people: John Metcalf, who invited me to write this book and provided welcome encouragement and sound advice throughout the process of writing; Noreen Mallory, Hugh Hood's wife, who not only gave me permission to quote at length from his writings but patiently answered my numerous queries, thus providing information that could not be obtained elsewhere; and my wife Hiroko, who helped with proofreading and the finding of misplaced books.

Abbreviations

AA *After All!* [*Collected Stories V*]. Erin, ON: Porcupine's Quill, 2003.

AM *Around the Mountain: Scenes from Montréal Life.* Toronto: Peter Martin Associates 1967. Rpt. as *Collected Stories IV.* Erin, ON: Porcupine's Quill, 1994.

AN *August Nights.* Toronto: Stoddart, 1985.

Bibliography J. R. (Tim) Struthers, "Hugh Hood: An Annotated Bibliography." *The Annotated Bibliography of Canada's Major Authors.* Vol.5. Ed. Robert Lecker and Jack David. Downsview, ON: ECW Press, 1984. 231-353.

DG *Dark Glasses.* Ottawa: Oberon Press, 1976.

FM *The Fruit Man, the Meat Man & the Manager.* Ottawa: Oberon Press, 1971.

FNF *Five New Facts About Giorgione.* Windsor, ON: Black Moss Press, 1987.

FRK *Flying a Red Kite.* Toronto: Ryerson Press, 1962. Rpt. as *Collected Stories I.* Erin, ON: Porcupine's Quill, 1987.

GB *The Governor's Bridge is Closed.* Ottawa: Oberon Press, 1973.

"H.H." "Hugh Hood (1928-)." *Contemporary Authors' Autobiography Series.* Vol.17. Detroit: Gale Research, 1993. 75-94.

IB *The Isolation Booth* [*Collected Stories III*]. Erin, ON: Porcupine's Quill, 1991.

Interview J. R. (Tim) Struthers. "An Interview with Hugh Hood." *Essays on Canadian Writing* 13/14 (1978-9), 94-112. Also available as Struthers, ed., *Before the Flood.* Downsview, ON: ECW Press, 1979 (same pagination).

LSOD *Light Shining Out of Darkness and Other Stories.* Selected and with an Afterword by John Metcalf. New Canadian Library. Toronto: McClelland & Stewart, 2001.

NGWS *None Genuine Without This Signature.* Downsview, ON: ECW Press, 1980.

SG *The Swing in the Garden.* Ottawa: Oberon Press, 1975

SS *Selected Stories.* Ottawa: Oberon Press, 1978.

SW *A Short Walk in the Rain* [*Collected Stories II*]. Erin, ON: Porcupine's Quill, 1989.

TT *Trusting the Tale.* Downsview, ON: ECW Press, 1983.

UA *Unsupported Assertions.* Concord, ON: Anansi, 1991.

YCD *You'll Catch Your Death.* Erin, ON: Porcupine's Quill, 1992.

1

Biographical[1]

Hugh Hood's fictions reflect both a fertile inventive faculty and a remarkable gift for preserving accurate and vivid accounts of geographical locations and atmospheres at specific moments in time. On the one hand, he can provide what he has called "the fundamental pleasure of recognition given by literary realism, not simply the naive pleasure of identifying one's neighbourhood, district or quarter, but the additional, much more complex pleasure of seeing one's place worked into the balance and design of the narration" (TT 127). On the other, he can take us, quoting the title of one of his short stories, to "Places I've Never Been," places containing characters and situations derived purely from his imagination. In the following biographical account, I shall often direct the reader to those parts of his fiction where he draws on autobiographical experience, but it should not be assumed that he was confined in his writing to subjects originating in his own life. (He set one of his early novels, *You Cant Get There From Here*, in Africa, a continent he had never visited.) One of his main literary strengths, indeed, was his skill to seamlessly blend fiction and non-fiction. The fictive elements will be stressed in later analyses of individual stories.

Hugh John Blagdon Hood, to give his full name, was born in Toronto on 30 April, 1928, the second of three children. His father's family derived ultimately from Scottish-highland and

---

1 I am indebted throughout this section to Hood's autobiographical account that appeared, under the title "Hugh Hood (1928-   )," in the Gale Research *Contemporary Authors' Autobiography Series*, vol.17.

west-of-England ancestry but more recently from Nova Scotia; his mother was French-Canadian, but from a family that had moved to Toronto at the end of the nineteenth century. As a result, Hood eventually became, as he told Kent Thompson, "imperfectly bilingual" ("Canadian" 21). He read French easily but admitted that his written French was "très imparfait" (see Garebian, "Hugh Hood" 94). In his short story "Brother André, Père Lamarche, and My Grandmother Eugénie Blagdon," Hood provides a vivid historical reconstruction, in his "documentary" style, of his mother's side of the family's way of life. A common factor in these diverse origins, inherited from the Scots and the French, was his constant but never stifling Catholic faith.

His early religious influences are lucidly and feelingly discussed in his essay "Before the Flood." There he explains that he was introduced to religious ideas and biblical stories through a combination of books and church attendance. From the Old Testament he encountered stories that "you turned over in your head with no power whatsoever to banish them from the imagination" (TT 11). Later, as he says, he "fell under the sway of parable, with the [Benziger Brothers'] *Bible History* and the readings from the New Testament, and equally under the sway of elementary theological reasoning in the *Catechism*," while his other early reading "served to propose subtle secular analogies of what was to be found in Scripture or Catechism" (14). All these literary experiences became a major influence on his subsequent writing.

He grew up during the 1930s in north Rosedale, which he was always at pains to identify as the residential source for the servants employed in "really rich South Rosedale" (GB 10), the affluent area just to the northeast of downtown Toronto. His life at this time is described at a semi-fictional remove in *The Swing in the Garden*, the opening volume of the *New Age* series. In terms of biography, the account needs to be read with caution—both Matt Goderich's parents are decidedly different in character from Hood's—but the settings are authentic, and the story of the development of his interests and activities seems accurate enough. After completing his elementary education at Our Lady of Perpetual Help School, he went on to attend De la Salle College, which appears as Oakland in his semi-fictional memoir "Silver Bugles,

Cymbals, Golden Silks." Other aspects of his life as a teenager in wartime Toronto are presented—again at a fictional remove—in the even numbered chapters of *Black and White Keys*, the fourth *New Age* novel.

He says little in his autobiographical fiction, however, about his other (non-religious) reading as a schoolboy; but in the 1987 introduction to *Flying a Red Kite*, in the first volume of his *Collected Stories*, he lays emphasis on his magazine route, delivering copies of the *Saturday Evening Post* and the *Ladies' Home Journal*. The indirect artistic implications of his undertaking this after-school job were considerable. He was now introduced to the flourishing world of popular fiction. Of even more importance was the appearance around 1940 of "new-fangled paperbacked books priced at 25¢," a phenomenon that, as he says, "did more to educate me to the possibilities of fiction than anything else" (FRK 11).

In the fall of 1947 he entered St. Michael's College, the Roman Catholic college of the University of Toronto, where he studied English and came under the influence of Marshall McLuhan, then a young (Catholic) professor beginning to formulate the ideas about communications that would make their first appearance in *The Mechanical Bride* a few years later and were to propel him into intellectual prominence—even notoriety—in the next three decades. McLuhan introduced him to the work of James Joyce, especially *Dubliners*, that had a profound effect upon his own writing. As far as extracurricular activities were concerned, Hood also took part in a drama production at his college, which led to his acting, under the direction of the famed Robert Gill, in several productions at Hart House Theatre and in independent student-initiated performances elsewhere. Among the actors in these productions were future celebrities including William Hutt, Kate Reid, Eric House, and Donald Davis. Fictionalized versions of these events are to be found in "The Ingenue I Should Have Kissed, but Didn't" and in the opening chapter of *The Scenic Art*, where much of the background detail is authentic, though Hood has taken liberties with the dates and ordering of productions.

After gaining his B.A. in 1950 and his M.A. in 1952, Hood worked briefly during the summer with the Toronto Works Department, and some years later this experience resulted in the much anthologized "Recollections of the Works Department," perhaps the best known example of his relaxed but poised style, deftly exploring the uncertain borderland between fact and inconspicuously crafted fiction. The next three years saw him at work on his PhD studies, when he became interested in what he significantly called "the truth-telling aspect of the poetic imagination," and devoted his doctoral dissertation to tracing out the links between "the mediæval view of modes of knowing" as exemplified in St. Thomas Aquinas and Dante and "the poetics of Wordsworth and Coleridge" in the Romantic period (Interview 22). This exploration into the history of ideas, an approach for which English Studies at Toronto were celebrated at that time, may seem esoteric, but it provided a solid intellectual foundation upon which Hood was later to erect his novels and short stories. It also helped in showing him "how to manage a long work" (Interview 21).

Moreover, this was not solely a period of academic study. During this time he met his future wife, Noreen Mallory from Brockville, Ontario (destined to become the "Stoverville" of Hood's later fiction). A highly gifted student at the Ontario College of Art, she was then lodging at the home of Morley Callaghan, the Catholic novelist and short story writer, whose interest in exploring moral and religious issues in fiction clearly had a stimulating effect on the subsequent work of her future fiancé.

On graduating in 1955, though unable to find a suitable job in Canada, Hood was offered a teaching position at St. Joseph College, a Catholic educational institution for women in West Hartford, Connecticut. But in November of the same year, Hood and Mallory became engaged, and they were married in April 1957 (Callaghan's son Michael being the best man). Hood worked for the next four years at West Hartford, where their first two children, Sarah and Dwight, were born in 1958 and 1961. It was there that Hood began to write short stories, a fact of considerable importance to be discussed in more detail in Chapter three.

In 1961, however, he was appointed to the faculty of the Université de Montréal, and so what Hood was later to call his "turbulent early years" ("H.H." 88) came to an end. The family moved to Montréal during the summer, and Hood was to live there, teaching and writing, for the rest of his life, another son

(John) and daughter (Alexandra) being born there in 1963 and 1965. Henceforward, the three principal locales in his writing were the Toronto of his childhood and early manhood, the area around his wife's home town of Brockville in southern Ontario (the Hoods built a summer cottage on Charleston Lake, near Athens, which they subsequently visited regularly during the summer, "cottage country" becoming a favoured setting in his work), and Montréal, where almost all his major fiction was written.

His first book of short stories, *Flying a Red Kite*, was published the year after his arrival in Montréal, and his first novel *White Figure, White Ground*, which explores his father's ancestral roots in Nova Scotia, appeared in 1964. Both were received as work of more than usual artistic promise. These were followed in 1967 by *Around the Mountain*, a collection of short stories subtitled *Scenes from Montréal Life*, in which he paid loving tribute, in the year of Canada's centennial celebrations, to the city (then hosting Expo) that he had made his new home. More novels followed, and in 1971 *The Fruit Man, the Meat Man & the Manager*, another book of short stories, appeared. It was at about this time that he settled into his habitual practice of interspersing the publication of full-length novels with volumes of short stories or non-fiction.

By the mid-1960s, he began feeling intimations of an extended work that demanded to be written, an endeavour to present in both historical and imaginative terms a sense of Canadian growth and aspiration during the twentieth century. This was an enormous undertaking, the most ambitious fictional project ever attempted in Canada, that preoccupied him until his death in the opening year of the new millennium. After a long period of planning, the first volume of *The New Age / Le nouveau siècle* (to give it its full bilingual title, though the volumes are in English) was published in 1975 as *The Swing in the Garden*. For the next quarter of a century, these volumes appeared regularly, punctuated by the appearances of the later short stories. In 1987, the first volume of *The Collected Stories* was published, and although it was not brought to completion it did include the volumes of his hitherto uncollected work, *A Short Walk in the Rain* and *The Isolation Booth*. As a result, all Hood's short stories, including juvenilia, are now available. Moreover, in the following year he enjoyed the honour of being admitted as an Officer of the Order of Canada.

As he came to the end of the *New Age* series, however, Hood's health began to fail, and he had to devote all his energies to the completion of the final books. He succeeded in this task, but the last volume, *Near Water*, appeared three weeks or so after his death on 1 August, 2000. *After All!*, a final collection of short stories written in the 1990s, appeared posthumously in 2003. He is buried in St. Denis Cemetery, just outside his beloved Athens, Ontario, where his gravestone reads: "Hugh Hood O.C. PHD / (1928-2000) / "No regrets."

2

Critical Considerations

I have called this book *God's Plenty*, echoing John Dryden's tribute to Chaucer, because I consider the most distinctive feature of Hood's short fiction to be his astonishing diversity. In his introduction to *A Short Walk in the Rain*, he observes that the experience of writing his early stories "taught me the unlimited range of possibilities inherent in this great literary form" (9). He clearly exploited this realization in his subsequent literary career. His work can be lightheartedly comic or profoundly serious (even, on occasion, both at once), ornate or casual in style, traditional or experimental in form and structure. To illustrate this remarkable quality, I would point to six stories, each chosen from one of his first six volumes: "He Just Adores Her!" from *Flying a Red Kite* for its unequalled blend of humour and seriousness; "Light Shining Out of Darkness" from *Around the Mountain* for its visionary quality; "The Dog Explosion" from *The Fruit Man, the Meat Man & the Manager* for its comic extravagance; "Going Out as a Ghost" from *Dark Glasses* for its moral complexity; "God Has Manifested Himself Unto Us as Canadian Tire" from *None Genuine Without This Signature* for its mischievous verbal excess; and "The Small Birds" from *August Nights* for its sublime simplicity. Others that extend the tonal and stylistic range could easily be found to augment the list (it does not include, for instance, a specimen of his celebrated "documentary fantasies" such as "Recollections of the Works Department"). Hood's motto, indeed, is encapsulated in the title of "Every Piece Different," and if this doesn't *quite* apply to all 129 short stories, the achievement remains extraordinary. It is difficult to imagine another writer of short stories or tales (apart perhaps from Chaucer) who could match this diversity.

Such variety can, however, prove an obstacle to an adequate critical examination of his work. An approach suitable to one story may well be hopelessly inappropriate to another. Or, to make the point in another way, a similar kind of variety to that displayed by Hood needs to be reflected in any extended discussion of his writings. Not surprisingly, such flexibility has not, in general, been forthcoming. Some excellent readings of individual stories have appeared, but the same cannot be said of attempts to come to terms with his work as a whole. There are many reasons for this, besides its quantity and range, and it may be helpful at this time to trace the main lines of critical interpretation from the earliest reviews onward, since such an undertaking reveals a curious change in emphasis over the years.

Hood was fortunate in the welcome extended to *Flying a Red Kite* (1962), his first publication. Not only did it receive wide coverage in the country's newspapers as well as the literary magazines, but the names of many of the reviewers now make up an impressive list of highly qualified writers and critics, though most of them were relatively little-known at the time. They include Munro Beattie, Kildare Dobbs, Arnold Edinborough, Robert Fulford, Dave Godfrey, Michael Hornyansky, John Mills, W. R. Percy, and F. W. Watt. I quote several of their comments when discussing *Flying a Red Kite* in Chapter four. Moreover, one only has to read through the digests of the leading reviews of Hood's early volumes of short stories in J. R. (Tim) Struthers's "Hugh Hood: An Annotated Bibliography" (321-44) to realize that, for the most part, these reviews were positive, even enthusiastic, and also that they stressed his variety of subject and treatment and his stylistic gifts. Some reviewers tackled the complex issue of his blending of fact and fiction, and some, when considering *Around the Mountain*, queried what they saw as a mixture of attachment and detachment on the part of the narrator. It is noteworthy, however, that virtually all were content to consider his work in terms of conventional realism.

But by the time *Dark Glasses* appeared in 1976, Hood had begun to attract a good deal of attention, especially with the well-publicized launching of the *New Age* series the year before. He had been quite extensively interviewed in the early 1970s, and academic scholars had begun to write articles on his work. As Hood made more and more statements about his ambitions and aims, commentators began to recognize the importance of his Catholic roots and to read his fiction, as he advocated, in allegorical terms. In *Dark Glasses*, he made the point even more conspicuous (though not wholly seriously, as we shall see in due course) by titling the final story in the collection "An Allegory of Man's Fate." This hint was taken up, all the more so after Struthers's long and informative interview appeared in *Essays on Canadian Writing* in 1978-9. Here Hood invited his commentators to regard his work as "a secular analogy of scripture" (32). By the time *None Genuine Without This Signature* appeared in 1980, despite Hood's insistence that he was "*both* a realist and a *transcendentalist allegorist*" (Hood and Mills 145), allegorical interpretations following the model of Dante were threatening to become the standard approach to his writing.

This situation was beautifully reflected in a critical exchange in *Books in Canada* in 1980. In the August issue, I. M. Owen published a review of *None Genuine*. Keith Garebian had contributed a scholarly introduction to the book that was included in the "text" edition but omitted from its "trade" counterpart. (This material was recycled by Garebian, with some omissions and alterations, in his Twayne study published three years later.) Owen reviewed the stories in what might be called the traditional way, and then took vigorous exception to the critical interpretation Garebian had offered:

> The most entertaining piece... is the introduction by Keith Garebian, who does his best to see Christian allegory in everything Hood writes. It reads like a parody of academic LitCrit at its most determined; but I fear it's serious. I fear even more that Hood may come to believe it—perhaps does already. (10)

Garebian replied with an aggrieved letter (cutely headed "Owen Hoodwinked," presumably an editorial title) in the November issue. It contained the usual sarcasm and righteous indignation characteristic of "Letters to the Editor" columns, but included one sentence that was clearly justified: "He is surprised to see that I find Christian allegory in Hood's works. I suggest to him that Hugh Hood would be more surprised if I did not make such a reading" (33).

This exchange is especially important because the lines are so clearly drawn. For the most part, academic criticism proceeded unperturbed with its allegorical emphasis. Garebian himself, in his Twayne study, even went so far as to write: "Hood has spoken so frequently about his allegorical method that a critic who does not read his fiction as allegory is either inordinately perverse or helplessly naive" (11). He is right to complain that critics of the early work "usually missed Hood's allegory beneath the documentary veneer" ("Hugh Hood" 102), but his own "sustained allegorical treatment of Hood's work" (105) can err in the opposite direction. It is hard not to agree with Owen when he complains of the critical attitude by which, once a writer is labelled as a Christian, it is assumed that "whenever he mentions a group of three he really means the Trinity." His assumption that, "if Hood describes a hockey game, the 12 men on the ice are hockey players, not allegorical representatives of the Apostles" (10), is surely a healthy one. Garebian's defence of these hockey players as "an Arthurian or Christian emblem" ("Owen" 33) notably fails to convince.

A middle course is surely needed here. Allegorical interpretation is a delicate operation that can be applied deftly or clumsily, either with taste or with the lack of it. To be fair, Garebian is not as narrow as some of his more extreme statements might suggest. Hood's allegory, he argues, "never loses its sensory appeal or allows its inner meaning to antagonize the literal reality under and through which the significance is maintained ... His imagination never becomes ... a mentality that ... denies man's commitment to the physical world" (*Hugh Hood* 12-13). Yet it has to be admitted, I think, that on occasion Hood himself pushed his allegorical preoccupations too far. Most notorious, perhaps, is his claim concerning the title story in *The Fruit Man, the Meat Man & the Manager*, set in a Montréal (Jewish) grocery: "The Fruit Man is God proffering the apple, and the Meat Man is Christ incarnate, and the Manager is the Holy Spirit moving the world" (Interview

38). Here the realistic and the allegorical levels remain embarrassingly separate. Aside from the dubious effect of having Jewish characters enacting a specifically Christian message, the fact that the Meat Man and the Fruit Man take on jobs in more prosperous stores without telling the Manager represents a bothersome split within the Trinity. Such an interpretation confuses rather than enlightens. I agree with Dennis Duffy when he writes: "One must be wary of taking on too heavy a cargo of meaning, even when setting sail with an allegorist" (133). An approach needs to be found that avoids the extremes of naïve realism on the one hand and totally generalized (abstract) allegory on the other. A realism that ignores larger meanings and an allegory that loses contact with the details of ordinary life are equally barren.

At this point, it is important that we look more closely at what we mean when we use the term "allegory," since part of the controversy surrounding the interpretation of Hood's work stems from the fact that the word conveys somewhat different meanings to different people. I depend here on an admirably clear and sensible discussion of the topic in the entry on "Allegory" (written by Northrop Frye) in *The Harper Handbook to Literature*. The basic definition reads as follows: "A story that suggests another story ... an allegory is present in literature whenever it is clear that the author is saying, 'By this I also mean that'" (12). No one is likely to disagree with this formulation, though I feel the need to point out that Frye is *not* presented as saying, "By this I *really* mean that." A higher meaning in no way denies or replaces a humbler one. But the *Harper* entry continues: "If we say that a work of literature 'is' an allegory, we mean that allegorical techniques are continuous throughout; but there are many such works which make only an episodic and sporadic use of allegory" (13). Furthermore, it is noted that the "imaginative effect" of many works "depends on the sense of a great variety of suggested meanings, and would be spoiled by the pinning down of such meanings to implicit alignments with specific conceptions" (13-14).

Difference and disagreements inevitably surface here. The *Harper* entry goes on to explain that in the Romantic period a distinction arose between allegory and symbolism, "the latter being preferred because of its greater suggestiveness and because it does not suggest that a poem can be fully 'explained' in other terms than its own" (14). Hood, it must be admitted, would have disagreed vigorously. Indeed, in his PhD thesis, as I have indicated, he argued for some essential connections between Dante's highly allegorical poetics and those of Wordsworth and Coleridge. On the one hand, far from welcoming a "greater suggestiveness" in Romantic symbolism, he declared: "I hate symbols; I don't mind images but I hate symbols because they propose an other-worldly truth which they never deliver" (TT 19). This is not the place to investigate the validity and consistency (or otherwise) of Hood's position, and such an inquiry would extend beyond my competence, but there can be little doubt that his encouragement of a full-scale allegorical interpretation of his writing led to what I for one consider an excessively rigid, over-intellectualized approach to his work. I'm thinking of Garebian's remark just quoted about the perversity or naïvety of those who do not read his work as allegory, or Barry Cameron's assertion: "I don't think a story like 'Doubles' can be fully understood without calling on Aquinas' concept of analogy" ("Incarnational" 90).

From what I have already written, it should be clear that, while I consider Hood's own comments on his own work to be of considerable value, I do not regard them as sacrosanct. On the other hand, I have never been impressed by commentators who habitually ignore the stated aims of authors and speak condescendingly of the "intentional fallacy." Although writers can fail to realize their ambitions, a statement of intention generally provides helpful clues to the reading of a given work. In Hood's case, however, such comments can sometimes prove misleading. He tended to emphasize a particular aspect of a story, presumably because he thought it was in danger of being overlooked, but in so doing left other qualities unremarked. Critics who *confine* themselves to his stated intentions are likely to become too narrow in their discussions. While taking due note of Hood's comments on individual stories, careful readers will also remember the title of his book of essays, *Trusting the Tale*, which echoes D. H. Lawrence's well-known dictum in *Studies in Classic American Literature*: "Never trust the artist. Trust the tale" (2). Though "never" is perhaps extreme, this is wise advice that also applies to classic Canadian literature.

Granted, Hood announced in an interview as early as 1972, "Everything I write is an allegory, there's no question about that" (Hale 37), but most commentators at that time were obsessed with his realism to the exclusion of any other literary mode. He may well have regretted that statement when he encountered the equally narrow focus of later allegorizing critics. Indeed, in another interview a year later he insisted that he was "not just an allegorist" (Cloutier 51), while his claim to being "*both* a realist... and a *transcendentalist allegorist*" (Hood and Mills 145) followed five years after that. It is surely a mistake to assume that every Hood fiction must invite the same kind of analytical approach. Because his work often responds to allegorical interpretation, there is no reason why all his narratives should aspire to a higher dimension of meaning. I can see no point, for instance, in scrutinizing "The Dog Explosion" in search of erudite profundity.

At the same time, Hood was always deeply conscious of the reflection of the divine or spiritual world on the secular or material world, and vice-versa. In the Struthers interview, he asserted: "I think bringing together the spiritual intelligence and the world of the senses and the world of the incarnate is the fundamental task of every thinker whether he's a poet or a theologian" (23). Or, he might have added, a writer of fiction. And because Hood is an artist, the most impressive statement of the principle occurs within a fiction when, in *A New Athens*, one of May-Beth Codrington's paintings is seen as presenting "the vision of the heavenly and eternal rising from the things of this world" (211). Such an approach can, I suppose, at least loosely be termed "allegorical," but more important, in my view, is the way Hood expects us to be aware of the one while experiencing or imagining the other. When the narrator in the central story of *Around the Mountain* arrives at the top of Mount Royal, it is not to transcend "the things of this world" but to look back down on them from above. The weakness of so much allegorizing of Hood's work is that it tends to leave the realistic level behind in its earnest search for abstract truth. In Hood's work, however, the realistic is illuminated and recognized as sacred by its relation to the divine.

In my account of individual stories within this book, I have often preferred to employ the term "moral fable," employed by F. R. Leavis a generation ago (and now, of course, unfashionable) when discussing such works as Dickens's *Hard Times* and James's *The Europeans*. "I have called *The Europeans* a 'moral fable'," Leavis wrote, "because a serious intention expresses itself in so firm and clear an economy of organization, and the representative significance of every detail in the book is so insistent" (59). Such a description fits Hood's work well, and allows for the almost "fabulous" departure from strict realism in certain of his writings that therefore draw attention to a larger meaning. At the same time it avoids the more rigid associations of "allegory."

Related to the subject of allegory are two topics about which Hood held strong but, from the viewpoint of most of us, unorthodox or even quirky opinions. These involve numbers and names. I believe that Hood's attitudes should be registered, treated with respect, but not necessarily accepted as matters of major significance to an appreciation of his writings. Numerology need not detain us long since its influence is found more obviously in his novels than in his short fiction. John Metcalf recalls in a memoir how Hood "organized his writing life under strange numerological schemes which made vital sense to him but which were incomprehensible to his readers" (*Aesthetic* 78). Fair comment. Hood admitted to Struthers that he had "some kind of fixation about numbers," yet insisted that they "are very important in all art" (Interview 39). This is partly because, as he points out, numerology is important within Christianity (the Trinity, four gospels, twelve apostles, forty days in the wilderness, etc.). He has also asserted that numerological symbolism "makes a kind of scaffolding for the imagination" (GB 128), and it certainly seems to have helped him in structuring his work. But awareness of these effects on the part of readers is another matter. Hood seemingly forgot that scaffolding is dismantled when a building is completed; the observer is not intended to see it. If a number has a clear and self-evident significance, so be it; but no extended piece of writing can proceed for long without involving numbers, and the practice of tracking down erudite meanings for all numerical references is counterproductive.

The use of names raises more complex issues. Serious writers are understandably careful about the names they choose for their characters, and Hood has left a detailed account of his agonizing over suitable names for the main characters in the *New Age* series ("H.H." 104-5). A devout Christian family should employ traditionally Christian names, so, at his wife's suggestion, he turned to the names of apostles: Matthew, Andrew, Philip. So far, so good. Such names are common enough and do not draw undue attention to themselves. But a problem occurs if names sound too suggestive. Appropriate names, outside the old game of "Happy Families," are rare in the "real" world. The more meaningful a name, the more difficult to maintain an illusion of credibility. Consider, for example, the "type" names in Restoration Comedy (Lord Foppington, Lady Wishfort, Horner and Pinchwife) or even in Dickens (Pecksniff, the Cheeryble brothers, Bounderby). When artifice or caricature is involved, such naming can add to the comic effect, but in works with tendencies towards realism, as soon as we become aware of the aptness of a name, we begin to doubt.

More often than not, names are chosen for reasons of euphony, or because they just "sound right," rather than for specific meaning. For instance, Alexandra Ellicott in "O Happy Melodist!" is a distinctive name well suited to a distinctive character. Fessenden is an unusual, memorable name that bestows an immediate sense of dignity to the protagonist of "Getting to Williamstown." On the other hand, Joe Jacobson, a seemingly ordinary name for the young Jewish writer in "Where the Myth Touches Us," becomes, when spelt out as Joseph son of Jacob, profoundly allusive as well. In "Fallings From Us, Vanishings," however, Arthur Merlin's name is too symbolic to be true, nudging us too insistently towards an allegorical reading.

When critical commentary is involved, two further problems arise, similar to those noted in the discussion of numerology. Either authors tend to employ names that do not seem appropriate, or commentators go to excessive lengths to find obscure meanings when it is highly doubtful that they are intended. Both tendencies can be illustrated from "Flying a Red Kite." Garebian reveals that Fred, the name of the protagonist, "is etymologically related to 'peace'" (*Hugh Hood* 15), though few readers are likely to pick up a subtlety of which Hood may not have been aware. At the same time, Fred's wife is called Naomi, a potentially interesting Old-Testament allusion, though no connection seems to link her with the character in the Book of Ruth. Garebian merely glosses it as "another biblical association" (14), which explains nothing. In "Nobody's Going Anywhere!" the father is Peter, whereupon Copoloff-Mechanic finds a link with St. Peter ("his namesake" 42), though the connection is by no means obvious. His wife is Helen, but no even remote reference to Helen of Troy is discernible, so the name is ignored. Moreover, in "A Solitary Ewe" the same critic justifies the name of another Peter because he is "a false prophet" who "reverse[s] the work of his namesake" (74). Heads I win, tails you lose.

Two other amusing anecdotes conveniently illustrate the random quality of the whole topic. Hood introduces a painter called Seymour Segal into two stories in *Around the Mountain*. Seymour is obviously an appropriate—arguably, too appropriate—name for a painter: "Seymour, as his name might suggest, could see things that I couldn't see immediately" (AM 12). Yet Seymour Segal was in fact an authentic painter friend and fellow hockey player of Hugh Hood; indeed, he illustrated some of the verbal sketches in *Around the Mountain* when they first appeared in magazines. Later, Hood even wrote the text of an illustrated book, *Scoring: Seymour Segal's Art of Hockey*, about Segal's work. The prime reason for using the name, of course, was its factual authenticity; its applicability is merely serendipitous. In "A Childhood Incident," on the other hand, the central figure is called Kate. Copoloff-Mechanic makes much of the fact that Katherine is supposed to mean "pure" (120). Again, this may or may not be a conscious additional subtlety on Hood's part (personally, I doubt it), but it is demonstrably not the principal reason for the name. Hood tells us that the story was derived from "an anecdote told to me by my sister-in-law" (SW 12), and Noreen Mallory confirms that it was based on an autobiographical experience of the sister-in-law whose name was Kate.

As for strained derivations, the prize must go to Copoloff-Mechanic's argument that Philip, Sanderson's first name in "The

End of It," should be interpreted as "lover of horses" (46). The only textual evidence she can cite is his wife's telling him to "stop horsing around" (239 [236]), surely a classic if unintentional *reductio ad absurdum*. In short, I see no possibility for any consistency of approach on this subject. If a meaning is obvious, it will be clear to all remotely qualified readers; if it has to be explained with reference to esoteric knowledge, it will prove more befogging than illuminating. Admittedly, there is no hard-and-fast line that can be drawn. Hood's now-unusual familiarity with the Bible may result in deliberate allusions that others will miss, but, for the most part, common sense rather than ingenuity should, I believe, prevail.

Finally, since I am insisting on the variety and diversity within Hood's short fiction, it is incumbent upon me to make some statement about the effect of these qualities on the unity of his short fiction as a whole, and especially on the claimed unity of individual collections. In the Struthers interview, Hood noted that his short stories "have tended to collect themselves into groups" (27), and Copoloff-Mechanic records Hood telling her that "he is preoccupied with the structural cohesion of all his short story collections; some, however, are 'arranged,' while others are 'deliberately arranged'." She infers from this puzzling statement that "some collections were written with a guiding theme in mind, while others were designed after the fact" (92n). I take this to mean that some (*Around the Mountain* being the purest and most obvious example) were planned in their present sequence from the beginning, while others consist of stories already completed that were subsequently placed in a considered and meaningful order.

One can readily agree when, again in the Struthers interview, Hood remarks, "it seems to me a better kind of artist will articulate every piece he does in relation to everything that he has done" (42), and also when he goes on to assert that an artist's individual works "gain by juxtaposition" (43). However, the first of these comments need imply no more than the observable fact that a major author's complete work is generally recognizable as a coherent *oeuvre*. As for the second comment, there is a sense in which this is a natural and inevitable process. Connections can almost always be made between different parts of a writer's work for the simple reason that common interests, attributes, and personal mannerisms are bound to recur. Indeed, it could be argued that virtually any two juxtaposed stories, whether by Hood or anyone else, can yield certain points of connection if one searches diligently enough. In Hood's case, this phenomenon will be augmented by his particular brand of Catholicism that will inevitably be reflected in much of his writing because his mind works in a particular and characteristic way. The resulting similarities will be readily discernible, but this does not mean that they were necessarily intended or planned by the author. Such a unified view is independent of any conscious arrangement or carefully constructed interrelation. The former will be the result of a common cast of mind, the latter of a gradually developed artistry.

An author's "deliberate" arrangement is another matter, though here it is important to insist that in fact Hood arranged his collections in an impressive variety of ways. *Flying a Red Kite* was a gathering, by Hood himself and two friendly editors, of what they considered the best stories that he had written to date. Since he had been experimenting to discover the extent of his abilities, the variety here is considerable, giving one reviewer, Michael Hornyansky, the impression that he was almost ostentatiously displaying the extent of his talents. As a result, attempts on the part of commentators to find a unity in the book have been unconvincing. Garebian finds that most of the stories "coalesce around two complementary themes—various gifts of the spirit, and the alarming 'doubleness' in life" (*Hugh Hood* 15). Copoloff-Mechanic regards the same stories as "attempts at moral, aesthetic or interpersonal enlightenment, whose success depends upon the ability of the protagonists to synthesize concrete and abstract, timely and timeless, daily and divine" (21). William Blackburn, reviewing the 1987 reprint, argued that each of the stories "is, in one way or another, about our ongoing struggle in the face of repeated failure" (183). Such generalized statements are so vague that they convey little: some reconciliation of opposites appears to be involved, but no individual story is thereby enriched by interconnection with another. On the contrary, they are made to sound similar whereas they are strikingly different in tone and effect. The first two stories in the collection reflect back interestingly on each other, as do the "documentary fantasies" ("Silver Bugles" and "Recollections"), and the concluding two stories are linked by their artist protagonists, but little more can be argued with any confidence.

Around the Mountain, in contrast, was conceived (like a novel) as a whole, and written, sketch by sketch, two a month, between January and June 1966, in the order in which they ultimately appeared. At the same time, there is an extraordinary variety of *kinds* of story within the book. It was, however, a successful experiment that Hood never repeated. *The Fruit Man* selects stories written between February 1957 and December 1969. The opening three stories form the "deliberately-related triptych" emphasized in an authorial note, but the connections, as I point out in the appropriate chapter, are so inconspicuous as to be imperceptible to all but the most determined of readers, while three other stories connected by Jewish subject matter are purposefully *not* placed together. The imagery associated with seeing, tinted spectacles, mirrors, etc., links many—though by no means all—the stories in *Dark Glasses*, and the same can be said for references to signs and signatures in some (but again, not all) of the contents of *None Genuine*.

From *August Nights* onwards, the stories are all presented in the chronological order in which they were written (with no omissions). Whether Hood chose to *write* them in a deliberate sequence is not known, but he certainly made no attempt to arrange them after the fact. Here, too, attempts to discover an overall unity prove unconvincing. Copoloff-Mechanic (129) quotes William French in the Toronto *Globe and Mail* to the effect that the only "discernible thread" in *August Nights* takes the form of "the mysteries of nature and interdependence of man and his natural environment" (though how this fits stories like "August Nights" and "Every Piece Different" is beyond me), while she herself falls back on "the idea that all aspects of existence are connected in a divine, coherent plan"—an odd argument, since the collection and its successors are notably less concerned with overt religious issues than his earlier work. Once again, broad thematic connections fail to engage with Hood's literary achievement.

In his later collections of stories, written while his major attention was directed towards completion of the *New Age* series, Hood appears to have abandoned whatever pretence towards unity of subject, style, or approach is arguable in some of the earlier volumes. The pleasure we derive from reading *August Nights*, *You'll Catch Your Death*, and *After All!* consists in an aesthetically pleasing uncertainty. We never know, as we proceed from one story to another, what will confront us. (This is a literary effect that academics tend to neglect.) One story may be richly comic, the next extremely touching, the next intellectually challenging. Attempts to trace connections (Copoloff-Mechanic's last chapter devoted to *August Nights*, or the noting by some reviewers of a preoccupation with birds and/or death in much of *You'll Catch Your Death*) can at best be considered only partly successful. It is more satisfactory to appreciate in these later writings an accomplished fiction writer revelling in his hard won freedom of both subject and treatment.

3

Starting from the States:

A Short Walk in the Rain, The Isolation Booth

In January 1957, three months or so before his marriage, Hood systematically embarked upon his career as a writer. Five years earlier, he had made an abortive attempt at writing a novel but abandoned it after forty pages. Now, however, the fact that he was about to enter an important new stage in his life provided added impetus, and in the next four and a half years, while at West Hartford, he wrote two novels (unpublished) and no less than thirty short stories.

Two statements in his introduction to *Flying a Red Kite*, where he documents these early days, are crucial for an understanding of his evolution as a writer: "I had then no formed sense of myself as potentially a Canadian writer," and "I was trying to learn to write fiction, by the method of trial and error" (15). It was, in many respects, a unique self-apprenticeship. He wrote almost completely in isolation from other writers, and his knowledge of the short story as a literary form was initially based on a wide range of reading that made no distinction between the "serious" or "artistic" on the one hand and the "popular" or "commercial" on the other. From the days of his magazine delivery route onwards, he had been exposed to an extraordinarily diverse list of writers: F. Scott Fitzgerald, Ernest Hemingway, Henry James, and Sinclair Lewis, but also Ray Bradbury, O. Henry, Damon Runyon, and James Thurber from the United States; Joseph Conrad and James Joyce, but also John Buchan, Somerset Maugham, and P. G. Wodehouse from Britain. He began without any literary preconceptions: "I had no theory of my own writing, and belonged to no school" (GB 127).

It will be noticed that no Canadian writers appear on these lists. Canadian literary nationalism would not come into prominence for another decade, so perhaps this is not surprising, but the issue is obviously complicated by the fact of Hood's residence in Connecticut. This turned out to be temporary, but might not have been. As it was, he naturally placed emphasis on American models and looked towards American markets. His younger brother Alex had already embarked on a lifetime career in the United States, and was in the process of becoming an American citizen. Hood might well have done the same. Questioned on this subject in the Struthers interview, Hood remarked:

> I have had no serious major influences in my work . . . from a Canadian writer . . . but there are two Canadian writers who have had some degree of influence upon me. One of them is Stephen Leacock, in relation to *Around the Mountain*; and the other is Morley Callaghan . . . Callaghan's work raised a number of questions in my mind, at various times in my life, about realism, for example, and about the transcendental Being, about Grace . . . But I wouldn't say that I was influenced by Leacock or Callaghan as an artist. I don't think they're good enough artists. (25-6)

A few years later, it may be relevant to add, Hood told John Mills that he considered Callaghan "a poor writer" (Hood and Mills 145).

Looking back on these years in 1987, Hood recalled what he considered "the grounds and principles" upon which he based his career as a writer of short stories: "Any story that I wrote would be aimed at magazine publication, but it wouldn't be a formula story or part of a series [like those by Runyon or Wodehouse]; every story would be different and new" (FRK 15). He was originally aiming at "a few wide-circulation magazines in which the fiction wasn't cut closely to plot-patterns" (10). He insisted on being "perfectly free to choose any subject, any anecdote or observation or fantasy or pure imagining that came under my notice . . . I hoped that with much practice and by the taking of infinite pains I might in time be able to write for *Esquire* and *The New Yorker* and the literary quarterlies and little magazines" (16).

These ambitions were never quite fulfilled. Hood had one story accepted and published in *Esquire*. This was "After the Sirens" (FRK 137-47 [124-35]), which was widely anthologized in subsequent decades. Hood claimed it as "about the first anti-nuclear war story to appear in print" ("H.H." 88), but John Metcalf, commenting on its inclusion in *Flying a Red Kite*, described it as the "only bad story in the book" (*Kicking* 149). This is somewhat unfair. The story was (and is) highly readable, and surely an acceptable, successful example of its (popular) kind, but Metcalf is, of course, right in describing it as "quite uncharacteristic of Hood's genius." Hood soon realized that his gifts lay in other directions, and it is significant that *Esquire* never accepted any of his subsequent (and subtler) submissions. As for the *New Yorker*, the magazine *almost* accepted "Recollections of the Works Department," but eventually turned it back. However, Hood succeeded in publishing regularly in "the literary quarterlies and little magazines," though this ambition was mainly satisfied in Canada rather than in the United States.

The first short story that Hood ever wrote, "A Short Walk in the Rain" (SW 29-47), did not achieve print until 1989 in the volume of the same title, yet it ranks high among his early work and will therefore repay consideration in some detail here. Hood, indeed, considered it "as good... as anything I've written" (FRK 18). The simple plot climaxes in a search—in the rain—by an Italian brother and sister, Angelo and Bella Mazzaferro, accompanied by the unnamed narrator, for their mother's unmarked grave in a Queens cemetery. It is, then, a simple story about "ordinary" people, apparently headed for a touching, perhaps pathetic conclusion in the tradition of Callaghan. But the telling is as noteworthy as the tale, and it includes elements that will characterize Hood's stories throughout his career.

The first sentence is highly revealing: "I arrived in New York a week before Truman's second inaugural and got a job in the mailroom at *Time*." Not the references one would expect as the first creative sentence of a Canadian author. Here Hood is obviously writing with an American magazine readership in mind; yet we note that the speaker "arrived" from elsewhere, and soon learn that he comes from Toronto. Since we know that Hood (uncharacteristically, it should be said) derived the main lines of the story from his younger brother who spent most of his life working for Time, Inc. (see "H.H." 88), we may assume that much of the detail is a transcript of Alex Hood's account. All this has no immediate bearing on the quality of the story, but it points to the care Hood took to meet the expectations of American editors and readers.

More obviously, as Hood acknowledges, the title and culminating scene constitute a literary bow in the direction of the ending to Hemingway's *A Farewell to Arms*, which "consisted of a short walk in the rain" (SW 9). Moreover, his simple, direct, sometimes colloquial but always efficient prose clearly benefits from Hemingway's example. At the same time, students of Canadian literature will notice other elements in the story which indicate that Hood also had the work of Callaghan in mind. Certain casually introduced details unostentatiously yet palpably evoke the Catholic attitudes of both the narrator and the Mazzaferros: not merely "a great big red-and-gold picture of the Sacred Heart" but the observation that Bella "was always giving people things" and that she "was the nearest thing to a real saint I ever saw." Hints of both writers eventually blend in the climax when the grave is approximately located: "Then, by God, the two of them knelt down, on that soaking sod, in a heavy rain, and recited the Rosary. It took about ten minutes. I could feel rainwater running down my back inside my shirt. Finally they got up." The setting and subject could be Callaghan's; the rhythms of the prose might be mistaken readily enough for Hemingway's if Hood had not succeeded in putting his own "signature" upon them.

Hood also had other personal contributions to make to the story. Readers of his later fiction will recognize a strong geographical/topographical preoccupation in the account of the narrator's approach to the Mazzaferros' apartment, and especially in the description of the drive out of Manhattan in heavy traffic. Moreover, he offers here an excellent example of the ambivalent or even ambiguous ending that was to become a feature of his work. After the scene just quoted, where the brother and sister's devotion to, and grief for, their mother seem unquestionable, the tone changes dramatically:

> A great big smile came across Bella's face. Angelo started to laugh softly.
>
> "Mama's really gone now," Bella said.
>
> Angelo echoed her. "Really gone. For good."

This is an example, comparatively rare in Hood's work, of what he calls "the surprise ending, the neat and sudden reversal of the reader's assumption," which he recognizes, against the received opinion of academic criticism, as "a staple element of the shorter narrative at any moment in its history all over the world" (FRK 12). In this case, however, it is not the actual ending, but leads instead to the final, and more characteristic, complicating paragraph:

> Nobody spoke a word all the way home in the car. I kept thinking it over; I felt as though they'd been laughing at me. Either I'd cheated them, or they'd cheated me, or somebody pulled a fast one somewhere. The whole thing was very mixed up.

At the last moment, we are required to rethink our attitudes to both the central character and to the narrator. What seemed clear and straightforward is clear and straightforward no longer. Even the apprentice Hood is a writer who makes considerable demands upon his readers. He freely acknowledged that he "learned an immense amount in writing 'A Short Walk in the Rain'" (11), and we can well believe him.

Of the thirty stories written in West Hartford, six were chosen for inclusion in his first collection, *Flying a Red Kite*, and four others eventually found their way into later gatherings. Of the remainder, those still residing in Hood's desk were published for the first time in *A Short Walk in the Rain* in 1989, while those that had been printed in magazines appeared in *The Isolation Booth* in 1991. In my opinion, few of these equal "A Short Walk" in quality. At this time, Hood was experimenting, finding out which kinds of story and technical approach were best suited to his own gifts. Inevitably, some of these early efforts succeeded while others failed, and he expressed his own opinions about their strengths and weaknesses in his introductions to the first three volumes of the *Collected Stories*. As has been noted, the stories written at this time taught him "the unlimited range of possibilities inherent in this great literary form" (SW 9), and he mastered a sufficient number of these possibilities for his subsequent mature work to become known for its remarkable variety.

Consider, for example, "The Strategies of Hysteria" (SW 55-63) and "That 1950 Ford" (SW 65-73), both set in West Hartford itself. These are readable but not particularly distinguished stories; they are linked, however, not merely by setting but by two principal characters, Mrs. J. Delta Williams the landlady ("closely modelled upon a certain landlady of mine" [14]) and Mr. Twombly the roomer (Hood's self-presentation, a sympathetic if slightly pompous figure whose like appears in several stories and eventually transforms and develops into Matt Goderich of the *New Age* series). More significantly, these are interrelated first-person narrations, one told by the man and one by the woman. Here is experiment indeed. It was generally believed at this period that male novelists were rarely capable of assuming a feminine idiom and persona and vice-versa. (This was long before political correctness and the absurdities of the "appropriation of voice" movement.) Hood was testing his technical and imaginative abilities here, and was sufficiently successful in employing a female narrative voice that he continued to do so, occasionally but regularly, throughout his subsequent career as a writer of fiction.

The stories themselves are fairly low-keyed, intended for casual reading. The first centres upon the landlady's bossy attitudes, while the ending of "That 1950 Ford" is implausibly contrived, with Twombly murdered by an irate, unbalanced neighbour. But Hood manages to create an authentic voice for Twombly ("... she's a very odd duck. She belongs to all those offbeat religious groups") and for the landlady ("... he passed beyond several years ago ... It was men like J. Delta Williams and Gus Funk who made West Hartford what it was"). Moreover, the writing of these stories clearly helped him to compose subsequent stories that interconnected creatively with each other, including the juxtaposed "documentary fantasies" in *Flying a Red Kite*, "Socks" and "Boots" in *Dark Glasses*, and the "Bronson" stories scattered through the later volumes.

Other experiments include attempts to write stories that relate specifically to the beliefs and practices of the Roman Catholic Church, particularly in relation to the contemporary secular world. Examples include "Which the Tigress, Which the Lamb?" (SW 115-22), a light-hearted comedy arising out of a potential scandal at a women's college (obviously based on St. Joseph) when an undergraduate is triumphant in a beauty contest, and "The Triumph of the Liturgy" (SW 107-14), representing the pre-Vatican-II American Catholic Church as organized, efficient, materially prosperous, but spiritually inert. This descriptive sketch demonstrates Hood's gift for clear-sighted social analysis, achieving what he described as "a mild satiric sting" (SW 19). But he soon abandoned such direct attempts to introduce sectarian religious issues into his writing. The best of these, "Cura Pastoralis" (FM 173-87), highly influenced by Callaghan in treatment, and successful in its presentation of a priest facing what would now be called a sexual harassment charge, was written in 1957 but not published in volume form until 1971, was the last of these stories to appear. Needless to say, this does not mean that Hood gave up presenting religious matters in his fiction; rather, he learnt to introduce them obliquely, and far more subtly, into his writing.

One such story that reflects his religious though not his specifically Catholic concerns is of particular interest, not because it is a complete success but because it shows him attempting to combine a number of fertile ideas that never quite form an artistic unity. This is "The Winner" (IB 41-51), which begins with a remarkable essay in perspective. We are presented with a view of the Toronto Exhibition grounds in November from the top of a gigantic Ferris wheel. This "angle of observation" is that of a "solitary workman ... bullied into the climb by his foreman" in order to make some correction to the mechanism. But his position suggests other traditional viewpoints: that of the God of the Old Testament or Zeus on Mount Olympus, for example. We are reminded of these associations when he "dropped his monkey wrench, hoping the foreman stood below it," a detail repeated in a subtler vein by Hood in the opening scene of *Be Sure to Close Your Eyes*, where the workman Charlie Rutter carelessly drops a faulty brick which falls close to the infant May-Beth. But this exalted viewpoint can also bring to mind the ancient image of a man poised at the height of the Wheel of Fortune.

The workman's "unconcerned glance" becomes an "amazed gaze" (note the conscious—even self-conscious—alliterative play here) when he becomes aware of the "bulging mushroom" of a tent still in use for the International Congress of Championship Evangelical Silver Bands. This tent becomes the setting for the opening narrative scene in the story, which somewhat awkwardly abandons the observing workman for a different but related figure, Harris Fudger of the Chippewa (*sic*) Salvation Army Band, an expert cornetist (anticipations of *Be Sure to Close Your Eyes* once again), who, though distinct from the workman, is similarly "solitary" and similarly bullied by his "Cyclopean bandmaster."

Fudger, possessed of one of Hood's highly suggestive but not excessively allegorical names, completes a brilliant cornet solo, then slips away to a local (authentic) bar to drink with his cronies (one of whom eventually makes brief appearances in the *New Age* series). But this is an act strictly forbidden by Salvation Army rules. Worse still, two initially puzzling references to a "blue paper" in his tunic are eventually explained when he announces to his friends that he has won a hundred and fifty thousand dollars in an Irish sweepstake. But the Salvation Army authorities share the keen observation of the original workman, and track Fudger down. He is summarily expelled, an action that sparks the moral climax of the story.

For Fudger, this initially seems a crushing sentence: "I can't go. Where would I go? I was brought up in the army..." We don't need a nudge from the moralizing side of Hood's nature to see here at least a faint echo of the expulsion from Eden, an enforced transition from an ordered, if constraining, existence to the unknown complexities and tribulations of a free but threatening world. In his introduction Hood describes the story as "a series of variations on the religious notion that riches... carry certain ultimate penalties" (14). But Fudger visits his bank, is inducted into the responsibilities of the rich, and returns to his friends in the bar, who now refer to him "obsequiously" as "sir." We may be reminded of the closing scene in Richler's *The Apprenticeship of Duddy Kravitz*, where the successful Duddy is at last treated respectfully and offered credit at the very moment he no longer needs it. But "The Winner" was written a year before Richler's novel appeared. The final sentence of Hood's story reads, "He had never felt so wealthy," and provides a poised if somewhat enigmatic conclusion in which innocence and experience, loss and gain, are subtly balanced.

"The Winner" is rich in invention to the point of indigestibility. On a first reading, it is difficult to follow the direction of the narrative, and the style, distinctive and effective as it is in individual instances, at times detracts from the narrative line. Hood himself refers to his attempt "to imitate the language of the oral fabulist, not a wholly successful undertaking" (14), and this is true. There is an occasional, almost embarrassing self-consciousness in the writing, as in the following extreme example: "O ye heavenly fair, ye gods, we thank thee in thy wisdom for having first made known to men that chief fruit of the malt and hop. I mean beer, blest cordial. Thus muses cornetist Fudger …" (But one doubts if he ever did.) Yet the sentiment, style aside, is one that carries the Hood's approval. The very next story in order of writing, "Marriage 401," contains the remark, "the senses are from God and so are the delights of the senses" (SW 100). So too are the delights and even the excesses of the effects possible within the English language. Hood has not yet fully controlled his art, but "The Winner" is evidence of an extraordinary potential.

Four other successful and propitious stories deserve mention, all of which can be seen as experiments with techniques that will eventually enhance his later work. In the first-person "Suites and Single Rooms, with Bath" (IB 117-27), an unnamed, thirty-year-old protagonist is separated from his wife after five years of marriage, and tries to explain to himself how the break occurred. His own attempt at self-justification is punctuated with recalled—or, more likely, at least half-imaginary—conversations with his wife, illustrating his side of the soured relationship. There is no narrative action in the conventional sense; the situation, brilliantly indicated by the title that specifies the setting but remains detached and offers no clue, is everything. The tone varies radically from the sardonically amusing and even witty to the pathetic and disturbing in its revelation of an unbalanced mind. All in all, it is remarkable for its psychological sophistication, a skill for which Hood is rarely praised.

Hood explains in his introduction that it was written for Robert Weaver of the CBC, who requested "a story specifically for radio broadcast by a single live speaking voice" (17). Ten years later, Hood wondered if it "might also be available to silent reading" (18), and it was promptly accepted and published by *Queen's Quarterly*. He hoped to discover whether readers would detect its radio origins, but got no immediate response. An oblique answer came, however, when *The Isolation Booth* appeared in print, since at least two reviewers singled it out as the best piece in the book. For my part I find myself, while in the process of reading, regarding it as a prose equivalent of one of Robert Browning's dramatic monologues, and this also provides a belated answer to another query. Hood had asked himself: "Would readers miss the effect of the pauses, the shifts in emphasis or pitch? If you subtracted the effect of the performance, would the story be disfigured?" (18). The answer is, surely, that the reader of a dramatic monologue is obliged to take over the combined function of actor and even stage director. He or she must insert the appropriate pauses, changes of pace, etc. And so here. A tall order? Not really, since this is what careful readers of any work must do when confronted by any piece of creative prose where there are nuances to be recognized and allusions to be picked up. "Suites and Single Rooms" is one of the most challenging as well as most successful of Hood's early stories, and constitutes a valuable experimental *tour de force*.

Another worthy experiment is "I'm Not Desperate" (IB 59-67), which takes the form of a philosophical conversation between two young men, Tony and another unnamed narrator, with the minimum of either plot or narrative. They are clearly Americans and presumably philosophy students at university, who argue in a pub over large quantities of beer about morals, French existentialism, honour and duty, conduct, and even the nature of jokes. As Hood notes in his introduction, it is a "serious parody" (15) that exemplifies the difference between Hemingway's style and his own. It is composed almost entirely of "allusive witty talk," to quote the opening sentence, and in terms of the fictional presentation of ideas, looks forward to Hood's later discursive pieces, notably "The Hole." One senses that he was deciding how far he could go in making philosophical argument interesting in itself as well as valuable as an intellectual exercise.

At an opposite extreme is "The Ingenue I Should Have Kissed, but Didn't" (IB 129-44), written after "Silver Bugles" and "Recollections of the Works Department" which were chosen for *Flying a Red Kite.* Here, Hood focuses on his experience as a not-very-good actor at the University of Toronto, a subject to be dealt with in more detailed and complex fashion in the first chapter of *The Scenic Art.* For Hood himself, it represents an extension of the essentially "slippery" form of "quasi-memoir" developed in *The New Age* into a "kind of meta-fiction" (IB 20), since the fiction itself becomes a meditation on the nature of narrative itself. The title-subject is left open within the text ("Maybe I should have kissed her ..."), but not in the title itself, as if the point is clarified—or fictionalized!—in the process of telling. All the characters in the story are presented under their own names with the exception of the "Ingenue" herself, who is only revealed in the Introduction as Kate Reid, later to become one of Canada's best-known actresses. To what extent the identification affects our response to the story is a moot question. Whether anecdote transforms into fiction by the very act of presenting it as a crafted narrative is another. Whatever the answers to these questions, Hood is here developing his mastery of "documentary fantasy."

"The Glass of Fashion" (SW 87-95), one of the most distinctive stories from the early years, belongs to a possible subgenre of the story, which Hood identified as "media folklore" (SW 16) and describes elsewhere as "a kind of story that I might almost claim to have invented" (IB 11). It can be defined as a story of contemporary life (variants can take place in commercial office buildings or commercial locations) which illustrates a representative pattern, an image, in Anthony Trollope's phrase, of "the way we live now." Hood's most detailed discussion of this kind of story may be found in "Floating Southwards," a short essay he wrote to accompany his stories anthologized by Metcalf in *Making It New* (1982), the story in question being "Breaking Off" from *None Genuine Without This Signature*:

> ... this story signals the significance of extremely complex patterns of group behaviour—and linguistic usage—using individual lives as enactments of social forms; the story has embedded in it an ongoing criticism of various types of communication ... I'm not talking about mere social history—any idiot can write social history—and I'm not primarily concerned with the multiplication of observed detail, although many of my critics have said that I am. I mean the way that membership in an army, a church, a big business, a social class, a language group, circulates like arterial blood ... into personal conduct in such a way as to make of occasional selected individuals immensely expressive representatives of what is happening in their world. (108)

Porky Valentine (a too-good-to-be-true name, but acceptable in a moral fable) is just such a representative man, a radio producer eager to enter the rapidly expanding television industry that clearly represents the future. He is proud to be from a non-Ivy-League university (American reference once again), because it suggests a desirable independent originality, until he discovers that "a couple of Yale men from the staff of another show" are in fact from Georgetown and Akron. He cherishes his apartment with a "de Kooning that had cost like Hell" till he becomes aware of a "terribly expensive Jackson Pollock hanging back-to-back with [it] in the adjoining apartment." Thinking that he detects a significant new trend, he moves way out of town to a well-wooded area, only to find a sometime business connection occupying the next lot. Finally, he decides to spend a summer in total wilderness in a virgin area of Algonquin Park (revealing Canadian reference once more), far away from the urban and sophisticated. Yet even here, there are tourists on the next lake, and when he returns to Manhattan civilization, he finds that all his associates "were tanned the colour of old shoes" and display other traces of similar back-to-nature endeavours. So much for the efforts to be "up to the minute—or even a little before the minute"; the Joneses are not kept up with so easily.

But what ultimately distinguishes this story, of course, is the quality of the writing—for example, the following sentence:

> He always regretted missing the war, as he might regret missing a hit show or the St. Lawrence-Queen's game; but his punctured ear-drums kept him in New York where he did mighty important work on morale-building home-front sustainers.

A remarkably flexible prose is required here in order to move from the criticism implicit in the opening part of the sentence to the breezily colloquial "mighty important," contrasting in turn with the jargon of the final words. The whole story is marked by an enviable ease and poise.

Finally, only as I reread this chapter after completing the rest of this book was I struck by the fact that I hadn't found space for discussion of a story as elegant and accomplished as "Educating Mary" (IB 145-59). Here the narrator is an elderly bachelor whose pompously formal prose style is caught expertly from the opening sentence onwards. Mr. Stewart promises to be a bore of the Polonius variety, but Hood is careful to ensure that, like Polonius, he is never a bore to read about. The plot involves his originally unsophisticated secretary and a nephew who eventually marries her. Mary is emerging "from the chrysalid state" and by the end of the story she has overwhelmed the nephew and is turning her attentions to Mr. Stewart himself. As Hood remarks in an explanatory comment: "He isn't educating her; she's educating him" (IB 20). Mr. Stewart's final comment—"I should keep my head. I must!"—is a cry of anguish, and we are at liberty to doubt if his determination will be strong enough, much as we doubt Charlie's "this time I want my rights, I'll fight, I'll fight" at the close of "A Solitary Ewe." It is, to be sure, a later story than most in this early collection, written indeed a few months after "A Solitary Ewe," and provides proof that, by the time Hood moved to Montréal in 1961, he was ready to enter his fictional kingdom.

4

Displaying His Wares:

Flying a Red Kite

In the early 1980s, John Metcalf, looking back at the flowering of Canadian fiction in the previous twenty years, hailed *Flying a Red Kite* (1962) as "the first book of modern stories published in this country," and added: "Or perhaps it might be more accurate to say 'traditionally modern.' These stories were in the line of descent of all modern stories. Relatively few people have grasped how centrally important this book is to Canadian literature" (*Kicking* 149). Moreover, in an interview at this time, he asserted: "It was Hugh Hood with *Flying a Red Kite* who signalled that we were joining the rest of the 20th century" (13). These are strong words, and are clearly intended to be challenging. It would be possible, for instance, to press the claims of two other short story collections that had been published a few years earlier. Mavis Gallant's first book, *The Other Paris*, had appeared in 1956, and Ethel Wilson's *Mrs. Golightly and Other Stories* followed in 1960. But Gallant was an expatriate living in France, and her book (not published in her own country until 1986) attracted little immediate attention in Canada, while Wilson's collection, though it gained a respectful welcome, was generally (and rightly) regarded as a coda to her novels rather than a significant event in the history of the Canadian short story. By and large, Metcalf, who wickedly points out that W. O. Mitchell's *Jake and the Kid* had appeared the year before Hood's collection and that the two books represent voices from two different worlds, is justified in his assessment—and in his judgment that Hood's stories "have withstood the passage of the years magnificently" (149).

Certainly, the book caused a stir in Canadian critical circles. Dave Godfrey, writing in the *Canadian Forum*, considered Hood's prose "as lyrical, precise, individual, and witty as that of anyone writing today" (229). Kildare Dobbs, in *Canadian Literature*, hailed it as "a subtle and generous book." In praising "Three Halves of a House" as "magnificent" and as presenting "a sense of the whole of Canada," he insisted: "Hood knows very well what he is about. He uses the literary past as he uses his own." He also emphasized something that could not, alas, be taken for granted: that Hood "has taken pains... to master the English sentence" (72, 73). F. W. Watt, in the *University of Toronto Quarterly*, welcomed "the outstanding collection by Hugh Hood" as the "happiest event of the year" in Canadian literature (391). Especially gratifying is the fact that these and other reviewers recognized and praised both the variety of Hood's subject matter and the quality of his style.

But it was Michael Hornyansky, writing in the *Tamarack Review*, who produced what I consider to be the most shrewd and perceptive review. He found the volume as a whole "brilliant" and commended the "skilful experiments with tense," but registered a single weakness that he found in a "gleaming" performance: "the fleeting sense that even as I am most caught up, I am still watching Mr. Hood perform." He grew "faintly aware of an Apprenticeship in progress behind the scenes," of being present at "a brilliant selection of toccatas, faultlessly executed," but demonstrating a little too emphatically that the young author was "getting his hand in" (87-9). Of course, Hornyansky was unaware of most of Hood's earlier stories that remained uncollected at that time, though he might have encountered "The Isolation Booth" and even "The Ingenue I Should Have Kissed, but Didn't," both of which had appeared in *Tamarack Review*. He would not know—though he seems to have instinctively felt—that *Flying a Red Kite* presented a shrewd display from the young writer's portfolio.

Hornyansky's response is a remarkable anticipation of the conclusions that I shall be forming in the course of this chapter. We find a Hood who has become aware of the breadth of his powers and is revelling in the opportunity to exhibit his talents. Whether the volume is ordered and shaped as a whole is arguable—Copoloff-Mechanic (ch.1) believes that it is, while I have doubts—but the four opening stories clearly divide into two related sets: two that Metcalf would call "traditionally modern," and two that artfully blur the boundaries between conventional fiction and documentary memoir. In addition, the two concluding stories, though fully self-sufficient, take on further resonances when we see them as both concerning artists—a young writer and an aging film-maker—both struggling with the challenging nature of their respective art forms. Hornyansky recognizes a precocious talent staking out an ambitious territory, with a self-conscious determination that can occasionally become too conspicuous. But he is prepared to acknowledge that Hood "knows exactly what he's doing and doubtless could show each place he's gone wrong" (88).

The opening story, "Falling From Us, Vanishings" (27-41 [1-17]) repays detailed attention here, not because it displays Hood at his best but because it shows him bubbling over with a multitude of ideas and techniques which are effectively realized but which he cannot fully control and unite. It opens elaborately and self-consciously: "Brandishing a cornucopia of daffodils, flowers for Gloria, in his right hand, Arthur Merlin crossed the dusky and oak-panelled foyer of his apartment building and came into the welcoming sunlit avenue." This is formal, sophisticated prose at the opposite extreme from the vernacular, yet a few lines later Arthur is humming a popular song of the period, and immediately after that we overhear his interior monologue.

The name "Arthur Merlin," we can see readily now with the gift of hindsight, flaunts Hood's allegorical interests yet at the same time strains credulity. (Twenty years later, the more experienced Robertson Davies, choosing a name for a character with Grail associations in *The Rebel Angels,* plumped for "Arthur Cornish," which is suggestive without seeming too symbolic to be true.) When we learn a little later that the surname of Gloria, Arthur's girlfriend, is Vere (truth), we cannot but feel that allegory is being *imposed* on the narrative, though it is true that decidedly few noticed this in 1962. The conspicuous allegorical superstructure is in fact pulling against the realistic detail.

Stylistically, however, despite the initial suggestion of fine writing (the "welcoming" avenue, maples that lean "encouragingly"), the opening is more successful. It helps to establish the somewhat pompous, over-literary, not-quite-of-this-world character of Arthur, against which Gloria is forced to rebel. At the same time, the switch to interior monologue, and therefore a first-person perspective, allows Hood to move into the casual, conversational style, which soon became his hallmark. This includes verb contractions ("I'll," "it's," "don't") and an early instance of the colloquial, generalized "you," which echoes throughout the book and is even more evident in *Around the Mountain*, where its regular employment establishes a sense of tonal continuity.

In addition, Hood reveals a capacity for the crisp and arresting phrase, as in the image of Arthur's Volkswagen engine "grinding like a coffee mill," or that of the doctor's widow in her contrasting antique "ghosting home from the drugstore" (the first, uncharacteristically comic use of "ghost," a word that develops serious connotations in the course of the story). He also displays a gift for articulate yet arresting dialogue, as in the exchange between Arthur and Gloria when he is astonished to discover that she considers Frank Sinatra "a foolish bald old man" (Sinatra was forty-five at this time, eleven years older than Arthur just as Arthur is eleven years older than Gloria):

> "Whom do you consider young, for goodness' sake?"
> "Any girl whose bust hasn't developed."
> "How do you tell about boys?"
> "There isn't any decent way," she said, laughing.

The period idiom in a nutshell. Subsequent dialogue is complicated by Arthur's congenital literariness and his obsession with quotation, but Hood manages their frustrated discourse (a more accurate word than conversation here) with assurance. At the climax, when Gloria exclaims, "You're haunted! You're a ghost-ridden man, you're a horror!," we can see that Hood has read Henry James with care, and the rhythms place the story in a literary as well as a temporal context. Hood is hinting that, if Arthur lives in the past, Gloria represents the equivalent of a Jamesian heroine in a post-Second-World-War situation.

This story is best appreciated, indeed, for its finely achieved "sense of period" (a phrase that occurs twice in the opening pages). Set on Long Island in 1961, it can be seen as a culmination of the West Hartford writings, with a more evident grasp of what Garebian calls "Hood's sense of texture" (*Hugh Hood* 16) than such efforts as "The Strategies of Hysteria" and "That 1950 Ford," produced four years earlier. In addition, he has now mastered the art of tapping far deeper emotional states. It is a story about time and personal attitudes to the past, and in his presentation of Arthur's complex attitudes towards Gloria and her mother as well as towards the past and the future, he achieves an admirable balance between sympathy and censure; Gloria's phrase "you poor dear idiot," is poignantly apt. I cannot consider adequate Garebian's view of Arthur at the close as "content and blessed with his memories" (18); the "glory" has fallen from him, and vanished.

There is a sophisticated confidence and subtlety in the writing here that must have seemed startlingly original to a Canadian literary generation for whom Callaghan and Hugh Garner were considered major practitioners. To take but one example, the detail of Arthur's ordering for Gloria a regular supply of daffodils to be kept in cold storage links neatly with his image of her as "primavera": "If he kept her like spring, she might never think of the eleven years' difference in their ages." But human beings cannot be kept in cold storage; time and love relationships cannot be frozen. Moreover, this cluster of image and idea is chillingly developed in the memory of Gloria's father, a victim of Pearl Harbor, trapped in death within his sunk ship. Cold storage indeed, and a painful gloss on Arthur's Keatsian quotation about the moving (not frozen) waters. His excessive literariness is thus integrated into the larger themes of the story.

In many respects, then, Hood's début appears dazzlingly precocious, as Hornyansky noted. However, close readers who happen to be Canadian will not read far without detecting an oddity. As the story proceeds, it becomes clear that the setting is the United States, later narrowed down to New York State. The geographical references include not only Pearl Harbor, but Philadelphia, Boise,

Cheyenne, New York itself, and finally Long Island. But the first specifically topographical references are to Roxborough Road and Rouge Hills, both suggesting Hood's Toronto. Yet there is no indication that Arthur, like the narrator in "A Short Walk in the Rain," is a Canadian immigrant. Moreover, in the flashback to Arthur as a little boy, we find that his parents' names, Alex and Margaret, are those of Hood's own parents. "Westport," mentioned a little later, may be judged neutrally ambiguous (New York State or southern Ontario?).

These are, to be sure, minor details, but important in showing that Hood had not yet recognized the desirability of keeping American and Canadian references separate. "Fallings From Us, Vanishings" was written in March 1961, four years after "A Short Walk," but almost exactly between them, in April 1959, he had written "Which the Tigress, Which the Lamb?" and later, as he notes, spoilt the story, originally set in Connecticut, by clumsily resetting it in Ontario, "introducing references to Wentworth County, Toronto, Kingston," with the result that "the texture of the piece became blurred" (SW 20). One of Hood's later distinctions is his topographical exactitude, his fidelity to local detail, and we can notice here a brief but significant glimpse of him in the process of mastering his art.

"Fallings From Us, Vanishings" was the last story he wrote before moving back to Canada. "O Happy Melodist!" (43-62 [18-39]) followed seven months later, with "Flying a Red Kite" and two other stories in between. As the placing within the volume indicates, it was deliberately written to form the second half of a diptych, as a mirror image of Arthur Merlin's story. Another doomed love affair is represented, a parallel study of incompatibility. Both central characters hold modest jobs on fashionable magazines; both are obsessed (though in different ways) with time passing; both appear self-sufficient yet highly vulnerable. And once again we find a version of American pastoral, with the untouchable Sandy Ellicott portrayed in her trendy New York apartment but also in the rural retreat of West Cornwall, Connecticut. (Hood makes much in his introduction of allusions to West Cornwall resident James Thurber's life and writings, although these seem of little importance to the overall effect.) But Hood is now more circumspect in his use of mythic allusion. Copoloff-Mechanic (25) is right to point out that the names of Alexandra and her sister Helen are classical in origin; but, more to the point, Hood doesn't make the mistake of calling his virgin-goddess figure Artemis. There is a reference to "Castle Perilous," and the view from her tower-like apartment suggests that of a (self-)imprisoned maiden from myth or fairy tale, but we are spared references to Danae or Rapunzel. Alexandra inhabits an American version of Tennyson's Palace of Art, which may collapse around her at any time, but Hood no longer feels the need to press home his allusions.

We are in the presence here of brittle but extremely skillful social comedy, yet the story contains a deeply serious core. The theme of a career woman's unmarried life was, of course, timely at this period, and Hood treats it sympathetically but guardedly, with a firm and shrewd originality. At the same time, we recognize the same carefully observed and precisely phrased descriptions ("that damned inconvenient floor-lamp shaped like a spear, the kind of thing that you might see in a production of *Macbeth* in Central Park," "A menu with six hundred illustrated items on facing pages, with a lot of little cards clipped to each leaf, with a special Jumbo-sized cocktail, and Chianti bottles hanging here and there"). There is an unobtrusive, relaxed wit ("If she stood up, five men would come near and ask what she wanted, and that was what she did not want"), and a taste for incongruous humour at the exposure of "terrible old Jim Savitt," who confuses anchovies and artichokes. The smart world of ostentatious name-dropping is admirably caught: "Jack and Jackie aren't here yet, they're still trying to arrive," an allusion rendered poignant but not outdated by the Kennedy assassination soon after the book first appeared). Above all, the society presented may seem to have liberated itself from moral concerns, but the story has not. Jim Savitt disqualifies himself by wanting to be married to Alexandra "even for six months," a remark she condemns as "deeply naïvely corrupt." And finally, we are offered one of Hood's enigmatic endings. Alexandra is apparently secure, self-sufficient, freed at last from Jim's attentions, with "her heart mov[ing] lightly." But the concluding paragraph moves back to her work as fiction editor surrounded (as we were told earlier) by colleagues who "couldn't read," and Hood leaves her making a considered but inconspicuous artistic decision and "wondering if anybody will understand." Her future is uncertain.

Michael Hornyansky found this story "entrancing" (88), while Kildare Dobbs was unimpressed, condemning "a false sophistication in the narrator" (73). I agree with Hornyansky. Dobbs appears to have overlooked the fact that Hood presents the story by means of an assumed sophistication that implicitly criticizes (I would argue, even "places") the subject matter. John Metcalf is, I believe, commenting more shrewdly on the same phenomenon when, in discussing the next two stories in *Flying a Red Kite*, he writes: "Hood has largely abandoned the flash and filigree of his earliest rhetoric because, I should imagine, his mastery of it bored him" (*Kicking* 152). Probably so. I would add, however, that this rhetoric was appropriate to the stories in which it occurs, and that he dropped it when turning to a very different aspect of his creative experience that demanded an equally different tone and style.

There are certainly no traces of "flash and filigree" either in "Silver Bugles, Cymbals, Golden Silks" (63-82 [40-62]), an account of Hood's association with his high-school band, or in "Recollections of the Works Department" (83-114 [63-98]), the product of a probably brief summer job repairing roads in Toronto. These stories gain their effectiveness from an art that conceals rather than draws attention to its artistry. At first sight, it seems as if these two narratives, with their sharply portrayed Toronto settings, represent a total break from his earlier flirtation with the American magazine market, but the truth is more complex. As he notes in his introduction, "Recollections" was in fact written while he was still living in West Hartford, and was "aimed specifically at *The New Yorker*." He describes it as "an essay in the genre which Thurber had created and *The New Yorker* made its own, the affectionate memoir of one's early life." Indeed, he "nearly sold it there" (20). Hood greatly admired Thurber's *My Life and Hard Times*, which he praised as "unquestionably the masterwork of a literary kind which Thurber may even have invented ... the loving, fantastic memoir of one's childhood and adolescence told in an exactly voiced idiomatic American English with all the refinements of fictional technique" (14). The words "fantastic" and "fictional" should be noted here.

Later in the same introduction, he commented that "nobody in Canada has ever identified 'Recollections of the Works Department' as a *New Yorker*-style memoir" (21), yet this failure is hardly surprising since the material is so conspicuously local and Canadian. Thurber may have provided the original inspiration, but Hood has so totally transformed it that the source is unrecognizable. His own prose here is decidedly "idiomatic" but it is idiomatic *Canadian* English. Thurber's work now seems dated, its unrelieved comic tone having long since lapsed into the oppressive, while Hood's version is crystal clear, highly readable, and as fresh as if written yesterday.

These stories are often discussed in terms of pure realism, but, as Metcalf has remarked, "it is a profound mistake to think of Hood as a 'realist'" (*Kicking* 152). Hood's own phrases are "super-realism" (GB 127) and "documentary fantasy," a term that evolved during an interview with Robert Fulford in 1975. Three years later, in the Struthers interview, he elaborates: "Documentary would relate to ... how one lives from day to day, what the world around us is really like," while documentary fantasy concerns itself with "the facts transformed by the image-making power" (82). As he told Fulford: "To me the words 'real' and 'imaginary' are not in any way opposed to one another. The wholly imaginary is what is most real" (77). In an even later essay he refers to these two stories as "semi-fictional memoir narratives" ("Elephant" 98).

Once again, Hornyansky provides a helpful if paradoxical comment. These stories, he observes, "have the fictional quality that distinguishes all good autobiography ... the Torontos sketched here convince us, not because we know they 'really happened' to the author but because he has realized them" (87). Ostensibly, "Silver Bugles" is a memoir of Hood's schooldays in "the famous Oakdale Boys Band," "Recollections" an account of a summer job after graduation working for the department that looks after the condition of the city streets. The former tends towards nostalgia, the ambitions and anxieties of school life exquisitely recaptured, while the latter (where the narrator is specifically named "Hood") is more carefree and comic in emphasis. Here the particularity of Toronto's buildings and road system is accurate to the minutest detail, and the apparent stylistic ease bears all the hallmarks of authentic memoir, the resultant vividness becoming, to use Hood's own term, "super-real." How much of the detail in these stories is truly autobiographical and how much invented cannot, of course, be determined with any authority, but Hood's whole literary career involves the blurring of the traditional fact/fiction distinctions which, as a result of modern psychological discoveries, are no longer recognized as sacrosanct. We now acknowledge, as Hornyansky implies, that all autobiography contains an element of fiction since, however eager a writer may be to record the truth, the facts of the past have already been distorted within our memories.

"Documentary fantasy" is therefore an apt term, and it is one that Hood develops later, especially in *Around the Mountain* and, more intricately, in the novels that constitute *The New Age*, notably *The Swing in the Garden*. In "Silver Bugles" and "Recollections," then, he found his own characteristic voice. Variety of tone and approach continue, and some of the subsequent writings are inevitably less successful than others, but henceforward we are considering a writer in full command of his mature creative powers.

"Three Halves of a House" (115-36 [99-123]) quickly established itself among the most highly praised of these stories on the part of early reviewers and commentators. Dobbs considered it "magnificent" (72), while for Dennis Duffy it was "one of the finest items" in the collection (137). Similarly, Hornyansky described it as "possibly the best story of the lot," adding, with what can now be seen as extraordinary foresight, that it was "certainly the most promising pledge of a novel to follow" (87). The story indeed looks forward, in numerous ways, to Hood's later work. The first "novel to follow," *White Figure, White Ground*, takes up the theme of heredity and "forbidden degrees of kindred," and focuses on another ancestral house presented within the traditions of Gothic. "Three Halves of a House" was also the first place in which the name "Stoverville" (= Brockville) appeared in print, and although the city is characterized there as a stagnant dead end, it gradually developed in Hood's imagination, along with the immediate area, as an emblem of Ontario's rural peace and tradition, primarily in *A New Athens* but also in the *New Age* series as a whole.

Above all, its original and highly effective structure represents a stylistic breakthrough. The story of the Bostons and the Phillipses and the Haskells is framed by passages of profound imaginative geography in which the stretch of the St. Lawrence east of Kingston is seen—or, rather, in Hornyansky's phrase, "realized"—as a unique centre both serving and served by much of the Canadian land mass and, indeed, of North America: "a third of the continent leans pushing behind the lakes and the river, the pulse, circulation, artery, and heart, all in one flowing geographical fact, of half the North Americans, the flow we live by all that long way from Minnesota to the Gulf." Here, the relation between non-fiction discourse and invented narrative, sometimes compared, sometimes contrasted, anticipates the literary method that Hood perfects in the individual sketches in *Around the Mountain* and employs in much of his subsequent work.

There is also, I believe, another reason why "Three Halves of a House" provokes references to full-length fiction. Dave Godfrey admitted in his review that he encountered difficulties in first reading the story, though he "finally caught on" (229); my own experience in coming to terms with the story was virtually identical. Godfrey doesn't elaborate, but my own feeling is that the narrative is a little too close-packed. The relationships are not easy to keep in mind during a first reading, and it may be that the story would have fitted better into the form of a novella. I am reminded of Hood's later comment about the title story of *A Short Walk*: "it contains the material of a long story ... I see that I have had to compress, to fudge, to move rapidly over events which should have taken longer in the telling" (SW 10). If that is true of his first story (though I'm not convinced that it is), it applies at least as well to the crowded effect I detect here (three halves, after all, imply crowdedness in themselves). I would have liked to see more of Ellie's father and of his relationship with his wife, and for the details of Grover Haskell's origins and earlier life. Maura Boston, it is interesting to note, proved fascinating to Hood just as "bicultural Angela" did in *Around the Mountain*, and she becomes a minor but memorable character in *The New Age*, where she is successful as a poet and an art curator, but never marries as she hopes to do here. Moreover, she ultimately returns to the Stoverville she finds so stifling in "Three Halves of a House."

If we know her subsequent family history, her presentation here becomes even more complex, perhaps contradictory. I have no intention to explore the aesthetic implications of this kind of hindsight, but merely record that it is an effect that can occur several times as we try to come to terms with Hood's *oeuvre*. Be that as it may, "Three Halves of a House" is an accomplished story, though I am not fully persuaded that it quite warrants the high evaluation that it has enjoyed. Academics may possibly overpraise its "problematic" quality rather than concentrating on its status as an achieved work of art; but its subtlety, its poignant presentation of disturbed emotional states, and its narrative and descriptive skill and complexity are not in question.

For the most part, the Canadian stories in *Flying a Red Kite* are superior to those set in the United States. Hood, we like to think, is more assured and comfortable when writing of his own people. There is, however, one notable exception, "He Just Adores Her!" (149-67 [136-57]), a demonstrable masterpiece that has passed almost unnoticed (perhaps because, nationalism being what it is, it is set out of the country), though Patricia Morley recognizes it as "the funniest story in the collection" (117).

This has been a misunderstood story, ironically, since it is essentially a story about misunderstanding. Hood reports that when he originally submitted it to *Esquire* (which had already published the manifestly inferior "After the Sirens,"), the editor was horrified: "This story *has four points of view*" (22)! Yet its effectiveness is dependent upon this fact. Hood begins by focusing firmly on the Lovelaces, Larry and Elizabeth, yet for much of the time we see them from the viewpoints of their apartment neighbours, Francis and Paula Rosebery, who eventually usurp the central place in the story. They hopelessly misinterpret both what they see and what they assume about the Lovelaces' private lives, but as readers we can (or should) know better, because we have already seen the Lovelaces for ourselves, beyond the distorting lens of the Roseberys' imaginings.

The Lovelaces are in their early twenties, the Roseberys in their mid-thirties, but the comparatively modest difference in age soon resembles that of a whole generation. Superficially, this is a delicious comedy of manners, with its comparisons and (more often) contrasts between the young and the not-so-young. The Lovelaces are endearingly uninhibited, if trendy and even, perhaps, slightly vulgar (as the first paragraph suggests); the Roseberys are solid citizens, a little dull, morally conventional, set in their ways, but dependable. The contrast in their styles is communicated by their artistic tastes. Elizabeth dresses in the height of fashion, and fixes up their old apartment, including a kitchen "in a contact paper which simulated bricks with ivy growing out of crannies" until it was "stunning and unrecognizable" yet obviously up-to-the-minute contemporary. She wants books for their bindings rather than their content, books that look impressive and fit in with her décor. Paula, knowing that "you would find that sort of thing in the decorators' magazines every month," refinishes junk furniture, paints and frames her own pictures so that their apartment "resembled no one else's." The Roseberys' taste (Telemann, Bach, etc.) may be prominently intellectual, but it is genuine, with Francis an amateur authority on eighteenth-century music; the Lovelaces' is represented by "a Tom Lehrer number" and Dvorak's New World Symphony "turned up very loud."

Hood's capacity for comedy may occasionally be equalled in his later work, but it is never surpassed. The two crucial scenes between the couples border on the farcical yet are profoundly revealing in terms of character. The farce is manifest in the situation but augmented by Hood's unerring stylistic skill. In the first, Larry is locked out of their apartment late at night because Elizabeth has fallen asleep after returning from a party in which liquor flowed freely. Francis discovers him in the hall calling "Poopsie-pie" through the keyhole. The process of waking her and persuading her to open the door is elaborate, but the scene ends as follows:

> ... at the fourth try she revived enough to roll out of bed and come to the door. She wasn't visible but nevertheless Francis felt his sense stir at the idea that she would be undressed.

> "Good night, Larry," he said decently, traitorously, and closed the door.
>
> The nosey bugger, thought Larry as his own door swung open ... She wavered in front of him, and he put his hands on her small hips, feeling their warmth delightedly through the gauzy slip. He kissed her with rapture, tasting stale gin.

Hood goes beyond the boundaries of simple "realism" here; the scene is full of complex implications, most of them communicated through style. Notice in particular "decently, traitorously," and the final sentence with the culminating last phrase.

The second scene occurs at the final revelation. Elizabeth has been away for several weeks, in fact seeking a better job in New York, but the Roseberys concoct various sensationalized scenarios ranging from "one of those quickie divorces" in Mexico to murder, with Larry having "walled her up in the cellar." Eventually, however, she returns, as the Roseberys discover one afternoon when, once again in the hall,

> they heard a bumping sound and their neighbours' door flew open. Elizabeth came falling out backwards to land with a thud on the floor at their feet. She was decently covered in an enormous terrycloth bathrobe but plainly had nothing on underneath. Francis caught a momentary glimpse of ivory inner thighs and averted his head. She looked up at them and they looked down at her.
>
> "We were wrestling," she said foolishly. Larry appeared in the doorway clothed, and approximately in his right mind.

This is a comic climax with a vengeance, but the full effect is only achieved with that brilliant "approximately" in the final sentence.

So far I have emphasized the comic, even farcical aspects of "He Just Adores Her!" because Hood has made them so conspicuous, but there is a more serious element within the story that needs to be recognized. Francis, as the quoted passages indicate, finds himself attracted to Elizabeth. The climactic scene disturbs him in a number of ways. Elizabeth's reappearance shatters the fantasies about her absence and makes them seem humiliatingly absurd, while the "glimpse of ivory inner thighs" brings home to him a full realization of his lust. Indeed, the presentation of the older couple throughout the story involves a psychological depth for which Hood is rarely given credit. Paula reveals herself throughout as the more perceptive, and generous, of the two. She recognizes his attraction, regrets it, but also understands it, and knows that he is far too morally responsible for the condition to become a serious threat. All this is skillfully established by Hood between the lines, as it were, of the situational comedy. Gradually we come to realize that Francis's ostensible dislike of Elizabeth ("Mrs. Lovelace whom he sedulously ignored... The bitch, he thought") conceals an infatuation he doesn't want to admit to himself. We also come to appreciate Paula's quiet confidence ("Men need women like me for the long pull"), her generosity of spirit and preparedness to acknowledge her mistakes ("He just adores her!... I think it's lovely the way he treats her"; "we made that story up... they're beautiful"), and above all her genuine love for her irritable and imperfect husband, justifying his unfashionable assurance that "passionless" and "loveless" are not the same thing.

In other words, the structural balance between the two couples is also maintained in our attitudes towards them. In accordance with traditional comic norms, we are basically on the side of the young lovers, and aspects of the Roseberys' character are decidedly unappealing, but they shouldn't be dismissed too readily. Hood presents them with a poignant sympathy while at the same time acknowledging their imperfections. Besides, they may even be right in their view that their own jog-trot relationship, if dull compared with that of the Lovelaces, is more likely to endure.

The opening four stories in *Flying a Red Kite* clearly divide into two related pairs. This has encouraged some commentators to find similar pairings throughout the book, but unfortunately such endeavours tend to lead to forced comparisons and distorted interpretations. Copoloff-Mechanic, for instance, insists on comparing Francis Rosebery in "He Just Adores Her!" with Peter Haggerty in "Nobody's Going Anywhere!," arguing that both "defer regenerating their world through physical and moral communion respectively. Just as Francis's excessive rationalism leads to a frigid marital life, so does Peter's superstition cripple his moral existence" (39). I'm not entirely sure what this statement is intended to convey, but find the generalized pattern totally misleading when compared with what Hood communicates through the words on the page. Significantly, Copoloff-Mechanic insists on the way the Roseberys "suffer a frigidity of the heart that is mirrored by their icy bedroom" (39) and fails to notice that the adjectives "icy cold" and "frigid" are also employed in references to the Lovelaces' bedroom (159-60 [148]). Moreover, while emphasizing Francis's "passionless ... rationalism," she never even mentions the instinctively physical attraction towards Elizabeth which becomes, as I have indicated, so important and complicating an element within the narrative.

Her treatment of Peter in "Nobody's Going Anywhere!" (169-84 [158-75]) is equally unsatisfactory. She roundly condemns him for his attempt "to evade the world" and for ignoring "the responsibility to initiate his daughter into the moral universe" (40, 41). On the contrary, the whole story concentrates on the fact that he *cannot* evade the world. A struggling artist, Peter is trying to protect his daughter from the dangers and distresses of human existence, and is here faced with the problem that every parent must face: how and when to introduce her to the harsh realities of injustice, suffering, and death. Sally has made friends with a Jewish Hungarian boy whose father dies of a heart attack after a stressful trip to New York to meet refugees (not an "uncle," as Copoloff-Mechanic claims [41]), who had been arrested while attempting to cross a border before leaving Europe. Both father and son had, in addition, been subject to racial intolerance on their journey back to Montréal, and the father dies of a heart attack soon afterwards. All this information is reported to her parents by Sally, who all too clearly "had no inkling what a Jew or a D.P. was" and is unaware of what she is saying.

Peter knows that "three and a half is too young for some kinds of experience," but circumstances force him to explain matters to Sally, only to be asked the dreaded but inevitable questions: "Won't you die?" ... "Will I die?" ... "Where do you go when you die?" Theirs is a Catholic family, but Peter himself has religious doubts: "Are you filling them with false hopes, crippling their little psyches, by teaching them a religion and the hope of immortality?" But he tells her about the traditional Christian heaven in the fond hope that he "had gotten the story right." This is a basic human situation, and Peter's dilemma is presented feelingly, with evident sympathy.

And he is rewarded. That night, he experiences "bright dreams," in which all the elements of the day's experience are jumbled into a pattern that ends positively. Finding himself playing cards with a shadowy opponent ("He couldn't see his opponent's face but he guessed who he was"), Peter is presented as about to draw the winning ace. But for Copoloff-Mechanic, his "sermon to his daughter concerning the resurrection of the spirit is revealed as a sham" because "winning for him depends upon mindless ritual" (42). This argument makes, I confess, no sense to me, especially since it seems to presuppose a hard rationalism comparable to that condemned in the Roseberys of the previous story. The underlying tone of Hood's narrative—and of all we know of his attitude to people and faith—is surely against it.

Thematically-minded commentators might well find links between "Nobody's Going Anywhere!" and "Flying a Red Kite" (185-96 [176-88]) on the ground that both stories concern themselves with close relationships between fathers and daughters. This similarity may well have encouraged Hood to place them together. But the two stories invite comparison not on account of their thematic similarities but because of the contrasting ways in which the stories are told. Both present their protagonists as moving from religious uncertainty to a more positive attitude, but in "Nobody's Going Anywhere!" the pattern is complicated by the decidedly ambiguous image of W. C. Fields (described at one point as Peter's "god") that serves as an enigmatic frame to the story. "Flying a Red Kite" is more straightforward in presenting a young man's emotional change from depression to confident faith while flying a kite with his daughter. Hood's narrator underlines the point within the text when, the subject of kites and kite-flying being introduced and designated "somehow holy," Fred Calvert acknowledges a kite as "a natural symbol." (This story was presumably written before Hood had fully developed his preference for "allegory" over "symbol" [see 28 above].) There is little difficulty, of course, in recognizing kites as images of aspiration. Whereas Fred had been depressed in his journey from downtown Montréal when the bus passed a cemetery and a "spoiled priest" was heard to comment, "It's all a sham… they're in there for good," the kite, when it at last flies, rises in the air towards the traditional location of the Christian heaven. Moreover, if we are prepared to interpret the structure of the story in this way, we can also appreciate the geographical movement from downtown Montréal to the Calverts' home halfway up the mountain—the traditional place to attain vision—when the kite-flying is successful and Fred "knew all at once that the priest was wrong."

These are the terms, I would argue, in which the text asks to be read. Any attempt to enlarge upon the allegory threatens to distort. John Mills offers a brilliant and sensitive (if brief) reading in his article, but other commentators have tended to go further. Copoloff-Mechanic, for example, sees the kite, hovering not merely over the story but over the whole collection, as "an emblem of [the] merging of divine love and mortal witness" (22), but this is a theological rather than a literary reading. To be sure, kites are borne on the wind, itself a widely recognized symbol of the spirit. Hood would have known W. O. Mitchell's *Who Has Seen the Wind*, and Mitchell's second novel, *The Kite*, appeared coincidentally in the same year as Hood's volume. But I see no reason why the kite should be seen as "hovering" over (say) "Fallings From Us, Vanishings."

In her next paragraph, Copoloff-Mechanic claims that it is the kite's "cross-piece" that makes a natural symbol, but this is not what Hood says; in fact, the cross-piece isn't mentioned until some six pages later. The same critic also wants the story to end with a "natural eucharist" (23), a bold and imaginative idea, but not, I think, Hood's. Certainly, the story ends by focusing on the juice of the crushed raspberries on the daughter's chin, but to interpret her song about the gingerbread man as indicating the "holy wafer" can hardly be termed anything less than desperate, if only because it detracts from the delicate moment of fulfilment experienced by father and child. When Hood wants a scene of natural communion, he makes it fully explicit, as in the picnic in the same location portrayed in "Looking Down from Above."

Garebian, though more judicious, can also over-interpret. According to him, in responding fully to Hood's story we should not only recognize the fact that the name Fred suggests "peace" (see 32 above) but also that the surname Calvert "forms an association with Calvary" (*Hugh Hood* 14, 15). Yet Fred, a married book salesman, seems a long way from qualifying as a Jesus figure, except in the most general sense in which the life of Christ provides a model for all believers. Here allegory appears to have severed any connection with realism, a procedure that denies an essential aspect of the natural symbol: that the cord forms an all-important link between the heaven-aspiring kite and its human controllers.

I have to admit, however, that my own reading might run counter to Hood's own. He informs us in his introduction that he intended the "flying red thing" in the final sentence to represent not merely the kite but "the Pentecostal tongues of fire which descended on the Apostles" (23; cf. Acts 2:3). This association is not likely to occur to most readers, not even (I would think) to many thoughtful Christian readers. It possesses, to be sure, an intellectual, theological, and even structural appropriateness: while the kite moves upward from earth towards heaven, the Pentecostal tongues of fire move in the opposite direction, from God to humanity. But I would argue that, although such an interpretation is available as an extension of the traditional, "natural" association, it is not essential. Hood admits (FRK 23) that the story originally contained three additional paragraphs that "moralized the meaning of the narrative." He wisely took the advice of a magazine editor and cut them, but may well have weakened the "Pentecostal" reference in the process. As the story now stands, if we respond like Fred Calvert to the "natural symbol" presented within the text, that is sufficient for a fully adequate reading. If individuals wish to venture further, well and good, but the resultant interpretation may then be of a story that they, rather than Hood, have written. And, by the same token, Hood himself may choose to interpret his own story in a manner that goes beyond what he has communicated within the text.

"Flying a Red Kite" can be regarded as the modernist short story *par excellence*. It exists as an example of autonomous art, detached from the situation of the writer. Fred Calvert may live on the slopes of Mount Royal and be a newcomer to the city, but his circumstances bear no other resemblance to Hugh Hood's. (Noreen Mallory tells me that Hood did in fact take his elder daughter on a kite-flying expedition, but the events have been fully subsumed into the texture of the narrative.) As a fictional creation, it exists at the opposite extreme from the conspicuously autobiographical "Silver Bugles" or "Recollections." This is a story remarkable for its impersonality; it contains all the desired qualities of a well-wrought urn, the notable artistic criterion of the period. Not so "Where the Myth Touches Us" (197-221 [189-217]). Hood describes it in his introduction, along with "Three Halves of a House," as belonging to "the kind of allusive, laboriously worked-out, syntactically complex, poetic stories one saw in the pages of *The Kenyon Review* and *The Hudson Review*" (20). It is subtly planned and structured, well paced, with verbal echoes and repetitions revealing considerable care and skill. That the subject is fiction writing, however, suggests that intimate personal experience is involved, and anyone reading it with even an elementary awareness of Canadian literary history will recognize factual and autobiographical elements that Hood has adroitly woven into his narrative but, arguably, hasn't been fully able to control.

Here are many of the more significant facts lying just beneath the surface of the story. David Wallace, an established novelist, is an obvious portrait of Morley Callaghan, as the description of his Toronto home (the now-famous 20 Dale Avenue), the broad lines of his biography, his writing habits, and the pattern of his literary career all attest. Joe Jacobson, the young and aspiring Jewish writer, though of Hood's generation, seems at first sight very different from his creator, but their circumstances are in fact significantly similar. Joe decided that, if he could succeed in having six stories accepted for publication, he would be justified in calling himself a writer, and it is no surprise to find Hood telling an almost identical story about himself ("H.H." 93).

But more immediate interconnections are involved. Hood has related how he became close friends with Callaghan's son Michael at university, and "used to go to the Callaghans' home for parties" at which "Morley was always ready to discuss his own work, and the abilities of would-be writers of my generation" ("H.H." 87). Moreover, Hood's wife Noreen Mallory has informed me that she believes Callaghan had a profound effect upon her husband's decision to become a writer. All these circumstances are directly reflected in "Where the Myth Touches Us." It may also be remembered that it was at the Callaghans that Hood first met his future wife, "who was at that time sharing an apartment at 20 Dale Avenue with two other young women" ("H.H." 87).

The main action in the story belongs, of course, to fiction. There was no clash of publication dates between any of the writers' books; *Flying a Red Kite* was, after all, Hood's first full-length production. But there are a number of less evident points of connection that prove intriguing. "Joe Jacobson" is, as I noted earlier, a disguised form of Joseph son of Jacob. In the Struthers interview, Hood recalls how, in the summer of 1956, he "used to go with Noreen over to the Callaghan's [*sic*] house and have these long, long [talks] from ten o'clock at night 'til three or four in the morning about the novel he was working on" (26). This novel, and the one that plays its part in the dénouement of Hood's short story, was *A Many Colored Coat*, whose title brings to mind the biblical Joseph son of Jacob. In addition, Hood rightly comments in the introduction that "Where the Myth Touches Us" is "obsessed with the kinds and modes of fatherhood and sonship" (21). The story begins and ends with a memory of Joe's dead father, and the action involves an implicit comparison between his biological father and his father in art. After the concluding confrontation with Wallace, Joe "thinks of the dedication to his book, TO MY FATHER, and thinks to himself, I'm glad it's for him, for my father, for my real father." How relevant is it, we may wonder, if we turn back to the beginning of *Flying a Red Kite*, to find that Hood's dedication is "to my father and mother"? While Hood's mother, unlike Joe's, was still alive, his father had died in 1959.

I am naturally aware that the arguments in the last few paragraphs will be considered absurdly irrelevant to a certain brand of literary critic, and to some extent I can sympathize with this view. I am by no means a passionate advocate of a primarily biographical or psychological criticism, but in this case I consider it not only appropriate but even essential. We cannot, I believe, come to a satisfactory and balanced view of the story and of its quality if we sidestep the obvious difficulties that form part of the story, its implications, and its reception. We cannot, for instance, ignore the fact that it is also about the implicit rivalry between one literary generation and another (as Wallace's outburst, "We're all competing," demonstrates). Moreover, it is clear that Wallace is portrayed within the story as a novelist who is past his prime ("the guy's written out"; "David had written nothing so good as his first half-a-dozen books for ten years"). Joe, it is implied, is poised on the brink of a successful career, and can easily be seen as a supplanter. All this is, to be sure, "fiction," but the exactitude of the "documentary" aspect of the story inevitably suggests the relationship between Hood and Callaghan. If we know nothing about the biographical undercurrents to the story, this need not matter. Yet an informed reading of the novel, the kind of reading that Hood demands, will necessarily recall the factual situation.

We face an interpretative dilemma here, and one that is crucial to any evaluation of the story. Was Hood making his own public declaration of independence from a former respected master? It seems highly unlikely. Anyone who knew him at all well will vouch for the fact that, highly ambitious and conscious of his own remarkable powers as he may have been, he was not that sort of man. Yet the fact remains that he published the story in Callaghan's lifetime. Can he have been unaware that it was almost certain to give offence? While this also seems unlikely, it appears to be the explanation. Because I have always been uneasy about this aspect of the story, I asked Noreen Mallory for her views on the matter. She obligingly told me of matters that have not, so far as I know, been made public in print, and are certainly not generally known, and she has kindly allowed me to reveal them here. Apparently, Hood wrote to Callaghan before the story was published to warn him that he was the model for a character who could easily be misunderstood. After the story was published, however, Callaghan was deeply offended, and cut off all communication. Ironically, then, the climax of the fictional situation anticipated the subsequent non-fiction events. Thus it would seem that a young Hugh Hood, underestimating the sensitiveness of an older writer as seemingly thick-skinned as Callaghan, made an unfortunate decision that dramatically concluded their personal relationship.

In purely literary terms, "Where the Myth Touches Us" is remarkable for its range of mood and tone, including the painfully humorous episode where the young Joe praises Wallace/Callaghan for a piece actually written by Irwin Shaw, and the wickedly comic moment when an earnest undergraduate asks "What do you do about myths?", duly glossed by the narrator as the "most dreadful" question of all. It leads, however, to the introduction of the title phrase, where "myth" is employed in a rather vague and (at least in my view) unconventional way. This results in a slight blur affecting our overall response. Yet it is an accomplished story guaranteeing in the sureness of its construction that Hood was approaching his maturity as a writer of short fiction. If it seems, with its early publication, to represent a somewhat regrettable lapse in taste, this can now be explained as the result of inexperience and naïvety rather than, to borrow a phrase from the succeeding story, "mutinous envy" (227 [222]).

"The End of It" (223-42 [218-39]) was being written early in 1962 when the publication of *Flying a Red Kite* was already in the planning stage. As Hood explains, his editors "felt that an additional story—if possible a brand-new one"—would be desirable in the interests of "a cohesive volume" (FRK 24). "The End of It" fitted the bill perfectly, and not merely in terms of title. He goes on to describe it as "a completely imaginary story" (meaning that, like "He Just Adores Her!," it was original in its conception and subject) and one "which imitates an art and the forms of that art, and tries to show how they function." The art in question is not fiction, which would have been a serious mistake after "Where the Myth Touches Us," but film. The central figure, Philip Sanderson, is a senior, aging producer at the National Film Board who is trying to decide the most artistic and effective way to shoot a documentary film entitled *A Walk Home from School.* But Hood is being somewhat playful and ingenuous in calling it a "completely imaginary" story, since this particular walk home, presented as that of Sanderson as a boy, duplicates Hood's own in Toronto from De la Salle College to Cornish Road, where the Hoods lived briefly in the late 1930s. In fact, personal experience and detached invention, fact and fiction, are here skillfully blended.

Hood himself had no personal experience of filmmaking; as he admits in his introduction, at the time of writing he didn't even know the whereabouts of the National Film Board premises in Montréal. But he was a keen movie watcher, both in cinemas and later on television, and he had characteristically acquired a remarkable amount of detailed knowledge about both films and filmmaking that was put to use in *The Camera Always Lies*, the significantly titled novel written a few years later, and later still in *Property and Value*. But although we learn a good deal about cinematography in the course of reading, it would be seriously misleading to imply that "The End of It" is a didactic story full of theories of art. If it were, the central section devoted to Sanderson's relation with Margery Endicott, the sometime wife whom he still loves, would be an irrelevant excrescence. This is, first and foremost, the portrait of an artist. In addition, it concerns itself throughout with the perennial matter of time passing, the clash (as in "Where the Myth Touches Us") between one generation and another, and ways in which the past can—or cannot—be recreated in works of art.

The opening scene, in which Sanderson and his junior assistants watch CBC footage of a famous mile race at the Commonwealth Games held at Vancouver in 1954, is a case in point. We soon realize that the filmmaker's interest in it stems from hopes for a clue towards solving a problem relating to his own film. He is impressed by the way in which it exists as a "single sequence" without any attempts to cut or dissolve, to zoom in or change a camera angle (all the admired, sophisticated techniques), and is shocked to learn that it was the result of serendipitous accident when a second camera was put out of action at the critical moment. Yet the scene makes an additional, perhaps subtler point. The race had taken place eight years before the "present" of the story, yet the excited response of those who watch it parallels that of the original spectators, even though the result is long known and the event a matter of history. Not only has an incident from the past been preserved accurately, but the emotional state surrounding it was caught so successfully that it is repeated at every subsequent showing.

That evening, Sanderson has a dinner engagement with his ex-wife, which similarly evokes a past, but one beyond the reach of film, accessible now only through memory and therefore unrepeatable. Thoughts of his childhood documentary inevitably return, and serious doubts begin to surface. Movies, like the race footage, though from the past, are no longer in the past but "are all in the present just as you see them." Although "Consciousness" is itself "a single sequence," can he risk such a sequence lasting fifteen minutes rather than four? In any case, a camera attempting to recapture his childhood past will inevitably "lie" in important details: there are no longer any streetcar tracks on Yonge Street, and the Packard showroom now displays Volkswagens. In this sense, at least, you can't go home again. He can photograph his (and Hood's) local church, but how can he "tell the audience in so many words [*sic*!] that it's the church of our mother of perpetual help"? He thinks suddenly, "*maybe I'll never get it*," and over dinner, faced with a past that so obviously cannot be recaptured, he admits, in a moment of devastating clarity, "I've been on the wrong track. What I've wanted to do can't be done on film."

That might well have been "the end of it," but Hood moves on to one of his enigmatic and intriguing conclusions. The following afternoon, Sanderson returns to the projection room without his assistants and examines the race footage in minute detail, then sits back "with an odd air of triumph" to watch the climax in solitude and silence while his "disembodied interior voice" responds with the spectators in the past "until the race was over." Has he at last found the key to his technical and artistic dilemma? Will the innocent spontaneity of his walk home from school be caught on celluloid at last? Or is a recreation in memory (which cannot be shared) now considered sufficient? We cannot tell, but some kind of resolution appears to have been reached.

The story is not remarkable for conspicuous stylistic effects, but Hood employs other methods to make it distinctive. Structurally, for instance, he uses various angles of vision, cuts, and changes of narrative viewpoint in contrast to the "single sequence" praised within the text. He also employs quotations to subtle effect. The first, an epigraph, from P. K. Page's "The Stenographers," aptly introduces the race and stadium imagery, but those familiar with the whole poem know that it contains an equally apt dreaming back to childhood (and even includes a walk home). The second, near the end, is from Coleridge's "Ode to Dejection," appropriate to Sanderson's sense of failure, but in the poem follows hard upon the famous phrase "My shaping spirit of Imagination," the recollection of which may serve as a salve to Sanderson's own dejection. And finally, of course, the title is richly ambivalent, suggesting at one and the same time the end of the race, the end of the film clip, the end of Sanderson's marriage, the end of the walk home from school, perhaps the end of the documentary project, and even the end of *Flying a Red Kite*. It is a masterly conclusion to a masterly collection.

5

Anatomy of a City:

Around the Mountain

According to Hood himself, *Around the Mountain: Scenes from Montréal Life* was "intended as a documentary/fantasy portrait of the city and its people, politics, folkways, geography, and appearance" (9)—in other words, a book that would display considerable variety within a firmly defined structure. In the Struthers interview, he ventured further: "A complete rotation around the mountain from east to west takes place, and the stories are calculated according to how high up the mountain they are" (45). Similar remarks appear elsewhere, but the statement is not, in fact, quite accurate. While it is true that the first story is set north and slightly east of greater Montréal, and the last west and slightly north (Hood seems to have depended on a standard street map in which the top was not straight north), the vast majority of the stories in between focus on the area of downtown Montréal just east of Mount Royal itself. Only the central story, "Looking Down From Above," much of which, like "Flying a Red Kite," takes place on the never explicitly identified Mount Royal, is centrally concerned with positions up or down the mountain.

More definite is the temporal progression. The twelve stories move from winter, through spring, summer, and fall, then back to winter again. They are not, however, rigidly confined to the months of the year. The opening story begins just before Christmas and extends into January, while the concluding one ends with an epiphanic moment on the following Christmas Day. The intervening sketches generally proceed month by month, with occasional overlaps backward or forward, though the seasons or festivals of the church year (Easter, Saint-Jean Baptiste) may be specified rather than the month itself. The cumulative effect fosters our growing awareness of different parts of the city, with its diverse inhabitants living their lives according to their own beliefs, interests, and limitations. The weather is constantly changing, and helps to establish a distinct overall mood in each sketch. Yet Montréal, with its mountain and its unique character, dominates, and we receive a vivid impression of the city at a significant moment in its history: 1967, the year of Canada's centennial and the celebrations (never themselves mentioned in the text) at the Expo site within the city. As Hood himself wrote, "I intended to create an encyclopedic record… that would enshrine an historical moment like the proverbial fly in amber" (18).

The book was originally produced as what might be called a personal centennial project, and it was hoped, by author and publisher alike, that it would serve as a keepsake for Expo visitors. The Hood family had settled in Montréal only six years earlier, so it was, in a sense, an account of his initial exploration of the city and its environs. Moreover, as an ambitious creative writer, he was intent upon producing a work of art of more than temporary interest. All these factors need to be kept in mind as we approach the book more than forty years later.

The original reviewers were somewhat puzzled but generally intrigued by Hood's blend of fictional and non-fictional techniques. John Robert Colombo suggested that he employed "two styles—the documentary and the dramatic, sometimes simultaneously" (quoted in 1984 Bibliography 341); Peter Gzowski shrewdly noted that the author and members of his family appeared "even in scenes that had been fictionalized" (70). Hood himself explained his position a few years later when he wrote of "tinkering around with a kind of fiction very close to fact," having become aware that "reporting, communication and the narrative art were coming closer and closer to one another" (GB 7).

Much of the unity of the book is achieved through consistency of style, which does not mean that there is no stylistic variation, but rather that Hood is careful to maintain the sense of a recurring tone or mood while at the same time producing all sorts of variations on the achieved norm. An important element in this effect is the narrator, and here I find Hood's explanations more confusing than helpful. "I wanted to adjust the narrator," he told Struthers. "It's not all the same narrator. People think they're all told by the same man; but they're not, really. They're told by quite different people" (Interview 44). This may be one of the occasions when we need to trust the teller rather than the tale—or, to be more circumspect and critically sophisticated, to trust the implied rather than the actual author.

It is true that the narrator is more prominent in some sketches than in others—in "A Green Child" he doesn't appear at all, and is barely present in "One Way North and South"—but for the most part we recognize a consistent and reliable figure. His wife, a daughter, and two sons make brief appearances in the course of the book, and the names—Sarah, Dwight, John—are the names of the first three Hood children. Sometimes, admittedly, the narrator seems conspicuously on his own—in "Bicultural Angela," "The Village Inside," and "Predictions of Ice"—yet he maintains his characteristic interest in exploring different parts of the city and a consistent eye for the clinching visual detail. Only in "Around Theatres" do we find a narrator noticeably different from the man we know, biographically, as Hugh Hood. My own impression is that, in the book as a whole, we find not so much different narrators as different aspects of the same narrator, a phenomenon common enough in first-person narrators in the poems of Wordsworth, acknowledged by Hood as a major influence.

This point brings us conveniently enough to the more general topic of Hood's influences. So far as structure is concerned, he is unusually prodigal in the listing of earlier books that he sees as having had an impact on the writing. These include Dante's *Purgatorio*, Spenser's *Shepheardes Calendar*, Wordsworth's *Prelude*, Dickens's *Sketches by Boz*, Balzac's *Scènes de la vie de province*, Turgenev's *Sportsman's Sketches*, George Eliot's *Scenes of Clerical Life*, Leacock's *Sunshine Sketches of a Little Town*, and even Brecht's *Threepenny Opera* (AM 10-11, Interview 51-53). Most of these supposed influences will be more obvious to the author than to his readers. Dante is there because of the claimed analogy of proceeding "around" Mount Royal to climbing the purgatorial mountain; Spenser is recalled because of the twelve part, month-by-month structure of his poem and a vague hint of pastoral connection; Brecht qualifies because he treated London as "an infernal and inverted pastoral" (Interview 53). Wordsworth, on the other hand, interests Hood through his poems about wanderers, walking tours, and his strong spirit of place, as well as for his "spots of time" (*Prelude*, 1850 text, 12:208).

The others are important for their ways of combining short pieces into a larger structure. Dickens, Balzac, and Eliot are listed in order to acknowledge the element of "Sketches" or "Scenes" in their titles. The remaining two are more obviously, and specifically, significant. Turgenev's book brings together a collection of stories of a particular area in Russia supposed to have been encountered when the aristocratic narrator goes out on shooting expeditions in all directions from his home. His first sketch in particular is prefaced by a meticulously detailed description of the area, while subsequent stories are also notable for the vividness of their topographical detail, though they tend to occur sporadically in the form of set pieces. Leacock's *Sunshine Sketches* is important because it evokes an idyllic pastoral tone and is written in a relaxed style: "he's thinking of that water-colour or pencil portfolio that an amateur artist might have collected" (Interview 52).

Oddly enough, the book that would seem to have had the most immediate influence on *Around the Mountain* is not mentioned by Hood in this context: Joyce's *Dubliners*. Here we find a series of sketches each set in a different part of the Irish capital, and each containing an "epiphany," a term Joyce used on numerous occasions though not, as it happens, when referring to *Dubliners* itself. In *Stephen Hero*, the early version of *A Portrait of the Artist as a Young Man*, Joyce wrote of the protagonist: "By an epiphany he meant a sudden spiritual manifestation, whether in the vulgarity of speech or of gesture or in a memorable phase of the mind itself" (qtd. in Scholes and Litz 253). Also relevant is a remark made by Joyce in a letter to a publisher: "The book is not a collection of tourist impressions but an attempt to represent certain aspects of the life of one of the European capitals" (ibid. 261). Hood had studied Joyce intensively under Marshall McLuhan, who "insisted on the central importance of the stories in *Dubliners*" (FRK 14). He would have been attracted in Joyce's book to the short narratives created not to narrate a strong plot but to lead to some moment of revelation. Joyce himself was most interested in collecting epiphanies that illustrated what he saw as the banality or paralysis of Dublin life in his time. Hood tended to be more positive, though the ending of "Bicultural Angela" and even of "The River Behind Things" would fit well into a Joycean fiction. In general, however, Hood's significant moments combine the qualities of Joyce's epiphanies and Wordsworth's visionary "spots of time."

Critically speaking, the main challenge for any consideration of *Around the Mountain* is to do justice both to the individual sketches and to the volume as a whole. There have been a number of helpful studies of several stories, and I shall be drawing upon these in the pages to follow. J.R. (Tim) Struthers's "A Secular Liturgy" is a perceptive general introduction. To date, however, the most detailed sketch-by-sketch account is Susan Copoloff-Mechanic's in her *Pilgrim's Progress* (1988). Unfortunately, this critique is deeply flawed, and it is important to show why. She begins, revealingly, by stating that the collection takes the form of "twelve monthly excursions, in which the narrator journeys through an allegorical landscape" (49), and I am at a loss to imagine a more misleading comment. The landscape in *Around the Mountain* is as specific, detailed, and vividly realized as it is possible for a literary landscape to be. That allegorical elements are also present can be assumed in any Hood fiction, but these, though occurring regularly, are decidedly secondary here. No adequate discussion of the text can neglect the centrality of Hood's "super-realism." T. F. Rigelhof, indeed, insists on what he considers "a fact so obvious ... that some people seem to miss it entirely: the central character in these stories is the island that's Montreal" (117-8).

A full response to the literary achievement of *Around the Mountain* is impossible without acknowledgment of the variety—in subject matter, tone, and narrative form—that is displayed as we pass from sketch to sketch. Even within each sketch, however, Copoloff-Mechanic goes astray because she tries to impose a rigid consistency of purpose, making no allowance for the balance of seriousness and humour or formality and casualness. By over stressing Hood's allegorizing tendency, she scants his corresponding respect for the "fundamental pleasure of recognition given by literary realism" (TT 127). In addition, she habitually emphasizes the negative aspects of the landscapes and mindscapes presented at the expense of their positive equivalents. (Examples will be noted as we focus on specific stories.) Hood's book concentrates neither on a single attitude nor on simple binary contrasts (ascent/descent, light/darkness). The moves from month to month and district to district permit him to present the diversity of peoples (English-Canadian, Québécois, Jews, Gypsies, etc.), social levels (poor, middle class, upper class), and atmosphere (in Robert Frost's phrase, both inner and outer weathers). There are naturally some deliberate connections and comparisons, but it is a mistake to think *exclusively* in terms of progressions and interrelations. Far more important is Hood's achievement in presenting this amazing variety present within the city while maintaining an artistic unity through his carefully controlled literary style.

Alas, Copoloff-Mechanic displays little or no interest in stylistic matters, so Hood's style, brilliantly described by John Metcalf as "that informal formality, that heightened vernacular" ("Afterword" 177), passes unregarded. Prominent, for example, is the colloquial ease, presented without any sacrifice of precision or even eloquence, that characterizes the writing throughout. One noticeable instance is the liberal use of contractions—"haven't," "don't," "they're" "I'll" (e.g., 33-4 [1-2])—that occur not only in spoken dialogue and interior monologue but also in direct narrative and descriptive passages. Another is the employment of a generalized "you"—"meeting your girl friend," "a lad of thirteen will hold the door open for you" (38 [7])—instances of which occur in all the sketches.

Hood himself draws attention in his introduction to "the pattern of verbal cross-references that I'd deliberately embedded in my composition" and "a continually varying level of style" (10, 14). Examples of the former include the phrase "one way north and south," included in the opening paragraph of "Light Shining Out of Darkness" and becoming the title of a subsequent sketch;

the related significance of north versus south in "One Way" and in "Looking Down From Above" which immediately precedes it; and the "unfinished apartment blocks" and "rubble" also in "Looking Down From Above" (93, 102 [81, 93]) balanced by "unfinished structures" and "rubble" in "A Green Child" (132 [131, 132]). The recurring "light/darkness" contrast throughout the book—in "The Village Inside'" for instance—also fits here. As for "varying level of style," the effect is well illustrated in the initial paragraphs of the opening story by the contrast between the considered formality of the first and the relaxed casualness of the second. And it is to this opening story that we should now turn.

At the opening of "The Sportive Centre of Saint Vincent de Paul" (33-47 [1-20]), the narrator (who bears a close resemblance to Hood himself) along with a friend (clearly the painter Seymour Segal about whom Hood was later to write a book) are making their way by car on a cold Montréal winter evening to the arena where they both play in a modest amateur hockey league. Much is made, as in all the sketches in *Around the Mountain*, of the particular sections of the city through which they pass. The slight plot involves a confrontation with a misbehaving team member, and subsequent queries about the fairness of what was, to all intents and purposes, his expulsion. At first glance, this appears straightforward enough. But Hood's fiction is seldom wholly straightforward, and there are subtleties and complexities here that soon reveal themselves. It may well be a tribute to the richness of Hood's text that, in exploring them, I often find myself coming to very different conclusions from Kent Thompson, a generally perceptive critic who wrote the first detailed analysis of this sketch, and Copoloff-Mechanic, who apparently owes much to his reading, though she never mentions it.

The title adjective is the first detail that needs to be glossed. In French, "sportif" means, simply, "sports" or "sporting," as in the designation of the hockey arena, "*Centre Sportif*." But its English equivalent means "playful or frolicsome … done in sport, rather than in earnest" (*Webster's*). The point is not merely pedantic; it offers a clue not only to the "amateur" nature of the hockey played within the sketch but also to the general atmosphere. The word suggests that Copoloff-Mechanic's description of the Centre as "an emblem of the postlapsarian arena fallen from unity" (52) may be too solemn, especially since Hood himself calls it "surely the most useful building in the community, churches and schools apart." Moreover, the first word in the story, "Snow" (as well as being echoed, in a typical Hood effect, by the last word in the book) is, Hood subsequently tells us, a deliberate bow towards the opening of *Bleak House*: "One of Dickens's richest and most *directing* sentences consists of the single word 'London.' I was so impressed by this little sentence that I virtually plagiarized it for the opening sentence of *Around the Mountain*" (UA 88). Hood does not expect every reader to register this connection, but it illustrates the cast of his creating mind. Unless we pay full attention to the words, and the literary associations of words, we shall be missing some of his subtlest effects.

I have mentioned the importance of "general atmosphere," and Hood, in the same context, refers to both Dickens's and his own openings as suggesting "a prevailing moral climate." This statement *could* be cited to justify both Thompson's and Copoloff-Mechanic's emphasis on the "moral" aspect of the story, and their rather dour critical readings, which I shall be discussing shortly. But this is arguable. Snow may be a depressing sign of cold and winter for some people, but for others it has more bracing connotations, and Hood, while acknowledging "winter twilight or blackness" on "this darkest week of the year," also clearly thinks of it in terms of the joys of hockey.

Here are examples of what I consider unjustifiably pessimistic interpretations. Both Thompson ("Hugh Hood" 58) and Copoloff-Mechanic (52) refer to a Montréal prison named after St. Vincent de Paul, yet Hood does not. One feels that, if he had considered such a reference important, he would have referred to it, especially since readers unfamiliar with the city would be unlikely to pick up the allusion. Moreover, Hood's own reference to St. Vincent within the text (quoted by Thompson but not by Copoloff-Mechanic) is to "a Saint of very charitable reputation." It seems to me a very dubious procedure to emphasize a negative reference not in the text at the expense of a positive one that is included. Similarly, Copoloff-Mechanic draws attention to the account of an act of violence on the part of "a member of the opposite team" (52) in which the referee lost the sight of an eye, suggesting that the narrator and his friend Segal are involved in rough hockey. On the contrary, the incident in question involved a totally different league from which the narrator dissociates his own team. In fact, he not only insists on the relative gentleness of their own league (significantly called "the Sportsman's League," which allowed "no board checking") but specifically notes: "In this city hockey is the chief social cement" (9).

All these factors are relevant to any interpretation of the story's ending. The team loses badly, due for the most part to poor play on the part of Fred Carpenter, one of its members guilty of "violating many silent agreements." Segal publicly rebukes him immediately afterwards, and he quits. Several games later, while they are enjoying a winning streak, Segal speaks to the narrator in the last lines of the sketch about taking "a pretty high moral line" and adds: "You know … if the position has a defect—I'm not sure that it has—it would be self-righteousness, wouldn't it?" The narrator comments: "I thought he was right, and said so."

Thompson, with characteristic caution, writes: "it would seem that Hood and his fellow players are all guilty of self-righteousness," that the offending player may represent "the failure of Christ in the 20th century," and wonders, tentatively, whether Hood, who sets the scene under an illuminated statue of the Virgin and Child is also alluding to a "rejection of Mercy" (58). But he admits that "ethical decisions … must be made," and grants that he "is not at all certain" that he has read the story correctly (59). Copoloff-Mechanic follows suit, but has no such qualms. For her, the narrator realizes that "his team lacks the spirit of mercy" and argues that Segal raises the issue in "a moment of self-recognition." She concludes (I am tempted to say, self-righteously!): "Their limited and self-righteous perspective has sentenced the appropriately named Carpenter to be their Christmas martyr" (53).

Let us look more closely at what Hood actually writes. Segal's speech is dignified and tactful. Carpenter's behaviour on the ice, he insists, is "dangerous," and as goalkeeper Segal is, of course, especially vulnerable: "You can get hurt … playing like that, and you can injure somebody else permanently." In other words, he is trying to avoid the kind of violent incident that Copoloff-Mechanic mistakenly attributed to their opposing team. Indeed, Hood may well have introduced the incident to give urgency to Segal's point. (It is also worth noting that the real-life Seymour Segal was critically injured in a hockey accident not long after the story was written, which prevented him from completing illustrations for *Around the Mountain* as had been planned.) Carpenter, on the other hand, who describes his habitual pattern as "I play, vomit, play," had apparently been drinking before the game; the narrator is uncertain, but another player reports: "You could smell it." He hardly seems to merit the title of "Christmas martyr." Moreover, as Hood writes it, the final exchange is decidedly equivocal. First of all, Segal is by no means convinced that their "high moral tone" has a defect ("I'm not sure that it has"). Second, when the narrator says, "I thought he was right, and said so," to what is he referring? He *could* be acknowledging self-righteousness, but he could with equal plausibility be agreeing only with the complete statement ("*if* the position has a defect"). And he could even be referring back to Segal's original speech, at the end of which he had asked: "Does anybody think I'm wrong?"

Now I have to admit that, in the 1994 introduction, Hood makes much of the religious aspects of the sketch. He draws attention to the significance of the name Carpenter, and notes that he is "made the scapegoat" for the lost hockey game. He also mentions the statue of the Virgin and Child (though emphasizing that it was an authentic realistic detail) and even points out that the words "building superintendent" in the same context refer "to the supreme authority principle at every interpretive level, from the building manager to Almighty God" (21). Hood certainly intended us to keep religious associations in mind; he is, after all, describing what was then a predominantly Catholic city. Thus, the narrator meditates on Pope Pius IX when driving up the street named after him, having just recalled "a parish church of daringly advanced design" of which he would have disapproved, while St. Vincent de Paul dominates not only the arena but, through its title, the story itself. All this is appropriate for the opening story, and needs to be registered. But if Carpenter is a scapegoat, he isn't an innocent one, and if his surname suggests Christ, it can only be as a Christ *manqué*.

The sketch's ending, I would suggest, is consonant with many of Hood's earlier (and, for that matter, later) conclusions, which are often ambiguous and thus thought provoking. He certainly raises the issue of "self-righteousness" but is not imposing it on the story. To assume a clear-cut moral judgment is surely unwarranted. Mercy is assuredly a desirable virtue, but does it take precedence over concern for self-protection or the protection of others ("he could hurt any of us")? On a moral level of interpretation, this is a disturbing question explored not as a philosophical abstraction but in the practical terms of "real life." Indeed, Hood would appear to be making Segal express a nagging sense of possible—but only possible—unfairness. (Do not most of us agonize over such incidents even when convinced that we are justified?) As I read the scene, Segal is asking not so much for agreement in self-criticism as for assurance, for support of his original "high moral tone." Like Thompson, I do not claim to be certain that I am interpreting correctly—or even certain that there *is* a correct interpretation—but am rather speculating that Hood is content to end on a note of questioning. In such situations, he may well be suggesting, how can any of us be certain?

I have written at considerable length on "The Sportive Centre" because, as the opening story, it establishes a pattern for what is to follow. Subsequent sketches can be considered more briefly, but "Light Shining Out of Darkness" (49-58 [21-33]) is important, not merely for its quality but because it introduces two central features that characterize the whole collection. These are the traditional yet still extraordinarily powerful image of ascent towards some kind of vision or epiphany, and the preoccupation with light and darkness (and their essential connection), which recurs in several later stories. Curiously enough, though the sketch displays an intense visionary quality that can legitimately be termed religious, it is told by means of wholly secular reference. There are none of the allusions to churches, popes, and sacred statues that we found in the first story ostensibly focusing on hockey, but a preoccupation with vision, enlightenment, and the creative aspects of art and imagination is evident throughout. The one possible exception is the title, ultimately deriving from the Gospel of St. John (1:5), but specifically, as Struthers remarks ("Secular" 112), borrowed from the title of a poem by William Cowper ("God moves in a mysterious way..."). Yet even this reference is given a significant twist: Hood follows Cowper in presenting light shining not in but *out of* darkness. The relation is much more complex than that of mere contrast.

The story begins, prosaically enough, with an elaborate piece of detailed description full of street names and topographical directions, out of which gradually emerge a sociologically informed picture of Montréal's residential downtown. Though excessively crowded and somewhat shabby, there is "an impression of delightful variety," and a few lines later reference is made to "the variety of customs and of wealth." There follows a scene in a local tavern identified by T. F. Rigelhof as "the Gérard Mercil Tavern, corner Saint-Hubert and Duluth" (118). It is focused upon "the Old Man, Petroff, the patriarch of Montréal gypsies," a people represented at first as inhabiting somewhat dubious margins of society, since Petroff has worked in circuses, "the Nifty Girlie Show," "the Bingo," and as accompanist to a dancing bear. Later associations, however, transform them, somewhat romantically, into an exotic, elusive, but obstinately free people. This tavern scene, in fact, functions merely as prologue to the visit to Tom, called by Hood in the introduction "King of the Gypsies" (21), though in the text he is no more than, in Petroff's words, "a fine young man who will replace me when I die."

The narrator, oddly uncharacterized and passive here, is none the less privileged to experience an unexpected vision. He moves with his friends out from the warm tavern into "black cold" and climbs an impressive but perilous outdoor staircase to the entrance to Tom's apartment. Admitted, he stands "blinking and looking around, a little confused by the wave of light and colour," but eventually makes out a series of "immensely delicate and detailed works of art, models of sailing vessels of the sixteenth and seventeenth centuries." These produce a poetic, almost magical effect, perhaps because, as Hood later makes clear to us in "Predictions of Ice," the St. Lawrence River is subject to freeze up during the winter. The scene looks forward in many respects to the haunting incident, also involving the St. Lawrence, in which Matt and Edie glimpse the image of the ghost ship beneath the ice at the end of the second chapter of *A New Athens*. But these exquisitely carved models, constructed by Tom himself, are free to sail the seas of the timeless imagination and become emblems of the gypsies' (and, potentially, humanity's) free spirit. As several commentators have noted, and as Hood has acknowledged (Interview 62), the vision represents a Wordsworthian "spot of time," and the text is studded with references to "works of art," "the life of the imagination," "feelings of a hidden and immense joy," "the possibility of goodness, of the memorable life." Hood's debt to traditional Romanticism is never more evident than here.

Eventually, of course, the group must return into the "deadly cold after midnight in February," but Copoloff-Mechanic is surely wrong to use this as an excuse for a gloomy exegesis: "Alone, divided, he is deprived of [the gypsies'] secular art of communion, at the heart of which is the vision of the eternal community" (54). Rather, like Lily Briscoe at the close of Virginia Woolf's *To the Lighthouse* (lighthouses produce light out of darkness), he has had his vision. Hood's intention was certainly positive. In the Struthers interview (62) he insists that "a scene like this can rotate in our imagination and seem to give special form to the rest of our life." All mortal visions at the top of holy eminences must necessarily end in a return to actuality. "What goes up must come down" (11), to be sure, but what has been revealed remains. To speak of deprivation rather than benefaction is inappropriate here. The emphasis of the sketch, as its title suggests, falls not on darkness but on light.

The final words of the story are, as so often in Hood, richly ambivalent. Coming back to make an unannounced visit to Tom and his wife some months later, the narrator discovers to his disappointment "that they had moved on." The phrasing evokes several associations. First, in strictly verbal terms, it constitutes a fruitful echo of "We moved off" in the previous sentence. But the phrase itself can be interpreted in at least three ways. On the level of realism they had simply moved elsewhere; if a dark reading is stressed, they can be assumed to have died (cf. "passed on" in the euphemistic language of obituaries); or, if a visionary possibility is allowed, they may be seen as having passed inscrutably into another dimension of experience. The gypsies are not, like the characters who appear in the other sketches, permanent residents but elusive birds of passage. At the same time, they have something to offer to Montréal: the memory of the exquisite sailing ships remains for the narrator—and for us.

Some of these stories, though decidedly accomplished in their own right, seem to have originated as illustrations of significant social and historical aspects of Montréal in the mid-1960s instead of arising from an urgent creative need. Two of them, "Bicultural Angela" and "One Way North and South" as well as, to some extent, "Around Theatres," confront the French/English split in Québec society. All are localized in the area immediately northeast of Mount Royal, and all fit appropriately into Hood's calendric scheme. Above all, social and political unrest is clearly evident, despite the official national euphoria represented by Expo, and it is worth remembering that *Around the Mountain* appeared in the same year as Hugh MacLennan's sobering *Return of the Sphinx*, three years before the FLQ kidnappings and the October crisis of 1970.

"Bicultural Angela" (59-68 [35-48]) is a poignant story of a love affair that fails to develop, the central character being an Ontarian who tries desperately to enter the Québécois segment of the broadcasting and television industry. She even changes her name from Angela Mary to Marie-Ange, but to no avail. As Thompson notes shrewdly, she is "rejected by her French-Canadian lover because she does not *have* his culture, and therefore, perhaps, cannot have him," while Struthers, just as shrewdly, claims that she "fails because she emulates, and eventually becomes, 'the mode'" ("Secular" 121). Hood, incidentally, was intrigued by the character he had created, and used her again in his full-length fiction, first in *A Game of Touch* where, quoting Thompson again, by "choosing to change her identity, she has lost her old one," and ultimately in *The New Age*, especially *The Motor Boys in Ottawa* where, as here, she shows familiarity (disconcerting in that context) with the General Agreement on Tariffs and Trade.

"One Way North and South" (105-117 [95-111]) focuses exclusively on the poorer Québécois and their discontents. The underlying threat of violence, imagistically heralded in "The Sportive Centre," comes to the surface here (and later in the dockside "Predictions of Ice"). Gilles O'Neill (whose name reveals somewhat mixed ancestry) is a garage mechanic too poor, it seems, to rise to the status of engineer, of which he appears capable. He becomes involved, impulsively yet reluctantly, in a minor riot and, in running off, meets up with an ex-school companion, Denise Gariépy, who has succeeded in rising in the social scale and is currently at university in the process of becoming a teacher. She befriends Gilles, encourages him to give up the non-productive politics of violent protest and to return to part-time study under her direction with the intention of bettering himself.

Inevitably a love affair develops which, though fragile and threatened by events beyond their control (Hood inserts an ambiguous, ominous note by referring to "[p]oor little Denise Gariépy" in the final paragraph), seems more promising than its equivalent in "Bicultural Angela," and at least has a chance of enduring. Once again, I am impelled to challenge Copoloff-Mechanic's unusually brief account. Convinced that all the stories in the second half of the book are "descent stories, marked by a sense of loss, conflict, and decay" (51), she insists that "descent towards *le centre-sud* is a one-way trip" and that "all subsequent excursions will meet with a similar dead end" (59). Oddly enough, she makes no mention of the two lovers, relying wholly on the topographical/sociological/descriptive sections of the sketch. But Denise *does* reverse the title's direction and is clearly making a vigorous attempt to assist Gilles in doing the same. Indeed, we are specifically told of Gilles walking "up the steep hill" as if he were "climbing out of a pit." This sketch does not support Copoloff-Mechanic's neatly schematic thesis.

"Around Theatres" (69-80 [49-64]), focuses on the moribund English-language theatre in the Montréal of that time, and compares it with the vibrancy of the French-language film scene. The narrator, who in "Bicultural Angela" hung out as a solitary figure in a record shop arguing about Haydn and observing the ups and downs of Marie-Ange's relationship with her Québécois *chansonnier* (and who is virtually imperceptible in "One Way North and South") now appears in the unlikely guise of an amateur dramaturge. Here Hood plays one of his habitual jokes, since this story, where the narrator has least in common with Hood himself, is the only one in which he makes oblique reference to his own name ("Any relation to Robin?"). The improvisational theatre in question flaunts words like "freedom" and "imagination," but these pall before their equivalents in "Light Shining Out of Darkness." Nothing much happens in terms of plot, and it could be argued that this is the least memorable sketch in the collection. Perhaps the most significant moment occurs at the close where the unsuccessful actor forced to turn cab driver observes that he "can always make a good living," but adds: "Well, at least a living…" Struthers draws attention to the felicitous ambiguity of that "good" ("Secular" 123).

These three stories justify their existence in the volume more for their subject matter than for their literary effects. "Le Grand Déménagement" (81-91 [65-79]), literally "The Great House-Moving," is very different. By contrast, it exemplifies Hood's gift for affectionate, comparatively light-hearted social and situational comedy, a gift developed in "The Dog Explosion" and in the more relaxed sketches of his later work. It is also the first story in *Around the Mountain* to present the narrator's domestic scene, which is endearingly portrayed, complete with the accurate names of Hood's wife Noreen and elder children Sarah and Dwight. His own birthday (as, later, in *The New Age*) is woven into the plot, and the world of family mores and anniversaries is rendered with an attractive directness. As Hood has observed, it is "by far the most personal of the twelve stories" (TT 41), and Noreen Mallory reports that the sketch is based on an actual incident. It is also, for the purposes of the whole collection, Hood's acknowledgment of the Jewish presence in Montréal, a subject he is to return to later in "The Fruit Man, the Meat Man & the Manager," "The Good Tenor Man," and "The Holy Man."

With its expert poise and warm humour, this sketch can legitimately be termed a minor masterpiece. The well-known tradition of Jewish humour may well have stimulated him here, the quick pace sometimes even offering a possible hint of the young Mordecai Richler. The presuming rabbi who browbeats the Hood-like narrator into running an errand for him through sheer force of personality, and the silent, hapless, helpless waggoner overwhelmed by circumstances may be close to stereotypes, but they are presented with equal convincingness and an admirable vigour. Above all, the narrator's self-portrait in the narrative section, half-amused, half-resentful, catches precisely the requisite blend of frankness and gentle self-mockery.

The story hasn't received much attention, though Metcalf justifiably reprinted it in his New Canadian Library selection. Hood regarded both this story and "Around Theatres" as overtaken by historical events. The custom of Montréal leases all concluding on 30 April, which sets off the action, ceased in the late 1970s, and as a result, he writes, "its mid-spring charm seems faded and bittersweet" (24). I beg to differ. Even if the specific circumstances have changed, the comic variations rung upon age-old themes (stingy landlords and complaining tenants, acts of generosity selfishly exploited, the ordinary man at the mercy of bureaucratic system) are as fresh and ingratiating—and in general terms as timely—as ever. Of course, commentators expecting profundity and social relevance will be unlikely to register the humour, and the resultant discussions lead to excessive solemnity and under-valuation. None the less, it is difficult to understand how Copoloff-Mechanic could describe the central concern of the story as "whether a spirit of common humanity can alleviate the burden of exile" (56)!

"Looking Down From Above" (93-103 [81-94]) is the centrepiece of *Around the Mountain*, the sixth out of twelve sketches, and is in some respects the key to the whole book. Fortunately, it formed the subject of one of the finest critical analyses that have yet been devoted to Hood's work, Robert Lecker's essay in *On the Line*. The following discussion is deeply indebted to that source, and consists of little more than a series of footnotes attached to that ground-breaking study.

Lecker properly emphasizes the fact that the narrative is divided into "three sections which explore the relationship among nature, time, space, and art" (100). This division is consonant with the traditional concept of a three-tiered universe comprising Heaven, Earth, and Hell, derived from Judeo-Christian lore and receiving its classic literary treatment in Dante's *Divine Comedy* and Milton's *Paradise Lost.* Hood adapts the concept to his own very different purpose. At this point, we need to recall the statement concerning *Around the Mountain* already quoted: "A complete rotation around the mountain ... takes place, and the stories are calculated according to how high up the mountain they are" (Interview 45). This is, as I have said, an exaggeration, but it is certainly applicable to "Looking Down From Above."

The central section establishes the fact that the narrator and his family (like the Hoods in the early years of their arrival in Montréal) live in an apartment building on Maplewood (now Edouard Bonpetit) on the north slope of Mount Royal, where Mme. Bourbonnais, assisted by "her industrious husband," is concierge. This may be regarded as the Hoodian equivalent of traditional "Middle Earth." In the opening paragraph, the narrator has worked his way from Maplewood around the northern side of Mount Royal and is proceeding down University (now université), in the direction, be it noted, of the dock area that is to form the setting for "Predictions of Ice," the "murderous neighbourhood" alluded to here. The Bourbonnais later encourage him to look higher rather than lower, but it is only in the third section that he reaches the top and can "look directly down on the Bourbonnais" and their picnic, and is able in the final line to generalize from his God-like perspective about "[h]uman purpose." Any reading of "Looking Down From Above" becomes much clearer when it is understood from the start that the setting is vividly realistic and consciously allegorical at the same time.

The sketch begins with the sentence: "Fair weather implies heightened perception in my book." Lecker appositely quotes a biblical echo, "Fair weather cometh out of the north" (though he attributes it to Proverbs when it actually occurs in Job 37:22). I am also inclined to suspect a hint from the famous statement in the opening chapter of Thomas Hardy's *The Return of the Native*, Egdon Heath being the subject: "Fair prospects wed happily with fair times; but alas, if the times be not fair!" (Hood was, of course, an admirer of Hardy.) The remark is appropriate for a collection in which weather (not always fair) and heightened perception are constant concerns. The concluding phrase "in my book" also deserves scrutiny. Lecker links it up with other references to "book" later in the story, and, referring to a passage close to the end of the second section, writes: "The 'book' here is doubtless 'my book' of the story's first line—a book which has changed" (115). However, the phrase "in my book" can also mean "in my estimation" or "so far as I am concerned," and it is clearly used with this meaning in "Bicultural Angela" (65 [43]). Hood (and/or the narrator) is presumably punning here. The double meaning enhances the resonance of the text.

Lecker's interpretation of the story as a whole seems thoroughly sound. The narrator *descends* to the "murderous neighbourhood," where he encounters a "small old woman, almost a dwarf," whose eyes reveal "fury... and extraordinary purpose," yet she is seen, despite her physical condition and situation, to be "full of life." This scene, while artistically memorable as an example of heightened realism, once again sparks literary associations. The meeting is comparable, for instance, to Wordsworth's with the Old Cumberland Beggar in the poem of that title and also with the decrepit Leech-Gatherer in "Resolution and Independence." In both poems Wordsworth is chastened by the difference between his own supposed problems and those of the people he meets, and the woman in Hood's story is certainly characterized as both resolute and independent. Moreover, when the narrator muses, "That woman am I. To her state must I come in time," I for one am irresistibly reminded of Hamlet addressing Yorick's skull in the graveyard scene: "get you to my lady's chamber, and tell her, let her paint an inch thick, to this favour she must come" (V i 213-5). Some readers will probably consider all these echoes far too academic, but Hood and myself were both professors of English and belonged to the same generation. My mind thinks like that, and I am convinced that his functioned in a similar way. Be that as it may, by the end of the section the old woman, as Lecker notes, has moved "up the hill" and is "standing on the top of the rise," while the narrator is now looking up from below. The reversed angle of vision is crucial. Moreover, the old woman, having ascended out of a world of darkness, is waiting for a light—a traffic light to be sure, but a green one.

The second section confines itself to the middle level. In the apartment house on Maplewood, the narrator, along with his family, makes the acquaintance of the Bourbonnais, who represent humanity at its best: hospitable, efficient, resourceful, responsible. They encourage him to look higher—"It was M. Bourbonnais who told me about the picnic spots on top of the mountain"—though, strictly speaking, "higher up" would have been more accurate than "on top of." At first he ventures on only a five-minute climb to an area where he often found the Bourbonnais on their days off, and where he joins them in a meal and a glass of wine which, as the allegorizing critics are justified in asserting, is clearly intended to be a secular Eucharist. But the setting, though qualifying as an ascent, remains worldly terrain, as indicated by the lovers who stumble over him at one point when he has stretched out on the grass.

The third section takes place two years later, after the Hood-like family has moved. One day, the narrator meets the Bourbonnais once again, and is shocked to discover that the husband is ill, and obviously dying. This realization prompts him to ascend higher, to the summit where, traditionally, spiritual seekers attain vision. And so it turns out, though, as Lecker notes perceptively, the vision is more enigmatic than we have been led to expect. "You have the sense of the world dropping away from you," yet: "The day wasn't sharply clear; outlines were blurred." In other words, despite the story's opening line, "heightened perception" is not affected by the weather, fine or otherwise. He looks down upon the Bourbonnais as if from a divine viewpoint, but it is found to be "a strangely mixed perspective." As Hood himself stresses in the introduction, by ending with the revelation that "Human purpose is inscrutable, but undeniable," he has transferred to humanity "two of the attributes of the Divine Presence" (11).

Hood here confirms Lecker's reading by acknowledging that "the speaker now seems to be haunted by an underlying dubiety" (25), while making the more general but important point that, while the book remains a "celebration," it is not as "joyfully affirmative" (13) as it may first seem. Lecker sums up his argument succinctly and cogently: "Fair weather does not always mean vision; light often shines out of darkness… Heightened perception is being redefined" (114). One of Hood's boldest effects occurs when, although the incident is now two years in the past, at the climactic moment the old lady of the first section is presented, at least in the narrator's memory, as still "waiting for her green light." It is hardly surprising that, looking back at the book a quarter of a century later, Hood wondered whether "Light Shining Out of Darkness" would have been "the right title for the entire work" (14). Yet he also observes that *Around the Mountain*, with the purgatorial implication of ascent to a point where one is vouchsafed a vision of paradise, is really saying the same thing.

"The Village Inside" (119-28 [113-26]) opens with a long passage devoted to topographical and historical background that takes up half its space. The solitary narrator is exploring on his bicycle an area of urban sprawl to the north of the city and becomes fascinated with the faint yet palpable signs of the sometime countryside still detectible within the bustling modern suburb. One particular "hundred-and-forty-year-old wooden farmhouse standing on a fifty-by-fifty plot of land" attracts his attention, and it duly becomes the subject of the story. This house belongs to Victor Latourelle, a septuagenarian farmer who had been born there, had farmed the local area, and is determined to die there. But his children have thrown in their lot with city life and deserted him. Gradually, his daughter Victorine bullies him into selling off most of his land, until all he has left is this "magnificent house," strikingly out of place at the corner of a "titanic parking lot." Here he intends to remain, living in an apparently dead past.

This sketch has been discussed in detail by two previous commentators, who come to almost totally opposed conclusions about its intentions and significance. Copoloff-Mechanic argues that "neither Victorine nor Victor is victorious: the former has disowned her past; the latter is severed from progress" (60). This is obviously true, though not perhaps the whole truth. One could retort that Victorine is not interested in the past or Victor in progress. On the other hand, one could claim that both are victorious: Victorine has obtained her "split-level ranch with copper plumbing" ("ranch" in the sense of a one-storey house with low-pitched roof "esp. one built in the suburbs" [*Webster's*]), while Victor holds on to his home despite efforts to evict him, and is able to retain the past in imagination, a faculty in which Victorine is notably deficient. Oddly enough, since she is generally prodigal with explanations of proper names, apart from recognizing (but not accepting) the obvious significance of "Victor," Copoloff-Mechanic makes no reference to the meaning of "Latourelle," preferring to think of him as an "Adamic refugee" (51). But one does not need to be fluent in French to recognize him as "the winner in the little tower," as Hood reminds us in his introduction (26).

Kent Thompson (whose article is never mentioned by Copoloff-Mechanic) reads the story very differently. Suspicious of any simple reading of the sketch as "a story about how the present swallows the past," with the narrator "lamenting the process" (cf. Copoloff-Mechanic's "pastoral tranquillity" [60]), he denies that Hood "is one to romanticize the past," noting for instance that the realtors are carefully not portrayed as villains but "deal fairly with M. Latourelle." He invites us to read the sketch not for its moral attitude but as "an experience of the imagination." The long introductory section, he maintains, is not so much a factual essay as an impressive example of "abstract history made personal and immediate," and he shows Hood "preparing the familiar landscape to lead to the point of imagination." Moreover, this "point," though he doesn't say so in as many words, is where, as Latourelle sits alone in a single lamplit room, the narrator sees a light shining out of darkness.

It should be noted that Hood himself acknowledged Thompson's essay, calling it "searching and substantially correct." His own commentary, however, draws attention to a unique response to the text that occurred during one of the Montreal Story Tellers' performances. He was reading to a small group at Vanier College which happens to be located in one of the areas described in the sketch:

> While I was reading the story—which seemed a natural selection for our appearance there—about half the students in the room, maybe fifteen of them ... got to their feet and moved quietly over towards the wide windowsills, where they sat or stood

> and gazed across at the very buildings I was describing... There were whispers of "It's them" and "That's like us"... (TT 126)

This is one of two such incidents illustrating "the fundamental pleasure of recognition given by literary realism, not simply the naïve pleasure of identifying one's neighbourhood, district or quarter, but the additional, much more complex pleasure of seeing one's place worked into the balance and design of the narration" (127). Those for whom "realism" has become a synonym for simplemindedness should take this situation to heart.

All that needs to be added, perhaps, are two glosses on Hood's title. Most obviously, of course, it alludes to the survival of the village, or at least traces of the village, in what is now city. As the narrator observes, "you can detect the ancient village inside the suburban growth." This effect is usefully described in a somewhat technical article by Douglas Ivison as "the palimpsest nature of urban space" (239), in which one layer of civilization covers but does not wholly obliterate an earlier one. But "The Village Inside" can be interpreted in another way, one more evident by the time the story has been read and fully experienced. The village is now inside the mind of Victor Latourelle, and, thanks to Hood, inside our own minds. Just as Latourelle can, through imagination, "see cattle grazing, his father working in their thick green truck [vegetable] garden, his uncle Antoine bent in a distant cornfield," so we too can experience the past as present, and say "That's like us."

"A Green Child" (129-38 [127-39]) might well be described as a mirror image of "The Village Inside," and the two can be regarded as yet another Hoodian example of a diptych. In the latter, suburbia has overtaken the past; in "A Green Child," it is in turn threatened by relentlessly approaching development ("Across the street a sign read: BRIGHT FUTURE CONSTRUCTION"). Where Victor Latourelle could imagine a lost landscape that gave him a form of solace, Thierry Desautels is deceived by an elusive apparition. "Hallucinatory," a word used in the last sentence of "The Village Inside," is also relevant here. "A Green Child" is remarkable as the only story in *Around the Mountain* where there is no hint of a mediating first-person narrator, perhaps because

Thierry's experience, what he "remembered or dreamed or imagined," is so ambiguous that it lies beyond interpretation. The very point of this vision/hallucination is that it is inexplicable.

Hood presents here his exercise in surrealist Gothic or post-modernist magic realism, call it what you will. Thierry, who sells television sets for a living and might therefore be called a dealer in apparitions, on two occasions encounters a mysterious young woman while on a bus, late at night, taking him back to his lodgings in the rapidly expanding eastern extremities of the city. Although apparently of flesh and blood (she is also visible to the bus driver), she seems to vanish, and Thierry becomes obsessed with finding her. Eventually, she passes him at high speed on a motorbike while he is out driving, and lures him into a "monstrous" cityscape of unfinished ramps and overpasses decorated by "semi-abstract, semi-representational figures ... many of great beauty, others purely grotesque." Here he becomes hopelessly lost and descends into unconsciousness and even death. The last sight he sees "looks like a test-pattern" from one of his TVs, but (and here an impersonal omniscient narrator steps in at the last moment) "what he really saw ... was a peculiarly distorted concrete woman."

Critical explanations of such a deceptive text are, of course, perilous. For Dennis Duffy, the girl, always identified by her green scarf, "could be lost Nature, instrumentalized by technological man into a reinforced-concrete fossil" (133), but in my view this doesn't take into account her more sinister aspects suggestive of a Belle Dame Sans Merci. Struthers's account is more circumspect: "His Beatrice ... has been hideously transformed, disfigured by 'the monstrous power and impersonality of the place' ... into a ghostly emblem of the lifelessness and the lunacy in modern society" ("Secular" 131). On balance, however, it is probably wisest to leave the mysterious as a mystery.

More fruitful is a consideration of the essay-like passage that Hood inserts into the middle of his narrative. This can be distinguished from the usual topographical accounts because it becomes a generalized meditation on the significance of images of "unfinished structures", "vacant lots," and "design without function," and their representation in contemporary film. Here we find another example of how "A Green Child" acts as a mirror image of the preceding story. Hood writes: "The effect is as if history were running backwards; instead of these buildings seeming the heralds of stunning development ... they seem ... to be the ruined monuments of a past describable now only by archaeological investigation." The broader significance of this experiment is underlined by Hood in his introduction: "the whole passage is the first instance of essayistic interpolation in narrative of a kind that I've used again and again in the books known collectively as *The New Age / Le nouveau siècle*" (16-17). Here, then, is the origin of Hood's mature narrative procedure that becomes so distinctive in his later work.

In the same introduction, Hood makes two other interesting observations. One is that Thierry's journey on the 95 bus paralleled Hood's own introduction to the area, his delighted discovery of "a new subdivision called rue Valdombre," and his realization that it was "the street of the valley of the shadow" (cf. Psalm 23:4) and that a "gross excavation ... lay next to it" (16). No invented street name could have been more appropriate; Hood's realistic fidelity and his allegorizing interests combine perfectly. He also makes an important gloss on his statement about history "running backwards" when he notes that if one travels to the site of rue Valdombre twenty-six years later, archaeological excavation would again be necessary: "The years have overbuilt it" (17). Here is a fascinating example of what can happen to a distinguished work of art over the course of time. "A Green Child" is not outdated by subsequent developments; on the contrary, a new dimension of meaning, a patina of additional profundity, has been bestowed upon it.

Perhaps the best way of approaching the somewhat uncohesive "Starting Again on Sherbrooke Street" (139-48 [141-54]) is to see it in primarily non-fiction terms as a search for "the essential Sherbrooke," one of the principal streets in downtown Montréal. Forty years ago (that is, in the 1920s), we are told, this street had been "a classically dignified enclave of great houses and tall old shade trees, gravelled carriage drives and wrought-iron gates." By the 1960s, these same great houses had become "headquarters of some important social institutions," and much of the street given over to "tall office buildings and apartment blocks, to a fashionable church, and to the Montréal Museum of Fine Arts." Sherbrooke Street is now more arts and fashion oriented, and decidedly more commercial.

Such an approach may help to explain the by-no-means-obvious relation between the frame material—an account of Hood and Seymour Segal transporting paintings for one of the latter's art exhibitions which Hood acknowledges "took place almost exactly as I have depicted it" (28)—and the fictional narrative concerning Christopher Holt, who is offered as a typical Sherbrooke Street specimen. The Hood-Segal narrative not only picks up on their friendship as presented in "The Sportive Centre" but reaches out to other parts of his work. The gallery where the paintings are to be displayed is the Galerie Anéantie, which appeared along with its owner Abe Shumsky in Hood's first novel, *White Figure, White Ground*, and will reappear briefly later in *The Motor Boys in Ottawa* and *Tony's Book*. The tone is light hearted, almost knockabout at times, and represents the modern "artistic" aspect of the street.

The main narrative involving Holt is more complex. The only connection with the Hood-Segal frame is that he turns up by chance outside the gallery while the paintings are being unloaded and the Hood-figure happens to have already met him at a local hockey stadium. Holt is a well-off, high-living English-Canadian who gives the impression of being a product of those "great houses" of forty years earlier. But he is presented satirically. He professes to a knowledge of art but "had an absurd air of connoisseurship unsupported by information," and his complicated but shoddy private life, torn between wife and "girl friend," is hardly impressive. Briefly in danger of losing both, after a period of separation he eventually returns to his wife, takes a "fresh grip on things," and in the final and most effective line in the sketch strides off "in the direction of the Ritz, tall, well-dressed, confident, untouched, a Sherbrooke Street man." "Untouched." As Patricia Morley was the first to point out (116), this adjective says it all. Holt is definitively "placed." None the less, the sketch remains somewhat inconsequential. One gets the uneasy impression that it exists only because a study of Holt's class and type was desirable in the interests of the book's social comprehensiveness.

A similar argument could doubtless be made about "Predictions of Ice" (149-57 [155-68]). Full coverage of Montréal as a city cannot omit the dock area, and this dark November story duly fills the gap. It is not, perhaps, one of the most memorable sketches in the *Around the Mountain*. Even Hood, in his introduction, says that it "needn't detain us long," and confines himself to linking its focus on politically induced violence with "One Way North and South," observing that the reader who "wants to see it as a chronicle of unrest and oppression ... has a perfect justification for doing so" (28). He then concludes on an even more ambiguous note by passing on to the final story and raising the postmodernist possibility—but only as a possibility—"that there are no true rereadings, only an interminable series of versions of the story" (29). There would therefore seem to be issues beneath the surface of the story that invite investigation.

A few facts will help. First, allusion is made to the Montréal longshoremen's strike "in the crucial summer of 1966." Second, it is important to realize that this sketch was written in the first part of June 1966, and that the book appeared exactly a year later. Hood, then, was dealing with up-to-the-minute news at the time of writing, and making reference to a surprisingly recent event at the time of publication. All this may help to explain why the opening paragraphs of "Predictions of Ice" seem closer to journalistic non-fiction than any other part of the book. True, there have been similar, quite lengthy, informative introductions earlier, in "Around Theatres" and "The Village Inside" in particular, but none of them sounds as close to the familiar prose of an established newspaper correspondent. When the narrative at last begins—"I can bear witness to the violence from direct observation"—it appears merely as a back-up to the earlier observations, whereas the opening passage usually serves as an introduction to the more significant main story.

The narrative segment here, though arising smoothly from what has preceded it, is remarkable in that it points towards a modern blood-and-thunder crime story that never quite manifests itself. The Hood-like narrator presents himself driving around the dock area at night "playing my favourite, rather immature, game of imagining myself a character in some spy or detective movie," and goes on to imagine the cliché images in such stories: "a man on the run, skulking in doorways, a hunted fugitive." And then, suddenly, he finds himself in a real-life scene where a Russian sailor has been beaten up by unknown assailants, apparently for political reasons. He plays the part of a modest Samaritan, alerting the crew of the victim's ship and seeing him carried on board. That is all, but it is recognized as "the damnedest confusion of life imagined and life lived." There is a sense in which this sketch belongs to the collection, not so much for the obvious reasons of comprehensiveness (the dock area, Cold War politics, the existence of a violence that is rarely witnessed) but as part of the continuing interchange, on which the whole of Hood's fiction depends, between the imagined and the supposedly "real." More than we might at first expect, "Predictions of Ice" raises *artistic* issues which are central to the book.

"The River Behind Things" (159-65 [167-75]) brings the whole book to an appropriate and effective close by juxtaposing two visits to a riverside area northeast of Montréal: one in summer, when the narrator takes his son to a small beach resort deserted in the middle of the week, where they dance and enjoy music in a deserted dance hall; the other on Christmas Day, when he returns alone and witnesses an enigmatic "solitary black figure, a man in a punt," jabbing away at the ice with a long black pole. Both incidents, Hood assures us, were autobiographical in origin: "The business about Dwight. We *did* actually go and dance ..." while the black figure "maybe a hundred yards away ... was doing exactly what's described in the story" (Interview 47). The two scenes, then, are studies in contrast: summer/winter, in company/alone, an atmosphere of familial solidarity and communion—

> "I love you, Dad."
> "And I love you"

—followed by an atmosphere of unease and foreboding. The effect is more complex than these simplistic categories suggest, but they indicate the structure upon which Hood builds.

The first scene is described as "an afternoon of great splendour," yet it is thoroughly domestic and filled with down-to-earth details. The excursion is arranged because the other children "were down with a mildly infectious summer flu"; Dwight goes to a park toilet and is surprised to discover "no water in there, just a hole"; he goes paddling and walks barefoot in the long grass; he recognizes a Beatles song on the jukebox, and asks if he can have a drum for Christmas. Ordinary incidents, simple, unpretentious, emotionally warming. The second scene contains the characteristic features of a Wordsworthian spot of time, but with intimations of mortality rather than immortality, yet also recalls the disturbing surrealistic vision at the close of "A Green Child." The final paragraph begins, "A breeze stirred," but there is no obvious "blessing" in it as in the opening line of Wordsworth's *Prelude*; rather, it is analogous to that moment of "visionary dreariness" involving the "naked pool" and the "girl, who bore a pitcher on her head" and the immediately following scene, significantly set at Christmas, with the "single sheep, and the one blasted tree" (see 1850 text, 12:248-306).

Because the first scene is commonplace in its details, it is often passed over without comment, yet it is essential to the full effect. The second scene, on the other hand, is regularly quoted and discussed, yet interpretations can be diametrically opposed. Hood himself complicated matters by sending out conflicting messages. In the introduction he refers at one point to "the menace of death in the book's closing paragraph" (14), yet a few pages later, quoting the final sentence, "the high hills rose ghostly from the melting snow and ice," he remarks: "I know what I meant to imply by that image, the recesses and secret places of Beatitude" (20). Not totally contradictory, perhaps, but hard to reconcile. One possible solution is to consider the paragraph as constructed out of a subtle mixture of associations and atmospheres. The "lonely black figure," as Hood also notes, "looks like a Dance of Death figure" (Interview 47), and the ending on "ice and snow" can be read as chilling. Yet the stirring breeze sounds at least potentially positive, and when the narrator says, "I raised my eyes to the source of the river," he is clearly echoing "I will lift up mine eyes unto the hills, from whence cometh my help" (Psalm 121:1). (And at this point, it is worth noting, if only parenthetically, that the title "The River Beyond Things" represents a moving image of eternity with deeply religious implications, a point of comparison/contrast with the frozen river of actuality.) Moreover, the ice and snow are in fact presented as "melting." Once again, Hood delivers conflicting messages. On the one hand, "it's downhill all the way back to the menacing surface of Lac des Deux Montagnes. What goes up must come down" (11). On the other, he is prepared to hint that the cycle continues and that "as things end … everything starts up again" (29).

Both Wordsworth and Hood are sometimes portrayed as incurable optimists, but in each case this is an inaccurate judgment. Wordsworth's spots of time can be moments of visionary exaltation (comparable with the experience in "Light Shining Out of Darkness"), but they can also be disturbing, like the well-known stolen-boat episode in Book One of *The Prelude* or the memorable scenes of desolation just quoted. Yet even the latter are said to "retain / A renovating virtue" by which "our minds / Are nourished and invisibly repaired" (*Prelude*, 1850 text, 12:209-10, 214-5). Much the same effect, I suggest, is achieved here when "all at once the scene composed itself into meaning." Hood may, in fact, have written better than he knew. In the 1994 introduction, he wondered whether he might have made "rather too prominent the sunlit high points in the design" (13). I believe, however, that a close and careful reading of the text, intent on avoiding preconceptions, will reveal an admirable *mixture* of attitudes and emotions, styles and forms. These vary from the uplifting to the desolating, and make *Around the Mountain* not only a rich portrait of Montréal at a notable period in its history but an admirable reflection of the successes and failures, joys and sorrows, of all humanity at all times.

6

Short Stories or Short-Story Collection:

The Fruit Man, the Meat Man & the Manager

I have argued that Hood's first published volume of short stories, though often divided into related parts, aimed to display the variety of his creative gifts in terms of subject matter, treatment, and style. On the other hand, it is obvious that his second was deliberately planned and executed as a story collection. Where did he go from there? The next volume, *The Fruit Man, the Meat Man & the Manager*, displays all the signs of returning to his interest in diversity. None the less, we are faced, even before the table of contents, with an authorial note that reads: "The first three stories in this book were written at the same time as a deliberately-related triptych. Human art and love are models of immortality." The stories in question are "Getting to Williamstown," in which a dying man dreams back to a desired landscape he never quite attained; "The Tolstoy Pitch," in which an American fiction writer ("Not small, not really big" [24]) is inveigled into a somewhat dubious book-of-the-film deal against his will; and "A Solitary Ewe," a sad love story in which the shy and quiet protagonist loses his girl to a more outgoing and flamboyant friend.

A "deliberately-related triptych"? Perhaps so, though Hood originally published these stories on their own in three separate magazines. However, even before the volume was published, when the first story—which had appeared in *Tamarack Review* in 1965—was reprinted in John Metcalf's highly successful school textbook, *Sixteen by Twelve*, Hood had elaborated his views in a commentary, "Writing 'Getting to Williamstown'." "Each of the three," he argued there, "uses a theme which I have found it important to write about," and lists them as the life of an artist, passionate love, and death. He then goes on to point out that he employs three quite different narrative techniques in these stories, explaining that "The Tolstoy Pitch" is "almost all spoken dialogue," "A Solitary Ewe" is "more a 'narrated' story," while "the methods of 'Getting to Williamstown' are mainly scenic, that is, symbolic and evocative" (87).

Agreed, but this is hardly an argument for an interrelated triptych. Moreover, a statement that "human art and love are models for immortality" is first found here, although its application to an argument involving structure is by no means clear. Besides, it is far too general a statement to provide a unifying subject for such diverse subject matter. No one, surely, would have recognized these three stories as in any way connected if Hood had not written his author's note. Some interrelations obviously exist between certain stories in the collection—those involving gentile encounters with Jewish culture, for example. But I detect no general connection that unites the volume as a whole. I fail to see how any *literary* links can be found between, say, "Getting to Williamstown," "The Holy Man," and "The Dog Explosion." The next two collections, *Dark Glasses* and *None Genuine*, for all their diversity do display some recognizable thematic elements in common, though each contains stories that don't quite fit, but *The Fruit Man*, despite Garebian's forced attempt to see it as "a series of panels about grace and penance" (*Hugh Hood* 24) and Copoloff-Mechanic's schema involving communion, communication, and community (66), is best considered as a further example of Hood's enviable versatility.

"Getting to Williamstown" (9-21) is remarkable for being experimental in the best sense of that much abused term; it is original in presentation without in any way suggesting the ostentatious or the difficult. It begins in what seems to be Hood's casual, documentary style, as in "Silver Bugles." We gradually discover, however, that the first-person narrative is regularly interrupted by italicized scraps of conversation, and eventually realize that the speaker, a Mr. Fessenden, is in hospital in a comatose and dying state. In his last moments he is reliving what now seem significant moments in his life. Williamstown is a small rural community in eastern Ontario through which the Fessenden family once used to drive from Montréal to his wife's family in Maitland, near Stoverville/Brockville. The husband had taken a fancy to the place, and longed to live there. But the practicalities of life prevent this, and it exists in his mind as a lost might-have-been—possibly a lost paradise, though there is nothing insistently religious about his vision within the text. At the close, he believes that he is returning to it for burial, and we are allowed to feel that he has at last returned to his imagined and perhaps spiritual home.

There is little narrative, but the whole is moving and deeply human. It is told by means of reminiscent flashbacks that blend naturally into each other. Although commentators have inevitably tried to allegorize the story and to find moral meanings within it, the emphasis is clearly on Fessenden's personal search for his version of the Jamesian "great good place," which is presented with loving precision through the vividness of memory. This story is a delicate construction that should not be burdened with a battery of intellectual interpretation. For all its focus upon the fact of dying, there is nothing sombre or melancholy about it. Indeed, John Metcalf came closer to the essence of the story than any of the academic commentators I know when, in his "Afterword" to *Light Shining Out of Darkness*, he wrote of "the joy and celebration that is 'Getting to Williamstown'" (176).

"The Tolstoy Pitch" (22-37), by contrast, avoids noticeable literary effect, depending upon "good clear prose" and "clean dialogue." It centres upon a respected, middle-aged writer of fiction, Frank Pastore, who faces a decision that has financial, artistic, and (though he tries to deny it) moral implications. His agent and a film producer want him to write a novel from a previously planned movie script so that it can appear just before the film release; the publicity involved will be of financial advantage to producer, publisher, and agent—and, of course, to the writer himself. On the other hand, the book will be presented, somewhat deceptively, as his own creation, and he fears that it will compromise his artistic integrity.

He eventually accepts, partly because he knows that a writer "cares about the world and the flesh, by definition" and is afraid that his increasing withdrawal from the contemporary scene will cause him to lose "that minute obsessed interest [he] used to have in the details of physical life, skirt lengths, peoples' [*sic*] incomes." This concern, encapsulating Hood's own best qualities, when linked with Pastore's later remark, "It takes a lot of guts to start writing parables" like Tolstoy, suggests that Hood may be brooding creatively on his own situation. The story was written in 1964, when he seemed to be turning away from his attempts while at West Hartford to write for *Esquire* and the *New Yorker* ("The Tolstoy Pitch" is mainly set in Connecticut) and considering his more recent move towards high art and "the sway of parable" (TT 14).

No overt comment is offered within the story on the rightness or wrongness of Pastore's decision, and commentators have disagreed on its interpretation. Copoloff-Mechanic argues that, in accepting the commission, Pastore is "devoting himself to the world" and will there "find his authentic mode of devotion" (72, 73). What I have called his artistic integrity, she dismisses as "artistic pride." Garebian, on the other hand, sees the story as chronicling "the pain of his compromise with materialism" and ending with his failure "to magnify his soul as an artist" (*Hugh Hood* 31, 32). Copoloff-Mechanic's reading is difficult to reconcile with the ending, where agent and producer (significantly described as the agent's "confederate") rejoice in their good fortune, praising Pastore as "a real pro, sincere, and a great guy." Garebian properly remarks that, while Pastore is certainly professional, he can no longer been regarded as "sincere." The critic is also perceptive in noting the balance within Hood's title, "the name of Leo Tolstoy bound in with a sales pitch for vulgar success" (31).

My own reading emphasizes this balance. It is inappropriate, I believe, to interpret this story, as Morley does, in terms of "comic villains" (111). The agent insists that it "isn't a sin to want to make some money," and Pastore grants that there is "nothing *wrong*" with the proposal. The producer is looking after his own interests, but, as Pastore also remarks, "he has to live, like the rest of us." Nor is Pastore himself portrayed simplistically, either by "abandoning the Tolstoy life and its world-rejection" (Copoloff-Mechanic 73) or by betraying his gifts for dubious riches. Indeed, he ultimately makes his decision when he comes to realize, regretfully, that he is "neither a saint nor a great artist." Yet Pastore does make reference to "the money changers in the temple," and the ending with agent and producer rather than with Pastore as protagonist suggests that, once he has agreed to the commercial proposal, he is no longer the centre of interest or importance. "The Tolstoy Pitch" is an absorbing moral fable that illustrates one of the many dilemmas confronting an artist in the modern world, and appropriately offers no easy solutions.

Little needs to be said here, I think, about "A Solitary Ewe" (38-54). It is a sad, wonderfully simple story presenting the shy, uncertain beginnings of a fragile love-romance that is selfishly and heartlessly betrayed. Critically speaking, the only difficulty of interpretation comes at the close when Charlie, outside his favourite restaurant, sees Janine and his sometime friend Peter "heads together, sitting in his customary corner." The last sentence reads: "I'll fight, it kept running through his head, this time I'll fight, this time I want my rights, I'll fight, I'll fight." Copoloff-Mechanic takes the statement at face value, though arguing that such a resort to violence would mean "retaliating with the same treachery" (74). This puzzles me, since defending one's rights can hardly be considered treachery, and even if it were, it would not be the "same" treachery. But in any case, Charlie seems to be protesting too much; there is nothing in the earlier part of the story to suggest that "this time" he will change character. However, as Morley observes, he may be "better off without Janine, but the mood is bittersweet" (109). Hood deliberately offers us a teasingly ambiguous ending; no single interpretation can be proven conclusively.

As an attempt to pierce the cultural divide between English- and French-speaking Montréal (Peter, although an "Anglicized Frenchman," has an advantage over the monoglot Charlie), "A Solitary Ewe," with its vivid evocation of a particular area of the city would have fitted comfortably enough into the scheme of *Around the Mountain*. Indeed, had Hood juxtaposed it with "Bicultural Angela," which displays a similar failed love affair but a decidedly different tone, he would have created a diptych far more acceptable than the triptych proposed here. As it is, the story exists impressively on its own, but tends to get overshadowed by the more elaborate but not necessarily more successful opening stories. It is time to insist that appreciation of the unique tone of the piece (so evidently different from both its predecessors) is more important than a search for fortuitous connections.

If Hood had wanted to present three other stories as a triptych, "The Good Tenor Man," "The Holy Man," and "The Fruit Man" would have been obvious candidates. All three share a Montréal setting, and in each case a gentile is drawn into sympathetic contact with the hitherto unfamiliar world of Jewish life and custom. All are strong stories, and deal, respectively, with human suffering and death, with a religious vocation, and with economic and commercial matters, yet when considered together reflect back and forth upon each other in creative fashion.

"The Good Tenor Man" (72-87) is best approached, initially, in the literary tradition of Ben Jonson's comedy of humours. Hannon, the central character, is a middle-aged man hopelessly set in his ways, in some respects resembling Francis Rosebery in "He Just Adores Her!," who takes regularity of behaviour to excessive extremes. Copoloff-Mechanic goes astray, I think, by condemning him immediately in moral terms. He is presented, rather, as a figure of fun to be laughed at rather than berated, "a man of immoderate attachment to habit and routine" (note the verbal richness of "immoderate" in this context). Thus he changes his razor blade regularly every third day, wears particular suits on particular days of the week, and continually counts such details as the number of Chevrolets, Fords, and Plymouths passing down the street, or the number of "average-sized steps" from his apartment door to the incinerator chute. Moreover, he eats "two Neilson's Crispy Crunch candy bars about an hour before bedtime," a habit since childhood (one of Hood's own habits, Noreen Mallory informs me). All this is absurd, but delightful. Imbedded in the opening account, however, is a one sentence paragraph that jolts the story towards seriousness: "What he couldn't defer or evade was death."

Change, then, has to be resisted because it is connected with the relentless process of dying. Even a new shop opening down the street arouses his initial suspicion, though he is drawn into patronizing Sam Rasher's Delicatessen because their Crispy Crunches are fresher than those at the grocery. As a result, this Irish Catholic is brought into contact with the Jewish proprietor, a "good tenor man in his day," who used to play saxophone with the big bands. This is a widening of Hannon's cultural horizons that, as readers, we welcome. Unfortunately for Hannon, it also draws him into a world of suffering and death. Saul's wife, who serves behind the counter, is blind as the result of a brain tumour, has only one kidney, and is now diagnosed with terminal cancer. "Hannon felt his scalp crawling."

The tone of the story has therefore changed radically, and changes again when Hannon, on hearing of Mrs. Rasher's condition, "wondered where he'd get his Crispy Crunches if anything happened," a remark that is simultaneously funny and chilling. The evidence of Hannon's self-centredness is repeated later when he finds a pencilled note, "CLOSED ON ACCOUNT OF DEATH," pinned to the shop door, and asks: "Where will we get our ice cream?" These remarks may be regarded as psychological rather than heartless. Hannon is sufficiently moved to visit the funeral home in order to pay his respects, but later, when he hears of the Jewish custom by which the family was watching through a screen, he "felt acutely resentful." And when the Indian woman at the cab stand (another "ethnic" whom he encounters at this time) forecasts that the Rashers will now "move to the States," he laughs. By the end of the story, this hasn't happened, but Hannon now slinks past the delicatessen and "misses his Crispy Crunches." The new horizons are blotted out as the humour turns sour. The final effect, partly poignant, is deeply disturbing.

An oddity of the story is the title, since "the good tenor man" is the Jewish proprietor rather than Hannon. Perhaps Hood is emphasizing the point that, as opposed to so much traditional humour, here it is the gentile rather than the Jew who is presented in stereotypical terms. In addition, Copoloff-Mechanic usefully points out that "tenor" has a double meaning, and fits Hannon not in musical terms but as one "holding on an uninterrupted course" (78). Furthermore, the immediate musical connotation associates the Rasher family with an awareness of harmony that Hannon lacks—hence the final sentence in which Saul and Sammy, father and son, show themselves capable of still making music together. However we interpret these details, "The Good Tenor Man" is notable for its masterly control of tone.

"The Fruit Man, the Meat Man & the Manager" (188-97) records how a (Jewish) grocery known for its honorable service is forced out of business by larger and more powerful interests, the whole process seen from the viewpoint of one of its admiring (gentile) customers. It is an absorbing story in its own right, a convincing example of Hood's "super-realism," but, as already noted, it cannot bear the additional Trinitarian burden that he tried to place upon it. Instead, his attempted allegorizing of the story detracts from its effectiveness (see 26-27 above). Hence the tale needs to be trusted rather than the teller. More impressive is the final touch, perceptively noted by Morley (113), in which the Jewish manager, after the closure of the store, sends a Christmas card to the customer in question, an emblem of human solidarity and decency.

But "The Holy Man" (102-118), I would argue, is the literary triumph of the three. Hood himself called it "a parody of the saint's legend" (Interview 81), though "parody" is, I think, a misleading term. On the surface it reads as a modern parable in the sense of a short, simple tale containing a moral or religious lesson. But many of Hood's stories would qualify under that definition; what makes this one special—and not so simple—is the way in which, just under the surface, we can watch Hood experimenting with subtle sub-genres of story. This complicating aspect is raised as early as the opening sentence: "As I'm not a Jew, how can I tell this story, current on Esplanade and Jeanne Mance and even as far west as De Vimy?" The conversational tone recalls Hood's early documentary fantasies as well as a great many of the sketches in *Around the Mountain*; indeed, "The Holy Man" would have fitted comfortably enough into that collection, with its bicycle-riding narrator who has a daughter named Sarah (cf. "Le Grand Déménagement," that also employs a Jewish background). Moreover, the family lives, we are told, on De Vimy, as did the Hoods between 1963 and 1967, and "The Holy Man" was written in December, 1964.

At first, then, this promises to be one of those stories close to non-fiction memoir, in which the sense of invented narrative is at a minimum. Yet the "story" is said to be "current" in a particular area of Montréal, suggesting a traditional if contemporary local legend. In fact, the narrator devotes the first five pages to establishing his credentials within the primarily Jewish community ("You? You're fine, just fine..."; "I have always held... that Christians are somehow Jews") before abruptly turning to what he calls "the story I'm telling," though the story itself hasn't yet begun. Once started, it seems at first to belong firmly within the traditional boundaries of literary realism. The early years of Menahem Luboshutz (Manny) are presented in an economical, matter-of-fact fashion, yet, as the narrative proceeds, it gradually takes on the fabulous quality of an ancient tale: "then everything changed; he became a saint..." Just like that, in the middle of a sentence. And when explanations are offered, they are full of unlikely transformations. Originally, "a nice ordinary [though Orthodox Jewish] young boy," he won a place at McGill (not easy for a Jew in mid-twentieth-century Montréal), and quickly "fell in with the theatre crowd, *nobody yet knows how*" (my emphasis), and "cut his earlocks." But then, after falling in love with a rich Jewish girl whose family "was reformed to the point of incredulity" and who "dropped" him under pressure from her father, he underwent another radical change, let "his beard flourish... his earlocks grow," and soon established "a well-merited reputation for holiness." This is the stuff of legend—even (in Christian terms) of a saint's legend; realism has been left far behind.

The first-person account now resumes, but it begins to tell of wonders. When Manny appeared on the crowded noisy *ruelles* of the Jewish area, the alleys "would grow still, the children gathered around him, moved by an unfamiliar need for quiet." A little later—even more remarkably, perhaps—"[c]rowds of pigeons on the street would fold their wings as he came by." He spends his time "walking the streets in the district, talking to people and telling stories." One of these stories is reproduced, and it proves to be an example of traditional parable—a parable within a parable, as it were. Moreover, before long, rumours of miracles begin to circulate: "I have heard from her friends that a child sick eight years of polio recovered the use of her limbs after minutes in his presence." Such a tale suggests the stories of Jesus; even the rhythms and word-order—"a child sick eight years"—recalls the Authorized Version.

The narrative resolution is worked out within the tradition of moral fable. When Manny becomes well-known as a healer, the father of the girl who had been forced to reject him seeks him out and pleads with him to accept her. Manny, of course, refuses, gently explaining that the older man "did [him] a good action" since the rejection led him to his life's vocation and fulfilment. No concern for the likelihood of the situation, and no consultation with the girl, who is now in love with someone else. More important is the appropriate symmetry—the rejecter rejected—structurally pleasing and morally satisfying. But the final sentence, with an exquisite detached dignity, tells us that the girl "treasured his legend in her heart through many years of a tormenting marriage." The art required to produce this illusion of simplicity is considerable, and Hood achieves it without apparent effort.

The Fruit Man is full of accomplished specimens of short fiction, and one can understand why Phyllis Grosskurth wrote in a review: "There wasn't a single story in this collection that I didn't like enormously" (43). None the less, however high the overall standard may be, some stories are undoubtedly more successful than others. I have already suggested that Hood's conspicuously technical experiments tend to prove less impressive and less original than those, like "Getting to Williamstown," where he has found the perfect, albeit unconventional way to tell a particular story. Here "Whos Paying for This Call?" (198-207) in particular exploits what Garebian perceptively calls "the first-person, avant-garde pop style . . . indiscreetly liberated from the niceties of punctuation, paragraphing, good grammar, and elegant syntax" (*Hugh Hood* 27). It portrays a post-Bob-Dylan showbiz-circuit poet who ultimately comes to recognize the inadequacy of his (arguable) gifts. Like so many of Hood's stories, it contains a skillful blend of the comic and the serious, the trivial and the weighty, but one suspects that it originates more out of a personal challenge to write in an alien style than out of a genuine creative urge.

Of "Places I've Never Been" (88-101), not quite so radical in its experimentalism, Hood has written: "What I have, in fact, is an exceedingly powerful sensory imagination which is able to persuade people of the utter authenticity of things I've never experienced except in imagination. That is why I wrote the story 'Places I've Never Been,' as a kind of clue to my readers, none of whom has ever been alerted by it" (Hood and Mills 146). The story of a Québécois terrorist who escapes somewhat improbably into the far north only to realize that he has fatally isolated himself is vividly and expertly written, but gives the impression that Hood is stimulated by the idea behind it rather than by the subject itself. The same might be said about "Harley Talking" (133-42), a technical tour de force told entirely in dialogue; the talk is convincing, but the collection of anecdotes seems inconsequential when compared with Hood's best work.

Of the rest, "One Owner, Low Mileage" (119-32) is highly readable and compares well with Hood's other studies of marital and family relations, and it even enjoyed the distinction of being translated into French by Hubert Aquin. But, alongside many of the stories here, it lacks substance. "Paradise Retained?" (153-61) is a fictive and less effective coda to two non-political reports on the Montréal Expo 67 available in *The Governor's Bridge Is Closed*, "The Singapore Hotel" (162-72) another contribution to office folklore, and "Cura Pastoralis" (173-87) an early pastiche of the Callaghan style written back in 1957, fully convincing without being particularly ambitious. But the two stories not yet discussed, "Brother André" and "The Dog Explosion," in their respective ways, are vintage Hood at his best.

"Brother André, Père Lamarche and My Grandmother Eugénie Blagdon" (55-71) belongs superficially with "Silver Bugles" and "Recollections." But there is, of course, a difference: while they drew upon Hood's own memories, however tempered by fiction (and we should take his just-quoted remark about "Places I've Never Been" to heart here), this story is dependent upon family tradition. All we can say for certain is that the basic biographical facts about Brother André's life are accurate enough. The narrator claims within the text that the story of Mrs. Moore and his grandmother on Amelia Street derives "very clearly from my mother's tales in my infancy," and as Eugénie Blagdon was Hood's own grandmother's name there seems no reason to doubt it.

In fact, the distinctive and significant characteristic of the story relates not so much to its historical authenticity as to the tone and attitude of the narrator. This is not quite Hugh Hood in his accustomed role as "a Catholic by birth, upbringing, and mature conviction" (AM 10). Instead, he projects a good deal of scepticism. On noting that, "like many another pious devotion of a less sophisticated age, the penitential intention is dying," he asks rhetorically, "Who needs it?," and then recounts a joke at the expense of miraculous cures. Of Brother André himself, he remarks that his "calling was that of a saint and anybody born much after 1845 won't very likely have such a calling." Miracles are downgraded to "inexplicable oddities." His personal memory of Brother André (which couldn't have been in "the summer of 1937," as he died in January of that year), while acknowledging it as a memorable event, places more emphasis on what would now be called the PR of the visit than the visit itself.

All this serves as preparation for the main episode set in Toronto in 1910, long before the narrator's birth, so the telling requires a considerable amount of historical reconstruction. And here, even more important than the factual details of a vanished age (reproduced with Hood's habitual concern for accuracy) is an imaginative recreation of the attitudes and assumptions of the period. Hood totally persuades us of the authenticity—and the gravity—of the episode. Mrs. Moore's dilemma—her fear of damnation because she "cursed God"—is treated seriously, and the community's concern comes across as both gratifying and genuine. Too often, critics approve a plodding kind of sociological fidelity without responding to Hood's capacity for imaginative sympathy—an empathy all the more impressive in contrast to the narrator's initial scepticism. It is as if the speaker is won over to the human dimensions of the story in the very act of telling it. "Brother André" is one of the indisputable successes of the volume.

"The Dog Explosion" (143-52), in which Tom Fuess, a playful young academic ("a bit of a kidder"), spreads a rumour that canine overpopulation will soon cause a world crisis of catastrophic proportions, can register a claim to be Hood's comic masterpiece, the supreme product of what he used to describe to his children as "Sportive play of imagination" (Interview 31). There is nothing quite like it elsewhere in his work. Tom insists that the idea "just came" to him, and one suspects that it "just came" to Hood also. In "Where the Myth Touches Us," the Callaghan figure David Wallace refers to "those lucky subjects," stories "that you don't have to build like you were building a house" (FRK 203 [196]). "The Dog Explosion" shows every sign of belonging in the same category. Once the central idea is obtained, the associated effects duly follow. Hood has great fun with journalistic writing-conventions: the inventing of outrageous possible side effects that could hinder concerted action ("High incidence of migraine among Pekinese on the pill"); parody of sociological jargon ("race, colour or breed…"); the scientific passion for acronyms ("Committee Against Native Instincts and Natural Energies"); or the sheer revelling in clashes of language levels (when Tom mentions the just invented crisis in his university classes, "students nodded wisely, as though they were wholly *au courant* dogwise"). Part of the richness of the joke is that it proliferates as quickly as the dogs in the rumour are supposed to multiply.

Needless to say, the story, though a monument to sheer fun, high spirits, and the joys of intellectual exuberance, is rarely discussed by critics. Only Morley (113), specifically emphasizing comedy, comes close to giving the story its due. Garebian passes it over as "merely playful" (*Hugh Hood* 32)—perhaps wisely, since it could well prove a cruel trap for earnest academic commentators, with results almost as hilarious as itself. Thus Copoloff-Mechanic solemnly argues that Tom's "perversion of the media disrupts social unity" and that he therefore "reminds us of the antichrist" (86, 88). The ripples of Hood's humour have spread further than he could possibly have anticipated.

7

The Morality of Vision:

Dark Glasses

Dark Glasses is unique among Hood's books of short stories in containing an epigraph: "For now we see through a glass darkly, but then face to face" (1 Corinthians 13:12). As Barry Cameron pointed out in a review, it serves as "a directive for understanding the meaning of the stories, which are laced with images of shadows, darkness, glass, light, and perception and with face to face confrontation with the self and others, with reality" (Review 146). But it is not a matter of "meaning" alone. Allusions to the epigraph, some obvious, some subtle, recur as leitmotifs throughout the volume, and Hood's artistry is displayed in the way in which they are arranged and controlled. The narrator of the title story admits to putting on dark glasses "to conceal my eyes from other people" (119); the aged protagonist in "The Chess Match" sees both pity and contempt in the eyes of a young relation, and thus recognizes his never-identified opponent, who is clearly death; in "Going Out as a Ghost," the speaker is "not permitted to see" (15) the prisoner he is trying to help. Although these effects are sufficiently broad in scope to prevent a unifying theme from becoming too conspicuous or insistent, they create the sense of a planned story collection rather than just a gathering of unrelated short fiction. It must be admitted, however, that the relation of several of the stories to the "dark glasses" schema—the minor "Socks" and "Boots" (22-35) and even the dark and disturbing "Worst Thing Ever" (87-96)—is by no means evident.

The focus in these stories frequently tends to turn on moral issues, but a caveat needs to be registered at this point. Too often, in my view, earlier critics have judged the characters too narrowly, condemning them on the basis of fixed principles applied without any reference to complicating human factors. These protagonists are generally faced not with a choice between right or wrong, good or evil, but between two or more possibilities of action, all of which are capable of leading to pain, hardship, or some form of injustice. Hood is interested in volatile human situations, not in fixed moral laws recognizing no exceptions,

The opening story, "Going Out as a Ghost" (7-21), provides excellent examples of this kind of dilemma. The unnamed protagonist suddenly receives a telephone appeal from Philly White, an acquaintance from his schooldays who has been imprisoned on a serious charge and requests help on the grounds of friendship and common humanity ("We are all responsible for one another"). Both his decent instincts and his Christian training tell him that he should comply, but he soon discovers that matters are by no means straightforward. White is guilty on many counts, including fraud, which means that, despite his high-toned appeal, he has himself behaved in a thoroughly irresponsible manner to his fellow beings. Indeed, he is irresponsible in the very act of preaching responsibility to the protagonist, whom (as soon becomes clear) he is trying to manipulate. Moreover, it is soon revealed that White "never, even by accident, said the plain truth." When a little later White phones again to ask for money, the protagonist regards such an appeal as the last straw. He refuses, and cuts off all further contact. Commentators find it difficult to resist judging this action as in some degree culpable; "in absolute terms," writes Copoloff-Mechanic, "he has denied Philly, and ultimately himself, the spirit of divine mercy" (97). Even Lawrence Mathews, generally a shrewder and more reliable literary commentator, remarks: "The protagonist ultimately fails to uphold the moral standard of God's love for man" ("Secular" 215). True, but he is not God, and can hardly expect (or be expected) to emulate God's standard.

Hood begins the story by describing his central figure as "a confused man," and we can now understand why. At the close he is sorely disturbed by the action into which he has been forced: "I did right (wrong), I did right, right (wrong), I did right..." (I have followed Mathews's lead in calling the unnamed main character "the protagonist" because he "agonizes" over his dilemma and is figuratively torn apart by conflicting moral imperatives at the end of the story.) That many commentators see the ending as the expression of an uneasy conscience is understandable—and, up to a point, true—but the conclusion on a tantalizing ellipse (the only example of such an ending in the whole book) suggests that this moral dilemma is one that cannot, given the conditions of this world, be solved. Hood does not judge the protagonist but rather sympathizes with his troubling situation—for which, of course, the smooth-talking but deceptive White is "responsible." Commentators should, I believe, adopt the same position. Indeed, I detect a crucial critical irony here: this is a story in which the responsive (and responsible) critic is committed to making a value judgment on the story by *not* making an inappropriate moral judgment on the man.

I have concentrated here on the moral aspects of the story because they are central to the plot, and also because their complexity is not always recognized. Hood's gifts as a moral realist are never more evident than here. But his artistry is conspicuous also, in such resonant imagery as the gorilla mask, pointing up "the human cast of the bestial shape"; in the Halloween setting, where evil is said to stalk abroad; in the superb ending portraying the innocent young Halloween visitor "going out as a ghost" who can be associated either with Philly White as a child or with the protagonist himself, who had originally suggested the same unimaginative ghost disguise. This is one of the most densely textured of all Hood's short stories.[2]

I do not consider "A Near Miss" (36-52) one of Hood's most successful stories, for reasons I shall explain shortly, but it raises important issues relating to interpretation and judgment and therefore needs to be discussed in detail here. Though totally

2 I have written in more detail about this story in my article entitled "The Atmosphere of Deception."

fictive in plot and characterization, many of its details are based on the early life and situation of Hood's wife and her family. Its subject is a young woman's inhibiting fear of men, and the psychological reasons for this condition. Although early scenes between Marnie and her father reveal him as wise and gentle, we eventually learn that it was the effect of his upbringing that caused her deep-seated attitude. At last, when he is dying, he tries to retrieve some of the damage he's done by saying: "I want you to believe—you *must* believe—that no proper man will assault you or abuse you. Believe this and don't be afraid." She later asserts that he thereby gave her "the freedom of the kingdom of men."

My bald summary suggests a dubiously didactic, even uplifting story, but "A Near Miss" is clearly more complex than that. In a characteristically thoughtful reading, Mathews interprets it as a challenge to "the expectations of readers schooled in the conventions of nineteenth- and twentieth-century psychological fiction" ("Hood" 177). He notes that the story "seems to develop … in conventional Freudian terms," argues that Hood "is challenging the assumptions upon which such 'psychological' criticism is based," and goes on to interpret Hood's viewpoint in terms of "enlarged vision" that combines religious and psychological insights (178-80).

All this is helpful, an admirable example of independent commentary. Its quality is demonstrated in literary-critical terms by the interesting—and surely revealing—fact that his reading of Hood's ending is totally opposed to that of Copoloff-Mechanic (who makes no reference to his article). After the father's death, Marnie organizes his funeral, and sets his photograph alongside the portrait of an ancestor who has been presented earlier as a specimen of ideal manhood. In the final sentences, she comments: "My friends, my gallery, these are not men but pictures. Men you have to touch." Mathews writes that this scene "reveals that Marnie has retained the freedom granted to her in the hospital room" (180). Copoloff-Mechanic, on the contrary, sees this ending as an admission, and argues that the "encouragement to meet the opposite sex 'face to face' is quickly forgotten" (102). Mathews is obviously right; Copoloff-Mechanic has missed the clear statement that Marnie now *distinguishes* between the ideal picture-men, the ancestor and her father, and "men you have to touch."

Even more interesting than this interpretative clash is Mathews's suspicion that his "sort of analysis is unlikely to convince a hostile critic that Hood's treatment of his material in 'A Near Miss' is artistically successful" (181). I am in no way a hostile critic, and I accept the general lines of Mathews's reading, yet I am convinced that in this case Hood hasn't fully realized his apparent intentions. First, the father's self-admitted "damage" is not made evident in the text. He comes across as loving, wise, and sympathetic. When he discovers an adolescent Marnie attempting to shave her legs under the influence of a TV commercial featuring Zsa Zsa Gabor, he remarks: "Never worry about what you see in TV commercials, Marnie; life's too short and we can assume them to be false." Surely sage advice: to warn her against the impure methods of the advertising and film industries is very different from a disparagement of natural sexuality. Later, social snobbery being in question, "Dad taught me that poor men are sometimes just as nice as people like us." Wherever Marnie picked up her prejudicial ideas, accurate or not, about inhabitants of "the incest-ridden back concessions," it wasn't from her father.

On the contrary, after admitting that she "never met a man who didn't make me feel threatened with rape," she claims to have "learnt the signals from Ted Harasymchuk and others." Harasymchuk (she almost never uses his first name) is presented as an uncouth, chip-on-the-shoulder art student she knew at college who, if not guilty of rape, clearly attempted seduction. The only other eligible male mentioned is Paul, the architect she eventually marries. He is described as "agreeable" and "gentle," and even associated with the picture of the ancestor on the wall ("he looked kind of varnished"). Mathews comments, "She has chosen safety, and she knows it" (178), but a safe marriage is not to be despised, and, in the absence of alternatives, Paul is far better suited to her than Harasymchuk. She may have married him because he wasn't "a sexual threat" but, the day before their marriage, she observes without any signs of embarrassment that "tomorrow night we'll be face to face" (note the echo of the epigraph, one that Copoloff-Mechanic oddly ignores).

Another puzzling feature of the story is that her father makes his plea *after* her marriage. That being so, what does "the freedom of the kingdom of men" imply? Any attempt to interpret it extramaritally would go well beyond anything authorized by the text. I cannot but come to the conclusion that Hood's reach has exceeded his grasp in this instance. The narrator raises too many troubling ambiguities, too many inadequate bases for forming a confident judgment, and if we are expected to form our conclusions (as sometimes in life) from incomplete evidence, the opposed conclusions of Mathews and Copoloff-Mechanic illustrate all too clearly the confusions that can result. Even the title is troubling. Marnie's last conversation with her father is alluded to, yet it has just been described as the sole occasion when she "got through to a man, really through," while a little later she asserts that "for once" she "got through the screen of another person's looks to the identity beneath." Why then "a near miss"—and are we supposed to extrapolate from these remarks any conclusions about Paul and their marriage? If there is ambiguity here, it lacks the rich enigmatic quality of Hood's endings at their best, when the ambiguity is easily recognized as deliberate, even calculating, and always contributing to the literary effect. The opening and closing stories in this collection are examples of different kinds of narrative equally successful in their consummate artistry. "A Near Miss," for all its intriguing readability, doesn't belong in that category.

Hood incorporated three early stories into *Dark Glasses*, all written in West Hartford between 1958 and 1961. Doubtless for this reason, they tend to fit into the concept and imagery of the collection only by some desperate forcing. Two need not detain us long. "Incendiaries" (53-62) concerns a couple who lose their first baby, possibly through unwise actions on the part of the wife, and later, when a second baby is on the way, let a young kitten burn to death through sheer carelessness. The commentators, forecastably, concentrate on moral judgment, though this can be exaggerated: their doctor describes the death of the baby as "purely accidental, a million-to-one shot." On the other hand, Hood is on record as stating that the story "is about irresponsible people" (TT 35). If we try to read it without preconceptions, we are more likely to be struck by the painful sadness of the catastrophes in human terms. The couple may, like the fatal meal when the kitten dies, be "rather silly," but they hardly deserve the traumatic disasters that overtake them. They are presented as pathetically fallible, and we can pity them even when they are open to criticism. Perhaps the context of the whole collection imposes an emphasis on their moral irresponsibility. By the same token, when in the presence of the major stories in *Dark Glasses*, "Incendiaries" appears somewhat slight.

"The Pitcher" (97-109) is a highly readable baseball story, although (unlike "Ghosts at Jarry" in the succeeding collection) only devoted ball players are likely to value it very highly. George Bowering describes it as "fabulous" (79), apparently in both the colloquial and technical senses of the word. A middle-aged businessman, Hod Gantenbein (known as Ganty), on receiving a large and unexpected legacy, decides to spend it "to enact his dearest fantasy": to become a major-league baseball pitcher. The most successful passages in the story are those involving the rackety characters in the training camp, where Hood, as it were, dominates the play on Callaghan's home ground. The narrative is crisp, the dialogue invariably convincing, but Ganty's success against all odds is so overwhelming that the story becomes little more than a sports player's wish-fulfilling fairytale. It is not a work likely to engage our deepest sympathies; to what extent can we admire a man who, once the magic wand is waved, thinks only in terms of playing ball? "The Pitcher" may record "a great triumph of human aspiration," but I cannot accept Copoloff-Mechanic's hermeneutical reading in terms of "Earthly Paradise," "grace," and "spiritual immortality" (107-8).

"The Chess Match" (76-86), on the other hand, belongs among Hood's finest achievements. While still in his early thirties, he succeeded in presenting the condition of old age from the inside with full conviction. The plot is simple enough. The 86-year-old Page Calverly is inevitably aware that he is engaged in a contest against death that he is bound to lose. We watch him slowly getting up in the morning, looking at his aged self in the mirror (thus conforming to a central image pattern in the collection), dressing, and preparing to attend the funeral of a younger relative. After the burial, he stumbles and falls to the ground, and is helped up by another relative. But he sees what he interprets as pity and contempt in the young man's eyes. Death has edged nearer.

The story is told entirely from Calverly's viewpoint, in an appropriately slow-moving and dignified prose. As Sam Solecki has written, "its brilliance lies in Hood's ability to create a style, an overall narrative voice and pace, that is an expression not just of an aging man," but of the man himself, catching "his hesitations, his qualifications, his careful discriminations between degrees of financial security" (346-7). The image of the chess match is regularly invoked, but only enough to remind us that the prospect of death is never far from the forefront of the old man's mind. Hood's insight into the preoccupations of old age is masterly: reluctance to look into the too-revealing mirror, the realization that "metaphors for sleep were all young men's metaphors"; the physical aches, stiffenings, and "leaps of the heart" during sleepless nights; careful manipulations in and out of the bath; continually shaking hands; thanks to God "for the invention of the safety razor"; and many more. Above all, it is a study in loneliness. Even at the funeral, Calverly keeps to himself; he is now "remote ... from the ordinary sequence of human affections." But (and this is a tribute to Hood's perceptiveness), this withdrawal from human contact is recorded in terms of an acutely human pathos.

Solecki's and my own focus on the writing is in striking contrast to Copoloff-Mechanic's astonishing misreading, which is both explained and invalidated by the unliterary, even anti-literary bias of her moral and religious preoccupations. These have to be recognized as secondary to (and subject to) what is presented in the words on the page. Calverly, she claims, is unable "to envision the immortal spirit within" and fails "to reconcile the material and spiritual concerns of being" (95, 109)—as if the 86-year-old had no pressingly immediate physical problems to require his full attention. Worse, his "dark glasses" (purely figurative, not in the text, and imported by the critic from the story's later surrounding context) not only "obscure the reality of the spirit," whatever that means, but "ultimately deprive him of his dignity and of his humanity" (105)! It is difficult to conceive of a more inaccurate account. Dignity and humanity are, of course, present—and even conspicuous—but only for those who respond adequately to the subtle potentialities of English prose. Hood's excellence when writing at his best will never, alas, be recognized as it deserves until critics become capable of reading and appreciating his work as literature and not as something else.

Response to authorial tone is particularly crucial in approaching "The Hole" (110–118). As Garebian notes in a brief but excellent discussion of the story, it combines "philosophic tenor and comic tone" (*Hugh Hood* 35). This is, of course, an unusual combination, but Hood is an unusual writer. Despite the fact that Laidlaw, the academic philosopher who is the central character, dies at the end, there is much in the story that is comic, not least the fact that one of the images we have come to recognize as a leitmotif in the collection, the image of seeing and experiencing reality, is itself parodied when in the opening sentence we find Laidlaw "looking at the hole of a doughnut," especially when the next step in the argument is: "How could he be looking at a hole? There was nothing to see." As Garebian explains, the doughnut hole "is Hood's witty way of satirizing the hole in Laidlaw's mind and the problem of the 'whole' in philosophy... we chuckle at Laidlaw's grave self-absorption and yet take the warning [of the danger of this kind of speculation] seriously" (36). Precisely. If, however, we turn to Copoloff-Mechanic's discussion of the story, and read that "the philosopher of 'The Hole' wears the dark glasses of metaphysics that blind him to the holy spirit that infuses all being" (109), we should realize immediately that the tonal subtlety of Hood's story is being missed. As in "The Chess Match," of course, these dark glasses are smuggled into the text by the interpreter.

When Laidlaw develops his argument further, he switches from doughnuts to candy, imagines a Minty Middle inserted in the hole of a Life Saver, and decides that "you were not really filling a hole, you were bringing together two pieces of matter which had no existential connection." (Given Laidlaw's imminent fate, "Life Saver" carries ironic connotations here, despite Hood's suspicion of the ironic mode.) Hood, of course, is poking fun, albeit gentle and good-humoured fun, at the practice of academic philosophy. When Laidlaw goes one step further still and pokes his finger into the doughnut hole, the waitress, who respects Laidlaw the professor but has experience of a non-philosophical kind, snickers. Hood then slyly opens a new paragraph with the seemingly innocent but potentially provocative sentence: "He ate the doughnut."

And so it goes on. To be sure, the story changes in tone as it proceeds. To quote Garebian again, "Hood's parody of philosophic reflection ... does not, however, reduce the high seriousness of the philosophic underpinnings" (36). Eventually, Laidlaw passes into a philosophic trance or perhaps into another universe. He has been considering the possibility that "there might be two universes," but later denies the possibility in what is described as "an extreme metaphysical step"—and dies. Clearly, Hood is flaunting his own artistic skill in controlling his story and the responses of his alert readers, but no critic appears to have noticed a further philosophical-cum-literary game that he plays at this point. He is deliberately breaking a classic rule of literary realism: that the thought of a dying person cannot be revealed by the writer if the person in question dies before announcing them (cf. the opening deaths in "Assault of the Killer Volleyballs"). In other words, Hood is also parodying a well-known theoretic "chestnut" involving the propriety of omniscient narration.

I am far from arguing that Hood is not serious. In his essay "The Ontology of Super-Realism," he writes that in this story he "tries to show a philosopher's intelligence actually at work, a hard thing to do." Metaphysical thought, he elaborates, "seems to take place in a non-verbal region of the mind, if there is such a thing, and therefore it's hard to write about, but to me an irresistible challenge" (GB 129). A little later, he brings up the analogy of sexual union that is considered by Laidlaw, concluding (like Laidlaw) that sex "is a metaphor for union, not itself achieved union" (131). My point is that Hood, being a writer and not a philosopher himself, explores the topic in writerly terms, and does so by invoking a variant of his highly favoured "Sportive play of imagination" (Interview 31). His narrative here contains an imitation of philosophical thinking—yet even the word "contains" takes us back to the holes in doughnut and Life Saver yet again. Hood delighted in this kind of intellectual problem, and fills his text with paradoxes and shifts of tone and philosophical jokes in the hope of throwing an oblique light on virtually unimaginable metaphysical questions. Laidlaw, in the serious play of literature, becomes a victim in this arena, but Hood's art focuses our attention on the metaphysical questioning to which he devoted his life.

"Thanksgiving: Between Junetown and Caintown" (63-75), one of Hood's subtlest stories, offers an ideal opportunity to demonstrate his mastery of the form by means of a detailed scrutiny of the opening paragraphs. "Certainly those places exist, go look them up! Do you suppose I've imagined this?" The opening lines sound like a *cri de coeur* on Hood's part, fed up with over-allegorizing critics and all those who play down realism, or what is called on the next page "hard reality." Junetown and Caintown themselves may sound obsessively symbolic, but are authentic small communities close to his beloved Athens, Ontario, just east of Charleston Lake. On the other hand, of course, his imagined readers are correct because he *has* selected them as appropriate names for his imaginative purposes. Moreover, we soon realize that the outburst is not Hood's but his narrator's—and a female narrator at that: "I don't like to speak frivolously of my own sex, and our sexual parts. All the same, Blue Mountain is shaped like a tit. I can't explain what I might have been doing, climbing up it like a flea on the breast of a goddess, but there we were." Not merely female, it seems, but feminist, a liberated narrator prepared to speak out. This impression is strengthened when we find her referring to her husband's "really *pathetic*" dependence on other people's opinions. This is in fact an exemplary entry into the story. We learn what we need to know economically but indirectly; we are shown, not told. Unless we read slowly and carefully, picking up the clues (the tone as well as the basic facts), we shall go astray.

But Hood is playfully deceptive even with his careful readers. When she describes her husband as "bounding joyfully on ahead, incurably hopeful, eager to placate when there is nobody to please, to mollify, no wrong to expiate," we detect an affection even in the placing criticism. She admits immediately that "it is exactly his folly that I love," and in the next paragraph, after establishing her rejection of Wordsworthian romantic excess—"You will not catch me prancing through meadows, nor does my heart lift at a soft breeze"—she admits (doubtless with exaggeration): "I am a dreadful mean woman. I am." Not, then, your average feminist—or at least not a feminist fitting the accustomed popular pattern. Nor your average feminist story. She recounts their parking at the foot of the mountain and her suggestion that her husband turn the car around to make the return easier at the end of the day. "Good thinking," he replies, and does so. Hardly an example of the relentless battle of the sexes.

At this point, it will be instructive to consult three previous literary-critical discussions of the story to see what aspects are emphasized and what judgments made. The earliest, by Mathews, is intent, as his title suggests, to reveal the "sacral" behind the secular surface of Hood's work. His two-page commentary is both sensitive and judicious, although, by the very act of drawing attention to a spiritual dimension, Mathews inevitably makes it appear more prominent than it is in Hood's text. The narrator, he writes, "undergoes an experience clearly presented as a secular analogue of salvation" ("Secular" 220). Fair enough, though he goes too far, I believe, in discussing her husband as "her saviour in a narrowly literal sense." I am not denying the presence of these hints towards a larger meaning; I am merely resisting the temptation to translate the literal into allegory and then abandon the primacy of the real.

Garebian repeats much of this, but adds one fact that is wrong and one interpretation that is arguable. The couple do *not* have "a thanksgiving meal in a farmhouse," a statement oddly contradicted by the interpretation: "What Mathews fails to see is that although the wife is not as 'dreadful' as she once was, she is still mean-spirited because, in failing to give thanks on Thanksgiving, she becomes symbolically a child of Cain—a creature incapable of ending her feelings of rivalry that ultimately close off her ranges of action and freedom" (*Hugh Hood* 35). No textual evidence is offered, and I can find none. He is possibly referring to the final "I said nothing" when her husband announces that he will drive, but this is as convincingly (I would say more convincingly) interpreted as accepting his leadership and foregoing her tendency to dominate. Copoloff-Mechanic, who inaccurately describes the ascent of Blue Mountain as "a pilgrimage" (104), follows Mathews even more closely, but interprets the ending in a way that contradicts Garebian (though without mentioning his response to this story). For her, the narrator discovers "that love and understanding lead away from Caintown" and that the whole experience leads "to her thanksgiving" (104, 105). Her claim that the narrator has "come to rely on her mortal and immortal saviours" (105) is highly exaggerated, but the main lines of her commentary seem to me sound.

In my own view, the "sacral" element in the story, though unquestionably present, is secondary to the presentation of the narrator's transformation in the course of the ascent and descent. (I find it significant, incidentally, that, contrary to standard allegorical patterns, the climax to her revelation occurs on the way down.) At the beginning of the climb, she is still amused at her husband's enthusiasm ("My woodsman, my model of crafty lore"). At the same time, despite her concern for "an access road to hard reality," she becomes taken up in the excitement of the adventure, even comparing it, albeit momentarily, to the ascent of Kanchenjunga or Everest. As she proceeds she refuses to comment on the view—"what can you do with a view?"—but when she takes over the lead she does so in no sense of triumph, realizing that one is not responsible for one's phobias and, since she's "not bothered by heights," she can't feel "superior." Her attitude, we note, is subtly changing.

The summit, ironically, is crowded with holidaymakers, including lovers (two of whom she falls over, as the male narrator does in the earlier account of a meaningful ascent, "Looking Down From Above") and a group of cheerful young Anglicans who are clearly not attaining spiritual insight. It is on the descent that a change occurs. They get lost in fading light, and the wife becomes frightened and even reduced to tears. But the husband remains calm, sensibly returns to the top, finds a fence that leads down, and follows it. "Oh, he was full of ideas." "Oh" still suggests affectionate criticism, but the rest implies praise. She is clearly uneasy about "[t]aking directions from him," but is now fully prepared to do so. "Damn it, he was right." Her silence as he drives home implies meditation over the changes in her understanding of herself, her husband,

and their marriage. Hood may suspect divine providence at work here, but he wisely doesn't impose any kind of overt religious conversion on his narrator. (It is *not*, I hope, necessary to argue that the story is no more an anti-feminist tract than a feminist one; Hood is clearly writing about the sharing of abilities and the acceptance of the skills of others.)

To conclude, all the commentators properly mention the female emblem at the opening (the mountain like "a giant woman's breast") and its male equivalent at the end (the "enormous boar" with the "biggest testicles" the wife has ever seen). These are carefully placed references on Hood's part, but they are not there to provoke glib thoughts about Freudian meanings. The former provokes the narrator into a specimen of her trendy vernacular ("like a tit"); the latter is registered, but conspicuously *not* interpreted as an indication of male threat. The woman now knows better. In the context of the story as a whole, these references are themselves placed, transcended (thanks to Hood's artistic skills) into a far more profound understanding of what is implied by "the essence of marriage."

In "Dark Glasses" (119-29), an unnamed male narrator attends an intellectual party in Montréal, at which he wears tinted Polaroid clip-ons to distance himself from people he dislikes. After being gratuitously rude to a fellow guest, he encounters the Leventhals, a social-activist Jewish couple, for the first time after the death of their son. Because he admires them, he now takes off his glasses to speak, but is confronted by a barrage of political theory that allows no room for human individuality or compassion. When he tries to offer condolences, he is himself rudely brushed off, and virtually dismissed. Putting on his dark glasses once again, he admits that he "could not bear the sight of them." So much for the basic plot. But our reading is complicated by the fact that we are forced to view the story through the same dark glasses as the narrator, who reveals himself as impatient, opinionated, cynical, and decidedly unlikeable. Remembering the epigraph to the whole book—"For now we see through a glass darkly; but then face to face"—we know that, in this case, the second alternative is not an option.

Like "Thanksgiving: Between Junetown and Caintown," "Dark Glasses" has been discussed at some length by Mathews, Garebian, and Copoloff-Mechanic, all of whom give adequate accounts of the ideas raised within the story. I find myself free, then, to focus on more literary issues. In terms of Hood's other writings, it is worth noting that the story could usefully be regarded as a reverse mirror image of "Light Shining Out of Darkness." Both take place in a Montréal February, and both unnamed narrators ascend in order to experience a significant encounter in an upper room. The opening sentence of "Dark Glasses" reads: "This story comes from the quality of the light," and the story could well have been called (albeit inelegantly) "Darkness Intensified by Light." In this setting, we realize that, paradoxically, "light can be dark." The narrator of "Light Shining Out of Darkness" undergoes a Wordsworthian illumination; the narrator here collaborates in creating an enveloping darkness.

Moreover, by choosing to tell the story in the first-person mode (and can it be significant that he gave the narrator his own age at the time of writing?), Hood compels us to experience the dark vision ourselves. We are required from the start to form some opinion of the narrator as we read. As early as the first paragraph, he makes a curious remark, "I'd needed the protection of the smoked lenses or imagined I had, which amounts to the same thing." This suggests a somewhat quirky mind, but the second paragraph is more telling:

> I don't think I had them on during dinner. I don't wear them around the house. To tell the truth, I feel pretty ambiguous about wearing dark glasses at any time, having read somewhere that hiding behind them is considered by psychiatrists to be a hostile act, which makes the person you're talking to uneasy and suspicious. Psychiatrists don't say what the content of the situation is when both parties are wearing dark glasses, but then psychiatrists are full of baloney anyway, so maybe I shouldn't worry about it.

"To tell the truth ..."? However "ambiguous" he may feel, his subsequent actions show that he puts on the glasses readily enough.

The claim that "psychiatrists are full of baloney" is noteworthy as much for its colloquial vocabulary as for its trendy facetiousness. On the other hand, the earlier part of the sentence, raising the issue of what happens when both parties wear dark glasses, reveals a shrewd intelligence. Moreover, as Copoloff-Mechanic perceptively points out (111), this is precisely what occurs later in the story when Leventhal's metaphorical dark glasses render any discussion impossible and cause the narrator to put on his own literal ones.

In the next paragraph he admits, as I have said, that he uses them "to conceal my eyes from other people"—that is, to prevent them from seeing him "face to face." This is followed by a remark about "compulsive acts," leading to the chilling statement: "Madness lies in wait all round." Few of Hood's stories are more dependent on the technique by which style gradually reveals character.

To say that the story is about seeing—or even, as in the concluding action, not seeing—is to risk the banal, but the narrator (surely like Hood himself) is interested in the way we see what we want to see. When he enters the house in which the party is taking place, he doubts if there were in fact "stuffed warhorses and arquebuses hanging above the gallery, but that's how I recollect the place, and the image establishes the tone." That last phrase seems to me crucial. Again, we see what we want to see; one thinks of Wordsworth's remark in "Tintern Abbey" (ll.106-7) about "what [we] half create / And what perceive." Later he insists that "light can be dark" but cannot tell why. Later still, Yetta Leventhal assures him that her husband will explain "how things really are," but he refuses to do so by asserting "you won't listen"—and he may well be right. The narrator had once considered the Leventhals "in the vanguard," and admired their courage and "persistance." Now they appear "shrunken, huddled together and feeble." His final putting on his glasses may indicate a deliberate decision not to see.

The last story in the collection, "An Allegory of Man's Fate" (130-43) rounds off the volume by drawing attention—even if somewhat equivocal attention, as I hope to show—to the allegorical element in *Dark Glasses*. At the same time, though no one (not even, perhaps, Hood himself) could have known it, this story also represents a beginning. This is the first of the "Bronson" stories that he wrote in his later years around the same protagonist. The others, for the record, are "We Outnumber the Dead" and "Bees, Flies and Chickens" (both from *August Nights*), "Jolene from Moline" and "Jill's Disappearing Nipples" (from *You'll Catch Your Death*), and "Plumbers" (from *After All!*). In addition, Bronson makes a tiny but memorable cameo appearance in *The Motor Boys in Ottawa*, the sixth of the *New Age* novels, published in 1985, and is a recognized but unseen presence in the final novel, *Near Water*.

Are these stories the scattered fragments of what might have become a unified story collection? No one can say for certain, but I doubt it, despite the fact that "Bees, Flies and Chickens" begins where "An Allegory" leaves off and "Jolene from Moline" contains references back to *The Motor Boys* and "We Outnumber the Dead." Otherwise, they vary widely in tone and situation, though Bronson (like Matt Goderich in *The New Age*) partakes of a number of the multi-faceted characteristics of his creator. As one passes from one Bronson story to another, he may seem at first to change disturbingly, but the new aspects eventually blend into the Bronson we think we already know. Like the narrator in *Around the Mountain*, he is notable for being presented sometimes as a family man and sometimes conspicuously alone. On balance, however, I believe that these stories are best considered within the contexts of the individual volumes that contain them.

A story entitled "An Allegory of Man's Fate" is clearly grist to the mill of any allegorizing critic. Hood himself initiates the process in the Struthers interview with a brilliant and sensitive account that is worth quoting in some detail:

> If you start thinking about building a boat, you're going to be led to all kinds of scriptural analogies—like the boat on the lake of Gennesaret where Peter says, "Lord, save me," or the building of the ark, or the sending out of the dove, all these

> things—and there's no way to deny or remove that from contemporary writing… You think of [Byron's] "my bark is on the sea [shore]." Or the boat in the poem by Tennyson about Ulysses… Or the opening of *The Cantos*: "And then went down to the ship," and off we go. Or *The Seafarer*. Think of the vast, vast iconography of building boats and sailing boats and sinking in boats. (32)

He goes on to specify *The Poseidon Adventure* and the *Titanic*, and for obvious reasons remembers "the loss of the battle-cruiser *Hood* in the action against the *Bismark*."

The commentators inevitably build on this foundation. Garebian quotes much of the passage and elaborates: "The boat-building is a holy task to Bronson, who never loses faith in himself… the completed boat is an emblem of man's self housed in the gifts of his own spirit" (*Hugh Hood* 38). Barry Cameron argues, reasonably enough, that "Hood invites us to read the whole story… as a type of man's travail through this world," but then goes on to see it ending "with a vision of apocalyptic bliss" (Review 146), which is arguable. Copoloff-Mechanic quotes both Hood and Cameron, and adds two flourishes concerning the finale: The Bronsons' "world model, fallen into fragmentation and confusion, is reconstructed the following spring—time of the holy resurrection, as well as their own." And, of the concluding sentence: "their amnesia is their blessing, and their bliss" (114).

Far be it for me to question the gist of all this (though I would question a number of the details). But the selective quality of what had been quoted from Hood deserves notice. He made much, for instance, in the Struthers interview of the autobiographical origin of the story: "we all had such a hell of a time the summer we were trying to build that boat and everybody got so furious with me, ha ha, for having inflicted it on them" (31). Moreover, Copoloff-Mechanic, though neither of the others, could have quoted his discussion in "Faces in the Mirror" (included in *Trusting the Tale*, published four years before her own book), where he wrote: "The lesson of 'An Allegory of Man's Fate' is simply this, 'if you want happiness badly enough, you can get it, but you'll have to be very tough, and afterwards you'll forget what a mean man you were on the way up'" (36). Later in the same essay, he explains that the story is "about trying to do something that you really haven't the talent or equipment to do" (38). Such comments seem to be describing a story totally different from that discussed by the critics.

When he came to discuss the title, Hood is equally revealing: "The title is intentionally heavy. The phrase 'Man's Fate' is one that I cannot hear without laughing. It is one of those resounding phrases that principals and politicians like to use when they assure us that 'the future lies ahead'" (TT 38-9). He even remarks that Bronson's impulse to self-improvement "is rather cruelly parodied in the story" because it "seems to cause everyone else enormous trouble" (39). But there is more. He continues, "One thing I particularly like about this particular story is the smoothness of the phrasing," quotes four examples of "phrasing which I mean to be poetic, in their linguistic poise," and then writes: "Read them aloud slowly, and you'll see what I mean" (39). The invitation to pay attention to language is totally ignored by all commentators on the story that I have read.

Hence the excessive and oppressive solemnity of earlier critics. Hood's account of the autobiographical element conveys a remarkable sense of familial energy, bickering, and frustration, which is clearly reflected in the words on the page, but has been consistently ignored—and perhaps not even noticed. "There is no difficulty that cannot be overcome" is described by Garebian as "a refrain, a chant or prayer of hope" (*Hugh Hood* 38) and by Copoloff-Mechanic as "Bronson's litany for triumph" (113). But in the text the somewhat pompous seriousness is leavened; the repetitions become comic, to the extent that he is prevented from finishing: "'There is no difficulty …' His wife and children cursed under their breath and he let the remark trail off." And later, when he completes the phase, Viv comments: "If you say that once again, at any time, I'll leave you." It is comic moments like this—Viv's blush while checking the contents of the kit and confronting a metal object "of decidedly suggestive shape," or the marital "pitched battle" that recalls a less sublime aspect of the Noah/Mrs. Noah story in popular tradition—that create its complexity, and the literary quality of the story. To be sure, there is a sense in which it is a story of "man's [and woman's] travail through the world," but—though you'd never know from the scholarly criticism—it is also a vigorous, emotionally varied, and extremely funny celebration of the trials, tribulations, and ultimately the modest triumph of an endearing human family.

8

Signs and Portents:

None Genuine Without This Signature

When Hood decided to call his next volume of short stories *None Genuine Without This Signature*, he was well aware that, in making the title of one of his finest stories do double duty, he would be encouraging both readers and critics to interpret the phrase as a clue to the unity of the whole volume. As might be expected, the reviewers—myself, I have to admit, included—took the hint. However, the phrase in question, as it occurs in the title story, is promptly surrounded by ambiguity: when the commercial production of fruit-flavoured "lotions, shampoos and soaps" is proposed, it is decided that the signature of Ma Hislop, the originator, should appear on each bottle, but there is no question that she should use her "real signature" (158, 161). The story itself, though serious in its intention, is the reverse of solemn—its alternative title is "Peaches in the Bathtub"—but Hood's clue has been picked up with decided solemnity.

The opening story, again presenting a warning in its splendid title, "God Has Manifested Himself Unto Us as Canadian Tire," is built on the conviction that the divine signature which should illuminate the things of this world has been parodied and vulgarized by commercial exploitation. Much of the text consists of an anthology of advertising signs or slogans, and "sign" appears in this sense, though not so flamboyantly or conspicuously, in many of the subsequent stories. The word also occurs in the sense of signing a contract, and various cognate words like "significance" and "significant" are employed elsewhere. Similarly, Don Stanley in "Crosby" takes over all the attributes of the crooner, including his signature—or "stigmata" (41)—in a metaphorical sense. On the other hand, "A Childhood Incident," an accomplished but somewhat inconsequential story that Hood took the trouble of resurrecting from his West Hartford years for inclusion here, seemingly offers no link of word, image, or idea. Copoloff-Mechanic, never at a loss, claims that it "examines the displacement of religious values as the signature of the contemporary psyche" (120), but this smacks of desperate word-juggling (the plot concerns a child accidentally locking another child in a steamer trunk!). Comparable sleight-of-hand uses of "signature" occur in critical commentary of other stories (see Garebian, *Hugh Hood* 47, and Copoloff-Mechanic 122, 126, 150).

When I reviewed this book, I remarked that the stories "lose much by being extracted and belong not only to the volume as a whole but even to the order within the volume ("Case" 239). That judgment is still defensible, but not to the extent that I once thought. *None Genuine* is not, I now believe, as integrated a collection as *Dark Glasses*, and certainly not a work like *Around the Mountain*, to which the just-quoted remark applies perfectly. Nonetheless, though in a less systematic but more creative or literary fashion than academic commentators suggest, most of the individual stories benefit from existing within the context of the others. Thus "God Has Manifested" displays links with the next story, "Breaking Off," in being preoccupied with modern cliché. On a thematic level, "Crosby," "February Mama," and "Doubles" all involve singers or songwriters. "The Woodcutter's Third Son" and "Doubles" interconnect structurally in their climactic scenes (lunches with women the protagonists admire) and also with "New Country" in the direction of their concluding sentences. "Crosby" and "Ghosts at Jarry" are part of what has been called (culturally and politically) the "conservative" element in Hood's work, with their common presentation of criticism, even hatred, for current developments in modern taste. A seemingly casual phrase in "God Has Manifested," "SOCIAL WORKER for God's sake" (7), takes on a literal meaning in "Gone Three Days." And so on. The extent to which these interconnections are merely the result of being stories by the same author written at about the same stage in his career is matter for debate, but for the most part *None Genuine* "works" as a collection while exemplifying the variety and diversity that we find throughout his writings.

Let us follow Hood's lead in his overall title by beginning with the title story (145-66), though it appears as the last-but-one in the book. It begins with an italicized epigraph-like line, "*Pick whichever title you like. Make your own movie*," which is completed by the story's concluding line, "*Cut and print it.*" This can be interpreted as offering two alternative ways of reading the text, either as erudite religious allegory ("None Genuine Without This Signature") or as simple comic entertainment ("Peaches in the Bathtub"). However, in my own view it is best read on both levels simultaneously, as more than comic relief but with the potentially pompous allegory leavened by down-to-earth fun.

Harry Felker, a highly successful travelling salesman, finds himself stranded in "Sweet Cream, Manitoba" (delicious name!) when his company goes broke. Taking temporary lodgings while contemplating his next move, he becomes aware that his landlady Ma Hislop, her daughter Peaches, and the latter's pharmacist boyfriend are experimenting with the already mentioned fruit-flavoured "lotions, shampoos and soaps." Hood's capacity for extravagant imaginative flights is clearly demonstrated here, even more so when Harry discovers Peaches immersed in the bathtub with "some liquid of unearthly smoothness and beauty" which she is "mixing" in a unique process roughly equivalent to that of treading grapes. Eventually, the four form a professional partnership to produce, distribute, and sell this new line of goods. The story ends with Peaches and her boyfriend married (the classic end of comedy), and Ma Hislop and Harry the salesman going east as "close business associates."

Most of the pleasure to be derived from this story concerns the various levels at which the details can be interpreted. To begin with the title, it refers theologically to the guarantee given by God that the works of his creation are intrinsically good; as Hood explained himself, it was meant to invoke "the primal guarantee of the actual, the authentic certificate of its existence which God provides" (TT 131). Realistically, however, it is an advertising gimmick by which manufacturers warn potential buyers not to accept the supposedly inferior substitutes provided by their competitors. And artistically, one suspects Hood to be implying that, when a writer publishes his work under his own signature, he is assuring his readers that it satisfies his own standards and is therefore worthy of their attention.

By and large, however, commentators have tried to keep more than one interpretative ball in the air at the same time. Garebian properly describes it as "a hugely entertaining secular analogy for scripture" and concludes that "the general mood is one of bliss" (*Hugh Hood* 49, 50). Copoloff-Mechanic admits that the conclusion "resists a moralistic hand" and that the story as a whole "appears to propose that goods and God can be sold at the same time," but claims in a final flourish that the "signature … is up to us to determine" (125). Yet both experience unnecessary difficulties when faced with Ma Hislop's non-real signature to be attached to each item, as if it were a parody or travesty of the divine word. But Hood is making two points simultaneously: first, the divine creation is good in itself, however much it may be tainted by human imperfection; and second, a human signature, however legitimate in human terms, cannot equal that of God. A similar complexity is evident in the detail of Ma Hislop and Harry going "east" at the end of the story. Both Garebian (50) and Copoloff-Mechanic (125) properly pick up the "east of Eden" allusion (Genesis 3:24 and 4:16) for an allegorical reading. But neither appears to notice that, on a realistic level, east of Manitoba implies commercial Ontario and the so-called "golden triangle," while, in another convention/cliché of North American comedy ("*Make your own movie*"), Hood has the pair moving traditionally towards the sunrise.

But Hood deserves the last word:

> In the title story "None Genuine Without This Signature" I make my salesman say, "I've always believed in the real presence." He means that to sell somebody something you have to be present at the point of sale—or represented there. You have

> to get the word to the outlets to put the goods across. Selling is strange, I say in the story, human. It is more than human; it is divine. The signature authenticates the goods. (TT 132)

Hood has acknowledged that "God Has Manifested Himself Unto Us as Canadian Tire" (1-11) was originally written as a piece to be read aloud with the Montreal Story Tellers, the group that used to give readings of short stories at high schools and universities in the Montréal area in the 1970s (TT 124). In other words, it was not written to be read silently, like the vast majority of his stories, but as a performance piece. John Metcalf, a fellow Story Teller, recalls that he "used to deliver it at a fast patter" ("Afterword" 177).

One's initial reaction on encountering the story might well be fears that it could never live up to its magnificently bold title—yet, almost miraculously, it does. Here we are introduced to A.O. and Dreamy, archetypal consumers who first met, appropriately, at Miracle Mart. They may at first sight seem blatantly satiric creations, crudely symbolizing a consumer society run riot. Hood saturates his prose with the rhythms and slogans of advertising. The couple is surrounded by the latest buys ("Tonight we've got a Coffee Magic superactivated dripolator"); their culture consists of reading about the next sale ("Canadian Industries 402, the *natural* shotgun ... Kills at any *reasonable* distance" [my emphases]); Dreamy is physically enveloped in bargains ("Hairspray, underarmspray, vaginaspray, and at the other end Desenex Foot Powder. Dreamy is covered ... triple-armour-proofed from head to toe").

But by the end of the story, they are regarded as a shockingly deprived, unfulfilled pair, babes in an artificial-*bonsai* wood, only half convinced that they must be happy since they "had it all or almost all," aware of a lack but unable to name it. For careful readers, however, the pathos of a self-imposed barrenness is intimated as early as the first paragraph: "Baby Car Seat by Travl-Gard conforming to all government safety needs. We'll never need one of those. Tossabed robes for car or boat, that's more like it." The essential aspects of living are replaced by ephemeral shoddy. "Who needs food?" asks Dreamy, "you can't grab a high on Hungry-Man dinners." Even making love is replaced by watching TV—for the commercials. Our reactions as readers move from a combination of amusement and contempt to an awareness of deep sadness.

Unfortunately, the reviewers and critics have tended, after acknowledging the obvious, to transfer their attention to irrelevancies. Copoloff-Mechanic notes that the first word of the story is "Wednesday—an allusion to Ash Wednesday" and notes that "A.O. inverts the Lenten observance" (117-8). But not only is there no mention of the church year, but the text makes clear that Wednesday is the day the ads come out "in the *Stars*." Dreamy and A.O. make their plans "[a]fter supper"; hence their shopping takes place "Thursday nights." Other critics have puzzled over the last five lines:

> Good taste is dead.
> Marx is dead.
> The sixties are over.
> Freud is dead.
> Keep on truckin'.

John Orange in his review worried about this—"Why would A.O. say those things?"—which is odd because he offers his own answer by noting that "the narrative voice becomes Hood's voice" (86). Garebian optimistically reads the last line as "Hood's implication that endurance may yield a richer perception" (42). Yet it seems to me obvious that A.O. is here registering his dependence on the transport companies to continue distributing material goods.

In any case, the major emphasis of critical focus ought, surely, to be Hood's style, his ability to sustain the relentless anthology of material excess without becoming boring, his tonal control that intersperses the listing of trade names with the cliché-ridden *patois* of consumerism, his rhythmic sense that converts the bombardment of advertising into a feast of sound. Hood himself has explained that, while he was writing the story, "the language of the catalogues turned before my eyes into a prayer, a kind of litany" (Letter 141). He is continually revelling in the quirks of language. To take a small, inconspicuous example, while discussing TV, A.O. comments: "It's terrible what you have to sit through to see something that's really worth watching." Hood is not reproducing everyday banality, since A.O. employs it to attack the programmes for interrupting enjoyment of the commercials. The cliché is thus both reversed and revivified. Or consider the possible depths and resonances of his remark, "If it weren't for Dreamy and me, who'd take care of the cost of living?" Whatever else it may be, "God Has Manifested" is a stylistic tour de force.

As I have indicated, "God Has Manifested" interrelates noticeably with two other stories in the collection. One of these is "Gone Three Days" (98-117), the opening section of which is also written to be performed. Here a mentally disabled boy, just rescued from an abusing foster mother by an understanding social worker, makes a badly timed bid for freedom and is only rediscovered after an extensive search. The incident is told first from the boy's viewpoint, then from the social worker's, and the "experimental" first section is therefore presented in the child's limited vocabulary. (Revealingly, Copoloff-Mechanic's discussion makes no mention of this technical and critically central fact.) We are faced with a battery of grammatically and syntactically unrelated words punctuated by meaningless sounds. John Metcalf, who once heard Hood perform it when they were reading together, admits that he "came almost to tears" (*Kicking* 25), but reading to oneself is a very different experience. To extract even a suggestion of meaning from the printed page entails a special kind of concentrated effort that runs the danger of converting story into coded puzzle. I am forced to agree with Cary Fagan's description of it as "a string of semi-coherent sensual experiences without the depth to convince the reader that a human mind is at work, even a deficient one" (136).

In two newspaper reports summarized in Struthers's 1984 bibliography, Hood rated the story highly and acknowledged allegorical interpretations of it. He described it as "the most difficult story he [had] ever written (286)," by which I assume he meant that it was the most difficult story to write, and claimed it to be "better than Faulkner's *The Sound and the Fury*" (285), which it all too clearly resembles. (One would like to think that he was misreported, but the remark is characteristic.) He agreed that it could be regarded as "a symbol for man's descent into hell," and elsewhere, in private correspondence, called it "Christological" and discussed the boy in terms of a scapegoat. All this encouraged Copoloff-Mechanic to liken the boy to Jesus wandering in the wilderness (16, 122). I cannot consider this helpful since there is nothing in the text (besides the conventional "three days" and the basic sense of suffering) to establish common ground between the mentally disabled boy's experience and that of the divinely inspired preacher of parables. If such was Hood's aim, I can only conclude that his artistry failed him on this occasion. In contrast, the second section narrated by the social worker is straightforward, effective, and highly readable, but as a whole "Gone Three Days" must be judged a bold but unsuccessful experiment.

"Breaking Off" (12-29) immediately follows "God Has Manifested" for several valid reasons. Here too Hood is preoccupied with a specific language—that of the office of a large corporation—and it is seen as disturbingly similar to the language of advertising:

> "Here's the constant-estimate-adjustment sheet for the third week of the current quarter, and the departmental breakdown, oh, and the extrapolation for the remainder of the quarter, and ... the in-field operations castings, and this is the divisional operations summary with three-previous-year comparison parameters."

Hood makes his point by flooding his text with the adjectival use of nouns now so characteristic of the Computer Age (itself an example). In addition to the flurry of examples in the passage quoted, we find "design efficiency," "office complexes," "building maintenance, "inner-city work-force comfort," and many more. It is typical of Hood that he should notice this phenomenon, incorporate it into his text, and revel in piling up specimens. But he also records it critically, as a degradation of English style.

Structurally speaking, "Breaking Off" balances the previous story in being a comic but sharply observed portrait of an ordinary couple finding their way in the contemporary North American world. Emmy and Basil are, of course, very different characters from Dreamy and A.O., and they are presented differently, most obviously in being fully realized characters with "real" names. In addition, they are seen convincingly within the context of their work, and they exist in a moral universe of which the earlier couple are totally unaware. Yet they are all prisoners of the linguistic deprivation already illustrated. This is neatly indicated when the narrator remarks of Emmy: "She had no moral vocabulary, but she had a complex moral life… She had no language to cover her behaviour." But "Breaking Off" is interesting in another way, one that combines language and structure. It follows the pattern of so many of the stories in *Around the Mountain*; beginning with a long passage about the office in Hood's best "documentary" style, it suddenly focuses on Emmy and Basil, taking them out of the office. We notice the style and tone changing, moving into dialogue as they begin to realize their mutual attraction, reproducing Emmy's inner thoughts and dreams, and then blending into courtship narrative as the scene shifts to her home.

And here, as so often, Hood's playfulness rises to the surface. A paragraph begins: "When Basil Mossington started coming to the house there was none of the low comedy that in times past was often associated with patterns of courtship." On the contrary, he immediately turns the story in the direction of low comedy with emphasis on Basil's faux pas with his potential mother-in-law (he piously condemns gambling while her "great ambition was to get back to Vegas") and his urination problems which reach a climax when Emmy catches him peeing in the kitchen sink. Hence the breaking off, and so back to the office, Basil's economical raffling of the birthday present that Emmy has now refused (thus profiting himself from the albeit modest gambling of others), and Emmy's continuing visions of "[s]evered heads, and other separated members." Breaking off indeed.

This story is, of course, a perfect example of Hood's fondness for "office folklore," and I have already quoted his account of the fictional sub-genre which he wrote with this particular story in mind (see 48 above). Emmy and Basil are "representative"; their story illustrates a class or generation or professional group of Torontonians at a particular moment in historical time, and "Breaking Off" therefore has a historical as well as a literary significance. But it has another significance as well. The title clearly refers to the failure of Emmy and Basil's relationship, though it includes a much subtler reference to office procedures, as the phrase "departmental breakdown" indicates, as well as Hood's concluding reference (still mildly risqué, at least in Canada) to "separated members":

However, in writing about the story he alludes to another, larger meaning:

> my central imaginative preoccupation ... is that of an enormous chunk of ice, a part of the glacier, separating itself off from the Arctic icecap and floating southwards in the current, gradually diminishing somewhat in size until it becomes an iceberg, smaller than at birth but still immense and capable of destroying the greatest human enterprise. The image is not found in the overt text of the story, except in the implications of the title. The social groups, the courtship patterns, which Basil and Emmy share, form a mass like that of the southward-moving iceberg with nine-tenths of its significance below the surface, but deadly. This isolated chunk of human culture—ourselves in the last third of the twentieth century—cannot speak to the times which went before, cannot hear their voices. ("Floating" 108-9)

This deep sense of a historical shift, as evident in "God Has Manifested" as in "Breaking Off," may not have been fully communicated in the story, but it casts its shadow. Emmy is presented as unable to understand her grandfather—she can't even begin to guess what his life has been, as if she can know nothing about "times past" or any sense of human continuity. Though ignorant of history, she represents a possibly climactic part of it. Hood was clearly worried about this development, and it contributes to the darkening of his vision in the 1980s and '90s.

"Crosby" (30-43) appropriately follows "Breaking Off" as a variant specimen of "office folklore," and offers the opposite situation of someone so identified with a past age that he is no longer able to operate in the changed present. It begins by evoking the wartime period when Hood, while an adolescent, hoped to become a singer in a band, material that he was later to develop in the fourth chapter of *Black and White Keys*. At a talent contest during the interval in a Toronto cinema, one of the competitors is an ambitious crooner about to change his name to Don Stanley, who has obviously modelled himself (notice the rhythm of his name) on Bing Crosby. He fails in his bid to enter show business, but pursues an initially successful career in the Canadian civil service. But his dress, mannerisms, and way of speaking still imitate those of the Hollywood star. The age of Crosby, however, inevitably passes, and in the pop world of Elvis Presley and Bob Dylan, Stanley seems outdated and reaches a dead end in his profession. The story ends with his anguished cry when Crosby's death is announced. Stanley recognizes the end of his cultural world.

This, then, is a story in which the historical changes within a generation are chronicled through the development of pop culture. Stanley is represented as one of the "sensitive barometers" of the period. By the 1970s, he realizes that the thirties and forties seemed "inconceivably remote," his own "upwards mobility" stalled because "it was impossible for him to wear sideburns or to let his hair grow long." (There are even echoes here of "The Glass of Fashion.") He comes to hate the new developments with a passionate hatred: "'Like hell, the times they are a-changin'. The times are staying right where they are'." But it is Stanley who stays where he is, professionally and culturally. He represents an extreme instance of the social pessimism registered in the early stories in this collection.

These issues are admirably presented in the story with the impersonality that had been associated, in the era of literary modernism, with objective history and major artistic achievement. But the times *were* a-changin' in all areas of life. Politically, the unity of Canada had been threatened by the success of the Parti Québécois in November of 1976, a circumstance that may well have been responsible for adding an extra, covert level of meaning to "Breaking Off." With the coming of an economic recession and the resultant financial cutbacks, the Canadian euphoria associated with the 1967 Centennial and Expo had faded. Culturally, modernism itself was being challenged; the Beatles song "Roll Over, Beethoven," recorded some years earlier, seemed increasingly to herald a pop future. In such a context, Crosby's death in October 1977 could not but mark the end of an era. Hood himself was deeply affected. "I can't realize yet how much I minded it when Bing died," he told Robert Fulford a few months later.

"I haven't felt anything so much in many years," Not long after, in a joint interview, Hood and John Metcalf together were quoted as lamenting "what they see as this country's cultural impoverishment" (qtd. in 1984 Bibliography 283, 285). This sense of cultural decline is discernible, under numerous disguises, in his subsequent work.

"Ghosts at Jarry" (44-56) is often classified as a baseball story, but this, though accurate enough, is also deceptive, since it raises important general issues and can be fully appreciated by any reader like myself who has never attended a game. The leading character, an Italian labourer named Mario, is an enthusiastic fan who quickly comes to dislike what was, at the time of writing, the new Olympic stadium in Montréal. For Mario it is spurious—the sward or turf "wasn't anything like grass"—and spectators found themselves lost in the "infinite space." Under the new dispensation, contact was "irretrievably lost." And he hated the roof design with its "hole in the sky" implying empty godlessness that he found especially unsettling. Mario therefore decides to invoke the power of imagination, which proves to be the main preoccupation of the story.

His solution is to go with his radio and (later) his portable TV to the old, derelict Jarry stadium and enjoy the game in the old, shabby, yet congenial surroundings. There he is joined by a solitary young woman with similar interests. And then, gradually, by hundreds of other enthusiasts—whether real or metaphorical "ghosts" is left uncertain. As Garebian notes, Mario "blesses the old and curses the new" (47). Once again we notice Hood's increasing unease with contemporary trends. It is important to stress, however, that Jarry is never sentimentalized. It had "the world's crappiest outfield" and is described as "the silly building." But it was built on a human scale and was able to accommodate human individuality, including a number of eccentrics who are vividly described. The new stadium is presented, implicitly, as lacking the divine signature; while the old, though described in wholly secular terms, is haunted not only by loyal spectators but by a hint of the never-quoted text, "where two or three are gathered together..." (Matthew 18:20). Certainly, this is one of Hood's most original, assured stories and, possessing a poignant elegiac quality, it tends to haunt the mind.

Though not one of his conspicuous major triumphs, "New Country" (65-76) can be regarded as a typical Hood short story, and not merely because it is set in the centre of the Hugh Hood country. He claimed to be writing about "the conjunction of Brockville and Toronto" (Interview 70), and this story treats the geography in between. More than that, however, he demonstrates his remarkable ability to turn an actual geography, the Highlands of Hastings, into a moral geography (Dante's, in the middle of a dark wood—and of life), and this moral geography takes precedence as we become more and more aware of a sense of death and foreboding. An elderly couple, Lester and Molly, on their way back to Stoverville from Toronto, find themselves talking about the deaths or terminal illnesses of people close to them. They then turn off to investigate "new country," and immediately the images of foreboding accumulate: "poorly-marked curves," a pick-up truck coming "around a curve, passing very near," fields slanting "down into obscurity," a "ghost town."

Whereupon Hood ends the story suddenly and enigmatically, the final sentence reading: "He speeded up, heading into a blind curve." The critics seem unanimous in assuming a fatal crash immediately afterwards, that the "new country" is in fact the land of death, but only because that seems to be the direction which the story is taking. One follows the words on the page and comes almost inevitably to that conclusion—unless this turns out to be one of Hood's surprise endings. I cannot help thinking that the accepted conclusion is too forecastable, and somewhat banal. If we read "allegorically," we can confidently assert that the couple are moving into the unknown. But can we with any confidence say more? The unknown may be the psalmist's "shadow of death," but must it be immediate? Can we honestly claim that the ending is any more definite than that? Might it not be Hood's intention (no need to be embarrassed about the word!) to create a story whose effectiveness depends on the fact that the expected fatal climax is left uncertain? In other words, this could be a story that is successful because it ends not on an extrapolated interpretation but on a nagging question-mark.

Despite its unusual Nevis setting, "February Mama" (118-33), the single creative product of a freighter trip Hood took in the late

1970s that included ports in the Caribbean, is also typical: as a specimen of "media folklore"; in the deft accomplishment of all aspects of the writing; in its fascination with the world of popular song; and in its vivid realistic setting continually spiced with hints at mythical, super-realistic overtones. Like the song that provides its title, the story exemplifies "that deceptively casual trademark of simplicity and smoothness of effect." But there are depths beneath.

Rafe Salvidge, whose artistic skills include the writing of song lyrics, has retired by becoming a resident and financial sleeping partner in the Peace Haven Inn on the island "paradise" of Nevis. His wife, Lois-Anne, however, runs a personal-management agency in Toronto, and joins him for only a week or two in a year. She arrives for a short visit at the opening of the story, and proves to be a tempting Eve in the Caribbean Eden (though we should not forget that Rafe has himself anticipated her by contributing to the dubious process of "developing" the resort). Rafe composes the words of the title song for her, and it is set to music by the director of the hotel band. Sniffing an international pop success in this reggae-style calypso, she takes it over and markets it, thus arousing financial ambition in the composer which might well lead to his ruin: "She would transport Errol to Toronto or New York as soon as look at him, lifting him out of all his life and dropping him into the media world without compunction, and very likely Errol would be burnt up in a month." A colonial parable, then, but constructed with the subtlety (missed by allegorical commentators like Copoloff-Mechanic who writes crudely of Rafe's "fall and damnation" [123]) that characterizes serious art.

"The Woodcutter's Third Son" (77-97), on the other hand, is anything but typical, at least in its opening pages. It is one of those stories which demand a distinctive style far outside Hood's usual range, one that possesses what John Orange has well described as "a slightly old-fashioned Jamesian air in syntax and diction" (85). Here is an example from the opening paragraph:

> After a single small measure of the delicate Moselle which arrived with the salmon, [Cecy] turned her glasses down. The first of them made the faintest of stains on the cloth, a pale circle the colour of

> a saint's nimbus in Victorian stained glass. Flamborough caught her troubled glance at the snowy expanse of stiff linen, now just that least peccant golden-ringed diameter removed from immaculate innocence. He said, "It will come clean."

The uncharacteristic upper-class setting naturally requires a greater stylistic formality and a correspondent verbal obliquity ("nimbus," "peccant").

The whole story is presented, again following a favourite Jamesian technique, through the consciousness of John Flamborough, a teacher of jurisprudence and also a politician. He is "a forty-year-old perplexed, confused, seeking man" who for some years has experienced "an obscure awareness that his life was turning in some new direction." Attending this sumptuous dinner party in the company of his wife, he finds himself seated next to the attractive daughter of a former colleague known by her pet name, Cecy. In the course of conversation, she explains to him the argument of Bruno Bettelheim's well-known book about the psychological significance of fairy tales, *The Uses of Enchantment*, but even before this he has become "enchanted" by her. Under what first seems a specimen of florid Jamesian polite repartee, we gradually come to recognize an erotic undertone as their *tête-à-tête* discussion about romance and fairy tale proceeds. At first, pondering the age gap between them, he persuades himself that he could "still just stay within hailing distance of this remote woman," but the association quickly becomes more intimate. Soon he has "covered Cecy's hand with his," a still meaningful gesture, we suspect, at this level of society. He recognizes her as a "minx," becomes aware of her "slender neck, whose nape invited a passionate salute," and is agitated by "an imaged and felt physical grab or clutch." Two pages later, as the conversation continues, he makes a pointed reference to "the face of the beloved."

All this reveals itself just below the surface of the text, which is ostensibly exploring the implications of Bettelheim's book. There is a sense, indeed, in which the story might well have been entitled "Where the Myth Touches Us." Cecy challenges Flamborough to name, without premeditation, the fairy-tale character whom he most resembles, and he immediately replies, "the woodcutter's third son"—in other words, "the spoiled favoured child of fortune" or, as his wife is to suggest later, "mother's spoiled darling." What Garebian calls "the analogy between myth and life" (48) becomes a principal theme. Flamborough acknowledges that he has been blessed with a "cloudlessly happy marriage," a "healthy pair of children," and "almost every blessing," but now feels the need to test himself, to "court temptation." He "had to see and know and yet abstain"—and Cecy is accessible.

At this point, Flamborough is caught between "the conflicting assertions of magical folklore" and the "sacred scripture" to which he had always conformed. And here, of course, we make contact with a recognizable Hoodian concern. Between the first part of the action (already discussed) and the conclusion, there is a middle section recounting Flamborough's thoughts in the immediate situation, his resulting tendency "to confuse folklore with divine revelation," and various other personal and national issues which, interesting as they may be, continue too long even (one suspects) for Hood's most confirmed admirers. Moreover, the Jamesian formality is now dropped and the discussion is conducted in Hood's habitual precise and flexible prose. By the time we return to Flamborough's relations with his wife and with Cecy, the dialogue is couched in more contemporary rhythms. With an innocence that severely strains this more realistic mode of writing, Flamborough not only invites Cecy to lunch, following up the Bettelheim challenge, but also, reverting to his traditional Christian code, invites his wife to accompany them! He is even surprised at her surprise, which reveals that their marriage is no longer cloudless.

The luncheon is forecastably brief, partly because he thereupon tells Cecy that he had invited his wife.

> "A child of ten would know better."
> "I'm incapable of deception," he said gloomily.

He also realizes that, being "neither a fairy prince nor a pilgrim," he is equally incapable of operating under "two contradictory notions of character." Cecy thereupon accuses him of smugness, and leaves. As the "mists of romance" clear, he finds himself, in the final sentence, "alone on a withered plain which at this stage began to slope downhill." The critics, who tend to emphasize the Bettelheim book at the expense of the incipient love affair, interpret the ending allegorically in terms of "spiritual damnation" (Garebian 49) or "moral downfall" (Copoloff-Mechanic 122), but an awareness of inevitable aging and gradual but relentless physical decline seems to me sufficient. His mid-life crisis has been acted out clumsily but revealingly; he is a sadder and (possibly) wiser man. The role of the woodcutter's third son is no longer feasible. This is one of Hood's most difficult stories, containing ambiguities that make various readings possible. It can therefore be regarded as either intriguing or frustrating. John Orange, who considered it "the best story in the collection," makes an additional, provoking observation: "the theme turns around and faces its author who is pointing an accusatory finger at his era" (86, 87).

Two stories remain, each excellent in its own way, one unique, the other supremely representative. "The Good Listener" (134-44) might be described as the wild card in the pack. It centres upon a man who moves from place to place, listening to other people's stories. This scheme enables Hood to juxtapose various stories and various devices with only the minimum of connecting narrative. At last, however, the man returns to his own home with numerous questions for his son, who is either absent or obstinately silent. The comfort that results from telling one's troubles is not extended to the good listener himself.

This is yet another of Hood's stories that has been interpreted in totally opposed ways. Garebian shrewdly likens the protagonist to "the inverse of Coleridge's Ancient Mariner because of his compulsion to listen rather than to unburden himself," but also describes him as a "confessor figure," and speculates that he might be "the Christ among us" (44). Copoloff-Mchanic, on the other hand, calls him an "impostor-Jesus," accuses him of "voyeurism," and condemns "the unholy nature of his confessional" (123, 124). Given the positive response of all the speakers except his own son, this seems improbable. Moreover, one clue artfully inserted into the text has not, so far as I know, been noted. In one of the rare narrative connections, Hood writes: "And ever that man goes through sleep to morning..." The opening five words echo, both verbally and rhythmically, a once-well-known line in a poem by W. H. Auden, published in *Collected Shorter Poems* as "The Wanderer" (suggestively alluding to the Old English elegiac poem of the same title), but earlier appearing as "Something is Bound to Happen" or "Chorus":

> Doom is dark and deeper than any sea-dingle.
> Upon what man it fall…
> That he should leave his house…
> But ever that man goes…
> A stranger to strangers over undried sea. (51)

Later, he "dreams of home," and in the last stanza the narrator calls on whatever persons there be to "Protect his house." Given the approval exemplified in this poem, Hood's listener should surely be regarded positively. Interpretations that look above all else for sacred analogies seem curiously prone to miss such obvious effects as the pathos evident in Hood's final paragraphs, where "there is nothing [at home] for him any more," he takes on a "curious invisibility," and leaves in search of "other places," a wanderer once more, and seemingly for ever.

There is no other story even remotely like this in the rest of Hood's work. It must be considered *sui generis*.

The concluding story, "Doubles" (167-89), begins with descriptions of a "strange geography" and an "extraordinary intermixture of night and day" at sunset, both in Saskatchewan, then moves to the fortunes in employment and love of two men and two women in Ontario. These two segments of the story are not adequately reconcilable at the level of plot, and it is therefore necessary to establish the artistic rationale for such an unusual structure.

The narrator (another of Hood's unnamed protagonists) is a highly intelligent rising pop star—the kind of person Hood might have become if his initial ambition to be a singer had come to fruition—who has been invited as a guest to a Saskatchewan summer school of the arts in what had once been a sanatorium. Unlike Thomas Mann's *The Magic Mountain*, however, it is located in a valley. Struck by the health of the youthful participants, he counters Mann's analogy between art and disease, and its accompanying geography of peak and lowland plain. The phrases employed here are "magic plain" and "magic valley." Immediately, then, we encounter the first examples of opposites or "doubles"; others will occur as the narrative proceeds. One day, he follows a path up from the school, expecting to climb a hill that will "form part of an increasingly high range of elevation." But this, of course, doesn't happen, since Saskatchewan is famous for its supposedly level prairies. He finds instead that he has "not climbed towards the peak of something" but rather "climbed up out of something." The significance of this distinction is never spelled out, but the subsequent narrative covertly reveals similar patterns in human lives. We emerge out of adolescence either on to a level plain or to a series of peaks that impel us to climb higher. The latter may seem more exciting and glamorous, yet both can contain magic.

On another solitary walk, he encounters an unusual sunset when both sun and moon are visible at the same time at opposite points in the sky. Moreover, each seems to partake, miraculously, of the qualities of the other. The moon appears to give "as much light as the sun," the moonlight containing the sunlight, while the sun exhibited "a moony, easy softness." Sun and moon are recognized, of course, as widely recognized sexual symbols, masculine and feminine respectively, and the mysterious way in which one seems to be concealed within the other serves as a striking image of the coming together of the sexes in marriage.

The image, the narrator tells us, "does it all," but a realization of its implications eases us into the human story. This begins with a flashback to the time when the narrator and his close friend, Fred Brookings, go through that anxious period for young men in their early twenties who are seeking permanent partners and ask themselves nervously: "Suppose we never meet anybody who would marry us?" The narrator starts dating Belle Markward, an attractive girl serving in the university coffee shop, yet comes to feel that there "was a ghost in her" and gets the uneasy sense that when she looks at him she was also seeing a ghost. Ultimately, she marries Fred, and he realizes that she had been "seeing somebody like me but not me." Later, however, when he encounters his bride-to-be, Flory Grundman, he realizes that Belle and Flory "looked alike" and that Flory was the ghost seen in Belle's eyes. One might say that a set of mixed doubles was involved, and that sun and moon reflected each other—doubly.

Coincidentally, the four meet again on a CN train when Belle and Fred are leaving on their honeymoon, and Flory and the narrator are going to Montréal so that he can meet her parents. A straightforward, subtle, but highly amusing scene ensues. Flory is the narrator's agent, and he is set for an international career in pop music (the climb to the peak); Fred is a school vice-principal (once out of the valley, he remained on the plain). But the climax takes place seventeen years later. The narrator is now famous—"Not Canadian-famous, really famous"—and Belle contacts him by telephone. In a scene subtly paralleling the close of "The Woodcutter's Third Son," they meet for lunch. He admits that he "could hardly keep [his] hands off her" since "love must have gotten mixed with desire," and a crisis seems imminent. It is forestalled, however, by the narrator's realization that, although Fred is still a vice-principal, she speaks of him with "enormous pride and love and confidence," and his own celebrity "meant nothing and less than nothing to her." He is left alone in the restaurant at the close, but in very different circumstances from Flamborough in "The Woodcutter's Third Son." Belle's final judgment on him is "You're all right, you are." The narrator thinks "about moons inside suns and *vice versa*, the one in the other," and his final revelation comes when he acknowledges music rather than life as the place where "vice" can mix with "bliss." The last sentence reads, "Bliss has a better sound," and Hood told Copoloff-Mechanic that he intended it to "sum up" not only the story but the book (127).

"Doubles" is not without its imperfections. The opening scene at the summer school is known to have been based on autobiographical experience, and this may explain why the narrator's thoughts and responses sound closer to Hood's than to a pop singer's, however cultivated. (It is difficult to banish the conviction that the singer in "Whos Paying for This Call" is decidedly closer to "realism.") Again, a paragraph about a percussionist playing impressively on a gong cymbal and then explaining that the piece was intended "for *fifteen* gongs of different sizes" is as potentially meaningful as the sun and moon imagery but is never integrated into the other musical references in the story. It remains one of Hood's more intriguing as well as more difficult stories, however, and (if my response is at all typical) it possesses the significant quality of revealing more subtleties at each rereading.

9

Every Piece Different:

August Nights

From this point onwards, a significant change comes over Hood's attitude to his short stories and their arrangement. "A Childhood Incident," in *None Genuine*, was the last story that he resuscitated from his file of earlier short stories to place in a current volume, and *None Genuine* itself the last book displaying any evidence of sustained, considered ordering. Henceforward, each collection was made up of stories reproduced chronologically in order of writing. This applies to *A Short Walk in the Rain* and *The Isolation Booth*, the later-published books of uncollected stories, as well as to *August Nights* and the two subsequent volumes. Even his two novellas are subject to this rule. "Weight Watchers" appears in its correct chronological position at the close of *August Nights*, while *Five New Facts About Giorgione* was originally slated as the opening story in *You'll Catch Your Death*. The evidence occurs in annotations to the typescripts now deposited in the Hugh Hood fonds, Special Collections, University of Calgary Library. In fact, the second novella was published separately between the two collections, so chronological ordering was maintained.

It would, I suppose, be possible to argue that Hood wrote the subsequent stories according to a carefully prepared schedule of related and developing subjects, but the stories themselves hardly support such a hypothesis. One only has to turn from "The Small Birds," the opening story in *August Nights*, about a family involved in watching a pair of swallows raising their brood under their summer cottage, to the succeeding story, "August Nights" itself, which chronicles the adventures of "Ollie's Dollies," a group of fanatical baseball supporters, to see that variety of literary experience (subject as well as tone) is Hood's main criterion—as, I maintain, it always was. The phrase "August Nights" (cf. 10) links them, but that is all.

The third story, "Every Piece Different" (36-47), is undistinguished as a story in itself, but essential in its subject matter to an appreciation of Hood's literary position at this time. Once again, the central figures are unnamed, though they are obviously based on himself and Noreen Mallory. While it opens with a sensitive portrait of the writer as seen from the viewpoint of his wife, most of the scene is taken up with a telephone call from his publisher, a conversation revealing disappointing initial sales of his latest collection of stories and sobering forecasts of his literary future, which notably qualifies his "habitual optimism." Since we know that this story was written in November and December of 1980, and *None Genuine* had been published the previous August (cf. "the book came out the end of August, right?"), it is reasonable to suppose that this is a precise account of the contemporary situation.

Towards the end of the story, the wife gives a shrewd explanation of why his work isn't more popular:

> "You're making every piece different... your style is to be a chameleon. You keep turning up in different places and different lexical domains ... and the audience has to re-learn all the assumptions every time they start a new piece. You unsettle them; they don't know where they are."

It's a brilliant assessment, an accurate account of Hood's practice not only in short stories but also in his full-length fiction, a point I emphasize in *Canadian Odyssey*, my study of the *New Age* series that was being written at the same time, where each novel belongs to a different fictional sub-genre. It is one of the main reasons, I think, why his work has not been accorded the major status it so obviously deserves.

Hood described the story soon after its completion as "a *cri du* [*sic*] *coeur* about how it feels to practise an art in Canada at the present time" (TT 122). The dilemma is poignantly expressed in the closing lines: "I've spent my life learning how to make these beautiful objects, and nobody wants them and I can't do anything else and I can't stop making them." Artistically, the story may seem too self-indulgent, too propagandistic, but the light it casts of Hood's attitude towards his art cannot be questioned.

August Nights, it must be conceded, is the most uneven of his mature collections. Three of the stories are best passed over as briefly as possible. "The Blackmailer's Wasted Afternoon" (90-100), in which the narrator is confronted by a mysterious accuser who is apparently the voice of his own conscience; "Moskowitz's Moustache" (113-122), a combination of "media folklore" and fantasy, in which a telecaster's moustache moves around face and screen; and "In the Deep" (151-9), where a Chilean sailor falls overboard in tropical waters and is borne to safety on the back of a giant turtle which, its duty done, vanishes as suddenly as it came. The first raises comparisons with Dostoevsky's Grand Inquisitor which it cannot live up to; the second was best summed up by Neil Bissoondath in an otherwise highly favourable review when he remarked that here Hood "tries too hard to be funny" (17); while the third, a variant, surely, on the Arion story rather than Jonah's, as Copoloff-Mechanic suggests (144), offers itself as a traditional fable without any meaning that doesn't appear simple-minded. Nonetheless, the book contains some of his finest achievements (including the novella "Weight Watchers"), and to these we shall now turn.

Though presented as a detached narrative with fictional characters, "The Small Birds" (9-19) is one of Hood's memoir-stories, the cottage-country setting clearly being his beloved Charleston Lake. What plot exists shows the family (though without the father) watching a pair of barn swallows nesting under the cottage. It is an engaging account of the beauty of the life process; we are witnesses to the continuing miracle of birth and growth.

A simple story—but Copoloff-Mechanic calls it "deceptively simple." For her it is "an allegory concerning the fusion of every realm of experience—national, social, aesthetic, and ultimately spiritual—under one roof, as the earthly counterpart of divine harmony" (131). There is nothing unequivocally wrong about this, but it has the unfortunate effect of turning a graceful, delicate, heart-warming narrative into a lofty statement heavy with significance. Moreover, she goes demonstrably astray when offering an illustration of this profundity. In a piece of straightforward description, Hood notes that the nest "was balanced over bare, flinty, ancient rock." She promptly allegorizes the detail, converting it into "an allusion to the rock of salvation" (132). But in context, it is all too clearly nothing of the sort. The nestlings are about to attempt flight, and the next sentence reads: "A fall would make mush of infant bones." The reverse of salvation is threatened here.

Oddly, she makes no reference to Hood's own brief but helpful discussion of this story in "Floating Southwards," where he writes:

> The most important sentence in "The Small Birds" comes close to the end. "Invisible influences crossed in the upper air." I originally wrote "Invisible voices crossed in the upper air," but realized at once that some captious critic would insist that voices are definitively invisible and so changed the word to "influences," which gives a pleasing suggestion of the in-flowing (*Einfluss*) of spirits, water or grace. "Crossed" fits in nicely too. The story builds up from our apprehension of the presence of spirits. (109)

"Captious" is ungenerous—"attentive," "close-reading" or "sensitive" would be preferable—but the importance of the comment lies in the demonstration of how Hood (along with all truly gifted writers) revised and improved his work through attention to logic and verbal precision. In the process, he shows the deftness with which a spiritual (not allegorical) dimension is introduced into the text. The "sacral" is indeed merged with the "secular" (in Lawrence Mathews's terms), but this is achieved by stylistic decisions made in the interests of literary effect. There is no formal allegory in "The Small Birds" but there is a delicate awareness of divine process.

"Cute Containers" (48-61) depends for its effectiveness not on its almost non-existent plot but on the richness and range of its ever-transforming imagery. The title derives from a joke about a desperate medical student who, faced on an exam with a question about the superiority of mother's milk over cow's, wrote: "It comes in such cute containers." The setting is Toronto's Yorkville, though not as the joke might suggest the liberated-sex Yorkville of 1960s hippies but the upscale, booming-real-estate Yorkville of 1980s yuppies. The opening scene is set between a sex shop and a nursing home, a juxtaposition that is offered somewhat pompously as "a type or abstract of the structure of human life"—yet that, within the mode of zany comedy, is precisely what it is.

The story is told from the viewpoint of Max Strathey, who grew up as a child in the earlier Yorkville, works for a firm called Datatronics (the zippy but meaningless name is part of the satire), and is both fascinated by and afraid of women. His somewhat exaggerated response to the title joke is, like the surrounding images, "multiplex," because he recognizes it as funny and politically incorrect at the same time. Max belongs, in fact, to a generation that is continually falling into the politically incorrect. He refers to the cute containers as "tits" and "jugs," thinks of Chickie Cochrane (the most prominent female character) as "Allen's squaw," refers to First Nation peoples as "Indians," and calls a female acquaintance (with perfect accuracy, of course) a "saleswoman." Hood is here "trifling with taboos," relishing the censored vocabulary of the period, in the same way that he delighted in the verbal absurdities of advertising in "God Has Manifested."

But the serious (though wittily explored) subject of the story is the transformation of real estate values. Allen and Chickie Cochrane (whom Max both watches and investigates) live idly yet comfortably enough in the funny-money circumstances of the period. They inherit a tiny wooden cottage "of great antiquity built no later than the 1870s" necessarily updated with stucco, brick, and insulated siding until it belongs in the category of "desirable residences." Beginning its existence as "practically a shithouse," it managed to survive into a period when "ordure and earth were transmuting themselves miraculously... into historian's gold." Even the original outdoor privy still survives as "an historic edifice, something that ought to be protected by Heritage Canada."

In some respects, this is the ant-and-the-grasshopper fable (a version of which Hood had told with indifferent success in his West Hartford days) revisited. Max himself lives in "a tiny disagreeable apartment in a Hillcrest highrise," pays $850 a month for what is really "a hovel" while the conspicuously idle Cochranes "owned one of the most famous houses in the city." He is an example of "the poverty of wealth"; they represent the reverse. But Hood rescues the unfortunate Max in a bold, elusive, enigmatic, and—in the best sense of the word—comic way. In the last, unexpected paragraph he feels "a tough resistant network growing up around him as though he were penned inside the trunk of a big old tree with hard springy branches forming ..." We have moved from the world of Aesop's *Fables* to that of Ovid's *Metamorphoses*, a development subtly anticipated by the images of change and transmutation that have characterized the real estate aspect of the story. But in this topsy-turvy setting, of course, it is the man rather than the pursued maiden who is rescued by Hood in his role as Ovidian *deus ex machina*. (It may be worth recording that Copoloff-Mechanic, who tends to miss verbal effects and non-biblical references, quotes the passage but fails to explain the literary allusion.) "Cute Containers" is not a story for humourless or sociologically-minded conformists; it is a study in witty extravagance, and as such is one of Hood's not-yet-recognized triumphs.

The two Bronson stories here, "We Outnumber the Dead" and "Bees, Flies and Chickens," though separated within the book, are best treated side by side. In "An Allegory of Man's Fate," we are introduced to the man and his family, and in the stories under consideration here, he is at first alone, then with his family once more. In "We Outnumber the Dead" (101-112) we are allowed to listen in to his inmost thoughts as he takes a country walk, and thus get to know him more intimately. It would be invidious in Canada early in the twenty-first century to describe him as an Everyman, but he may reasonably be thought of as representative of any thinking, white, middle-class male in Ontario—a Hugh Hood, perhaps, though without the creative gift.

The scene is, once again, the lakeside cottage, obviously located in the vicinity of the Hood cottage on Charleston Lake.

Bronson is alone in the natural world; the only other human being within sight or sound is a solitary trail biker passing along the private road. Our awareness that the account of the boat building in the first story was based on a similar incident involving the Hood family encourages us to regard Bronson as Hood's *alter ego*. Throughout, he displays the same keen interest in everything from the cosmic to the trivial that was characteristic of Hood himself. The "enormous old rocks" on the property lead him to try to imagine the unimaginable geological upheavals of aeons ago (as Matt Goderich is to do, much later, in *Near Water*). But soon he is examining with equal curiosity the distinctive tread marks left by the motorcycle tires. Nothing is beneath his notice.

Moreover, his thoughts from time to time express themselves in extraordinarily vivid imagery that once again unites creature and creator. He recalls an American bittern seen for a moment the previous evening, with its bright green legs that only Bronson or Hood would liken to "frozen solid lime popsicles" with the colour of "some 1980 Lada automobiles" (Hood once owned a Lada). A little later, after the motorcycle has passed, he encounters "a ghostly grey caterpillar moving slowly along the tire tracks" which seemed "double-ended like a ferry-boat," suggesting "the look, and very much the action, of a self-propelled concertina." Anyone who fails to notice and relish such verbal effects is missing a high percentage of the satisfactions that Hood's writing can offer.

This caterpillar becomes the second protagonist within the story. Bronson foresees the need to remove it out of the track of the probably returning trail biker. The creature's life thus becomes associated with his own, and as a result he begins to think of "the need of the living to ... take up arms against the opposition." And this leads, in turn, to an elaborate (and decidedly Hood-like) meditation on population statistics and the dilemma of the non-specialist faced with apparently scientific data frequently linked to conflicting theories. The bug's view is ultimately seen as analogous to the limitations of human thought on the mysteriousness of the universe. By now, Bronson has come to see it as a "friend and ally." Its sense of deliberation and purpose is impressive, even humbling. Copoloff-Mechanic justly remarks that the caterpillar "comes to embody the sacredness of all life" (140). Bronson's gesture in assisting and protecting it thus becomes an emblem of his commitment to the living rather than the dead.

Hood's passion for variety is illustrated in the fact that, while "We Outnumber the Dead" is the most serious and probing of the Bronson stories, "Bees, Flies and Chickens" (135-50) chronicles a "farcical fantastic dream." Despite the beginning and ending, which present and then resolve one more crisis involving the boat from "An Allegory," this story, as the bald title-list suggests, is no more than a series of unrelated misadventures strung together and attached to the family when they pay a brief visit to a cottage other than their own. Bronson, strongly persistent in "An Allegory," observant and thoughtful in "We Outnumber," is "silly ass" here, a "curious but irresolute motorist," somewhat bumbling and ineffectual yet likeable throughout. The other side of summer-cottage life is now emphasized: flies, mosquitoes, even bees which, in the absence of the customary owners, have turned at least one wall into a gigantic honeycomb. The chickens belong to a long-forgotten advertising song from a long-abandoned 45-rpm disc singing the praises of Kentucky Fried. The single narrative segment at all resembling a plot, in which the daughter leaves an unlucky peacock's feather in the cottage owner's house, whereupon he promptly dies, could form the basis for a Gothic-style story but is here accepted as bizarre coincidence.

As a whole, this story ought to be a pointless mess; in fact, it's refreshingly original—and extremely funny—in its presentation of ordinary, unrelated oddities that raise an echo in the experience of most readers. Copoloff-Mechanic's attempt at allegorization—the boat as emblematic of the church, the solemn acceptance of Viv's casual "it was like being in hell" (but why the bees and the sweetness?), the final skinny-dipping in their own lake as a "secular baptism" and a regaining of "paradise" (143-4)—loses all contact with the everyday world that Hood is at pains to record and celebrate. This light soufflé of a story cannot sustain such ponderous commentary. Better to recognize that Hood is enjoying himself in an endearingly relaxed way and that, if we are sensible, we enjoy following him. From a literary standpoint, there is nothing remarkable or distinctive about "Bees, Flies and Chickens"—except that he gets away with it.

* * *

In "I've Got Troubles of My Own" (62-76) Hood offers a study of up-to-the-minute moral complexity. The unnamed protagonist from whose viewpoint, and in whose language, the story is told is explicitly offered as an example of "the new woman" ("Single-parent status") with no certainty about the paternity of her four-year-old daughter. A generation before, she would have been frowned upon, perhaps socially ostracized, but times and attitudes change: "She had imagined herself 'bearing the shame' or 'facing up to her disgrace' but there wasn't any shame or disgrace. People applauded. Brave girl. Gallant new woman." Hood is careful to offer no moral judgment one way or the other, traditional or revisionist, but the very fact that the story is presented through her consciousness implicitly tilts the balance in her favour.

But Hood adds complications. She tries to find tenants for the old farmhouse which she had bought, impulsively and perhaps foolishly, in the hope that it would ultimately become her permanent home. This makes her a landlord at a time when, as she discovers, "the drift of legal interpretation over the past decade [i.e. the 1970s] has favoured the tenant" and popular sentiment often regards landlords in a decidedly hostile light. But this is not all. The tenants, eventually found for her by the realtor from whom she had bought the farmhouse in the first place, turn out to be "Indians," the husband as the result of a job injury on compensation that suffers "interruptions," his wife pregnant. Needless to say, they fail to maintain their rental payments, and the protagonist is forced to press for eviction. Moreover, to add to her difficulties, she works as a local investigative reporter with a reputation for fearlessly "uncovering injustice in fairly high places." But the tables are now turned. The tenants flee before they are evicted, leaving the place filled with dirt and ordure of all conceivable kinds. The protagonist is left on the defensive, passionately denying that she is a "mean landlord."

Though Hood might be suspected of stacking the cards rather heavily against her, such a supposition would be unfair. He is working, in fact, as he so often does, within the tradition of the moral fable, which flourishes on the construction of situations in which the pros and cons of moral action are finely balanced. We judge at our peril. The currently politically correct stance is revealed as containing its own double standard. Copoloff-Mechanic writes of the protagonist's "indifference" to her tenants, her "lack of charity," and accuses her of being "[m]ore concerned for her house than for the welfare of those it shelters" (137). All this is justifiable comment, the kind of comment the protagonist herself might have made in one of her journalistic exposés. But it is, essentially, the case for the prosecution. Here is her own statement of defence:

> "I've got to think of myself. I'm not your mean landlord. I'm a person with problems too. I've got a little girl. I work for a living. I have to get income from my house. I can't provide anyone with free rent. Nobody's entitled to a free ride through life. I'm not listening, I tell you, I'm not listening, do you hear?"

The lady doth protest too much? Perhaps, but what she says is equally justifiable on its own terms. The tenants signed a contract and failed to honour it. Their behaviour in her house was thoroughly irresponsible, and even Copoloff-Mechanic admits that they were "delinquent." It is all very well to invoke charity and Christian forgiveness, but charity can be said to begin at home, and Christian forgiveness should operate in both directions. (A comparison with "Going Out as a Ghost" is fruitful here.) Hood, as I have said, may stack the cards against her in terms of plot, but in terms of literary effect he tells the story from her perspective and allows her the advantage of the last word. We should try to imagine what the story would sound like if told from the standpoint of the tenants. This is a literary work in which the emphasis is less on stylistic matters (though the protagonist's vernacular speech is effectively reproduced) and more on the building up of the moral dilemma—*our* moral dilemma as we read and try to interpret the story. Whether we judge her leniently or harshly, we should acknowledge that Hood has manipulated his material with amazing skill.

The only interpretative difficulty presented by "August Nights" (20-35) is paradoxically its lack of difficulty. It reads as a straightforward, skillfully written, totally realistic account of two baseball fans, Treesha and Slither, and their relations with two (American) members of the Montréal Expos. They produce banners praising their favourite players, and even an enormous cake when one of them has a birthday. All this promises to lead to romantic liaisons but: "Nothing happened." In the last section, they put on a roller skating display in a stadium parking lot that deflects the attention of many supporters from the game. The team eventually loses the divisional championship, and the two players drive off—cliché of clichés—to "sunny California" without even noticing them.

Since Hood gave the story's title to the volume as a whole, one would suspect it to have special significance, but no "higher" meaning is readily discernible. Copoloff-Mechanic tries hard: "the baseball competition, ... with its frustrations and disappointments, reminds us of the natural limitations imposed on human beings in any physical context" (129-30). But this sounds banal, and bears little relation to the main interest of the story which lies elsewhere, in Hood's lively presentation of the young women. Their slangy dialogue sounds convincing (at least to me), and they are gently laughed at without ever being made to look ridiculous. On the level of pure story, "August Nights" is decidedly well done, and its bittersweet tone is effective; but it can hardly be considered outstanding.

With "Evolving Bud" (77-89), we find Hood in local-historical style, subtly demonstrating the changing lifestyle in cottage country in the 1970s and 1980s. Set at Charleston Lake and centring on "the Landing," it brilliantly evokes the time in the mid-1970s when it was "a grand place ... for the youngsters ... where they could enjoy themselves and stay out of grief." But soon afterwards a "special kind of money began to circulate around the Landing, loose money, beer-drinking, dirt-biking money, snowmobiling money," and the old-fashioned hotel once famous for its cuisine now has "a sex-show on Friday nights and a country-and-western concert on Saturdays which often blurred into Sunday morning." Hood has no equal in finding exactly the right word (note "blurred") and the right concrete detail to indicate a significant economic and social change.

Here the background is ultimately more important and memorable than the plot, which takes the form of one of Hood's "representative" narratives. The main characters are Billie, one of the original "youngsters," and two of her boyfriends. These are Arnold with his "acres" of condos (whom she eventually marries) and Bud Charland, an inscrutable member of one of the local families ("Never had much to say for himself and looked like an otter"). Two scenes sum up their fortunes. In the first (behavioural), "one of the comic fiascos that go down so well as half-hour sitcom segments on television," Billie and Arnold are engaged, meet Bud at a newly opened SnowTrail Clubhouse, and the two men establish a close, temporary, macho-male friendship devoted to snowmobile runs and ice-fishing excursions, during one of which Arnold significantly "hooked the legendary thirty-three pound pike through a hole in the ice." Of course, he lands Billie too. In the second (social-historical), Billie's family subsequently encounter the "evolved" Bud in a noisy "muscle-car" complete with "enormous sideburns," a "long cigar," and an "unknown girl ... on his right, no visible daylight between them." The country rube is now no more than a parody of the contemporary city slicker. This is Hood, if not at his best, at one of his bests. No detail exists merely for its own sake; every word counts. The social history may be depressing, but his deft chronicling of its relentless development is exhilarating.

"Quicker Coming Back" (123-34) may be most accurately described as a moral realist's exercise in pornography. If this sounds unlikely, Hood's own words can be quoted in support. Since his own written comments on his later work are uncommon, it is especially instructive to consider his remarks in the introduction to *A Short Walk in the Rain*, where he contrasts this story, in the interests of what was and is "permissible," with the tameness and naïvety of his early story "Marriage 401," written back in 1958. He observes that the present story, written in 1983, "is obsessively concerned with the double question of what you can and can't do, sexually, and what you can and can't say about what you do. I wanted 'Quicker Coming Back' to move towards the condition of pornography, and apparently it did so. Some of its readers have found it sufficiently stimulating" (18).

Characteristically, Hood's eye and ear for sexual allusion and innuendo are seen to be as keen as for scenic detail. The unexpected setting of the story makes this clear. Gracie Falconer and her "live-in lover" Dan Perrot (whose surname, mentioned only once, is probably an allusion to a west-country river prominent in the opening section of *Tony's Book*) are on a walking tour in the west of England, and the text is littered with accurate and perceptive images of modern English rural life: the inn "featuring four-poster canopied beds and full snack service in every room"; the "lightly-constructed, quaint, countryside imitation shopping-centres"; the "up-market tearoom" offering "West-Country thick cream" at high prices. The references to sexual practices and accessories are listed with a similarly keen relish, though Hood interestingly follows the traditional prime rule of pornography by never actually specifying details, which therefore remain titillating.

One gets the distinct impression, however, that Hood wrote the story as an intellectual exercise or challenge, to establish how far he could succeed in a genre with which he is not (and doubtless had no wish to be) associated. His keen interest in all aspects of life, of course, requires that he include generous presentation of sexual as well as other central aspects of human experience, and *The New Age* duly includes a number of such scenes, both heterosexual and homosexual. He clearly enjoys the challenge of introducing textual subtleties for which run-of-the-mill pornography is not renowned. How many times do we read it before noticing the inconspicuous pun in the title, or the *double entendre* in the listing of Gracie's sexual preferences, "the permissible bringing up the rear"? At the same time, need we be considered excessively prudish if we feel that this is an experiment which, amusing and skillful as it is, does not need repetition? Above all, however, it is important to note that the "moral" segment of "moral realism," downplayed for much of the story, comes significantly to the fore in the implications of

Gracie's final thought-provoking question: "'Corrupt,' why do I think 'corrupt'?"

The excellence of "Weight Watchers" (160-215), over and above the interest in its plot, the clarity and wit of the writing, and Hood's characteristic blend of the comic and the serious, is to be located in its construction. On the surface, it is a representative, almost banal eternal-triangle story of a middle-aged man, his no-longer-attractive wife, and a younger woman. The divorce-courts, we might say, are full of them, and that fact provides Hood with the critical focus for his story.

It begins in the key of comedy. In her single apartment, Patsy Lambert, an attractive young woman conscious of fashion and contemporary trends, is intent upon slimming. Once, we learn, she had been "obese." She views herself in two mirrors, tries to "pinch an inch," performs exercises recommended in women's magazines, and realizes to her satisfaction that she is succeeding. The narrative voice is that of a detached, somewhat amused, but sympathetic observer, primarily male (her fashionably brief bathing suit is noticed as conveying "the effect of stringently qualified modesty"). The tone is calm and relaxed, but there are danger signals. Patsy has obtained her furniture from a burned-out apartment house, and reference is made to an "obscure odour of burning" and "lingering impressions of combustion." This could be a threatening world.

The scene changes in the second section, where another woman, Ethel Merriman, is portrayed in the office of a psychoanalyst, Dr. Harcourt. She seems as different from Patsy as it is possible to be: no longer young ("at forty"), decidedly unsure of herself—and "about ninety pounds overweight" ("oh dear, where was the lower jaw? Gone, quite gone"). She proceeds to break down or, from Harcourt's viewpoint, "acted out 'crying hard; unrestrained; abject'." There are still touches of humour here; at the same time, she almost qualifies as a grotesque. The next section, entirely in dialogue, shows Ethel arguing with her husband Frank, who is angry at being expected to accompany her to the next session, refuses ("I won't and that's final"), but, as we learn later, capitulates. Some of the exchanges border on slapstick—"And so you're seeing a psychiatrist?

God, you should have your head examined"—but the seriousness of the situation increases. Back now to Patsy, celebrating because at last she has achieved her goal of weighing in at ninety pounds—exactly the amount, we notice, that Ethel is said to be *over*weight. She celebrates by buying an expensive dress in "the high-fashion starved look," but then, immediately feeling hungry, goes to a local restaurant because "[s]omebody had to see her tonight." Somebody, of course, does, and (of course) that somebody is Frank.

The individual scenes, though apparently discrete and fragmented, are now seen to be subtly contrived. Four of the five main characters in the story have been introduced, and the main patterns of relationship made clear. Moreover, the dominant sets of imagery, eating and weighing, are established and their interrelation made clear. The climax of the fourth section, the beginning of Patsy's association with Frank, clinches the point: "She sensed his eyes travelling up and down her non-stomach and non-waist. He was simply gobbling her down."

The quick cuts between scene and scene suggest the art of the cinema, and at this point Hood introduces another cinematic device: the flashback. We suddenly find ourselves witnesses to an earlier period in Frank and Ethel's marriage, and both style and tone change dramatically. The writing becomes more formal, lyrical, as if conjuring up the dignity and courtesies of a bygone age. This now prosaic couple once experienced a dimension of love comparable to that communicated by the Song of Songs, which is duly quoted. Yet the imagery of eating, traditionally associated with sexual passion, continues; words like "hunger," "fasting," "appetite," "abstinence from nourishment" recur in an amatory context. This culminates in Ethel's remark that love-making "increases by what it feeds on," recognized as a quotation but not identified as Hamlet's description of Gertrude's early love for his dead father (I ii 144-5). The allusive style is taken up once more when, Ethel's overeating being in question, Frank also echoes (and parodies) Hamlet by saying: "Get ye to a sauna, go" (cf. III i 146-7). The undertones in the text are considerable—and ominous.

We return to the present with an uneasy sense that both Fred and Ethel have coarsened over the years. After Frank's cruel outburst at the joint meeting with Dr. Harcourt ("My self-esteem won't allow me to appear in public with her... Look at her!"), Ethel in despair goes on an eating binge, courtesy of a Chinese-takeout service. Here even the list of dishes transforms itself into a paean of sensual excess: "The little won tons seemed to resemble the grey matter of the brain: wrinkled; fleshy; soft in the mouth." An expertly involved stylistic climax—but Ethel passes out in the toilet. Simultaneously, Frank entertains Patsy at the restaurant again, where she tries to confine herself to non-fattening salads and broccoli but is tempted by Frank, in a cunning reversal of the Adam and Eve story, with "a canapé, a Ritz cracker thickly smeared with cream cheese and topped with a slice of pepperoni. "'Eat!' he commanded." Then back to Ethel next morning, and her attempts to recover with a hot bath, during which she sees in front of her "the sagging heavy abdomen, the blue veins, the rolls of fat rising out of the water, an island of floating flesh bobbing gently as if independent of itself... I look like a beached whale, she thought savagely." Hood's manipulation of his material and his stylistic mastery are here unparalleled.

But now, at the half-way point in the story, Hood changes tack yet again. The immediate action stops once more as we are forced to consider the situation from a broader perspective. A new character is introduced, Judge Le Mesurier, his surname subtly bolstering the imagery of weighing and balancing—as Copoloff-Mechanic justly remarks, "he 'measures' the degeneration of contemporary society" (146). Appointed to preside for the first time over the newly introduced "no fault" divorce procedures, he seeks the advice of Dr. Harcourt, thus initiating a troubled discussion of what the latter calls "the status of marriage today." Suddenly, the specific situation of Ethel, Patsy, and Frank becomes a representative example of a current social problem. Some readers of Hood will regard this as a lapse into didacticism, but the effect is best understood in terms of structure. What has hitherto been presented as a personal story emphasizing human actions and responsibilities is now examined in terms of philosophy, morality, justice, and even social and religious principle. "Are there any remaining grounds," Harcourt wonders, "for treating [marriage] in the traditional Christian terms as a sacred relationship which is supposed to endure for ever, even beyond the grave?" At once, we view the narrative in an entirely new light. Moreover, not the least of the complications Hood introduces into his story is the fact that sympathy is now due not only to those who experience heartache and the breakup of hitherto settled ways of life, but to those, like Harcourt and Le Mesurier, required to advise and judge in matters that have momentous personal implications.

If this ninth section had not been included, no reader would suspect that anything was missing. The narrative now continues where it left off, but we approach the rest of the story with a different attitude. Although Hood does not insist on the allusion (though Judge Le Mesurier recalls part of it later in the text), he is in fact suggesting that, when human beings put asunder what God has joined (see Matthew 19:6), the decisions are necessarily made by people who, if I may be allowed another old-fashioned quotation, know not what they do (Luke 23:34). Careful readers will approach the last half of "Weight Watchers" with these uneasy reflections in mind.

The story now moves crisply, economically, towards its conclusion. We see Ethel in another session with Dr. Harcourt, understandably ill-tempered, but increasingly unreliable and pathetic. And by contrast we see Frank imperturbably enjoying himself with Patsy on a canal holiday. But then the focus turns to Patsy, once more alone. A section begins: "In September Patsy sat sweating and terrified in her apartment; appetite tore at her will." In other words, she is taking over the condition that had earlier characterized Ethel. She desperately procures "proper balance-scales", a phrase recalling both her first efforts with cheap scales and now the balancing scales of justice. Following that troubling intimation, in the first court scene, when the judge has the chance of urging some sort of reconciliation, he realizes that Ethel and Frank have "made their minds up" and that the "counselling stuff is a charade." This becomes even more evident in the next section in which Frank is precipitately moving in with Patsy, who is now putting on weight at an alarming pace.

The two concluding sections take place at the courthouse, the viewpoint shared between the judge and Frank. Here the judge sees Patsy for the first time, and is immediately struck by the fact that she "looked like a clone, an identical twin" of Ethel, only younger. Later, Frank watches her as she comes "wobbling" from the witness stand, sees the judge glancing from Ethel to Patsy, and knows what he is thinking. The divorce is now ratified, legalized, but, as Frank is about to leave, his eyes fall on the court stenographer: "Rather a pretty girl, thin." The story ends.

Copoloff-Mechanic mentions the last twist of Hood's narrative knife in the course of her discussion, but in her summation moves back to Dr. Harcourt's passionate view of a "total breakdown of the notion of charity or compassion or self-sacrifice" in the contemporary world. "What Hood wants the reader to see at the conclusion of *August Nights*," she claims, "is the fall from unity that is the result of starving the partnerships that alone confer continuity upon human experience" (147). But such a reading interprets "Weight Watchers" as sociology rather than literature. In fact, it plays down all that makes Hood remarkable *as a writer*. Had the sociological lesson been Hood's main point, the rest of the action (which includes Patsy's returning obesity, presented in terms of personal crisis but also with a sharp, almost pungent humour) would be irrelevant. Hood's ending may well be bleak in its attitude to contemporary developments in modern Canada (a subject that will return in my final chapter) and sardonic if we judge by the tone and implications of the final phrase, but we cannot help, if we are perceptive readers, being exhilarated by the skill with which Hood brings his story to a perfect structural close. That is, indisputably, the right ending to the story—one which suggests a recurrent pattern, an "open ending" with the prospect of "no exit" at the same time. A proper response to the story holds all these emotions and conclusions in an *artistic* balance.

10

Art in Crisis:

Five New Facts About Giorgione

This novella about a scholar convinced that Giorgione never existed, originally intended to serve as the opening long story in *You'll Catch Your Death* but in fact published separately in 1987, presents serious readers and commentators with a major literary-critical challenge. Hood is writing, I am convinced, on a subject of extreme importance both to himself and to us all, yet for many the book bears witness to what are often considered his literary weaknesses. Characteristically, John Metcalf lays down the main challenge in the following passage:

> Many readers have problems with Hugh's meanderings down byways of information, his asides, his digressions... Other readers feel that Hugh's disquisitions are an essential part of his charm. The novella *Five New Facts About Giorgione* would be a good starting point for coming to some decision about this argument. I found the book maddening. (*Aesthetic* 81-2)

No "decision" on this matter will be arrived at here, but I hope that the terms of the argument can be clarified.

For my part, though I can understand Metcalf's viewpoint, I find the book fascinating (albeit sometimes somewhat frustrating) because it reveals Hood wrestling desperately with issues central to his own art and to his way of looking at the world. That it is flawed artistically must be conceded. The narrative often rambles with apparent aimlessness in a way that is wholly uncharacteristic of Hood at his best, and the opening chapter moves uneasily between high realism and seemingly crude caricature. Moreover, there are curious shifts in subject, style, pace, and tone, and even some startlingly abrupt changes in narrative perspective. In addition, one obvious difficulty is that his chosen subject presupposes considerable background knowledge of some quite esoteric aspects of Renaissance art; this forces Hood into elaborate explanations that sometimes threaten to swamp the plot.

Yet it would clearly be improper to write off the novella as an unfortunate failure; Hood was too experienced and too talented a writer for the awkwardnesses and irregularities of the text to be explained away by incompetence. He has not, I think, been able in this instance to control and resolve the full implications of all the issues raised. There are times, indeed, when one is tempted to think of him as a juggler trying to keep too many balls in the air at the same time. Yet the main idea upon which the book is based carries the unmistakable marks of intellectual urgency. *Five New Facts*, I am convinced, is a highly ambitious undertaking that did not quite succeed in maintaining its full impact. All the more reason, then, to examine it in some detail and try to unravel the pressing issues, even obsessions, that went into the writing.

The only substantial discussion of this novella published to date is Alex Knoenagel's "The History of Art and the Art of History: Hugh Hood's *Five New Facts About Giorgione*," which appeared in *Mosaic* in 1994. He interprets the book as primarily concerned with the vexed question of historiography and the recent challenge (associated with the name of Hayden White) to the assumption that the practice of history can ever be truly subjective. The novella is, he argues, "a provocative contribution to the historiographic debate," raising "basic questions about the nature and ethics of historiography ... and about the responsibilities of the historiographer toward his/her readers" (124). This is an informative, well-researched, though dryly theoretical scholarly article containing a number of useful insights, and anyone interested in the novella will benefit from reading it. None the less, perceptive as it is, it treats the book almost entirely as an intellectual discourse rather than as a work of art. Knoenagel *uses* the novella to illuminate an intellectual problem, and shows little interest in it for its own sake. In any case, the historiographical debate is only one of several issues that Hood considers—and not, I think, the most important one. If one must isolate a single topic which the novella is "about," it is the ways in which art and artistic research and discussion are regarded in the contemporary world. *Five New Facts* is best appreciated at the outset not in terms of Giorgione and the "Giorgionesque" (a subject I shall be considering shortly) but in terms of Neil Tarrant the protagonist: his character, interests, theories, and ambitions.

Like Matt Goderich in *The New Age*, Neil is an art historian; unlike Matt, he is presented as totally alone, without family or relatives and with only a few friends. He lives in an apartment where walls are covered with reproductions of details of Renaissance paintings (their significance becomes clear later), but this constitutes an inner sanctum to which he never admits others. It is a private world in which he is passionately involved, even obsessed. In Toronto, his only acquaintances whom we hear about are Betty Frits and Huey-Jack Dubois, denizens of the Nag's Head tavern, which Neil uses as a sort of private club. Betty is his upstairs neighbour, successful as an estate administrator, whose interest in art is confined to commercial value, which is dubious because not readily forecastable. She provides Neil with occasional evaluation assignments, but takes the view that "All you could do with a painting... was look at it" (13-14). As for Huey-Jack, an oil tycoon for whom money is everything, the cultural achievements of the past are irrelevant and expendable: "All these burrheads are finished and fading out. Ain't no reason why anybody gonna pay attention" (20).

In other words, Neil, with a "university appointment... of unimpeachable dignity and authority" and "the coming young man in his field" (14), inhabits a social world in which all that he values—professionally, intellectually, and emotionally—is considered of no account. This, surely is a situation familiar to anyone committed to the arts and the humanities in our time. Even Pierre de Chenonceaux, the distinguished (fictional) art authority at the Louvre, who accepts Neil's conclusions about Titian as the painter of *Fête Champêtre*, does so primarily in the spirit of science, convinced by the technological proof of his arguments. When Neil asks: "What becomes of the Giorgionesque?" all he can reply is: "What indeed?" (23). Neil's excitement at the prospect of his discovery leading to the rewriting of modern art history means nothing to him.

In other words, *Five New Facts* is centrally concerned with a crucial, potentially life-changing discovery by the protagonist, who dreams that he will be able to "revise all the books" (20) and even emend the "Story of mankind" (59). Yet he also knows that such a discovery, after provoking a few sensationalist newspaper headlines, will not cause the slightest ripple of change in what it is now fashionable to regard as the "real" world. Neil knows that in Huey-Jack's blunt response, "his very reason for existence had been called into question" (21). Hood himself, I am convinced, experienced similar feelings, especially in the last fifteen years or so of his life. That is what makes *Five New Facts* so important a statement, whatever reservations we may have about parts of its artistic execution. I have called this chapter "Art in Crisis" not merely because of the consequences if Neil's "facts" about Giorgione are found to be correct but because the whole significance of art (despite exalted auction prices) is under threat in the modern world.

Ultimately, I shall be offering a reading of the novella that will show how Hood explores this topic in his own artistic (if sometimes flawed) terms. First, however, since many readers may not be sufficiently informed about the background upon which Neil's case against the historical existence of Giorgione rests, it will be helpful to summarize the artistic situation surrounding both Giorgione and the Giorgionesque. Giorgione (c.1477-1510) and Titian (c.1489-1576) are generally regarded as the two dominant figures in the remarkable development of Venetian painting at the turn of the fifteenth and sixteenth centuries. Yet although much is available in historical records about Titian (one of whose paintings—invented by Hood—becomes important to the plot of *Great Realizations*), Giorgione remains a decidedly shadowy figure. Moreover, Luigi Coletti notes that the enthusiasm for Giorgione's work at the time of his early death resulted in "a sudden confusion in attributions between Giorgione's paintings and those by other contemporary artists, especially Titian" (7). The latter is traditionally recognized as Giorgione's pupil, and art critics frequently—one is tempted to say rashly—speculate on the extent to which Titian may have finished or altered the work of his sometime teacher. Indeed, a surprising number of paintings claimed as Giorgione's have, over the years, been re-attributed, by apparently expert scholars, to Titian. This is true of several of the paintings Hood mentions in his text, including *Fête Champêtre* (10-11, 22-23, also sometimes called *Concert Champêtre*), *The Concert* (11), and the *Sleeping Venus* (23-4). Terisio G. Pignatti's magisterial *Giorgione: Complete Edition*, published in 1969 and in translation by Phaidon in 1971, which Hood may well have consulted, dismisses Giorgione's claims to the first two, but accepts the third.

The Castelfranco altarpiece, which becomes the chief focus as providing the final 'fact" in Hood's novella, is another matter. According to Pignatti, the painting's "authority and its importance in Giorgione's *oeuvre* have never been doubted" (97), though after both he and Hood had written at least one alternative attribution has been suggested. But the painting was crucial to Hood's argument for more pressing reasons. In 1978 one authority, Rudolf Wittkower, called it "one of only two works undoubtedly by [Giorgione]" (qtd. in Knoenagel 124), and at the beginning of the twentieth century, though Hood may not have been aware of it, the poet and classicist A. E. Housman declared that it was "the only picture which is known with certainty to be his" (59). These statements may be dubious, but, exaggerated or not, they indicate why any attempt to argue convincingly that Giorgione never existed would have to come to terms with this painting.

In the course of his meditations, Neil finds himself speculating whether, in Knoenagel's words, "Giorgione may be the pseudonym for a specific artistic development rather than an actually existing human being" (130). Neil's own thoughts are more religious in reference:

> Was this single unknown personage of all-inspiring genius the presence in the air from whom descended like angels in the firmament a generation of painters of unrivalled originality and

> beauty? Wasn't the word "Giorgione" a name for the heavenly providential inspiration of an historical movement, a word without concrete embodiment, the name or one of the names for the Paraclete? (36)

According to Knoenagel, Hood "was not the first to think in these terms" (130). He cites Herbert Cook's comment as early as 1900: "The result [of recent scholarship] has been to reduce the figure of Giorgione to a shadowy myth, whose very existence at the present rate at which negative criticism progresses, will assuredly be called in question" (qtd. 131). It is tempting to speculate whether Hood had encountered this statement. Cook, indeed, may well be the "great authority" who claimed that some new expert would eventually "proclaim the purely mythical status of Big George" (10).

Be that as it may, while almost all the authorities accept at least a small nucleus of authentic paintings, many have expressed considerable skepticism about his output. Edgar Wind acknowledged that the bulk of his work was "either unknown or completely uncertain" and wrote somewhat suspiciously of "the strange assortment of pictures that form the so-called *oeuvre* of Giorgione" (7, 20). The distinguished and influential Italian scholar Robert Longhi was prepared to assign many of his works to Titian, while Coletti granted that "a recent school of thought" would "replace Giorgione by Titian as the reformer of Venetian art," and admitted "how difficult it is to feel reasonably sure about any picture" (8, 31). Since Hood wrote, Jaynie Anderson has written: "Were it not for the existence of Marcantonio Michiel's notes on Venetian painting [written between 1525 and 1543], cynical twentieth century historians might not have allowed Giorgione to exist" (53). Thus Hood was only taking to a radical extreme a general scholarly unease that has a long and continuing history.

We are now, I hope, in a better position to approach Hood's text, and perhaps the first point that should be made, to counter Knoenagel's somewhat overearnest reading, is that, for all the seriousness of the subject, Hood is capable of inserting an element of the mischievously and imaginatively playful. For example, we need to keep in mind, as Knoenagel apparently does not, that Neil

Tarrant is a fictitious art historian attempting to cast doubt on the existence of a painter generally accepted as historical. Hood is serious here, genuinely concerned with the reliability or otherwise of traditional attributions, but such a position is not incompatible with a strong sense of fun. There is a "what if" quality about the story that should not be underestimated: what if one of the most admired painters of western art, about whom scholarly specialists have written at length, should prove a myth? It is a question intriguing in itself, and clearly stimulated the writer to assemble a convincing case. Moreover, Hood found here a topic where his consuming interest in the blending of fact and fiction could be readily exploited. *Five New Facts* presents the Giorgione question from an imaginative perspective rather than an academic one.

The novella opens in a supposedly "traditional English pub" but one in downtown Toronto offering "the illusion of hoary antiquity" (7). Not quite what it seems, as Knoenagel notes (137), its tables are "oak-veneer" and its frosted glass panels "fake." It is, however, Neil's favoured watering hole, where we first find him reiterating to himself his revolutionary thoughts about *cinquecento* painting. We learn that the Venetian "ground beneath his feet was swampy and marine" and that no other place on earth had "evoked such ambiguous findings" (9). Before long, he has come to regard the painters of the period "as myth-ridden as their works" (18), doubts the very existence of Giorgione, and considers that authorities who attribute *Fête Champêtre* and *The Concert* to him rather than to Titian are "genuflecting before a ghost of their own creation" (11).

All these matters that are going to prove important and controversial are raised in the first five pages of text. Others follow soon after: a reference to "an acute conscience" (14), the asserted location of numerous false Constables in the richer residential areas of Toronto. In addition, as Knoenagel (127-8) astutely revealed, a mischievous piece of fictionalizing on Hood's part occurs when three out of the four claimed authorities on Venetian art (14) turn out to be nothing of the sort. A brief conversation between Neil and Betty is then interrupted by the entrance of Huey-Jack, who gives the impression of being materialism and vulgarity personified. At first he seems a grotesque parody as well as a failure in tone on Hood's part, but we soon realize that he performs several significant functions within the form of the novella: he too is not what he seems (he possesses "two advanced... degrees from the University of Tulsa" [17]); he represents the world of crude power in which a scholar like Neil is forced to operate; and his talk reminds us that romantic Venice is situated cheek by jowl alongside Mestre, "one of the biggest oil ports in the world" (19). So ends the first chapter, which presents us with a bewildering number of disparate topics yet, for all its rough edges, encourages us to read on.

At the beginning of the second chapter, Neil is approaching Venice—predictably via Mestre, which "smelled bad;" and seemed to offer an "insult... to antiquity" (21, 22). But even when Mestre has been left behind, Neil is confronted with troublesome ambiguity: a "strange church/cinema which used to be dedicated to Santa Margherita and is now sacred to the luminaries of the silver screen," the saint herself described as a "ghostly presence" (29). So far, so good. But at this point, I am bound to say, the narrative thread of *Five New Facts* falters. Hood includes a number of details in the interest of local colour (more of that later), but here the plot virtually grinds to a halt. The comparison between Toronto and Venice (a favourite Hood topic that recurs in *Property and Value*) is apt enough, but is it strictly relevant to Hood's purpose? At any event, we hardly need the blatant digression about the woman whose dog was lost on a flight between Toronto and Regina or a discourse on the special meaning of "gondola" in the context of Canadian hockey. Neil later watches an eccentric elderly man bargaining for a freshly caught fish, but the episode belongs more in a travelogue than in a novella. Here, I suspect, Hood could not resist downloading his recently acquired interest in Venice at the expense of his art. The details may be interesting in themselves, but they fail to cohere. We learn a little about Lorenzo Lotto and Sebastiano del Piombo (and will learn more in the next chapter), but the momentum of the story slows down.

It is possible, indeed, that Hood's hesitations and conspicuous digressions reflect Hood's attempted presentation of Neil's confused psychological state. In the light of subsequent events, could it be that the art-historian's conscience is troubling him, that he is beginning to have second thoughts about the consequences of upsetting the apple cart of Venetian art history? His mood, as presented here, seems curiously reluctant to focus on the reason for which he came. Such speculation is, of course, superfluous, since there is no clear evidence for it in Hood's text. I raise it, however, to indicate how Hood seems to have found difficulty, at this stage in the writing, in controlling the direction of Neil's thoughts and actions. As a result the narrative progress within the chapter appears oddly slack.

In chapter three, Neil spends most of his time meditating in the Carmini Church in front of Lorenzo Lotto's *Saint Nicholas of Bari* and in the church of San Giovanni Crisostomo in front of Sebastiano del Piombo's's *San Giovanni Crisostomo with Six Saints*. These sessions are crucial to the formulation of his theory ("Now we're getting somewhere" [36]), and by the end of the chapter, when he receives formal permission to re-examine documents (in fact, fictive documents) relating to the Castelfranco altarpiece, he is well prepared to argue the case for Titian rather than Giorgione as the painter. In the present section, Hood cannily (though somewhat confusingly) moves in and out between third-person informative narration and Neil's personal interior monologue. It is an impressive piece of writing, but not without its problems. The chief difficulty lies in the fact that Neil is an expert whereas most of Hood's readers are not. Much of this chapter, indeed, takes the form of a crash course on the two painters in question. The information becomes fascinating, if my experience is at all typical, only when it can be reinforced by reproductions of the paintings at the reader's elbow.

But how much can Hood legitimately ask of his readers? To expect readers of a book, even a short fiction, about Giorgione and his work to have some prior acquaintance with the main materials (Titian as well as Giorgione) is surely not unreasonable. But to expect familiarity with Lotto and Sebastiano del Piombo as well is another matter. Rough equivalents in other arts would be a novel about Wordsworth requiring readers to have on their shelves at least the selected works of Robert Southey and Thomas Campbell, or one about Mozart assuming record collections adequately stocked with Salieri or Boccherini. A matter of tact is involved here. In an ideal world, an edition of *Five New Facts* would contain good colour illustrations of all the paintings mentioned in the text, but the time is not yet. The information presented in this chapter can be frustratingly difficult to grasp at a first reading. Personally, I have, after numerous readings, come to find it intellectually absorbing, and well worth the trouble of mastering. But that, ironically, is part of the problem. I have to acknowledge that the effort of adequately understanding this specialized material seriously detracts from any smooth and straightforward coming-to-terms with Hood's plot. The bracing clarity and illumination provided by the greatest art is at this point lacking.

Fortunately, the narrative regains momentum in the fourth chapter. The focus changes from Neil's arguments to his emotions. We hear, for the first time, that he "had not undertaken the study of these works of art in the cheap spirit of revisionism" (48). Perhaps, though back in Toronto, as we have seen, he had boasted that if he could discover "five new facts about Giorgione"—he has already found three and confidently expects the remaining two to reveal themselves at Castelfranco—he "could rewrite modern history" (19). If a contradiction is involved here, it is a decidedly revealing one, and increases our interest in Neil as a character. Furthermore, the details of his journey to Giorgione's reputed birthplace are not just mere local colour; they reflect the suspense and tension in Neil's mind.

The narrative here is crisp and convincing. At the same time, if we know something of the historical situation, we can appreciate that Hood is playing with history in his fiction. "We have the documents," the diocesan official remarks, and acknowledges that some of the most significant ones had been discovered by Neil "three years since" (53). But in actuality documents for the altarpiece are embarrassingly absent, and Anderson assures us (83) that the discovery of further documentary evidence is unlikely. The apparent climax occurs when the two men examine the (invented) correspondence and discover—conveniently—that the affectionate diminutive used for the painter indicates Titian rather than Giorgione. This means that Neil's "five new facts" are now in place—though we realize if we have been reading carefully that, strictly speaking, several of them are not so much facts as shrewd, perhaps convincing, but ultimately unprovable deductions. I say "apparent" climax because, as we soon learn, the crucial action is just beginning. An ecstatic yet also morally troubled Neil returns to Venice, plans to make enlargements of the acquired evidence the following day, goes to bed—and is suddenly confronted by a "mysterious figure."

In the last paragraph of the fourth chapter, Hood's style changes dramatically: "Towards midnight the wind rose high… there came an explosive sound… a violent gale snapped his windows open on their rickety hinges" (60). This sounds more like *The Mysteries of Udolpho* than a late twentieth-century novella about art history, but it prepares us, along with earlier uses of "ghost" and "ghostly" for a supernatural visitation. As might be expected, the apparition itself is ambiguous. It is obviously not a ghost in the traditional sense of the word, since, as a ghost, it could only be Giorgione's if Neil's conclusions about his non-existence were wrong, and this is clearly not the direction the story takes. Despite the mysterious, thunderous atmosphere, the apparition is in no way spooky; indeed, instead of experiencing fear and horror, Neil believes that "something intolerably good and important was about to take place" (63, but notice the ambiguous juxtaposition of "intolerably" and "good"). This is a "vision," and is clearly a product of Neil's conscientious unease; to adapt an earlier, already quoted phrase in the novella (11), it is "a ghost of [Neil's] own creation."

And at this point, we may well be reminded of another distinguished fiction writer, Henry James, whom Hood obviously admired. Indeed, Knoenagel (141) perceptively noted two palpable allusions to James within *Five New Facts*: Neil Tarrant's surname echoes that of a prominent figure in *The Bostonians*, and an early sentence ("He sat, Neil Tarrant, scratching at the frosted panel…" [10]) follows syntactically the opening sentence of *The Wings of the Dove*. Since, if we except the somewhat bizarre "Third Time Unlucky," this is Hood's only ghost story in anything close to the conventional sense, it would not be surprising if he had James's supernatural stories very much in mind while writing. Indeed, he may have been influenced by James's story "The Right Real Place," written some two years after "The Turn of the Screw" and collected in *The Soft Side* (1900). Here the widow of a major author invites a young writer to write his biography, placing her husband's study and papers at his disposal. But as close investigation of his life proceeds, both wife and biographer become conscious of his disapproving presence, and eventually see his protesting ghost in the doorway, whereupon the project is abruptly abandoned. The circumstances are different, but the general principle is remarkably similar. Knoenagel criticizes Neil's immediate abandonment of his research and his determination to "*proceed no further in this business*" (67) as highly unlikely. This would be so if *Five New Facts* were a purely realistic fiction, and if I am right about hints of his earlier reservations, the encounter with the self-created "ghost" would explain such action as undertaken in a spirit of deep inner relief. But, like so much of Hood's short fiction, this is moral fable, and leads to a troublesome and ambiguous moral climax that occurs after his return to Toronto. It is not enough to zero in on the potentially sentimental "*You don't meddle with peoples'* [*sic*] *dreams*" (69). Hood's point ultimately becomes provocative, and it has disturbing consequences that Knoenagel (along with the reviewers I have read) ignores.

This remark is shown to be decidedly double-edged when he is reunited with Betty Frits at the Nag's Head. She invites him to assess and evaluate a painting, with a probably forged signature, that the owner hopes to be an A. Y. Jackson but is apparently "afraid that it's really by Fred Banting." When faced with the hope that he'll "come up with an affirmative judgment" against all the probabilities, Neil replies, blandly and astonishingly: "I expect I will" (72). This can only mean that the dreams one doesn't meddle with can also include those of an owner seeking considerable financial gain. This is a very different Neil from the person in the first chapter who claimed that Constable "painted about 400 canvases in his lifetime and over 600 of them are in Forest Hill and Mississauga" (15). His final words, when asked about his Venice research, are simply "No . . . I found nothing," which is technically untrue and suggests that he has abandoned some of his principles along with his revolutionary discoveries. A distinct whiff of corruption is evident on the final page. As so often in Hood, a last twist of the knife (or turn of the screw) forces us to reconsider all that has gone before.

Five New Facts is a puzzling text to read and appreciate. Before summing up, however, I should draw attention to an additional mystery surrounding the novella's date of writing. Hood was meticulous in inscribing such details on the title pages of the typescripts now deposited in The Hugh Hood fonds, Special Collections, University of Calgary Library. He records that a typed outline of [the] story idea" for *Five New Facts* was written in late December 1984, and the "final draft" between September and December of the following year. At this time it was intended for publication as the opening story in *You'll Catch Your Death*. These dates fit neatly and logically into the pattern of his writing during this period, and there is no reason to doubt them. Yet a record of his travels abroad insists that his "first ever trip to Italy" took place between April and June of 1986, presumably undertaken—at least in part—in preparation for writing the Venetian scenes in *Property and Value*. This date is also vouched for by Noreen Mallory.

Given this firm evidence, there seems no alternative to the conclusion that Hood wrote *Five New Facts* while relying on maps and guidebooks before he had ever set foot in Venice. Although I originally felt this to be impossible, further consideration persuades me that, though improbable, it can—and, indeed, has to be—accepted as possible. It is certain that he relied heavily for details of the Campo Santa Margherita on the relevant pages in James (Jan) Morris's *Venice*. There is also a slightly self-conscious air about the local information revealed in the Venice scenes, and one should never underestimate either Hood's capacity to write about "Places I've Never Been" or his delight in inventing documentary fantasies in which much that appears factual is in reality the product of a keen imagination. In addition, this circumstance could account for some of the apparent hesitations and uncertainties revealed by a careful reading of the text.

Ultimately, we must admit that *Five New Facts* fails to cohere as an artistic unity. None the less, there is much that can be admired. The initial idea, the mythical status of Giorgione, is absorbing as an intellectual construct, and its presentation within fiction enables Hood, as imaginative artist, to indulge his inventiveness while simultaneously enjoying some oblique fun at the expense of established experts (e.g., the somewhat unfair reference to "that old fraud Berenson" [40]). At the same time, he clearly admires the tracking down of clues and the elaborate detective work involved; Neil's research is presented with lively interest and sympathy. The descriptions of Venice, however obtained, carry conviction while we read, and the climactic apparition is managed with skill and tact. The whole is set within the Toronto-based frame which, whatever other reservations we may have, firmly establishes Old- and New-World attitudes to life in relation to the past. Moreover, as I have argued, the fast-changing reactions to humanistic studies in his own time were deeply troubling to Hood, and are communicated with impressive urgency.

Yet it is difficult to reconcile all these individual yet divergent effects, to see how they combine to form an achieved whole. One gets the impression that Hood has too much to explore—and to assert—in this book, that all sorts of pressing but possibly contradictory issues and emotions are struggling for expression. As a result, readers do not feel sure of their bearings, and are frustrated at the apparent lack of connection between parts. For those of us who share his interest in this kind of artistic speculation, the book is likely to be regarded with affection, but with a realization that we return to some parts of the narrative and tend to scant others. The assurance, not to mention the impersonality of major art, is not present here. *Five New Facts* is clearly the work of a highly talented writer, but it leaves us in a disturbed frame of mind. Part of this was obviously deliberate, but it is disturbing in a way that for some readers, including Metcalf, fails to satisfy. Crisis in art indeed.

11

Miscellany of Tones:

You'll Catch Your Death

You'll Catch Your Death maintains Hood's partiality for fictional variety. Tonally, the contents range from varieties of Gothic in "Third Time Unlucky" and "Last Remake of Nosferatu," through the bizarre fancifulness of the second part of "Disappearing Creatures" and contrasting forms of sexual comedy in the two Bronson stories, to the unique and poignant idyll of "Deanna and the Ayatollah"—the surprise and arguably the triumph of the collection. The overall standard of this collection is gratifyingly high. Only one contribution can be considered an at least comparative failure: "Getting Funding" (21-29), a spoof on chatty CBC interviews and governmental funding for the arts in an age of multiculturalism. Written for publication in an anthology edited by Metcalf, or "the poet Metcalf" as he is called here in one of Hood's private jokes (26), one feels that it would have been more effective if written by Metcalf himself. Funny enough in its rather obvious way, and sensitive as usual to the jargon-ridden banalities of "Canajun" speech, it lacks the accompanying pathos—and therefore depth—of "God Has Manifested." "Third Time Unlucky" (31-43), an unexpected and somewhat anomalous excursion into the half-ironic, half-horrendous supernatural, is likely to prove puzzling on a first reading, and it is arguable if a careful rereading ultimately repays the effort. Other tales like "Rig Flip" (79-88) and "Hot Cockatoos" (139-50) are absorbing enough, but exist mainly on the level of plot-suspense.

The remaining eight, however, represent Hood at the peak of his highly versatile powers.

I have already commented on the darkening of Hood's vision in his later years, and this is well illustrated by the opening story, "More Birds" (9-19), which initially gives the impression of being a straightforward, pleasantly informative account of foreign travel, a product of Hood's first visit to Italy in the summer of 1986 (the story was written in September of the same year). In terms of the structure of the volume, as the title implies, it neatly balances "The Small Birds," which opened *August Nights*, but the earlier account of the celebration of nesting swallows is replaced by a depressing tale of human exploitation and cruelty. The narrator, who in this case can safely be identified with Hood himself, is visiting Ravenna, and finds the interior of San Vitale an exhilarating array of saints and birds: "Birds or other kinds of winged creatures cast in the form of birds." Similarly, the interior of the mausoleum of Galla Placidia "is filled with the forms of birds." He welcomes their presence in the mosaics as "some imaginary aviary of the artistic consciousness" and as an offering to God representing by the powers of flight "the supreme expression of human freedom." But later, as he waits on a railway platform during his return journey to Bologna, he encounters a wagonload of cartons containing caged birds being shipped in appallingly cramped conditions "on a survival-of-the-fittest basis," bound—if they survive—for the local pet trade.

His comment is as simple as it is bitterly succinct—"I began to think of the trains to the camps" (i.e., the Nazi extermination camps of the Second World War), and then, in another of his telling one-sentence paragraphs: "We will do anything, you know. Absolutely anything." All *he* can do by way of recompense is, in a gesture of compassionate but futile sympathy, to whistle to them sequences of musical notes that seem to offer a temporary comfort. When his connecting train arrives, he takes his place in a first-class carriage, and becomes aware that he is weeping. What began as a fulfilling artistic excursion, an appreciation of "the inexhaustible splendour of the mosaic," ends in a heartbreaking vision of evil.

"Last Remake of Nosferatu" (103-116), the second story set in Italy, is an unusual attempt in the Gothic mode, which Noreen

Mallory confirms was based on an actual episode occurring on one of their Italian visits (*Nosferatu* was a film version of *Dracula*). The story centres upon an ancient and decaying inn named—with an un-Hood-like irony—the Albergo Santo Spirito (Inn of the Holy Spirit). But it is presented as a place of death and suffering rather than life and promise. An English-speaking couple, Luke and Meriel Springford, clearly modelled on Hood and his wife like Alfie and Brenda in "Life in Venice" in *After All!*, have persuaded the *padrona* (owner) to allow them to stay there for two nights, though they are clearly unwelcome. She accepts them only because she fears the loss of her licence, and a ghost-like effect is created later in the story when the proprietress of a local restaurant insists, "There is no one at the Albergo Santo Spirito. No one has stayed there for many years." She dismisses the Springfords as if they too were dubius apparitions.

The opening sentences read as follows:

> Signora Nerittini moved as though in a trance past the reception desk and into the shadowed hall, tripping over Bruno whose massive rump protruded from beneath a rich-bottomed chair. The old dog stirred in his sleep and began to wheeze awfully, the body alternately inflated and deflated by struggle for breath.

This represents a deliberate formal style emphasizing troubling details and an oppressive atmosphere. The subsequent vocabulary draws on Italian tags (*padrona*, *contado*, *fiaschi*) and comparatively obscure English or Anglicized words (napery, gonfalon, camionettes, armoires). Emphasis falls on the darkness of the rooms, the coldness of the stone floors, the old-fashioned spaciousness of dust-covered furniture, and a disturbing emptiness. Before long, we hear of a "sense of the unreal." Only outside the inn is there evidence of "hints of daily realism, the ordinary and credible."

None the less, in accordance with the eighteenth-century traditions of literary Gothic popularized by Ann Radcliffe in *The Mysteries of Udolpho*, supernatural fears and anxieties are ultimately allayed. The explanation for the mystery is that the brother-in-law of the *padrona* is dying, and in fact dies on the second night of the Springfords' stay. Yet when, after a night spent "in a state of alarm and apprehension," the couple leave, they are presented efficiently, prosaically, and inevitably with a fully-itemized account. Moreover, in an effect that we may recognize as characteristic, Hood blends a somewhat playful humour with the standard but semi-parodied Gothic machinery of "whispers in the dark, footsteps, cries and sobs, and finally a long mournful howl." Coincidentally, the decrepit—and smelly—dog dies on the same night as the brother-in-law. Moreover, the grounds of the inn are inhabited by eleven tortoises, who are said to have lived there (the numbers remaining suspiciously constant) since the *padrona* was "a little girl." Yet when the Springfords eventually emerge out of the ominous place, down into the world of ordinary reality, "they overtook a dignified procession of eleven tortoises headed in the same direction." The "Nosferatu" suggestion of supernatural horror dissolves in comic but charming absurdity, yet the illusion is maintained by the verbal triumph of "dignified."

"It is an almost unknown fact of contemporary history that ..." So begins the paragraph-long opening sentence of "Deanna and the Ayatollah" (45-55); it ends with the claim that Deanna Durbin, the Canadian-born child film star, who retired from Hollywood in her late twenties, and the man who ruled Iran after the fall of the Shah in 1979 "lived next door to one another" near Paris "for several years." The matter-of-fact tone carries all the confident conviction of Hood's earlier "documentary fantasies," and this story represents the climax of that Hoodian genre in the way in which it expertly blends historical fact and imaginative fiction.

Although it may seem ungracious to try to unravel what Hood has so expertly entangled, a few facts about the main characters may be useful as a preliminary to further discussion. The Ayatollah Ruhollah Khomeini was born in 1900, Deanna Durbin in 1921. Durbin retired from films in the late 1940s, married the director Charles David in 1950, and eventually settled close to Paris. I have not been able to establish precisely how close their properties were in Neauphle-le-château, but Hood's claim that they lived next door for years is not borne out by the historical facts. The Ayatollah did not arrive in Paris until October 1978, and left for Iran on

1 February 1979. Consequently, Hood's time-references—"at the beginning of the seventies," "about 1974 or 1975," etc.—belong to fiction. Furthermore, he makes no mention of the complicating fact that the Ayatollah's wife was with him at this time.

Once these points have been established and understood, we are left free to appreciate the story for what it is: a whimsical fantasy masquerading under the disguise of historical realism, portraying with extraordinary grace and charm a supremely unlikely relationship that might have been feasible if our world were constituted a little differently. The solemn-minded may well wish to dismiss it as "the acme of frivolity," to quote the Arab guards' verdict on the retired film star, but Hood is presenting his own oblique commentary on the failure of humanity to live and let be in terms of religious practice and alternative life patterns. This story belongs to the category of Hood's "what if" creations: for all its documentary-fantasy qualities, it aligns itself firmly with romance, its January/May relationship played out against a background of walled gardens and "the pleasures of courtly retreat."

This set-up partakes, of course, of the simplicity of fable: the Ayatollah as "opposed to all things Western" and Deanna as icon of that most prominent of Western institutions, Hollywood. Yet the two are surprisingly close in some respects. The old man "had not at this time ... taken on his shoulders the full burden of worldwide celebrity which Deanna Durbin had been forced to bear from childhood." Moreover, Hood is not averse to introducing the baldly incongruous and even absurd. Deanna encourages the Ayatollah to develop an "image," recommending a black burnoose—and even, irony of ironies, discussing his appearance and charisma in the terms of Walt Disney cartoon characters: "'You don't want to be a Clarabelle Cow ... when *Daffy* Duck came along he ... well ... he had chemistry. He had insouciance. He had *flair*'." Serious art here masquerades as comic grotesque. Stylistically, this can be illustrated by a scene where Hollywood directors with fake invitations are debarred from Deanna's select parties: "Hired limos drifted soundlessly back to Paris, housing studio biggies and their muttered discontents." To introduce into one short sentence the high-class abbreviation "limo," the journalistic "biggies," and the Freudian "discontents" reveals the art of a master. It is difficult to think of any other writer, with the possible exception of Metcalf, who could tread the fine line between the sublime and the ridiculous so skillfully. While obviously vintage Hood in its exquisite range of effect and the capacity to move from the farcical to the touching from moment to moment, there is nothing remotely like "Deanna and the Ayatollah" anywhere else in his work.

The fourth and fifth of Hood's Bronson stories ("Jolene from Moline" and "Jill's Disappearing Nipples") both appear in this collection. Bronson has been established in earlier stories as a representative Canadian middle-class man of the period, father of a lively but close family, and also as solitary thinker about the natural world and the responsibilities of humanity. In the stories here, he is presented as middle-aged, with the children "grown up and living in distant places" (121); somewhat surprisingly, however, his portrait is expanded by offering him as an example of *l'homme moyen sensuel* in situations that, albeit in very different ways, clarify his sexual nature.

In the first of the two stories, "Jolene from Moline" (57-67), we at last discover his unexpected profession in commercial marketing, where he is, among other things, a sought-after speaker at seminars with special reference to fast-food outlets. Hood thus returns to his interest in commercial clichés explored in "God Has Manifested," though in somewhat less exaggerated a style. None the less, the sessions in which he is involved speak for themselves: "Use of pre-packaged relishes and condiments in speeded-up takeout service," a discussion on "control of excessive paper napkin use," and his keynote address: "*Meeting pure-food standards in franchised operations.*" In addition, this is a late example of his interest in "media folklore," a phrase Bronson uses himself in relation to the conference.

But the central situation concerns his relationship with Jolene, a graduate student assigned to him by the conference organizer as a personal chauffeur and general assistant. She is presented engagingly with an innocent enthusiasm ("I feel that franchise food is more important even than rock and roll") and a pronounced but not excessive middle-American accent ("I think our old people have the same rahts as everybody and especially the raht to socialize with dignity"). Bronson, who later "feels pleasure at the impression of Jolene's soft dry cool palm in his as she leads him to the respondent's bucket seat" at the first session, is sufficiently impressed—and attracted—to insert her rock-and-roll remark into his final presentation. The moral climax arises when, at the reception following his lecture, the two of them are "instantly left alone on a davenport" in "what must have been a familiar behaviour pattern here", at which point Bronson suddenly realizes: "She's only here for you to fuck." Not surprisingly, he rejects the pattern. After all, he is happily married, and earlier parts of the story record intimate conversations with his wife. Giving his address to Jolene, and promising his help if she ever needs it, he ceremoniously kisses her hand; they part, and "he hasn't heard from her yet."

It is a touching story told with a rare delicacy and tact. At the beginning, we hear of fog and heavy rain, a recent plane crash at Kansas (where the conference is taking place), rising foods and the possibility of cyclones. These hint at crises and dangers that by the end of the story are shown to contain potential symbolic significance. They serve as backdrop to a situation that might have developed stormily but, in the event, didn't. In the final lines, when Bronson is on his way home, he "hopes someday to go back." Yet we can be sure that this is no more than a wistful passing dream of what might have been existing outside the world of reality as well as outside his ultimate desire.

From the half-facetious, light-hearted title onwards, Hood writes in a relaxed style, and displays a gift for successfully presenting the essential details of a landscape—in this case, the details that Bronson with his focus on marketing naturally notices. "They snake into mid-morning traffic on an Interstate access past the other seven motels, Burger King, Chicken Ranch, a pair of soaring golden arches and ... the logos of chains never seen at home." There is much humour (Bronson adapts Blake's religious aphorism for his marketing purposes by asserting, "all hamburgers are One," and later announces: "In the beginning is the logo"). But Jolene increasingly occupies a corner of his mind, and thoughts of her recur regularly but not obsessively. Against this teasingly ambiguous background, Hood deftly succeeds in constructing an essentially temporary, poignant, and deeply human interlude.

Not only is a semi-facetious title for "Jolene from Moline" repeated for "Jill's Disappearing Nipples" (117-26), but the opening sentence is similarly calculated to startle: "Nobody ever figured Bronson for some kind of pervert or pornographer." No, indeed. We recall "Quicker Coming Back" in *August Nights*, and Hood's claim that in that story he wanted "to move towards the condition of pornography" (SW 18). Of course, we are soon reassured. Bronson was "if anything frightened by sexual display" and would even cross a road to avoid "involuntary inspection of explicit posters" (a nice example of Hood's use of playful euphemism to gain an effect of near-pomposity) when passing local blue-movie theatres. The Jill in question is Jill Adams, an attractive British film actress of the 1960s, and the story focuses ultimately on the technological possibilities provided by VCRs. Part of Hood's joke stems from the fact that the suggestion of pornography here, as in the effect of most pornography elsewhere, is a deception, the subject of his story with the provocative title being yet another example of "media folklore."

The main action, depicted as an example of "innocent" curiosity, involves Bronson's frame-by-frame examination of his tape of *The Green Man*, in search of a few microseconds of filmed nakedness. The first climax is presented as follows:

> If twenty-four frames were being exposed per second (or whatever the correct speed is), Jill's nipples were visible for about two-fifths of a second, or about eleven frames. He accessed the stop-action mode at about the fifth frame and gazed and gazed at a tiny segment of life captured thirty-four years earlier and stilled into eternity. There they were. They would be gone before another second began. Gather me, he thought, into the artifice of the temporal.

This is an unostentatious but highly skilled specimen of prose. Bronson (like Hood himself, one suspects) is inexpert so far as technical details are concerned—he is unsure of the correct speed—but he has at least managed the rudiments of the jargon: "He accessed the stop-action mode…" Suddenly, however, the scene is transformed (temporarily, at any rate) into a Proustian moment: the past recaptured for an instant in time. Moreover, at what one might call the pornographic moment, Bronson, again resembling Hood in his obsessive habit of quotation, is not only reminded of Wordsworth ("gazed and gazed" presumably deriving from "I Wandered Lonely as a Cloud") but deliberately applies—and reverses—Yeats's famous lines from "Sailing to Byzantium": "gather me / Into the artifice of eternity."

A little later, he is diverted into thoughts about the socio-political implications of the technology he is manipulating ("Democracy in action"). Bronson's pornographic inclinations thus prove to be as fleeting as the eleven stimulating frames. And almost immediately, the second climax occurs when Viv interrupts him ("Why, you dirty thing!"), he presses the wrong button, and unintentionally erases the crucial sequence. My employment of the term "climax" here is, of course, deliberate. Hood has built the physical process of pornographic theory into the very structure of his story. Bronson, if he ever really desired a fully sexual satisfaction, is deprived of it, just as pornography invariably defrauds its patrons by offering a mechanical, artificial stimulation as inferior substitute for a natural fulfilling act.

It is characteristic, however, of Hood's art at its finest that he doesn't terminate the story at this point. Viv (like, say, Paula Rosebery in "He Just Adores Her!") is understanding of human frailties in general and those of her husband in particular. Far from making a "scene" or denouncing his action, she sympathizes, and tries to make up for his loss.

> "You poor lamb. Come on, let's go up."
>
> She put her arm entreatingly around his waist and together they mounted to their bedroom. Maybe the pornographic impulse had its uses after all.

Ironically, the whole episode concludes with an example of traditional (non-pornographic) comic closure. What on a casual reading may seem little more than a skillful *jeu d'esprit* is in fact a thought-provoking comment on the nature of comedy itself.

Part of the interest of "Two Bridport Tales' (69-78) stems from the enigmatic authorial note that precedes them. Hood writes: "The word 'tales' is used in the title in view of John Metcalf's well-known aversion to employment of this term in literary discourse." Metcalf's attitude is conveyed most succinctly in the interview that opens his *Kicking Against the Pricks*: "When I arrived in Canada in 1962, the Canadian story was more tale or yarn. I *hate* that word. Tales about lumberjacks and prairie farms. Heavy on plot and light on brains, style, and elegance" (13). It is clear that Hood (praised for his short stories on the same page) interprets the word in a radically different way. Indeed, it is possible to argue that this gathering of local stories develops into a discussion of the meaning of "tale."

Most dictionaries tend to treat "short story" and "tale" as synonyms, but once again the *Harper Handbook to Literature* is helpful in offering a more thoughtful definition of "tale": "A simple short narrative with a story-teller's air." This is precisely how Hood employs the term here. The speaker (clearly based on Hood himself, who visited the Dorset town in 1982 and 1987 while investigating his ancestral west-country roots) is presented as being admitted by the tenant into the house in which Hood's English ancestors had once lived. The tenant, who becomes principal speaker and teller of the tales, is "Mistress Minnie Dunford, eighty-one, brave, purblind, blue with damp cold." She proceeds to reminisce about her life and local memories. Two "tales" in particular are recounted. The first involves the local rector who assembled a valuable collection of antiques as perquisites from his parishioners, only to have it stolen in an impudent burglary after leaving the district. (This detail, incidentally, seems to have been influenced to some extent by a section in Metcalf's "The Lady Who Sold Furniture"—but that, as they say, is another story.) The second is about a local undertaker who is himself ironically buried at sea. Both depend for their effectiveness on Hood's remarkably convincing reproduction of the local dialect, the interest falling as much on the teller as on the tale.

But Hood doesn't content himself with what might be seen as an art of ventriloquism. Of the rector's story he notes that it "lay so ugly on the tongue as to make one's mouth pucker" and observes that Thomas Hardy (Bridport is in the heart of the Hardy county) "was full of similar jokes upon the comfortable," and adds: "I wondered whether the Hardyesque was born out of the grimness of the place ... or whether the wry tone of Bridport anecdote derived from unconscious imitation of the supreme artist by the folk who lived under his eye." Subsequently, Mistress Dunford tells the tale of the undertaker, whose surname, Vye, is important in *The Return of the Native*. It can be regarded as a classic specimen of what Hardy, in the title of a volume of short stories, called "Life's Little Ironies."

Clearly Hood's sense of "tale" is broader than Metcalf's; those offered here are indeed notable for "brains, style, and elegance," which earlier Canadian yarns lacked. One thinks of more substantial English examples: Chaucer's *Canterbury Tales*, Coleridge's "Rime of the Ancient Mariner" ("And till my ghastly tale is told ..."), not to mention Hardy's own *Wessex Tales*, though that collection does not conform to the *Harper* definition. "Two Bridport Tales" may be a minor achievement, but it represents a decidedly successful study in atmosphere. We bring away from it not only the old lady's characteristic speech patterns and Hood's skill in recreating it but a memorably gritty awareness of a now unfamiliar culture. As Hood comments, it exists "at the edges of counterpoised realities."

"Disappearing Creatures of Various Kinds" (89-102) deserves consideration at this point because it neatly juxtaposes what Hood designates a "story" and a "tale," though the distinction is not that of the *Harper Handbook*. The opening account of the sparrow that nearly comes to grief when venturing inside a wall partition is simple and unremarkable, told for its human (and avian) suspense, but its mildly bizarre quality is outclassed ("I can top that") by the wonderfully improbable tale that follows it. The narrative connection between the two is tenuous but ingenious. At the conclusion of the opening story, one of the protagonists tells it to another, claiming the incident as one that "happened ... to a friend of mine." It is offered, then, as an orally-communicated anecdote (duly identified as a "tale" as distinct from the previous "story"), but there is no attempt as in "Two Bridport Tales" to reproduce the words and cadences of the original teller.

The difference lies, ultimately, in the intrinsically unlikely nature of the plot. Who but Hood, one wonders (at least in his generation), would have thought of introducing a lovelorn hippopotamus into southern Ontario cottage-country? In this instance, *pace* Metcalf, we accept the absurdity of the tale or yarn for the sake of the pleasantly and variedly amusing effects that Hood can extract from it. This tale represents an excuse for art, not an escape from it. Despite the fact that the narrative begins with a potentially fatal road accident, Hood's prime aim here must be acknowledged to be comic entertainment. The situation makes a number of humorous effects possible. Thus the collision between car and hippo is described as "like driving head-on into an enormous stationary mattress." The incident is, of course, newsworthy, but the tale is set in those unliberated days when the mating urge of a hippo could be a sensitive topic for TV: "The biological cycle of the male hippopotamus was perhaps an improper topic for public debate." When at last the "great beast" responds to a local farmer's simulated call with "a tremendous sucking sound," it is likened to "the noise which a mammoth rubber plunger might make in some leviathan of a sink." Such sentences are self-justifying, and they tempt us to hope that the biblical echoes ("great beast," "leviathan") will not encourage some scripturally informed but humourless critic towards an earnest allegorical interpretation.

Such a reading would be understandable but in the event erroneous. Hood can change from serious to comic at will—and back again. The plot may end with the successful recapture of the animal ("re-enacted twice so that the moment could be preserved on colour videotape"!), but a traditional tale should contain a moral so, when the farmer, asked how he was able to imitate the mating call of a female hippopotamus, replies simply, "I made it up," the narrator can declare: "And so . . . we see that our sympathies can reach out and touch all creatures from the largest to the very least" (cf. the often-criticized moral at the close of "The Ancient Mariner"). And Hood's story (which extends further than the tale) ends with the authorial comment: "In this way our lives radiate allegories and symbols at all times." He seems to be playing here, but playing seriously, with the whole vexed question of literary-critical approaches to his work. Yes, the allegorical meanings are always available, but they must not be forced against the meaning and tone of the text. The scene remains richly comic but with a hint of higher significance. In its unostentatious and even hilarious way, "Disappearing Creatures" may be seen as, paradoxically, one of Hood's more profound achievements.

"Well, it's a long story and it isn't over yet." So begins "Don't Bother Coming" (127-38), which illustrates Hood's remarkable capacity to trace the ways in which a combination of geographical, historical, and sociological factors can combine to mould the lives of individuals. In this case, the area in question is the "desolate" region around Tupper Lake in northern New York State, the time span encompasses half a century between the early 1940s and the time of writing in the late 1980s, and the individuals are Alice Gracie, "spinster" and teacher, and her nephew Dan Lippard, who eventually becomes a successful architect. In twelve brief but closely packed pages, Hood is able to construct a powerful revisionist view of North American life in the mid-twentieth century. Basically, it is an account of the degeneration but also the resilience of a culture.

Beginning with solidly based historical background, he soon finds that he has to go into minute and even acrimonious detail to explain once-accepted social attitudes and assumptions that have now changed out of all recognition. He is at pains to reconstruct a period when television wasn't "invariably a dreary wasteland" and was still a medium through which it was possible to make contact with art, a time before "a half-baked and muddled—even addled Freudianism—had invaded our minds," when unmarried women could still command respect before the onset of the "thoughtless, stupid, uncaring, ill-informed" voices of the mid-sixties. Irascible? Reactionary? Perhaps, but he is making a point of considerable importance: that such women, under a cloud of disapproval and sexual suspicion for a generation, "were the models of today's independent powerful wise women who are increasingly directing our lives; yesterday's old maid is today's feminist empress." Which doesn't sound so reactionary after all. This insistence is necessary, Hood would argue, as prelude to a balanced view of Alice's relationship with, and profound influence upon, her nephew's subsequent career.

Aunt Alice took Dan under her wing, as it were, while he was still in high school. His father was a civil engineer, but Alice introduced him to more artistic subjects like architecture and stage design. They explored these subjects together "with a dreadfully enjoyable sense of complicity," and for Dan at this period her relationship with him became "the closest tie of his life." But time passes, and early relationships fade. Alice's influence on him is evident when, after two years of civil engineering at university, Dan switches to architecture, but, after he marries and his career becomes international in scope, his life "turned further and further away from its beginnings." The process is familiar, but in this case leads to an unexpected sequel. A generation later, Dan is informed that Alice has had a stroke and is dying. Although by this time she was "not much more than a shadow in his surface imagination," he immediately decides to make the journey from Montréal, though his mother says "Don't bother coming" because she considers it a waste of time. But he comes, and his presence, against all the odds, revives her.

An improbably positive ending, reverting to Hood's earlier optimistic mode? Not really. The story that begins as a historically significant saga has been skillfully transformed into a philosophical fable. We are expected to accept it not naïvely at a level of rose-tinted realism (though such inexplicable medical "miracles" are on record) but as a symbolic statement of faith in the power of human bonding. Realism, we might say, is transcended here as it is in a late Shakespearean romance in the interests of a higher imaginative purpose.

"Don't Bother Coming" is remarkable for the ultimate rejection of its title, for its impressive historical texture in its earlier pages that authentically reinterpret the standards of an age, and, within the text of *You'll Catch Your Death*, as the one contribution that looks back to more visionary earlier works like "Flying a Red Kite" or "Light Shining Out of Darkness." In a collection where "Death" appears to be emphasized, the expected does not occur. While it hardly cancels out the darker stories around it, it is eloquent evidence in favour of Hood's concern for variety of tone and sentiment as well as style.

"You'll Catch Your Death" itself (151-61), the concluding story that gives the volume its title, is clear and straightforward, and in normal circumstances would not invite any extended comment here. Set for the most part in a pet shop in Montréal, it opens with a superb evocation of a contemporary underground shopping mall setting that shows Hood's super-realism to best advantage. Given his increasingly critical response to developing aspects of modern life, we might expect this description to be a prelude to a sombre or even satiric story, but in fact it develops, despite its sad ending, into a heartwarming account of human kindness and co-operation. Maggie, a bag lady, becomes known in the pet shop as "the bird lady" because of her obvious love for the birds on display. The staff unite to give her a beautiful though slightly injured parakeet (an avian equivalent of Maggie herself?) and for a few months she is blissfully happy in looking after it. Unfortunately, she falls sick during a harsh Montréal winter, and both Maggie and parakeet are found dead of exposure and starvation in her modest apartment.

Hood tells "You'll Catch Your Death" with characteristic skill and convincingness. Further literary-critical comment seems unnecessary, but the subject of the story provides an excellent example of how Hood moulds his narrative in order to set up subtle interconnections with other stories in the volume, and so creates links that do much to give the collection a greater thematic and structural coherence than we might otherwise expect. These links involve birds in the case of "More Birds," "Disappearing Creatures," and "Hot Cockatoos," and the more pervasive theme of death (or, in some cases, a close brush with death), which characterizes a majority of the stories within the book.

Before proceeding with this argument, however, I need to clarify one detail. "More Birds" may well leave the impression that Hood is protesting against all instances of keeping birds in cages, but this is not the case. The Hood family itself kept parrots for several years, and this fact explains the brief but noticeable appearance of various members of the parrot family in "Disappearing Creatures," "Hot Cockatoos," and the concluding story. Hood's complaint, it would seem, is against inappropriately cramped confinement.

All four bird stories, moreover, concern themselves not merely with birds but with the relations between birds and human beings. The narrator of "More Birds" finds his "heart breaking" after the experience on the railway station. Leonora in "Disappearing Creatures" is a keeper of caged birds, but the focus is on the fledgling sparrow which she hopes eventually to return to the wild. "Hot Cockatoos" is about a compulsive collector who takes to crime in order to improve his collection. Here in "You'll Catch Your Death" a reciprocal companionship between bird and human being is established when the slightly deformed parakeet is presented to the frail but sympathetic bird lady.

The title shared by both book and final story reminds us that death is also a prominent topic in these bird stories. In "More Birds," only half the birds bound for the shops in Bologna are expected to survive the journey. The narrator in "Disappearing Creatures" explains how, in nature, "the hardly-maintained balance between energy output and nutritional intake fails," at which time "Death ensues." In the troubled ending of "Hot Cockatoos," the birds are released by the police, resulting in a stunning image of colour and brightness suggesting a triumphant freedom, but: "It will be Christmas in six weeks and the nights will grow very cold." The birds, then, are doomed, like the parakeet and bird lady here. Moreover, of the remaining nine stories, death figures prominently in three and near-death in two others, while "Deanna and the Ayatollah" ends with the latter's realization that "he is dying."

These details may seem unimportant, even trivial, but they help us to come to some conclusions about Hood's attitude to the unity and coherence of his later volumes. If we consider this book as a collection, we cannot help but be aware of the shadow of death overhanging so many of the stories, while the positioning of the first and last stories, while obeying his later principle regarding order of writing, serendipitously underlines the thematic preoccupation with both birds and death. But no attempt is made to unify *all* the stories. Allusions to birds and death are absent from "Getting Funding" and minimal in the two Bronson stories. Hood included these stories, it would seem, simply because he had written them during this period. It is therefore fair to draw the following conclusions. Interconnections between individual stories often exist, and if they do an attentive reading will duly reveal them; if, however, one sets out with a determination to look for them when they are not obvious, one runs the risk of overlooking other more important literary effects that are intrinsic to Hood's art.

12

Late Harvest:

After All!

The stories that eventually made up *After All!*, Hood's last collection of short fiction, were written between September 1991 and December 1996. During this period, *You'll Catch Your Death* and *Dead Men's Watches* (the tenth volume of *The New Age*) were published, and *Great Realizations* (the eleventh) was in preparation. *Unsupported Assertions*, a collection of essays, had just appeared, and he was about to begin work on the concluding volume of the *New Age* series, *Near Water*. All this activity suggests that Hood was an energetic as ever. Unfortunately, however, his health was beginning to fail, and he decided to devote the whole of his attention to the successful completion of the novel-cycle. As a result, he made no attempt to publish the collection, which in normal circumstances would have appeared in 1998, and it remained unpublished at the time of his death in the summer of 2000.

For the most part, these stories were shorter than usual, all but three of them being between six and eight pages in length. Whether this represented a deliberate striving for succinctness, or resulted from a physical slowing down while still conforming to a preconceived plan, is uncertain. It is clear, however, that his desire for variety of subject matter, style, and approach was as keen as ever. The stories here include vignettes of everyday life, fantasies, problem stories, satires on the excesses of modern civilization, documentary sketches, stories that amuse, stories that entertain, stories that set one thinking, stories that disturb. All are written with the stylistic elegance, and filled with the inquiring intelligence, that had come to be expected from him.

While it must be admitted that this is a somewhat uneven collection, ten out of the seventeen stories are of high quality and deserve attention here. The rest may be listed briefly. The volume gets off, in my opinion, to a rather shaky start. "Bit Parts" (9-14) is based on the hypothesis that we all exist within the dreams of others. A woman becomes aware, originally in "bits," of her lover as glimpsed in dreams, and he is eventually dreamt into existence. This is one of Hood's more whimsical "experiments," intriguing but not without a hint of the pretentious. "Swedes in the Night" (23-30), on the other hand, is a straightforward story of two young women on a European train who are assaulted in their apartment by two "enormous blond statuesque foul-smelling Swedish youths," clearly drunk. The women hold off until help comes, but the story, though readable enough, appears to lead nowhere in particular.

"A Subject for Thomas Hardy" (63-70), is about a dubious real estate manipulator, and "A Gay Time" (79-86), in which a new addition to an office department is suspected of being a company spy, both belong in the "office folklore" category, but do not qualify as memorable. "How Did She Find Out?" (107-114) tells of a businessman husband's obsessive conviction that his wife is trying to poison him for the insurance money; it is a shrewd presentation of a particular mania, but, accomplished as it may be, it is hardly designed to bring out Hood's best strengths. The other two, "Pain Control" (127-33) and "The Messages Are the Message" (135-42), are little more than vignettes that tend to hang fire. The former doubtless draws on Hood's experience of physiotherapy during his health problems at this time, while the latter (beginning promisingly, "Fanny finally bought a modem and it just about finished her off") suggests more "Sportive play of the imagination" (Interview 31), since Hood himself never used a computer. But in both instances, the narrative records a case history rather than a narrative proper. All this being conceded, we can proceed to a discussion of ten stories showing that, even in the last years of his life, he could write with originality, authority, and finesse.

"Assault of the Killer Volleyballs" and "Too Much Mozart" are remarkable in that, although they both focus on violence and sudden death, the atmosphere created is certainly not tragic, and in the second instance even aspires to the condition of comedy. Here, to be sure, is "experiment" (and I must confess that, on a first reading I failed to detect much merit in the volleyballs story), but not in the sense of avant-garde technical effects or insistent typographical departures from the customary. Closer examination, however, should reveal that in both of them bizarre subject matter is presented through styles that change drastically as the stories develop, and would doubtless be considered inappropriate if they were not so obviously deliberate, so evidently moulded by Hood for his particular purpose. A focus on style is, I believe, the most likely way of elucidating at least some of their oddity.

The title, "Assault of the Killer Volleyballs" (15-21), is obviously an allusion to *Attack of the Killer Tomatoes*, a notorious film of 1978. Hood is clearly bringing his "Sportive play of imagination" to bear upon the phenomenon of the horror movie, but he casts his net somewhat wider than that. It embraces the appeal of fantasy in modern culture, Hollywood film conventions, and the way our response to violence has been affected by various recent developments in "the media":

Consider the opening paragraph:

> Mother heard the sound from the attic first, a rhythmic spong-ing noise, insistent and impossible to identify, a rebounding, bonking agglomeration of thumps. A sound that might be made by an Airedale trapped in a bass drum. This happened at dawn on a Monday morning when everybody was still asleep.

The first four words and the last sentence could not be more ordinary, evoking a simple domestic scene. But "spong-ing"? "bonking"? Onomatopoeic words not listed in the dictionary. But then "agglomeration of thumps"! And we have barely recovered from this clash of language levels before encountering the mind-boggling simile involving the Airedale and the bass drum. This could well be Hood's most extraordinary stylistic gambit.

After some naturalistic dialogue between Mother and Dad, the volleyballs descend from the attic and kill them both, Hood defying (as in "The Hole") the realistic convention that thoughts or spoken words should not be reported if there were no survivors in a position to record them. The prose relaying this event varies between the scientifically specialist ("slightly prolate spheroids") and the vividly vernacular ("crazy arcs and whirls"), blending into the clinically descriptive ("sounds that accelerated alarmingly in tempo and increased in volume as the deluge of balls mounted in pressure"), where "alarmingly" is personal and "deluge" has metaphoric power although both are encased in the detached language of physics. With no human beings to observe the subsequent unfolding of events, the prose takes on the impersonal quality of an official report ("a case... very unusual in forensic record. The bodies showed many minor subcutaneous lesions"), though the occasional bizarre image stands out: "They might have been the marks left by the passage of a fleet of colossal gumballs." Reference to the possibility of "a collective intelligence directing the movement of [the aggregate of spheroids]" suggests that a religious element may be introduced, but this collapses in an analogy to "the flight instincts of a flock of Canada geese."

The relentless course of the volleyball attack is chronicled in this tight-lipped, "objective" approach until the scene narrows down to the local sheriff's military-style "cantonment," which appears to be identified as a prime target. There follows a description of "the fleet of squad cars... lifted up and thrown across the village green to land crushed and flaming in front of the hardware store"—clearly a parody of the customary car-chase-cum-stunt-display that provides a climax in the average Hollywood B movie. But then, when the volleyballs have moved onward towards other objectives, the deputy-sheriff enters the ruins, and returns to deliver the simple word, "Spiked!" The meaning is evident though somewhat off-centre (spiked guns? rendered ineffective?) unless one recognizes the technical volleyball meaning: "to hit (a ball in the air) with a powerful, overarm motion from a position close to the net so as to cause it to travel almost straight down into the court of the opponents" (*Webster's*). Hitherto, the choice of volleyballs as the agent seems as gratuitous as tomatoes, but the single word indicates that we have been witnessing a game transformed into a deadly contest, where the balls have taken upon themselves the roles of belligerent human participants. Fantastic? Absurd? Surrealist whimsy turned sour? Possibly all of these, but also an image of our capacity to invent and become engulfed by our own horrors. A fanciful invention, but also a warning parable for our times.

"Too Much Mozart" (31-37), a response to the two-hundredth

anniversary of Mozart's death commemorated widely throughout 1991, was commended in several of the reviewers of *After All!* as one of the most appealing stories in the collection. However, none that came to my attention commented on the odd fact that a decidedly comic story should climax on what ought to be a terrifying example of multiple homicide. Here, as in "Assault of the Killer Volleyballs," one feels that Hood wanted to see how far he could go in combining within a single succinct narrative radically conflicting acts, emotions, and responses. And once more his chosen style provides the key.

The opening paragraph is again crucial:

> The distressing incidents of the closing weeks of 1991 have been the occasion of much curious but fruitless speculation among members of the concerned public, without any systematic inquiry's [sic] having yielded an account of these matters satisfying alike to the subtlety of the trained investigator and the grosser perceptions of the mass of opinion.

This sounds like the abstract, essentially gutless prose of, say, a sociologically inclined academic writing for a newspaper with pretensions towards intellectual coverage. The same style continues for several paragraphs full of pompous cliché, through which we have to search for details of the main subject. The "distressing incidents" gradually become "the tragedy," "the dreadful event," "the fateful year," until finally we hear of "infamous mass slayings." We also register the unlikelihood (to say the least) that this established narrative voice will be capable of giving, as promised, "a clear, full and responsible description of the entire matter." We can be sure, however, that the Hood who, as we have seen, once read Hemingway with attention is obviously writing in this way with a purpose.

All this is perplexing, not least when we learn that the main slayings took place "at the Burger Heaven outlet in East Sequoia." Moreover, as soon as the human narrative begins, the style of the opening pages falls quickly away and is replaced by one that is crisp, concrete, unostentatious, and continues to the end. This conspicuous change in the writing is as incongruous as the original cliché-ridden officialese. And here, perhaps, we may find a clue to Hood's purpose. There is a very real sense in which the story is a study in incongruity as it manifests itself in our world. We are soon introduced to Merle Huggins, seemingly average guy, but protagonist and perpetrator. He is said to show a "keen interest in folk and western, with some blue grass," yet is capable of discriminating between classic and "bottom of the barrel" Mozart. Formal decorum is also flouted. When Huggins gets into a fist fight with a young student in a supermarket after an argument about (of all things) the "two doubtful 'Lambach' symphonies, K. 45a and 45b," what could be a disturbing incident is rendered farcical when "they rolled along the aisle towards the pet food, where they toppled a pyramid of economy-sized cartons of Purina Dog Chow."

Further incongruity, relating to U.S. attitudes to violence and gun possession but with wider implications, follows when Huggins buys a bulletproof vest from a "gun boutique" and tries it on at home. "His wife Eleanor noticed this but thought nothing of it." Just before the shootings, when she asks him where he is going, armed, in the middle of the night, and he replies, "Going to get me some Mozart lovers," her subsequent comment is: "Naturally I thought he was only kidding." When the killings follow immediately, we can hardly take them seriously. And this is precisely Hood's point. Huggins is made to reveal his motive with his dying breath—"Too much Mozart"—as if that explained everything. It is an ending as real as it is incongruous, incongruous *because* it is real.

Nowadays it is fashionable to ignore all aspects of a writer's life when considering a literary text. In this case, however, certain biographical details can throw valuable light on Hood's motives for writing as he did. First of all, "Too Much Mozart" was written in December 1991, the end of the "Mozart year," and it is likely that Hood, on record as considering Haydn the finer musical genius, had become more than a little tired of the constant stream of Mozart performances, especially on radio, at this time. (The story's title, incidentally, contains a probable allusion to "Mostly Mozart," the name currently given to several Mozart festivals and music series.) In addition, Hood was writing, in Montréal, exactly two years after the "Montréal massacre" (6 December 1989), when thirteen women were killed by a psychopathic anti-feminist. Canadian newspapers duly gave considerable coverage to the anniversary throughout the 1990s and beyond. These two events apparently came together in Hood's mind, and so encouraged him to write a story that brought the seemingly irreconcilable subjects together. The presentation of a world that was both absurd and dangerous may well have nudged him in the direction of the "postmodernist" mode to explain something of the mixture of fascination and distaste (but always acute interest) that he found in the world (the "new age"?) evolving around him.

"The Bug in the Mug" (39-45), in which friends of the female narrator, alone in her house, encounter an "enormous bug" and trap it in what turns out to be her favourite coffee mug is a totally different kind of story. The potentially horrendous is again seen to intrude into the domestic world of everydayness. However, the "bug" (evidently a species of moth) is large but by no means "enormous," and, when safely dead, is found to be a thing of beauty. Horror is briefly invoked, even whipped up, but eventually dissipated, tamed, and the bug is ultimately displayed as a conversation piece on "the rec room wall." Yet it features, if not as horror, at least as *other*, part of an unknown world the narrator, for once, encounters.

This is another *tour de force* on Hood's part, told by an unnamed narrator whose character is brilliantly presented through her speech rhythms, and who is soon revealed as more complex than expected. She is given to endearingly human exaggeration ("Every woman has a right to her own coffee mug. The National Action Committee on the Status of Women has decreed this to be a fundamental female right") or to gruesomely bizarre imagery ("The poor little handle, broken off and all alone, like Van Gogh's ear"). But how do we respond when, embarking on a systematic search for her lost mug, she quotes Christ's parable of the woman who loses a single piece of silver (Luke 15: 8-10)? The reference seems to partake more of parody than of analogy. Moreover, when she has found it, instead of gathering her neighbours in celebration, she alludes to another of Christ's speeches: "Who can drink from that cup?" (cf. Matthew 20:22-3 or Mark 10:38-9), The implication is, to say the least, ambiguous.

I raise this topic for two reasons: first, because religious allusion is decidedly less frequent in these later books, and the Divine/human analogy so evident in earlier stories seems far less insistent here; second, when Wally cites William Blake's famous remark about "an immense world of delight" (cf. "Marriage of Heaven and Hell," Plates 6-7), she fails to recognize it, and can only say: "Come again?" What are we to make of this? Indeed, to ask what "The Bug in the Mug" is about can lead to embarrassed uncertainty. But perhaps such questions lead in the wrong direction. Perhaps we should be content to sit back and enjoy the story simply as performance art. The speaker's idiom is perfectly caught; she can be both funny and touching, as well as possessing a solid and saving common sense. The action, such as it is, is beautifully paced and controlled. Our attention is invariably engaged. This is a narrative, I suggest, that should be enjoyed as pure entertainment. No solemn interpretations, no pompous concerns about relevance, no allegory. This is excellent, absorbing *writing*, and there is no reason why we should ask for more.

"Life in Venice" (47-53) is the last, and arguably the best, creative product of Hood's visits to Italy from the mid-1980s to the early 1990s. In terms of plot it is the simplest, and one of the most straightforwardly autobiographical; Alfie and Brenda are no more than shadowy stand-ins for Hugh and Noreen. When the Hoods stayed in Venice in 1988 and 1992, they indeed stayed at the Hotel Airone (its address preserved in Hood's notes), and Noreen Mallory has acknowledged in conversation that the incident involving the carrot-scraper occurred just as Hood recorded it.

The title, of course, is an allusion to Thomas Mann's *Der Tod in Venedig* (*Death in Venice*), and provides an immediate indication that the story is likely to concern itself with language and the interrelations between languages. Not, however, the language for which one turns in search of help to phrase books and tourist guides, nor "the kind of language you find in Berlitz," but the language of everyday need in all its complexities and puzzlements. A constant preoccupation with the challenge of communicating in a foreign language is paramount. The problem of communication may now be recognized as a cliché, but it is real enough, and suitably parodied before the pitfalls of a *foreign* language becomes an issue, when Brenda's "I can't understand a word you're saying" is followed by Alfie's attempted explanation through plugged sinuses: "It's somethig from the canals, I don't thig it's catchig."

The resultant search for *una farmacia* is itself punctuated by another illustration of the uncertainty of language, since they find themselves passing "S. Simeone Grande (much smaller than S. Simeone Piccolo, why?)." But the topic is brought to a climax when they finally track down the elusive drugstore and examine its window display:

> Shampoos. Bathing caps. A tower built of little green boxes with blue trim, bearing the legend *Pomata balsamica: uso esterno*. At the top of this column of little boxes stands a small jar bearing the elegant triangular logo enclosing the simple announcement: VICKS.
>
> And below that in red: VapoRub.
>
> "*Posse avvere un*'" (jar, what's jar?), "*un' bottiglia ... un vasetto piccolo di VapoRub, per favore?*"

Here the visual and the auditory blend, as do inner thoughts and the outward attempt at understandable speech.

Misunderstandings need not, however, be confined to language. Back at the hotel with the hardly-won VapoRub, they assume optimistically that the proprietor, "used to seeing them retire in mid-afternoon," will ignore "the groans and sighs that now emanate from room 14, where Brenda is giving Alfie a neck and back rub." And there follows a bravura passage in which the sound is as eloquent as the meaning, all the human senses expertly brought into play (I use the word "play" deliberately):

> "*Pomata balsamica* is *onguent vaporisant* in French," murmurs Brenda luxuriously, as she slides glistening odoriferous palms around the base of Alfie's neck ...
>
> "Vaporizing ointment," he now remarks drowsily. "Trilingual," whispers Brenda. Aren't we civilized, they think, staying in a small hotel, counting pennies ... The back rub issues in embraces and kisses blended with the heady scent of balsamic unguent.

The style here does not draw attention to itself but, once noticed, is recognized as without parallel.

But the quest for *Pomata balsamica* serves as a mere prologue to the more central quest for a carrot-scraper. As in "The Bug in the Mug," Hood is here enjoying himself in chronicling the pleasures of the light-hearted and the commonplace, and once again devotees of the profound and the universally meaningful should turn their attentions elsewhere. The linguistic misadventures continue. They can find no Italian expression for "carrot-scraper," but sally forth in search of a hardware store, though uncertain of the

Italian for that as well. When they at last discover the store and look in the window they see sink-stoppers but "don't even know the French name for sink-stopper"! The proprietor speaks neither English nor French but

> smiles with great charm and asks, "*Inglese*?"
> "*Canadese*!" they exclaim proudly.
> Friendliness washes miraculously across this cagey Venetian face. "*Ah, si, si*, Toronto. Eastern Avenue. Centre Island!"

But the story is not destined to collapse into a paean to Canadian multiculturalism. They turn to "some non-verbal means of communication" to convey the meaning of "carrot-scraper." Mime fails, but Brenda (like Noreen Mallory, an artist) attempts a drawing of "what she considers to be the unmistakable outline of a swelling carrot," only to realize, when the Italian expresses embarrassment and anger, that "her rendering of a carrot is widely open to misunderstanding." However deficient the characters may be in Italian, Hood's capacity to find the oblique but perfect way of presenting the situation cannot be doubted.

All (of course) ends happily. Alfie miraculously finds the right (or at least comprehensible) words, the purchase is made, and the scraper lasts for twenty years ("Unlike your ordinary Canadian article it is built to last"). Whenever used, it recalls the area of Venice in which they found it, including "the mysterious interior of S. Nicolo *dei mendicoli* ("Why *mendicoli*?") and the image from that church of the Virgin Mary, evidently their protectress through Venice and the unending perils of language. The charm, difficulties, and even the religious aura of Venice is delightfully caught in a beautifully achieved trifle that reveals itself as decidedly more than a trifle. Yet, because it lacks an *important theme*, no Canadian critic seems to have noticed it.

"Plumbers" (55-61) similarly concerns itself with the comic but frustrating aspects of everyday living. It is also the last of the Bronson stories, though a reference to further contact with "Jolene and Bubba" (see YCD 65) suggests that Hood might have been contemplating a further story that never got written. Here Bronson, as in the initial "Allegory of Man's Fate," is confronted with a complicating domestic situation in his Montréal home. At first we find him in his bath intent on those "bathtub games" that we all indulge in but rarely acknowledge: chasing soap, floating his washcloth, inserting a toe in the tap. A classic example of Hood's deftly impressionistic and playful style. But "the most tension-relaxing time of the day" is rudely shattered when his wife Viv announces a crisis and Bronson, in a wonderfully apt but incongruous image, "[r]ises to the surface like a victorious U-boat in a World War II film."

The crisis naturally concerns plumbing, and is described in traditional but currently unfashionable mock-heroic terms. Two weeks earlier, a "plumber of Herculean force" had arrived to fix a blockage and eventually emerged brandishing his plunger "like the great sword of Durendal of Roland or Arthur or some other epic hero." (Hood knows that it was Roland's but Bronson does not.) This Hercules engaged in non-epic labours, however, doesn't know his own strength and ruptures a pipe with his plunger. Hence the usual discomforts and misadventures of modern home repairs. What is forecast as a three-day repair takes nineteen, and then the Bronsons are left with a major plastering job. Moreover, Bronson, as if in bond with his home, suffers his own internal problems in the form of stomach pains. The house plumbing is presented in terms of human anatomy and vice-versa: "'Here's your leak,' he said, pointing to a long irregular slit down one side of the excised member. Bronson thought that the object resembled a lacerated bowel. His stomach quivered sympathetically." We laugh even as we sympathize.

But the crisis passes, like that of the boat-building caper in the first Bronson story, and is ultimately forgotten. Hood ends with a bow to "Time the disguiser. Kindly Time." It would be easy to underestimate the subtle art of this unassuming but totally achieved story. A now aging and even ailing Hood is able to find subject matter for effective and satisfying stories in the ordinary, not immediately promising events occurring around him. Even the single-word title is evidence of his gift for a difficult, ultimate simplicity that never lapses into the trivial.

"Deconstruction" (71-77), another brilliant one-word title, could have been called, though lamely, "*A New Athens* Revisited." Here we look back to the countryside of the Stoverville, Westport and Lake Superior Rail Road that played such a significant role in the second novel of the *New Age* series. There Matt Goderich, following the lead of Hood and his family, scoured the local area looking for physical remains of the historical BWLSRR, which served the immediate environs of Athens and Forfar Junction between 1888 and 1952. Now, a generation later, the narrator and his girlfriend (once again stand-ins for Hood and Noreen Mallory, though less intellectual) make similar investigations, finding the spot where the tracks intersected with those of the Canadian National: "We stood on either side of the meeting-point admiring the simplicity and elegance of the small gaps in the rails that allowed the crossings."

As in *A New Athens*, "Deconstruction" insists on how it is possible to "trace the life of the region" in these survivals from the historical past. Moreover, in the story the protagonists are aware of plans to reopen the line as a tourist attraction, with gourmet meals served in a rehabilitated restaurant car: "What a good idea for a summertime excursion package! Romantic!" But here, Hood's later and darker awareness takes over: "This is no country for good ideas... It was too bright an idea; it never had a chance." Almost immediately, they hear an approaching "warlike sound" which, as it approaches, is likened to "a dragon or a giant beetle or something out of the Apocalypse, snouted, armoured, almost completely inhuman." It turns out to be an infernal machine that tears up the track as soon as it has passed over it. "The steel rails might have been toothpicks or matchsticks hanging from the devouring claws; it was a terrible sight." The account is offered, it will be noted, in the uninspired diction ("Romantic!" "terrible") of the ordinary-guy narrator. But Hood inconspicuously and expertly takes over to provide a depressingly eloquent final sentence: "At its slow determined pace the unpurged image of destruction on wheels went on its way, unwinding the meaning of a hundred and fifty years, which must now sink back into the lines of an old map, and from there to nonentity."

The story serves as a dark coda to a period of southern Ontario history, and is fully justifiable at this level. But Hood's title is profoundly deliberate in its implicit reference to the movement in literary theory prominent at the time of writing. Here, emphasis was placed in any text on what was *not* stated, or on enigmatic passages that might provide unintended, unconscious meanings. Close scrutiny was undertaken not in the interests of literary appreciation so much as to assemble evidence that could be used, as it were, against the writer, a primarily destructive procedure. Only the title hints that the ostensibly realistic narrative (Noreen

Mallory again affirms that it was based on an authentic episode) serves as an image for a contemporary and comparable intellectual trend of which Hood passionately disapproved. Though this effect hardly qualifies as allegory in the strict sense of the term, it is one of the relatively rare instances in his late work where two distinct meanings coalesce at the level of image.

Hood's continuing ability to provide the unexpected is well illustrated by "A Catastrophic Situation" (87-98), one of the longer and more elaborate stories in the book. Here we might say that he is being almost perversely experimental by working in a backward-looking fictional mode. The setting is France, the family rich, well-established, clearly belonging to what used to be called polite society, and the whole story told in a way reminiscent of a Victorian realistic novel. The main relationship is between an eighty-four-year-old artist and his eight-year-old grandchild, and it is interesting to observe Hood, here and in the succeeding story, "There Are More Peasants Than Critics," experimenting with the interaction between old and young (or at least younger) that he had initiated with "Deanna and the Ayatollah."

Structurally, the story divides into five parts, written from continually changing perspectives. In the first, the main members of the Chénonceaux family question the grandchild Fossette about a "master drawing in his most finished late style," her portrait which her grandfather ("admired by *both* Picasso and Bonnard") has given her to hang in her room—that is, to enjoy, not to hoard as a speculation. The old man works up in the attic and will admit only the grandchild into his sanctum. The family, described with a piquant, almost Dickensian sharpness, are blatantly materialist, regarding the portrait primarily as an object of financial worth. In the second section, reproducing the child's first-person viewpoint, we come to realize that the old man is setting his affairs in order, destroying all his paintings that he does not accept as exemplifying his highest standards. In the central third section, between the old man and the young girl in his studio, the artist makes his position clear on a favourite Hoodian topic, property and value: "I've a right to do with my property just as I please... These works are mine, and their only value is the marks I've made on them." He insists on destroying (note another variant on the "deconstruction" theme here) a portrait of his daughter, the child's mother, which could be sold to the Japanese "for another million" but "I botched the job and I won't allow it to be seen." The child covertly burns the cut up rejected paintings in the furnace, appreciating the effect ("They blaze up like fireworks") in a scene reminiscent of the burning of the banknotes in the fourth chapter of *Reservoir Ravine.*

With section four, we return to the family again, and further interrogation of the grandchild. They begin to realize what the old man is doing, are appalled at the financial loss involved, and lament the fact that "we're faced with a potentially catastrophic situation." Fossette asks her grandfather in the final section what this means, thus creating the motive for a traditional didactic "message" (fully justified, it should be stressed, by the conventions in which he is working). He begins whimsically by defining the phrase as "a very unusual period of life . . . when the very old and the very young turn the tables on the wise folk. It's a game where the powerful lose." Later, he describes it as an illness: "It's called greed." In opposition, he proclaims his own artistic values: "I want to preserve my few good things and destroy all the bad. I want to allow nothing to leave here that I can't approve, no matter what the cost. I will not allow them to compromise me or to traffic in my signature" (cf. *None Genuine*). This does not represent Hood's own practice—as we saw, he published *all* his short fiction, even the early failures, when putting together *A Short Walk* and *The Isolation Booth*—but it is an ideal which he certainly approves. Moreover, though the "message" is baldly stated in the above summary, in the full text it is presented in fully human terms, the old man at the end of his life passing on to his grandchild his deeply-felt principles, unrecognized by the intervening generation, in the hope that a new age will come to appreciate them.

The story ends, somewhat abruptly, at a meaningful moment. The old artist is presented as resembling "some figure from the plates of William Blake, some allegory of Adam triumphing over dissatisfaction" (a reminder that Hood's earlier allegorizing tendency is still available, still employed where appropriate, but subtly muted here) as he disposes of "almost the last of the large late oils, an end-of-the-millennium pastiche of the painting of the whole previous century" (a remark with possible relevance to the story itself). Entitled with obvious irony "A Postmodern Family at Teatime," it presents the family members, including Fossette, in an exaggerated manner ("Sargent's treatment of the Sitwell family is cruelly parodied"). But the artist extracts the grandchild's image before "attacking" and destroying the rest of the canvas. He will not treat Fossette like the others, yet her image becomes "flat and meaningless out of context." The implication is presumably twofold: Fossette escapes the symbolic erasure of the previous generation, but her true portrait is the one hanging in her bedroom, where he has presented her in a style appropriate to her qualities.

Hood's most radical (yet delightful) venture into the area of experimental fantasy may well be "There Are More Peasants Than Critics" (99-105). Like "A Catastrophic Situation," it presents the meeting of old and young, in this case an "ordinary man like us ... an office worker in the middle way of life" and Katie, a twelve-year-old girl described improbably yet intriguingly as "one of those natural truth-tellers thrown up by human society from time to time." But there is a strong thematic as well as formal link between the two stories. Yet again the subject of property and value is raised in connection with the world of art and creativity. These stories are wholly separate, very different in tone and style, but one cannot help suspecting that Hood's writing of the first led him to follow up by writing the second.

The story opens with an unnamed protagonist having a remarkable dream that offers itself as a classic narrative, "a complete work of art." One may think of the famous story of Coleridge's composing "Kubla Khan" in a dream, a difference being that the dreamer has no difficulty in remembering it and writing it down. Moreover, he is not a gifted writer, not even an especially imaginative person, but he recognizes quality when he sees it, and realizes that he has been blessed with some kind of creative inspiration, "an irradiation whose source is only to be guessed at ... something given, ordained elsewhere and not to be traced back." At the same time, however, complications arise. On the one hand he is reminded of the parable of the prodigal son and realizes that "the parables of Christ could never have been copyrighted"; on the other hand, "It is his alone! ... This is a *valuable property*" (my emphases). He imagines trying to sell a superb slogan to an advertising agency: "How can you tell the secret without, as we say, giving it away ... They'll steal it!" ("as we say" drawing attention to an example of inconspicuous yet profound wordplay).

One odd feature of "There Are More Peasants" is the fact that this is a seven-page story in which the first five are taken up with introductory exposition. Only then does the protagonist make the essential decision to consult his twelve-year-old niece and invites her to lunch at McDonald's. (A similar locale is featured in the third chapter of *Property and Value* itself, described in terms of "some fairy-tale encounter … Where else should loving encounters take place in late twentieth-century romance if not in McDonald's?" [69, 70]). We catch a glimpse here of the subtly interrelating cast of Hood's mind.

Within this archetypally popular setting ("The restaurant will be very noisy, no chance of being overheard"!), rendered with an accurate and vivid realism ("Chicken McNuggets," "a quarter-pounder with cheese," even Hood's ubiquitous "Daffy Duck" in doll form as a featured extra), the uncle asks advice on publishing strategy: should he attempt a popular or a critical success? He receives the reply indicated in the title, finding it "strangely persuasive, even compelling, gnomic," though it is hardly profound and in no way resolves the issues raised. Still, Katie's approval is welcome, indeed valuable to him. He takes her home, returns to his typewriter, and, in one of Hood's trickiest endings, he "starts to type out the last and definitive version of the story that you are about to read … " But of course we don't.

At a first reading, the imbalance of exegesis over action is disturbing. Further consideration, however, should reveal that the story is not primarily about uncle and niece but about the act of creation itself, its challenges, temptations, and responsibilities. "He will be judged by the way he delivers the narrative." The plot provides a resolution as an appendage. Above all, it cures the uncle of proprietary selfishness. His realization that he might be offered "all the kingdoms of the earth" for film rights (Matthew 4:8) recalls earlier references to Christ's parables. He now sees that no one can "possess" a myth. Ultimately, then, the story is recognized as itself a parable, and so beyond the dictates of standard realism. Only the most naïve of realists would object to the lack of customary form, logic, and consistency. It partakes of the reality of dream, far more compelling (at least in my view) than the rather self-conscious whimsy of "Bit Parts." It is sufficient that the narrative "charms and delights"—like the dream itself.

The last two stories to be discussed surprise because they display new aspects of Hood's writing that, even after thirty-five years, he had not attempted before. "Finishing Together" (115-25) is perhaps the most classically constructed and succinct story he ever produced. Hood was knowledgeable about music, both classical and popular, but this is his only story about professional musicians working as a group.

It is divided into four parts that become increasingly personal as they proceed. The opening section is as objective a piece of writing as can be imagined. The three musicians, a man and two women, are introduced and their forming of the Warshow Trio (violin, cello, piano) described, along with informative details of their repertoire and notable musical qualities. The only hints of personal significance occur in a brief reference to their resemblance to each other, "like loving siblings," and the earlier sentence: "Harold, Sylvia and Nella complemented and balanced each other so finely, as they developed their repertoire, that they seemed almost like brother and sisters." In the second part, which covers their early days travelling under uncomfortable conditions, a more personal note is introduced when Harold "remembered admiring Sylvia's back and shoulders, curved over the shrouded cased cello." Moreover, the narrator remarks on their maturing "personal relations" as they "work together in conditions of revealing intimacy."

In the third part, we learn that "by now, four or five years into their association, it was clear to [Harold] that [Sylvia and Nella] half expected him to fall in love with one of them." When, a little later, the narrator explains that the "ever-varying power relationships among members of chamber-music groups are always troublesome," we know that the troubles are likely to be sexual as well as musical. It becomes clear that, for a number of quite complex reasons, Harold is inclined to favour Nella the pianist. This sexual emphasis rises to a climax in the concluding section. The group established the practice of booking adjoining rooms in motels, Harold in a single, Sylvia and Nella in a double. The management, we are told, "now and then made faces about unlocking the communicating door, as though the trio—serious musicians—might be getting up to some odious sexual romp." Eventually, however, Harold discovers that the women bolt the door, and in the course of time is informed that they are lovers and he is excluded. The story ends with the three of them still together as musicians "at least for the moment," but with the possibility that Sylvia and Nella may break away to form the Warshow/McBride Duo.

A prominent feature of this story can only be described adequately as the chasteness of its style, almost totally devoid of metaphor or imagery. It is admirably clear and precise, able to explain complex musical issues to the inexpert and to convey subtleties of human response without an excess of emotion or any hint of moral comment. The title is, of course, richly ambivalent. Technically, it refers to the ultimate test of true musicianship, since "[f]inishing successively, especially in slow tempos, can expose ineptitude in a chamber group." In terms of plot, however, it provides an unexpected resolution of the eternal-triangle situation, since it is the two women who in private life are "finishing together." The special qualities of the story, however, may well be more evident to fellow practitioners than to general readers. It is the inconspicuousness of Hood's art that is so remarkable. His style in no ways draws attention to itself, yet it proves to be the perfect vehicle for the effect he requires.

The final story, predictably, is very different. For forty years, Hood earned his living as a teacher of English, first at St. Joseph College in West Hartford, later at the Université de Montréal, yet, with the arguable exception of "Which the Tigress, Which the Lamb?," not until "After All!" (143-52), the last story he ever wrote, did he choose as a fictional subject the world of teaching and administration. Into it he poured all the frustrations and dissatisfactions that characterized arts disciplines at that time, the disastrous period marked by political interference (and correctness), compromise, and intellectual decline. However, though one detects a palpable sense of anger and disillusion behind the writing, the story is poised, emotionally restrained, and even, in a laconically tight-lipped way, comic.

"After All!" is a classic example of one of Hood's moral fables. The plot, if one stops to scrutinize it, is highly improbable, yet in its very excess it is perfectly suited to Hood's purpose. A Graduate Studies sub-committee on admissions agrees to accept Molly Spencer, a student confined to a wheelchair, who proceeds to claim all sorts of rights to offset her "physically challenged" status. These include "the right to put her exam answers on audio cassette," to hold up classes in the event of her lateness lest she be "deprived of some important part of a discussion—to which she was entitled by right," and the right to tape lectures, with all the physical and technological problems of positioning microphones that this entails. In other words, she becomes a disruptive influence for her teachers and fellow students alike.

In the event, she turns out to be an impostor. The "chairperson" (who narrates the story), seeing her by chance on a Métro platform and, recognizing that she is in fact able-bodied, follows her into a department store and attempts to lay a charge against her. She retorts that she has "been doing some research for a sociology thesis on the life-styles of the physically challenged." The teacher thereupon finds himself "checkmated," at risk of being charged himself on a gender harassment charge. The whole sequence possesses an absurd, zany quality that is at the same time uncomfortably pertinent to current attitudes and assumptions.

I make no apology for giving away the plot, since the art of the story lies in the telling. The narrator, as indicated, is "the department chair," who reveals himself as patiently good-humoured, anxious not to be considered illiberal, reluctant to be acknowledged as an "authority figure," easy-going to the point of ineffectiveness, incapable of steering with any success between the conflicting duties and responsibilities that confront him on all sides. He begins by trying to explain the departmental bureaucracy and making a joke of its complexity ("Am I making myself clear?"). We gradually become aware of his preparedness to use every contemporary cliché or politically correct euphemism available: "Ms. Spencer," "departmental chairperson," "finalized our decision," "affirmative action," "physically challenged," "manipulative behaviour," "life-styles," etc.

To an outsider, some of the details may seem exaggerated, and probably they are. Yet who, within a modern university, has not met the likes of "Rina Baldwin, who never votes to reject a female applicant, no matter how borderline she may be"? The narrator's attitude is highly revealing:

> I've discussed this with her and she says it isn't prejudice, it's affirmative action. "So be it" is what I say. We here have to live with each other in the department after these borderline cases

> have done their three or four years and then gone on. WHY BE TOO INSISTENT ON STRICT STANDARDS? The loud inner voice of corruption.

A similar revelation occurs a little later when the narrator agrees, against his better judgment, to allow the candidate in question to supply taped answers to exam questions. "I had my doubts but I went along. Kind of makes me think of Adolf Eichmann, that formula does. I had my doubts but I went along." Now, after almost fifty years, it may be necessary to explain that Eichmann (1906-62) was a Nazi war criminal snatched out of Argentina by Israeli agents, accused of being involved in the extermination of millions of Jews, tried and executed. His defence was that he merely obeyed the orders of his superiors. The analogy is as chilling as it is provocative.

These are but two instances in the text where sarcasm and bitterness break through. Elsewhere the tone is surprisingly relaxed, patient, more in sorrow than in anger. Once again Hood has "something to say," but the way it is said is all-important. We sympathize with the narrator, recognize his basic decency, know that in his shoes we would almost certainly have done the same. We may not believe in the likelihood of such a story occurring "in real life," but it has the application, the resonance, of a disturbing parable. A proper reading of "After All!" will respond to the artistry while simultaneously acknowledging the validity of its message.

A volume that contains "Assault of the Killer Volleyballs," "The Bug in the Mug," "Life in Venice," "Deconstruction," "A Catastrophic Situation," and "After All!" demonstrates an astonishing variety that, I submit, fully justifies my insistence on "God's Plenty." Hood was a dedicated, serious artist, and his contribution to Canadian literature has been incalculable. But for all the seriousness, he remained playful, sometimes almost puckish, always eager to insert hidden effects into his work, even if most of his readers were unlikely to recognize them. One final, perhaps trivial, yet characteristic instance of his quirky and prodigal genius may be noted here. The first word of the first story in this collection is "After"; the last word of the last is "All!"

List of Short Fiction

Details of time of writing are drawn from Hood's own listings in *Collected Stories*, his "Floating Southwards," J. R. (Tim) Struthers's 1978-79 "Bibliography," and the Hugh Hood fonds, Special Collections, University of Calgary Library.

"After All!" (AA) Written Dec. 1996.

"After the Sirens." (FRK) Written Jan. 1960. Published in *Esquire*, Aug. 1960.

"Allegory of Man's Fate, An" (DG, SS, LSOD) Written Dec. 1973 – Jan. 1974. Published in *Journal of Canadian Fiction* 3 (Winter 1974).

"Around Theatres." (AM) Written Feb. 1966. Published in *Parallel* 1 (Jul. – Aug. 1966).

"Assault of the Killer Volleyballs." (AA) Written Oct. 1991. Published in *Carousel* (University of Guelph) 9 (1993).

"August Nights." (AN) Written Oct. – Nov. 1980. Published in *Canadian Forum* 61 (Aug. 1981).

"Bees, Flies and Chickens." (AN) Written Oct. 1983.

"Bicultural Angela." (AM) Written Feb. 1966. Published in *Canadian Forum* 46 (Aug. 1966).

"Bit Parts." (AA) Written Sep. 1991.

"Blackmailer's Wasted Afternoon, The." (AN) Written Sep. 1982.

"Boots." (DG) Written Nov. 1969. Published in John Metcalf, ed., *The Narrative Voice* (1972).

"Breaking Off." (NGWS) Written Jan. 1979.

"Brother André, Père Lamarche, and My Grandmother Eugénie Blagdon." (FM) Written Apr. 1964. Published in *Alphabet* 13 (Jun. 1967).

"Bug in the Mug, The." (AA) Written Aug. 1992.

"Catastrophic Situation, A." (AA) Written Dec. 1993.

"Changeling, The." (IB) Written Dec. 1960. Published in *Canadian Forum* 41 (Mar. 1962).

"Chess Match, The." (DG) Written Jun. 1960. Published in *Fiddlehead* 53 (Summer 1962). Discussed in some detail by Solecki 346-7.

"Childhood Incident, A." (NGWS) Written Jun. 1960. Published in *Salt* 12 (Winter 1974-5).

"Crosby." (NGWS, LSOD) Written Nov. 1977. Published in *Saturday Night* (Jan. – Feb. 1978).

"Cura Pastoralis." (FM) Written Feb. 1957. Published in *Contact* (Sausalito, CA) 3 (Aug. 1962).

"Cute Containers." (AN) Written Sep. – Oct. 1981.

"Dark Glasses." (DG, SS). Written Sep. 1971. Published in David Helwig and Joan Harcourt, eds., *73: New Canadian Short Stories* (1973). Discussed in detail by Mathews in "Secular" 217-220.

"Deanne and the Ayatollah." (YCD) Written Sep. 1987.

"Deconstruction." (AA) Written Oct. 1993. Published in *Carousel* (University of Guelph) 10 (1994).

"Disappearing Creatures of Various Kinds." (YCD) Written Oct. 1988. Published in John Metcalf and Kent Thompson, eds., *The Third Macmillan Anthology* (1990).

"Dog Explosion, The." (FM) Written Dec. 1969.

"Don't Bother Coming." (YCD) Written Oct. 1989.

"Doubles." (NGWS) Written Dec. 1977. Published in *Fiddlehead* 118 (Summer 1978).

"Educating Mary." (IB) Written Jul. 1964. Published in *Montrealer* (Sep. 1965).

"End of It, The." (FRK, SS) Written Mar. 1962. Published in *Tamarack Review* 24 (Summer 1962).

"Every Piece Different." (AN) Written Nov. – Dec. 1980. Published in *Waves* 11 (Winter 1983).

"Evolving Bud." (AN) Written Nov. – Dec. 1981.

"Fable of the Ant and the Grasshopper, The." (IB) Written Jan. 1959. Published in *Yes* 13 (December 1964).

"Faithful Lover, A." (SW) Written Jan. 1957.

"Fallings From Us, Vanishings." (FRK, SS) Written Mar. 1961. Published in *Montrealer* (May 1962).

"February Mama." (NGWS) Written Feb. 1979. Published in *Descant* 30-31 (1980-81).

"Finishing Together." (AA) Written Dec. 1994.

Five New Facts About Giorgione. Written Sep. – Dec. 1985 (doubtless revised later). Discussed in detail by Knoenagel.

"Flying a Red Kite." (FRK) Written Jul. 1961. Published in *Prism* 3 (Spring 1962). Discussed in detail by Mills, "Hugh Hood" 95-101, Tranquilla, and Zimmermann.

"Friends and Relations." (IB) Written Jun. 1960. Published in *Seven Persons Repository* 6 (Spring 1973).

"From the Fields of Sleep." (SW) Written Aug. 1961, rev. Jun. 1979.

"Fruit Man, the Meat Man & the Manager, The." (FM, SS) Written Sep. 1966. Published in *Canadian Forum* 48 (August 1968).

"Gay Time, A." (AA) Written Nov. 1993.

"Getting Funding." (YCD) Written Oct. – Nov. 1986. Published in John Metcalf, ed., *Carry On Bumping* (1988).

"Getting to Williamstown." (FM, LSOD) Written Jan. 1964. Published in *Tamarack Review* 34 (Winter 1965). Discussed in detail by Hood in "Writing 'Getting to Williamstown'" in John Metcalf, ed. *Sixteen by Twelve* (1970) 87.

"Ghosts at Jarry." (NGWS, LSOD) Written Sep. 1977. Published in John Metcalf and Clark Blaise, eds., *78: Best Canadian Short Stories* (1978).

"Glass of Fashion, The." (SW) Written Nov. 1957 (see SW 17; dating at 173 is a misprint).

"God Has Manifested Himself Unto Us as Canadian Tire." (NGWS, LSOD) Written Nov. 1975. Published in Joan Harcourt and John Metcalf, eds., *76: New Canadian Stories* (1976).

"Going Out as a Ghost." (DG, SS, LSOD) Written Jan. 1974. Published in *Fiddlehead* 101 (Spring 1974). Discussed in detail by Mathews, "Secular" 213-17, and Keith, "Atmosphere" 128-37.

"Gone Three Days." (NGWS) Written Oct. 1978.

"Good Listener, The." (NGWS) Written May 1979.

"Good Tenor Man, The." (FM) Written Jun. 1962. Published in *Encore* 3 (Oct. 1963).

"Grand Déménagement, Le." (AM, LSOD) Written Mar. 1966.

"Granite Club, The." (IB) Written Oct. 1966. Published in *Journal of Canadian Fiction* 1 (Winter 1972).

"Green Child, A." (AM, SS) Written May 1966. Discussed in detail by Duffy 133-5.

"Harley Talking." (FM) Written Jan. – Feb. 1969. Published in *Quarry* 20 (Fall 1971).

"He Just Adores Her!" (FRK) Written Feb. 1961. Published in *Montrealer* (Jan. 1962).

"High Fidelity." (SW) Written Jun. 1960.

"Hole, The." (DG) Written Dec. 1970. Published in *Canadian Fiction Magazine* 7 (Summer 1972). Discussed in detail by Garebian, *Hugh Hood* 35-7.

"Holy Man, The." (FM) Written Dec. 1964. Published in *Tamarack Review* 37 (Autumn 1965).

"Hot Cockatoos." (YCD) Written Nov. 1989.

"How Did She Find Out?" (AA) Written Oct. 1994.

"I'm Not Desperate!" (IB) Written Jan. 1960. Published in *Exchange* 1 (Nov. 1961).

"Incendiaries." (DG) Written Dec. 1957, rev. Jan. 1974. Published in *Grain* 2 (1974).

"Ingenue I Should Have Kissed, but Didn't, The." (IB) Written Apr. 1962. Published in *Tamarack Review* 25 (Autumn 1962).

"In the Deep." (AN) Written Nov. 1983.

"Isolation Booth, The." (IB) Written Mar. 1957. Published in *Tamarack Review* 9 (Autumn 1958).

"I've Got Troubles of My Own." (AN) Written Oct. 1981. Published in *Malahat Review* 67 (Feb. 1984).

"Jill's Disappearing Nipples." (YCD) Written Sep. 1989.

"Jolene from Moline." (YCD) Written Oct. 1987.

"Last Remake of Nosferatu." (YCD) Written Oct. – Nov. 1989.

"Life in Venice." (AA) Written Sep.1992.

"Light Shining Out of Darkness." (AM, SS, LSOD) Written Jan. 1966. Published in *Saturday Night* (Apr. 1966). Discussed in detail by Rigelhof 115-20.

"Looking Down from Above." (AM, SS) Written Mar. 1966. Published in *Prism International* 6 (Autumn 1966). Discussed in detail by Lecker 99-120.

"Marriage 401." (SW) Written Nov. 1958.

"Messages Are the Message, The." (AA) Written Nov. – Dec. 1996.

"More Birds." (YCD) Written Sep. 1986.

"Moskowitz's Moustache." (AN) Written Nov. – Dec. 1982.

"Near Miss, A." (DG) Written May 1964. Published in *Fiddlehead* 94 (Summer 1972). Discussed in detail by Mathews, "Hood" 172-81.

"New Country." (NGWS) Written Dec. 1978.

"Nobody's Going Anywhere!" (FRK, SS) Written Feb. 1962.

"None Genuine Without This Signature, or, Peaches in the Bathtub." (NGWS). Written Oct. 1977.

"O Happy Melodist!" (FRK) Written Oct. 1961.

"One Owner, Low Mileage." (FM) Written Feb. 1967. Published in French translation (by Hubert Aquin) in *Liberté* (mars – avril 1969).

"One Way North and South." (AM) Written Apr. 1976. Published in *Tamarack Review* 41 (Winter 1968).

"Pain Control." (AA) Written Nov. 1996.

"Paradise Retained?" (FM) Written Oct. 1967. Published in *Tamarack Review* 46 (Winter 1968).

"Perfect Night, The." (IB) Written Sep. 1957. Published in *Story* (Jul. – Aug. 1963). Discussed in detail by Mills, "*Sciptible*" 256-9.

"Pitcher, The." (DG) Written Sep. 1961. Published in *Canadian Forum* 43 (Apr. 1963).

"Places I've Never Been." (FM, SS) Written Feb. 1969. Published in Stephen Clarkson, ed., *Vision 2020: Fifty Canadians in Search of a Future* (1970).

"Plumbers." (AA) Written Nov. 1992.

"Predictions of Ice." (AM) Written Jun. 1966. Discussed in detail by Vauthier, "Une vue" 189-98.

"Presents for an Anniversary." (SW) Written May 1959.

"Quicker Coming Back." (AN) Written Sep. 1983.

"Recollections of the Works Department." (FRK) Written May 1960. Published in *Tamarack Review* 22 (Winter 1962).

"Regulars, The." (SW) Written Jul. 1960.

"Rig Flip." (YCD) Written Sep. 1988.

"River Behind Things, The." (AM, SS) Written Jun 1966. Discussed in detail by Duffy 135-7.

"Season of Calm Weather, A." (IB) Written Jan. 1961, slightly rev. before publication. Published in *Queen's Quarterly* 70 (Spring 1963).

"Short Walk in the Rain, A." (SW) Written Jan. 1957.

"Silver Bugles, Cymbals, Golden Silks." (FRK, SS, LSOD) Written Dec. 1961.

"Singapore Hotel, The." (FM) Written Mar. 1969. Published in *Fiddlehead* 84 (Mar. – Apr. 1970).

"Small Birds, The." (AN, LSOD) Written Sep. 1980. Published in John Metcalf and Leon Rooke, eds., *82: Best Canadian Stories* (1982).

"Socks." (DG) Written Nov. 1969. Published in John Metcalf, ed., *The Narrative Voice* (1972).

"Solitary Ewe, A." (FM) Written Feb. 1964. Published in *Literary Review* 8 (Summer 1965).

"Sportive Centre of Saint Vincent de Paul, The." (AM) Written Jan. 1966. Discussed in detail by Thompson, "Hugh Hood" 58-9.

"Starting Again on Sherbrooke Street." (AM) Written May 1966. Published in *Parallel* 1 (Nov. – Dec. 1960).

"Strategies of Hysteria, The." (SW) Written Feb. 1957.

"Subject for Thomas Hardy, A." (AA) Written Dec. 1992.

"Suites and Single Rooms, With Bath." (IB) Written Nov. 1961. Published in *Queen's Quarterly* 79 (Autumn 1972).

"Swedes in the Night." (AA) Written Nov. 1991.

"Thanksgiving: Between Junetown and Caintown" (DG, SS, LSOD) Written Nov. 1974. Published in *Canadian Fiction Magazine* 18 (Summer 1975). Discussed in detail by Mathews, "Secular" 220-22.

"That 1950 Ford." (SW) Written Sep. 1957.

"There Are More Peasants Than Critics." (AA) Written Sep. 1994.

"Third Time Unlucky." (YCD) Written Nov. – Dec. 1986. Published in *Rubicon* 10 (Fall 1988).

"Three Halves of a House." (FRK) Written Oct. 1960. Published in *Tamarack Review* 20 (Summer 1961).

"Tolstoy Pitch, The." (FM, SS, LSOD) Written Mar. 1964. Published in *Fiddlehead* 79 (Mar. – Apr. 1969).

"Too Much Mozart." (AA) Written Dec. 1991.

"Triumph of the Liturgy, The." (SW) Written Dec. 1958.

"Two Bridport Tales." (YCD) Written Nov. 1987.

"Village Inside, The." (AM) Written Apr. 1966. Discussed in detail by Thompson, "Formal" 205-12 and Vauthier, *Reverberations* 152-76.

"We Outnumber the Dead." (AN) Written Sep. – Oct. 1982. Published in *Prism International* 21 (Spring 1983).

"Weight Watchers." (AN) Written Oct. – Nov. 1984.

"Where the Myth Touches Us." (FRK) Written Nov. 1960. Published in *Queen's Quarterly* 69 (Summer 1962).

"Which the Tigress, Which the Lamb?" (SW) Written Apr. 1959, rev. Jun. 1964.

"Whos Paying for This Call." (FM, SS) Written Dec. 1969. Discussed in detail by Garebian, *Hugh Hood* 27-28.

"Winner, The." (IB) Written Oct. 1958. Published in *Jubilee* 3 (Spring 1976).

"Woodcutter's Third Son." (NGWS) Written Nov. 1978.

"World by Instalments, The." (SW) Written Oct. 1957.

"Worst Thing Ever." (DG) Written Apr. 1969. Published in *Intercourse* 12-13 (Jan. 1970).

"You'll Catch Your Death." (YCD) Written Dec. 1989.

Other Works Cited

NB: Details of Hood's volumes of short stories, and some other frequently cited items are listed under "Abbreviations" (16).

Anderson, Jaynie. *Giorgione: The Painter of 'Poetic Beauty,' including Catalogue Raisonné.* Paris and New York: Flammarion, 1997.

Auden, W. H. *Collected Shorter Poems, 1927-1957.* London: Faber, 1966.

Bissoondath, Neil. "Quiet Skill and Overkill." Rev. of AN. *Books in Canada* 15 (June – July 1986), 16-17.

Blackburn, William. Rev. of *Collected Stories I: Flying a Red Kite. Canadian Book Review Annual 1987.* Toronto: Simon & Pierre, 1988. 183-4.

Bowering, George. "Modernisn Could Not Last For Ever." In his *The Mask in Place: Essays on Fiction in North America.* Winnipeg: Turnstone, 1982. 77-83.

Cameron, Barry. Rev. of *Dark Glasses. Fiddlehead* 115 (Fall 1977), 145-7.

—. "'Incarnational Art': Typology and Analogy in Hugh Hood's Fiction." Rev of J. R. (Tim) Struthers, ed., *Before the Flood. Fiddlehead* 133 (July 1982), 89-91.

Cloutier, Pierre. "An Interview With Hugh Hood." *Journal of Canadian Fiction* 2 (Winter 1973), 49-52.

Coletti, Luigi. *All the Paintings of Giorgione.* London: Oldbourne, 1961.

Copoloff-Mechanic, Susan. *Pilgrim's Progress: A Study of the Short Stories of Hugh Hood.* Toronto: ECW Press, 1988.

Currie, Sheldon. Rev. of NGWS. *Antigonish Review* 45 (Spring 1981), 104-5.

Dobbs, Kildare. "Memory Transfigured." Rev. of FRK. *Canadian Literature* 16 (Spring 1963), 72-3.

Duffy, Dennis. "Space/Time and the Matter of Form." *Essays on Canadian Writing* 13/14 (Winter/Spring 1978-9), 131-44. Also available as J. R. (Tim) Struthers, ed., *Before the Flood.* Downsview, ON: ECW Press, 1979 (same pagination).

Fagan, Cary. Rev. of NGWS. *Canadian Book Review Annual 1980.* Toronto: Simon & Pierre, 1981. 136.

Fulford, Robert. "An Interview with Hugh Hood." *Tamarack Review* (June 1975), 65-77.

Garebian, Keith. *Hugh Hood.* Boston: Twayne, 1983.

—. "Hugh Hood (1928-   )." Robert Lecker, Jack David, Ellen Quigley, eds., *Canadian Writers and Their Works. Fiction. Volume 7.* Toronto: ECW Press, 1985. 93-151.

—. "Owen Hoodwinked." *Books in Canada* 9 (November 1980), 33.

Godfrey, Dave. "Turning New Leaves." Rev. of FRK. *Canadian Forum* 42 (January 1963), 229-30.

Grosskurth, Phyllis. "There's No Doubt He Loves the Place." Rev. of FM. *Saturday Night* 86 (December 1971), 42-3.

Gzowski, Peter. "Why Montreal is Canada's Parnassus." Rev. of AM. *Maclean's* 80 (August 1967), 70-71.

Hale, Victoria G. "An Interview with Hugh Hood." *World Literature Written in English* 11 (April 1972), 35-41.

Harper Handbook to Literature, The. Ed. Northrop Frye, Sheridan Baker, and George Perkins. New York: Harper & Row, 1985.

Hood, Hugh. *After All!. The Collected Stories* 5. Foreword by W. J. Keith. Erin, ON: Porcupine's Quill, 2003.

—. *Around the Mountain*. 1967. The Collected Stories 4. Introduction by Hood. Erin, ON: Porcupine's Quill, 1994.

—. *August Nights*. Toronto: Stoddart, 1985.

—. *Be Sure to Close Your Eyes. The New Age/Le nouveau siècle 9*. Concord, ON: House of Anansi Press, 1993.

—. *Black and White Keys. The New Age/Le nouveau siècle* 4. Downsview, ON: ECW Press, 1982.

—. *Camera Always Lies*. 1967. New Canadian Library. Toronto: McClelland & Stewart, nd.

—. *Collected Stories, The*. 5 vols. See under individual volumes.

—. *Dark Glasses*. Ottawa: Oberon Press, 1976.

—. *Dead Men's Watches. The New Age/Le nouveau siècle* 10. Concord, On: House of Anansi Press, 1995.

—. *Flying a Red Kite*. 1962. *The Collected Stories 1*. Introduction by Hood. Erin, ON: Porcupine's Quill, 1990.

—. *Fruit Man, the Meat Man & the Manager*. Ottawa: Oberon Press, 1971.

—. *Game of Touch, A*. Don Mills, ON: Longman Canada, 1970.

—. *Governor's Bridge is Closed*. Ottawa: Oberon Press, 1973. [Essays]

—. *Great Realizations. The New Age/Le nouveau siècle* 11. Concord, ON: House of Anansi Press, 1997.

—. "Hugh Hood (1928-)" *Contemporary Authors' Autobiography Series*, Vol. 17. Detroit: Gale Research, 1993.

—. *Isolation Booth, The. The Collected Stories 3*. Introduction by Hood. Erin, ON: Porcupine's Quill, 1991.

—. *Light Shining in Darkness and Other Stories*, Selected with Afterword by John Metcalf. New Canadian Library. McClelland & Stewart, 2001.

—. *Motor Boys in Ottawa, The. The New Age/Le nouveau siècle* 6. Toronto: Stoddart, 1986.

—. *Near Water. The New Age/Le nouveau siècle*. Toronto: House of Anansi Press, 2000.

—. *New Age/Le nouveau siècle, The*. 12 vols. See individual volumes.

—. *New Athens, A. The New Age/Le nouveau siècle* 2. Ottawa: Oberon Press, 1977.

—. *None Genuine Without This Signature*. Downsview, ON: ECW Press, 1980.

—. *Property and Value. The New Age/Le nouveau siècle* 8. Toronto: House of Anansi Press, 1990.

—. *Reservoir Ravine. The New Age/Le nouveau siècle* 3. Ottawa: Oberon Press, 1979.

—. *Scenic Art, The. The New Age/Le nouveau siècle* 5. Toronto: Stoddart, 1984.

—. *Short Walk in the Rain, A. The Collected Stories* 2. Introduction by Hood, Erin, ON: Porcupine's Quill, 1989.

—. *Swing in the Garden, The. The New Age/Le nouveau siècle* 1. Ottawa: Oberon Press, 1975.

—. *Tony's Book. The New Age/Le nouveau siècle* 7. Toronto: Stoddart, 1988.

—. *Trusting the Tale*. Downsview, ON: ECW Press, 1983. [Essays]

—. *Unsupported Assertions*. Concord, ON: House of Anansi Press, 1991. [Essays]

—. *White Figure, White Ground*. Richmond Hill, ON: Pocket Books, Simon & Schuster of Canada, 1973.

—. *You Cant Get There From Here*. Ottawa: Oberon Press, 1972.

—. *You'll Catch Your Death*. Erin, ON: Porcupine's Quill, 1972.

Hood, Hugh, and John Mills. "Hugh Hood and John Mills in Epistolary Conversation." *Fiddlehead* 116 (Winter 1978), 133-46.

Hornyansky, Michael. "Countries of the Mind II." Includes rev. of FRK. *Tamarack Review* 27 (Spring 1963), 80-89.

Housman, A. E. *The Letters of A. E. Housman*. Ed. Henry Maas. London: Rupert Hart-Davis, 1971.

Ivison, Douglas. "A Reader's Guide to the Intersection of Time and Space: Urban Spatialization in High Hood's *Around the Mountain*." *Studies in Canadian Literature* 23 (1998), 238-49.

Keith, W. J. "The Atmosphere of Deception: Hugh Hood's 'Going Out as a Ghost'." In John Metcalf, ed., *Writers in Aspic*. Montréal: Véhicule Press, 1998. 128-37.

—. *Canadian Odyssey: A Reading of Hugh Hood's The New Age /Le nouveau siècle*. Montreal and Kingston: McGill-Queen's University Press, 2002.

—. "The Case for Hugh Hood." In his *An Independent Stance: Essays on English-Canadian Criticism and Fiction*. Erin, On: Porcupine's Quill, 1991. 234-40.

Knoenagel, Alex. "The History of Art and the Art of History: Hugh Hood's *Five New Facts About Giorgione*." *Mosaic* 27 (March 1994), 123-44.

Lawrence, D. H. *Studies in Classic American Literature*. 1923. New York: Viking, 1964.

Leavis, F. R. "*The Europeans*." In his *Anna Karenina and Other Essays*. London: Chatto & Windus, 1967. 59-74.

Lecker, Robert. "Hugh Hood: Looking Down From Above." In his *On the Line: Readings in the Short Fiction of Clark Blaise, John Metcalf, and Hugh Hood*. Downsview, ON: ECW Press, 1982. 99-120.

Mathews, Lawrence. "Hood and Evil." In J. R. (Tim) Struthers, ed. *The Montreal Story Tellers*. Montréal: Véhicule Press, 1985. 176-87.

—. "The Secular and the Sacral: Notes on *A New Athens* and Three Stories by Hugh Hood." *Essays on Canadian Writing* 13/14 (Winter/Spring, 1978-9), 211-29. Also available as J. R. (Tim) Struthers, ed., *Before the Flood*. Downsview, ON: ECW Press, 1979 (same pagination).

Metcalf, John. *An Aesthetic Underground: A Literary Memoir*. Toronto: Thomas Allen, 2003.

—. "Afterword" to Hugh Hood, *Light Shining Out of Darkness and Other Stories*. Toronto: McClelland & Stewart, 2001. 173-8.

—. *Kicking Against the Pricks*. Downsview, ON: ECW Press, 1982.

Mills, John. "Hugh Hood and the Anagogical Method." *Essays on Canadian Writing* 13/14 (Spring 1978-9). 94-112. Also available as J. R. (Tim) Struthers, ed., *Before the Flood*. Downsview, ON: ECW Press, 1979 (same pagination).

—. "A *Scriptible* Text." Rev of IB. *Essays on Canadian Writing*, 50 (Fall 1993) 256-63.

Morley, Patricia. *The Comedians: Hugh Hood & Rudy Wiebe*. Toronto: Clarke, Irwin, 1977.

Orange, John. Rev. of NGWS and *Reservoir Ravine*. *Fiddlehead* 133 (July 1982), 85, 87-8.

Owen, I. M. "The Hood Line: Father, Son, and Holy Ghost." *Books in Canada* 9 (August – September 1980), 9-10.

Pignatti, Terisio G. *Giorgione: Complete Edition*. London: Phaidon, 1971.

Rigelhof, T. F. "Tales Catching Tales." In his *This Is Our Literature*. Erin, ON: Porcupine's Quill, 2000. 111-33.

Scholes, Robert, and A. Walton Litz, eds., *James Joyce. Dubliners. Text, Criticism, and Notes*. New York: Viking, 1969.

Solecki, Sam. "Fiction" (Letters in Canada 1976). Includes rev. of DG. *University of Toronto Quarterly* 46 (Summer 1977), 346-7.

Struthers, J. R. (Tim). "Bibliography of Works by and on Hugh Hood." *Essays on Canadian Writing* 13/14 (Winter/Spring, 1978-9). 230-94. Also available as Struthers, ed., *Before the Flood* (Downsview, ON: ECW Press, 1979 (same pagination). Superseded for the most part by the entry immediately following.

—. "Hugh Hood: An Annotated Bibliography." In Robert Lecker and Jack David, eds., *The Annotated Bibliography of Canada's Major Authors*. Vol 5. Downsview, ON: ECW Press, 1984. 231-353.

—. "An Interview with Hugh Hood." *Essays on Canadian Writing* 13/14 (Winter/Spring, 1978-9), 21-93. Also available in Struthers, ed., *Before the Flood* (Downsview, ON: ECW Press, 1979 (same pagination).

—. "A Secular Liturgy: Hugh Hood's Aesthetics and *Around the Mountain*." *Studies in Canadian Literature* 10 (1985), 110-35.

Thompson, Kent. "The Canadian Short Story in English." *World Literature in English* 11 (April 1972), 15-24.

—. "Formal Coherence in the Art of Hugh Hood." *Studies in Canadian Literature* 2 (Summer 1977), 201-12.

—. "Hugh Hood on the Expanding Universe." *Journal of Canadian Fiction* 3 (Winter 1974), 55-9.

Tranquilla, Ronald. "John Updike's 'Toward Evening': Hoodwinked." *American Review of Canadian Studies* 26 (Spring 1996), 67-82. (A comparative study of Updike's story and "Flying a Red Kite.")

Vauthier, Simone. "Changing Metropolis and *Urbs Eterna*: Hugh Hood's 'The Village Inside'." In her *Reverberations: Explorations in the Canadian Short Story*. Concord, ON: Anansi, 1993. 152-76.

—. "Une vue du Montréal de Hugh Hood." *Études Canadiennes / Canadian Studies* 19 (1985), 189-98.

Watt, F. W. "Fiction" (Letters in Canada 1962), containing rev. of FRK. *University of Toronto Quarterly* 32 (July 1963), 391-4.

Wind, Edgar. *Giorgione's Tempesta, with Comments on Giorgione's Poetic Allegories*. Oxford: Clarendon Press, 1969.

Zimmermann, Jutta. "The Modernist Aesthetic: Hugh Hood, 'Flying a Red Kite' (1962)." In Reingard M. Nischik, ed., *The Canadian Short Story: Interpretations*. Rochester, NY: Camden House, 2007. 175-89.

Index of Short Fiction

NB: Page numbers here refer to first editions of each collection.

General Index

About the Author

W. J. Keith, FRSC, is Professor Emeritus of English at the University of Toronto. He is the author of numerous books and articles on Canadian and English literature, including *A Canadian Odyssey* on Hood's twelve-volume novel series.